JACK KEROUAC
AND THE
LITERARY IMAGINATION

PREVIOUSLY PUBLISHED WORK

The Feminized Male Character in Twentieth-Century Literature (1995)
Girls Who Wore Black: Women Writing the Beat Generation (with Ronna Johnson, 2002)
Breaking the Rule of Cool: Interviewing and Reading Beat Women Writers (with Ronna Johnson, 2004)

JACK KEROUAC
AND THE
LITERARY IMAGINATION

Nancy M. Grace

JACK KEROUAC AND THE LITERARY IMAGINATION

Copyright © Nancy M. Grace, 2007

First published in 2007 by
PALGRAVE MACMILLAN™
175 Fifth Avenue, New York, N.Y. 10010 and
Houndmills, Basingstoke, Hampshire, England RG21 6XS.
Companies and representatives throughout the world.

PALGRAVE MACMILLAN is the global academic imprint of the Palgrave
Macmillan
division of St. Martin's Press, LLC and of Palgrave Macmillan Ltd.
Macmillan® is a registered trademark in the United States, United Kingdom
and other countries. Palgrave is a registered trademark in the European
Union and other countries.

ISBN-10: 1-4039-6850-0
ISBN-13: 978-1-4039-6850-0

Library of Congress Cataloging-in-Publication Data

Grace, Nancy McCampbell.
    Jack Kerouac and the literary imagination / by Nancy M. Grace.
       p. cm.
    Includes bibliographical references (p.) and index.
    ISBN 1-4039-6850-0 (alk. paper)
       1. Kerouac, Jack, 1922-1969—Criticism and interpretation. 2. Spriritual
    life in literature. 3. Myth in literature. I. Title.

    PS3521 E735Z66 2007
    813'.54—dc22   2006050992

A catalogue record for this book is available from the British Library.

Design by Macmillan India Ltd.

First edition: January 2007

10 9 8 7 6 5 4 3 2 1

Printed in the United States of America.

Transferred to digital printing in 2007.

For Ronna

TABLE OF CONTENTS

ACKNOWLEDGMENTS

I think of any author to be like the tiny fish that Virginia Woolf's female narrator in *A Room of One's Own* imagines bringing to shore. The metaphor describes the moment when an idea is caught, but Woolf's portrait of the fish as "insignificant . . . the sort of fish that a good fisherman puts back into the water so that it may grow fatter" strikes me as an apt image of an author, who alone is insufficiently equipped to write a book, no matter of what kind. If we do not acknowledge this reality, then it is best that we throw ourselves back into that stream and look more closely at the world in which we live. A book is always a collaborative venture. No author can claim *not* to have benefited from the inspiration, support, and guidance of others. In my case, there are many who have contributed, and I will try to thank them all as best I can.

Jack Kerouac and the Literary Imagination would not exist without a generous one-year leave from The College of Wooster that enabled me to spend a year reading, researching, and shaping the argument and its narrative. With the support of the Henry Luce III Fund for Distinguished Scholarship at The College of Wooster, I was able to spend an additional semester completing the manuscript. Faculty development funds from the College allowed me to secure permissions and an indexer. I extend my sincere gratitude to R. Stanton Hales, president of the College from 1994 to 2007, for supporting my scholarship.

Much of my research was conducted at the New York Public Library, one of the most beautiful and peaceful of places to work in the United States. Isaac Gewirtz, director of the Berg Collection that houses many Kerouac manuscripts, was most generous with his time and expertise, as was Stephen Brooks, also of the New York Public Library.

Farideh Koohi-Kamali, my editor at Palgrave Macmillan, deserves tremendous thanks for recognizing merit in the proposal that I submitted to her. Her faith in the project and the integrity of Kerouac's writing shepherded the book to completion.

I appreciate the kindness of Julia Cohen, of Palgrave Macmillan, who admirably kept me on track. John Sollami also deserves much gratitude for his careful reading and appreciation of Kerouac's art and legacy.

The editorial staff of Macmillan India Limited provided respectful and meticulous copyediting and production services.

I am grateful to City Lights Books and the estate of Jack Kerouac for giving me permission to quote copiously from Kerouac's novels, poems, journals, and letters. It is my hope that his passionate and lyrical voice dominates this interpretation.

A number of others have helped make this book the centerpiece of my scholarly life over the last four years. Megan Cameron and Elizabeth Miller, a political science and English/sociology major, respectively, at the College, contributed valuable research support; thank you for the time you spent in libraries tracking down obscure data for me. Kathie Clyde, administrative associate with the English department, not only worked with me to guarantee that permissions were secured but she is also the best of readers; without her keen eye and intelligence, the manuscript would not have been formatted so professionally, and without her humor and sincerity, my spirits would not have been buoyed so often on dark winter mornings. To Candace, Gwen, and the late Jim Fyfe, thank you for providing me a place to write in a city that I love. Susan Bowling helped me understand that a writer and scholar's life is worthwhile and manageable. Ishwar Harris guided me in matters of theological scholarship, Peter Veracka of the A. T. Wehrle Memorial Library at the Pontifical College Josephinum in Columbus, Ohio, provided critical research assistance, and Mark Graham contributed invaluable insights toward my understanding of Buddhism. Tim Hunt and Jennie Skerl encouraged me with their belief in and insights about the text. My Wooster colleagues Carolyn Durham, John Gabriele, Deb Shostak, and Shirley Huston-Findley supported me at all points with their friendship, wit, wine, and love of writing; you make my tenure at Wooster a pleasure. To Hans Johnson, much love and gratitude for making us part of your family. Marcia Holbrook showed me how important humor, friends, pets, and basketball can be. Marianne Bowden, my sister, is the best friend, fan, and role model a woman could ever have.

Two others warrant special recognition. Ronna Johnson provided expert guidance, which helped reshape the book. Thank you for your time, generosity, candor, and faith in my abilities. Our friendship and scholarly collaboration over the last ten years has transformed my life. Tom Milligan, my husband, is responsible for seeing me through all phases of this project. Without you, who always counsels me on the value of the life of the mind, I would not have pursued a project that has pursued me for almost twenty-five years. Thank you for your gargantuan spirit and belief in our communion.

Finally, to the memory of Jack Kerouac, much gratitude for always reminding us of the majestic human potential flourishing amid our many human foibles.

LIST OF ABBREVIATIONS

In-Text Abbreviations

Angels	*Desolation Angels*
Atop	*Atop an Underwood*
Beat Soul	*Beat Down to Your Soul*
Blonde	*Good Blonde and Other Stories*
Blues	*Book of Blues*
BS	*Big Sur*
Dharma	*Some of the Dharma*
Letters 1	*Jack Kerouac Selected Letters 1940–1956*
Letters 2	*Jack Kerouac Selected Letters 1957–1969*
MCB	*Mexico City Blues*
OAM	*Old Angel Midnight*
Pomes	*Pomes All Sizes*
Portable	*Portable Jack Kerouac*
Portable Beat	*Portable Beat Reader*
Road	*On the Road*
Satori	*Satori in Paris*
Sax	*Doctor Sax*
Scattered	*Scattered Poems*
WW	*Windblown World*

INTRODUCTION

In early 1954, Jack Kerouac composed a short narrative titled "AREMIDEIA AND THE PARACLETE: Religious Fancies for Western Believers" (*Dharma* 43–45). *Paraclete*, a term of Greek origin meaning intercessor, teacher, advocate, and comforter, is associated in Catholic tradition with the Holy Spirit sent by Christ to comfort his disciples; Aremideia, another name for Maitreya, is the first Buddha that is to follow Gautama.[1] Kerouac's story about this spiritual comforter is a religious teaching conveyed by a narrator who declares himself to be everything and everybody, and, as a short prose poem immediately following the lesson declares, this narrator is more truly Aremideia than the legal name "John Kerouac." Announcing that Aremideia will write the Jack Duluoz Legend "to rid himself of his earthly attachment and identity" (47), Kerouac at age thirty-two considered himself a man with a holy mission to be achieved through life, language, and art. Only a short time after his meteoric rise to fame following the publication of *On the Road* (1957), many readers concurred. Some, such as Seymour Krim, in his introduction to Kerouac's *Desolation Angels* (1965), appeared unafraid to set the bar especially high for the Beat Generation's best known spokesman. Claiming to speak for all "who were purged by [Kerouac's] esthetic Declaration of Independence, that time itself will use and exhaust his 'Duluoz Legend' and that he will then go on to other literary odysseys which he alone can initiate," Krim declared that Kerouac needed to "scale the new meanings that a man of his capacity should take on" (xxxvi). In other words, he needed to deliver repeatedly new messianic messages—the old ones, no matter how valid, would not suffice.

This was not the way Kerouac had begun life on March 12, 1922, as the youngest child of working-class French-Canadian Catholic parents in Lowell, Massachusetts. His family inhabited a world that mixed immigrant hardship with hope for a better socioeconomic future, both enveloped in the rituals of Catholic mystery and the myth of America as the Promised Land. It was a provincial enclave in which young Catholic children would kneel with their mothers in front of the twelve stations of the cross at the Lowell Grotto while their fathers worked in factories or struggled to keep small businesses solvent. Kerouac's mother, Gabrielle, while feisty and independent, steadfastly maintained her Catholic faith; on the contrary, his father, Leo, refused to attend mass (Nicosia 24). From Kerouac's own admission, he inherited his mother's penchant for the divine, which, when combined with the traumatic experience of the early death of his older brother Gerard who succumbed at age nine to rheumatic fever, endowed him with a visionary perspective on the world. The incense-filled and moth-swarmed world of his childhood however, eventually gave way to more conventional, secular interests as Kerouac developed into a strong student and successful athlete in the Lowell public school system.

Even as a teenager, though, he pursued literature and questions of life's philosophical and spiritual import, first with his Lowell friend Sebastian Sampas and later with his Columbia University friends Allen Ginsberg, William Burroughs, Lucien Carr, and Hal Chase. The treatises of Oswald Spengler and Fyodor Dostoyevsky, among others, centered his thinking on a new vision that he and his friends purported to build for the new world.[2] His letters and journals attest that he read, wrote, talked, and thought deeply about the difference between bourgeois culture and the artistic life, finding in companions such as Ginsberg "a kindred absorption with identity, dramatic meaning, classic unity, and immortality" (*Letters* 1: 81), as he wrote in 1944. At the forefront of his thinking were always questions about the existence of God, the Creator's purpose for all forms of life, the concept of mind, the nature of sin, the existence of evil, a hostile/indifferent/benign cosmos, self and other, the definition and function of time, care and compassion, and salvation.

For much of his adult life, he immersed himself in the serious study and practice of a religious life to achieve salvation for himself and others. The writing of literature—which he defined as "the tale that's told for companionship and to teach something [. . .] of religious reverence, about real life, in this real world which literature should (and here does) reflect" (*Satori in Paris* 10)—became the vehicle for completing this mission. In fact, writing for *Pageant* magazine in 1958, he characterized the term *beat* in "Beat Generation" as not "tired, or bushed, so much as it means *beato,* the Italian for beatific: to be in a state of beatitude, like St. Francis, trying to love all life, trying to be utterly sincere with everyone, practicing endurance, kindness, cultivating joy of heart" (*Blonde* 51). Kerouac's famous expression of this life's work is the ineffable "IT" from *On the Road,* a narrative that is just as much about finding God as it is about finding freedom and America. *On the Road* presents no rational explanation of where IT resides or what IT means, but as Ben Giamo notes, if one traces IT throughout Kerouac's prose and poetry, one will discern that he experimented with various meanings, ranging from "romantic lyricism to 'the ragged and ecstatic joy of pure being,' from the void-it of the Great World Snake to the joyous pain of amorous love, and, finally, from Catholic/Buddhist serenity to the onset of penitential martyr-hood" (xix). Kerouac defined the word for Allen Ginsberg in 1955 as "True Mind itself, Universal and One, . . . mind is IT itself, the IT" (*Letters* 1: 461). Toward the end of his life, IT reflected Kerouac's return to the conceptual framework of his French-Canadian roots: "All I write about is Jesus" (Plimpton 118). As I elucidate in this introduction and the chapters that fol-low, these pronouncements identify the intricate paths on which Kerouac traveled, a lifetime's journey that via his literary imagination transformed spiritual, cultural, and aesthetic materials into enduring mythology.

Near the end of his life, Kerouac attempted to clarify this configuration, as he explained to Ted Berrigan in a 1968 *Paris Review* interview:

> What's really influenced my work is the Mahayana Buddhism, the original Buddhism of Gotama Sakyamuni, the Buddha himself . . . The part of Zen that's influenced my writing is the Zen contained in the haiku . . . but my seri-ous Buddhism, that of ancient India, has influenced that part in my writing that you might call religious, or fervent, or pious, almost as much as Catholicism has. Original Buddhism referred to continual conscious compas-sion, brotherhood, the dana paramita meaning of the perfection of charity. (Plimpton 117)

In tone, the interview suggests that Buddhism (of which it appears he had some rudimentary knowledge in the early forties, most likely through his reading or the chinese author Lin Yutang, and seriously pursued from 1953 through 1957),[3] coupled with his belief in Catholicism and his development as a writer, contributed to a smooth integration of complex and contradictory belief systems. The process, however, was anything but smooth, as Kerouac struggled to meld the two according to a logic that allowed him to pursue his art. Periodically, he determined to abandon each of them, but never did. What persistently perplexed him was the recognition that both Catholicism and Buddhism, but most strongly the latter, teach that personal and human salvation is beyond the Word, which left him with the paradoxical belief that while words must be used to create and to communicate truth they are fun-damentally incapable of doing so. Therefore, as his poetry intimates, one must move beyond words to sound and, ultimately, beyond sound itself, or, as he wrote in *Some of the Dharma*, "CROSS YOUR EYES AS YOU READ THESE WORDS: - TRUTH IS NOT IN THE LETTERS" (313). But despite this realization, he remained convinced that the primary purpose of words must be to convey comfort and enlightenment for readers (*Dharma* 278–79), as he prophesized in this poetic passage, also from *Dharma:* "Of universal salvation (Just as Dostoevskii / Came close to being a Writing Christ) [. . .] / . . . I am Writing Buddha" (312). Clearly, Kerouac found himself caught between his need for the loss of self through spiritual enlightenment and his intense desire to write, between his effort to believe the Buddhist teaching that words are mere figures of speech and his need to continue the ego-driven project of the literary myth of the character he called Jack Duluoz.

Kerouac referred to the corpus of his work, primarily his thirteen books of prose as well as his long poem cycle *Mexico City Blues* and the prose poem *Old Angel Midnight,* as the Duluoz Legend, the Quebecois pseudonym for most of his first-person narrators (*Letters* 2: 285). The Legend, he wrote, formed "ONE BOOK . . . in which everything, past, present and future . . . is caught like dust in the sunlight." Considering himself and the Legend "like Rembrandt in front of the mirror," he vowed the following: to "treat 'myself' like in third person and discuss my own vanity—nothing will be concealed in the end" (*Dharma* 277–78). He often noted that what he also described as a series of installments in book form (*Letters* 2: 386) was autobiographical, which the Legend clearly is. Readers encounter characters that are thinly veiled representations of Kerouac's family and friends, and settings correlate smartly with cities, towns, and landscapes from his biography, particularly the city of Lowell.

However, he maintained with equal fervor that he was writing fiction. For instance, many events and people in Kerouac's life make no or only minor appearances. Little is revealed of his great friend Lucien Carr; his first wife Edie Parker, his second Joan Haverty, and his third Stella Sampas; his sister Caroline (Nin); and his childhood friend Sebastian Sampas who was fatally wounded on Anzio beach in 1944 (Maher 115, *Vanity of Duluoz* 160). Ginsberg, although playing a fairly prominent role under the pseudonyms Carlo Marx, Irwin Garden, Adam Moorad, and Alvah Goldbrook, is minimally sketched compared with Neal Cassady, Gary Snyder, Gregory Corso, and William Burroughs. Even these are somewhat unstable figures, shifting slightly from one text to another. Duluoz himself, whom Kerouac described as "fictions" in a notebook for *Satori in Paris* (1966), wears pseudonymic masks, appearing as Sal Paradise in *On the Road,* Ray Smith in *The Dharma Bums,* and Leo Percipied in *The Subterraneans.* In these respects, the Legend adheres faithfully to Kerouac's description of it in a letter sent to Carolyn Cassady: "Then before New Year's I finish the grand on the road, the plot of which I ben [*sic*] working on since 1948 [. . .] all along and with W. C. Fields road [. . .] with all of us fictionalized, I'm Ray Smith (actually I'm Duluoz but Ray Smith is the hero and he will be a Buddhist)" (*Letters* 1: 442).

Significantly, the Legend's shifting character names, attached to a recognizable type such as Duluoz the American French-Canadian Catholic Buddhist, situated the texts in Kerouac's mind as a mid-twentieth-century version of Joyce's *Finnegans Wake,* "one great dream with a unified spontaneous language lulling out the report forever so that in my sleep-bed the uproar continues—and the uproar, like the uproar of FINNEGANS WAKE, has no beginning and no end" (*Letters* 1: 516–17). The Legend as a whole recycles, as does the *Wake,* forms and voices that appear to be new characters but often present only slight differences in the underlying types emanating from the all-encompassing voice of Jack Duluoz.

Like all memorable characters, the Duluoz who developed out of this milieu is paradoxically unique, yet generic. A mixture of the Greek surname "Daoulas" (Jones, *Nine Lives* 66), which Kerouac identified as "a variation on the Breton name 'Daoulas'" and an intended signifier of his Breton heritage (*Satori in Paris* 101), "Duluoz" praises and mocks the hero of his legend much as did Joyce's Stephen Dedalus (*Portable* 6). This link is enhanced by the soft echo of "Dedalus" in "Duluoz," connecting Duluoz to, one, the Greek Dedalus, creator of the labyrinth who crafted the wax wings used by his son Icarus in a fatal attempt to reach the sun, and, two, St. Stephen, the first Christian martyr after whom Joyce named his character. As Kerouac stated in *Vanity of Duluoz,* Duluoz is also akin to Stephen Hero, Joyce's adolescent attempt to create a legendary version of himself. In imitation of both Stephen Dedalus and Hero, Kerouac envisioned Lowell as the New World version of Dublin (*Vanity of Duluoz* 106). Duluoz, then, based on Kerouac's stated intentions and the intertextual nature of his name, reifies an image of the flawed artist, youthful and mature, attempting to capture the shimmering aftereffects of his earthly presence.

This mantle of classical and modern heritages renders Duluoz distinctly American, an identity reflected in the hybridity of his name with its lingering resonances of French-Canadian, Greek, and Irish heritage. The name is so distinct that it seems unique, narrowly signifying a unitary external referent; yet contrapuntally it is so distinct that it shatters signification into multiple selves. This American character assumes many guises, most notably in the different names that he assumes in the Legend. At one level, these evince Kerouac and his publishers' efforts to avoid possible libel actions and to clarify the fictional nature of Kerouac's art. But at another, they reflect the mercurial sociological reality of the human name—a significant, although under-unacknowledged, component of the nineteenth- and early twentieth-century American experience.

American history is filled with stories of immigrants whose names were changed, sometimes callously or unintentionally by immigration officials who could not understand or spell a name correctly. However, individuals often voluntarily changed the spellings of their names to blend into Anglo-American culture, as did many Native Americans and East Europeans. Some even took on entirely new names to start new lives or avoid criminal prosecution. As many experienced, fresh identities could easily be found or forced upon one. In the New World, one's past could be quickly obliterated, leaving one either blissfully free of a cultural heritage and/or, as in Kerouac's case, proudly mournful of those Old World connections undergoing erasure. Certainly the many variants of the name "Kerouac" in both Canada and the United States, including "Kirouac," "Kyrouac," "Carouac," "Kirouack," and "Keloaque," and his fascination with the etymology of the name that he often parsed and reinvented in the Legend imply that Kerouac was cognizant of the plasticity of names and individuality in the New World (Maher 6), in other words the ease with which the American self could claim, reject, or create its ethnic, national, and personal heritage. The very name "Duluoz" underscores this national and literary artifice, reinforcing the Legend as neither a purely fictional nor purely autobiographical portraiture.

Ann Charters posits that this turn may have been influenced by Kerouac's reading of Herman Melville's *Pierre; or, the Ambiguities* (1852) in a 1949 edition introduced by Henry A. Murray (*Portable* 310). Kerouac frequently cited Melville as a progenitor of his work, but it is Charters's reference to Murray's interpretation of *Pierre* that provides fertile ground for a clearer articulation of the literary imagination that generated the Legend's unifying device. Like Duluoz, Melville's Pierre Glendinning is based on the life of its author who exuberantly deployed florid conceits, gothic tropes, and sermonic discourses to plumb the psychological depths of his fictionalized self, or "self image," in a narrative about the tragedy of Christian hubris (xx). Unlike Duluoz, Pierre does not tell his own story, but the nameless "I" who recounts Pierre's fall from socioeconomic and Puritan Christian grace is a distinct human presence who, as Murray writes of Melville, shares "a peculiar intimacy with his hero" and takes his side unequivocally (xx–xxi).

The narrator never hesitates to address readers directly and ask them to comment on his hero and the human condition, at times the distance between Melville and the narrator seeming to vanish entirely. Chapters 17 and 18, for example, violate the narrative design to present Pierre as a great but misunderstood American writer, a youthful iconoclast who inexplicably declares that despite conventions demanding history be written either contemporaneously with the events it records or according to the dictates of "the general stream of the narrative," he will do neither: "both are well enough in their way; I write precisely as I please" (1930, 272). Melville added these chapters after he had completed the narrative and was negotiating with the Harper brothers, whose refusal to grant him his customary royalties of 50 percent drove him to revengeful revision. This break in the narrative stance may have contributed to Kerouac's belief that fiction could function as the most personal expression of not only artists' philosophical and theological positions but also their visions of the nature and plight of a writer in a capitalist culture. Certainly the similarities between the themes addressed by *Pierre*'s narrator and Duluoz, as well as the construction of each as highly conscious of its readers, coupled with the blending of autobiography, fiction, and philosophy, underscore a genitive correspondence between nineteenth-century romance and Kerouac's Beat innovations.

Then contemporary readers of *Pierre* soundly damned the book for its bizarre actions, stilted dialogue, its failure to be another *Typee* (a genre with which they felt comfortable), and its disregard, as the *Southern Literary Messenger* reported, for fiction's obligations to "delineate life and character either as it is around us, or as it ought to be" (Higgins and Parker 48). While the novel was "rediscovered" in the 1920s, it remains one of Melville's most underappreciated works, no doubt partially because Melville failed to meet reader expectations by separating his personal life from public art. Similar interpretations of Kerouac's first-person narrators occurred almost immediately after the publication of *On the Road,* with Kerouac bearing some responsibility for this trend that has produced considerable criticism misinterpreting his corpus as straight autobiography while frequently ignoring or undervaluing the literary nature of the texts. The current trend in Kerouac scholarship, like that of Melville's nineteenth-century readers, presupposes that autobiographical writing is inferior to fiction and cannot sustain stylistic innovation.[4] Kerouac, however, by describing the Legend as a mirror image of himself as the artist and as the artist catching motes of dust in the light, blurs the boundaries between the crude categories of fiction and nonfiction. James Jones makes this case in *Jack Kerouac's Nine Lives,* claiming that "[Kerouac's] own term for his autobiographical saga, the Duluoz Legend, implies a hero who is at once mythical and historical. The putative historicity of a legend, moreover, fits into a strategy to blur the distinction between fact and fiction that novelists have used ever since *Don Quixote*" (15). Kerouac's movement away from the novel of social and psychological realism as represented by his first published novel *The Town and the City* (1950) to autobiographical fiction as represented by *On the Road* (1957) through *Satori in Paris* (1968) announces the creation of a character who by its very development demands that one reconsider the relationships between fact and fiction, veracity and mendacity, autobiography and the novel.

There now exists a rich body of critical theory generated by contemporary scholarship in history, literary studies, psychology, and gender studies that reveals the complex epistemological realities with which writers deal, particularly writers such as Kerouac who employ themselves as templates for a fictional persona. These reassessments convincingly challenge the belief in an essentialist self, moving readers beyond the assumptions that, first, autobiography and memoir are historical documents obligated to report a life as material and linear fact and, second, that such texts should focus on *what* the subject *has done* or *what has happened* to the subject. Multiple narrative "I's" operating in any text written about the self have thus been unveiled. In Kerouac's case, the texts themselves eschew linearity in favor of a style and content that better suit the movement of one's mind, creating a narrator whose reliance on memories distinguishes processes by which human cognition creates itself and others.

When dealing with Kerouac, known as "Memory Babe" and who by all accounts had extraordinary powers of recall, one may erroneously conclude that anything the writer identifies as "real" or based on memory is a reliably accurate report of the past. But even when recalled with the belief that memories are accurate, memories combine reconstructing and copying processes. Some are "flashbulbs" or mental copies of the perceived, but many are *constructed* and *reconstructed* through retrieving, losing, and adjusting cognitive materials over time. Memories remain substantially accurate as one ages, particularly for seminal events in one's life, but distortions occur as older memories are reconstructed to correspond with current self-perceptions, often tilting toward self-enhancement (Thompson et al. 72). Consequently, memories are far from being uninterpreted or unmanipulated copies of prior events. Like the language with which one reports them, memories mediate reality through creative processes basic to human cognition.

Psychologists identify different types of memory, including sensory, short-term, semantic, and episodic, but the one most relevant to Kerouac is autobiographical (or personal) memory, defined as recollections of specific events from one's past that often seem like a reliving of the phenomenal experience. The form and content of autobiographical memory remains somewhat ambiguous, but mental imagery, similar to but distinct from visual (perceptual) imagery, is an important mnemonic device to enhance the specificity of the remembered experience as personal and contribute to the feeling that the stories told are accurate and believable.[5] Visual imagery and narrative are also considered key components. Kerouac himself identified these as structural elements upon which his literary production relied, such as tics (sudden visions of memory), sketches (prose descriptions of remembered scenes), ecstasy (prose and verse accounts of meditative experiences), visions (prose passages concentrating on a single individual), and routine (the prose acting-out of daydreamed roles) (*Dharma* 342).

Additionally, autobiographical memories are frequently recovered as narratives told either to others or oneself. Discursive elements are included or excluded, in part depending on the language and narrative structures available. Significantly, the memories one tends to retain are those that have been rehearsed or practiced by repeatedly telling them to oneself or others: the personal or folk story, in particular, functions as a verbal rehearsal to shape and reshape memory (Rubin in Thompson et al. 53). Repetition can lead to distortion, but overall the stories are believed to constitute the basis of the remembered self (Schank and Abelson 1).[6] The structure of the rehearsed narrative also mirrors the narrative forms of social discourse, indicating that memory recall is a discursive social act defining a social group (Rubin 54).[7] Narrative, then, is not only, as historian Hayden White claims, "a mode of discourse, a manner of speaking, and the product produced by the adoption of this mode of discourse," but also an essential way of thinking (57). Another way of putting it is to identify self-representation as self-creation, personal and cultural history as constructed through the interaction of language and memory, and life writing as a fictional form to some degree.

By approaching prose as a continual shifting of form characteristic of life writing and fiction, Kerouac collapsed and expanded categorical distinctions to create and record the life of Jack Duluoz through the essential human practice of storytelling. From this standpoint, the Legend conflates truth-fact distinctions, questions the correlation between and the nature of figuration and referent, and produces a hybrid form of history and fiction—whether called fictionalized autobiography or autobiographical fiction, both being appropriate terms for the Legend—resisting the impulse to rest firmly upon either.

As both process and product of Kerouac's persistent defiance of literary categorization, Duluoz and his Legend are nothing if not a vibrant representation of the nation's mythic heritage as a New World grown out of and superseding the Old. I concede that it may seem outmoded to speak of literary characters such as Duluoz or American literature and culture in general in terms of myth and myth criticism, especially in light of comments like that of Philip Fisher who declared in the early 1990s that scholarly "interest [in American Studies] has passed from myth to rhetorics."[8] While the perspective of myth relies upon the retelling of a "fixed, satisfying, and stable story" that naturalizes historical experiences, rhetorical analysis reveals multiple language systems with not only the persuasive power of myth but also what Fisher calls "the action potential of language and images." Rhetorics, he concludes, are "the servants of one or another group within society" (Greenblatt and Gunn 232). The Foucauldian perspective on discourse underlies my own assumptions about memory and narrative articulated above. Indeed, many of the arguments that constitute *Jack Kerouac and the Literary Imagination* draw upon and expose the processes of rhetorical agencies, especially the many diverse "servants" Kerouac used to create his Legend, as the remainder of this introduction will elucidate. However, whenever an author intentionally names his literary protagonist after accepted mythic and literary heroes, as well as labels that same protagonist's story a "Legend," a reader may be best served by investigating the extent to which myth, itself a powerful form of rhetoric, operates within that author's imagination and in the literary texts that arise therefrom.

Readers will find a touch of Northrop Frye's, Ezra Pound's, T. S. Eliot's, and Thomas Mann's approaches to myth criticism in the following chapters, and cyclic visions of human history propagated by the Italian philosopher Giambattista Vico (1668–1744) and the German philosopher Oswald Spengler (1880–1936) appear as well. But the primary formula that I have applied, and I admit on a grand scale, to interpret the conflation of Kerouac's spiritual and literary quests via Jack Duluoz is that of Nicholas Berdyaev (1874–1948), the Russian political philosopher and propagandist for Christianity. Berdyaev is a name no doubt unrecognized by many contemporary readers, but his philosophy of the mythic nature of human history parallels with a fascinating degree of similarity that articulated in the Duluoz Legend. As such, Berdyaev provides a lens through which one can more clearly imagine the world as Kerouac saw it. Again, this is not to say that postmodern (anti-myth-critical) approaches to Kerouac are not insightful but rather that a perspective more analogous to Kerouac's own may disclose features of his art that have long rendered it both controversial and endearing within post–World War II cultures, particularly in the United States.

Berdyaev rejected the definition of history as "objective empirical datum" (21), a revisionist stance that, excluding his unabashedly uncritical defense of Christianity, is not unlike that of many today and without question in line with Kerouac's refusal to accept a positivist vision of human stories. However, Berdyaev's perspective deviates from contemporary turns to rhetorical or discursive theories of social construction by defining history as a myth itself. Contrary to contemporary contentions that myths are socially derived narratives grounded in fiction as well as fact, Berdyaev posited that "myth is not fiction, but a reality . . . one of a different order from that of the so-called objective empirical fact. Myth," he continued in *The Meaning of History*, "is the story preserved in popular memory of a past event and transcends the limits of the external objective world, revealing an ideal world, a subject-object world of facts" (21). The Berdyaevian understanding attempts to undermine the Enlightenment separation of mind and body as well as the naturalistic vision of human existence as "a minute fragment of the universe" (22), positing that all humans carry within themselves a whole world that can be revealed by subjective investigation. Within the human-as-world, traces of past epochs defy erasure, continuing to surface in the present as what Berdyaev calls factual, or historical, stories. Only by plunging oneself into oneself to re-member these stories can one fathom time and history, which according to Berdyaev is not an external, alien, and dictatorial super reality, but the manifestation of one's essential self: the development of self-consciousness.

Berdyaev did not discount historical criticism that eradicates false beliefs, but he contended that any historical tradition is valuable only insofar as it symbolizes a people's destiny and that the symbolism itself is the source of knowledge of the union of historical reality and self-knowledge, a position compatible with Kerouac's visions of the self-in-the-universe. In turn, Berdyaev advocated that the connection between revelations of self-knowledge and historical traditions be given the highest regard. For example, one should be able, he wrote, "to discover within [one]self the profoundest strata of the Hellenic world and thus grasp the essential of Greek history. Similarly, the historian must discover within himself the deep strata of Jewish history before he can grasp its essential nature" (23). Such mythologies, he concluded, allow human beings to apprehend the reality of the divine, what he called celestial history, and in so doing history becomes "a great and occult act of remembrance" through which one gains self knowledge as well as understanding of oneself as "an inalienable participant" in the mystery of life (23). Another way of extrapolating this philosophy is to place it along side Thomas Mann's belief that historical characters illustrate one's life as a mixture of movement according to prearranged scripts and free will. Life, then, is always simultaneously the succession story and the genesis story (Ellmann and Feidelson 675), a position consistent with Kerouac's figuration of self and character as both type and original.

This holistic—and I venture even mystic—vision of self and history undergirds the Duluoz Legend, especially Kerouac's rendering of his narratives as the fictionalized autobiography of an American male who repeatedly plunges into and out of his interior world, in the process making visible not only himself but also the myriad others who have preceded him and will succeed him.[9] As I have already noted and as a number of his biographers have detailed, Kerouac's interior world early on was in broad strokes populated by Catholic precepts, French-Canadian lore as propagated by his small immigrant community in Lowell, and more general twentieth-century beliefs regarding America as the promised land. As he matured, elements of literary as well as sports heroism, Buddhism, family obligations, human sexuality, Cold War politics, and popular Hollywood entertainment culture, among others, colored the inscape. I have identified four seminal themes to demarcate the permeable boundaries of this world, establishing a focus for mythologies that nurtured Kerouac's interior explorations and nourished the Berdyaevian celestial history that appears in the Duluoz Legend. Each will be discussed below as mutually exclusive, although it is important to recognize that in reality they are integrally bound and as filtered through Kerouac's imagination, they effectively dismantle barriers between high culture and today's commercial and popular culture.

THE AMERICAN MASTER NARRATIVE

A pantheon of American histories and characters that seem to exist suspended outside of time embodies Duluoz's tales, producing a textual imperative conflating personal and cultural history such that Kerouac could read his personal history into the master American narrative. This is the nation's essential story of manifest destiny, the open frontier, youth, individual liberties, nature as welcoming yet wild, the right to own property, economic prosperity, the spirit of individual and group resistance, the messianic exporting of American values to improve lives across the world, and the assimilation of everyone into a great unified whole.[10] The myths that have systemically been built upon and sustain these beliefs and values, creating a "fault line" between the ideal and the real (Fisher 31), began as patriarchal and racist but have over the history of the United States proved flexible enough to accommodate some redemptive political and cultural changes. Kerouac's characters, particularly Duluoz, as products of this tradition tend to resist the angst-ridden and spiritually bereft, twentieth-century antihero as well as the media stereotype of the Beat writer as a dangerous nihilist threatening America's familial security from within.

At the same time, Kerouac recognized in the master narrative its hidden prejudices. For example, in a May 19, 1950, journal entry in which he recorded his dreams of his deceased old brother, Gerard, he wrote,

> I think [Gerard] is my original self returning after all the years since I was a child trying to become "un Anglais" in Lowell from Shame of being a Canuck; I never realized before I had undergone the same feelings any Jew, Greek, Negro, or Italian feels in America, so cleverly had I concealed them, even from myself, so cleverly and with such talented, sullen aplomb for a kid. (*WW* 259)

Since in this text he blamed himself for not seeing more clearly the larger sociohistorical reality of his and others' conditions, we can surmise that either he did not recognize or he refused to acknowledge the ways in which American political and social cultures consistently manipulate discourse to create invidious distinctions between ethnic and racial groups. In fact, self-blame, a reverse doppelganger of the myth of American self-reliance, is one of the most pernicious and insidious methods by which hegemonic power is constrained. But despite his blindness toward that discursive reality, Kerouac at some level clearly understood himself as someone who had bought into a myth that lacked integrity. By plumbing his interior world through his literary imagination, he created a vision of the common American experience that began a critique of the supremacy of the master narrative.

Central to this vision was Kerouac's efforts to escape the ego-focused corporeal world alongside his conviction that the material realm, including the human body, is the only seat of eternity. It was in the American corpus—mythological, geological, and the sentient—that he saw eternity most explicitly acknowledged, and it is the Duluoz Legend that dramatizes his efforts to reconcile the apparent contradictions in these beliefs. For instance, at one level, the discrete narratives, each to a greater or lesser degree, question gender such that belief in gender's grounding in stable sex and sexuality distinctions is effectively undermined, or "troubled" as philosopher Judith Butler argues. In keeping with Butler's assessment of gender as "an identity tenuously constituted in exterior spaces through a stylized repetition of [bodily] acts—that formulate the illusion of an enduring gendered self," Kerouac transforms the master narrative through attention to parodic proliferation in particular, disparate components of the Legend ultimately revealing what Butler identifies as a "perpetual displacement [that] constitutes a fluidity of identities [suggesting] an openness to both gender resignification and recontextualization" (Leitch et al. 2500–01).

At a second level, Kerouac's critique assumes the form of twentieth-century inheritors of American mythology to be those who although forgotten or marginalized by the reality of American socioeconomic and political systems still manage to live hope-filled independent lives. These he imagined to be African Americans, Native Americans, other ethnic groups, and the Depression-era hobos—those unwilling to accept inferiority in the face of systemic discrimination: those who by claiming the mythic discourse for themselves rob the narrative of at least some of its dehumanizing strength. Writing to his friend John Clellon Holmes in 1952, he included himself among these groups: "I'm not American, nor West European, somehow I feel like an Indian, a North American Exile in North America—In New York I'm a Peasant among the Solomons . . . A HOBO LIVES LIKE AN INDIAN" (*Letters* 1: 381–82). In this case, his denial of being an American advances his critique of the master narrative, implicitly asking whether one can be an American in a system that subverts its very belief in the essential self by forcing particular individuals into psychological or physical exile based solely on categorical signifiers.

THE AMERICAN FOLK HERO

Interestingly, however, while engaging in critical assessment of himself and thereby the master narrative throughout the Legend, Kerouac remained unwilling or perhaps unable to relinquish it. The Beat Generation, he contended, inherited the legacy of nineteenth-century folk heroes such as Johnny Appleseed (1775–1847), the Swedenborgian Christian missionary who traveled Ohio, Indiana, and Illinois planting apple trees and spreading the Christian Gospel; and James Bridger (1804–81), a rugged mountain man and legendary teller of tall tales who helped open the West to fur trading and eventual expansion through Utah into Oregon (*Lonesome* 173).[11] By recognizing and claiming these American ancestors, Kerouac established as his and

the country's mythic grounding a melding of masculine independent rugged-
ness with feminine Christian tenderness and communal charity, both tem-
pered with the spirits of commercial and theological entrepreneurship.

In 1960, as he composed *Lonesome Traveler*, he foregrounded this modern-
day folk hero by projecting these values onto the hobo, with whom he idein-
tified, envisioning this impoverished soul who as "childlike and proud
remained hopeful amidst hopelessness" (173). Calling himself "a hobo
only of sorts" (after the publication of *On the Road*, he had realized that
his writing had brought him some monetary success), he retained belief in
the American dream and in the alienated and downtrodden who struggled
to sustain that promise. In the hobo tradition of what he called "foot-
walking freedom" (*Lonesome* 173), that of Johnny Appleseed and Jim
Bridger, Kerouac embedded himself and constructed an American hero,
Jack Duluoz, who as a self-appointed savior of the world straddles plains
and mountains as well as popular and elite cultures. From youth to middle age, that character is blessed with a fundamental optimism, courage,
and perseverance that allow him to shed elements of a Euro-American past
that haunts but fascinates him.[12]

THE AMERICAN LITERARY ROMANCE

The contradictions of American history revealed through Kerouac's
Berdyaevian probing of the nation's myths and heroes are exposed in the very
literature that dominant American culture during Kerouac's lifetime honored
(and still to this day honors) as the supreme voices of the American consciousness. He was especially drawn to American romantics, including
Thoreau, Hawthorne, and Melville as well as to some of their modern suc-
cessors, such as William Faulkner and Thomas Wolfe. Within this tradition,
Kerouac was exposed to and schooled in the struggle to shape a new national
literature that for each generation would stand apart from the old. In particular, the American Renaissance provided him with a template for the construction of succession and originality narratives in his search for spiritual
and aesthetic certitude. As I will argue in subsequent chapters, the Duluoz
Legend incorporates elements of the master American narrative and the
American folk hero within the literary context of the often-referenced definition of American romance, Hawthorne's pronouncement in *The House of
the Seven Gables*. It is worth quoting in full:

> When a writer calls his work a Romance, it need hardly be observed that he
> wishes to claim a certain latitude, both as to its fashion and material, which he
> would not have felt himself entitled to assume had he professed to be writing
> a Novel. The latter form of composition is presumed to aim at a very minute

fidelity, not merely to the possible, but to the probable and ordinary course of man's experience. The former—while, as a work of art, it must rigidly subject itself to laws, and while it sins unpardonably so far as it may swerve aside from the truth of the human heart—has fairly a right to present that truth under circumstances, to a great extent, of the writer's own choosing or creation. If he think fit, also, he may so manage his atmospherical medium as to bring out or mellow the lights and deepen and enrich the shadows of the picture. (vii)

Hawthorne identifies elucidating the truth of the human heart as the central purpose of a romance. This truth, which Hawthorne believed existed "in an attempt to connect a bygone time with the very present that is flitting away from us," must suffuse the work at all points. Kerouac himself in 1949 composed, in a letter to Charles Sampas, Sebastian's brother, a meditation on time, life, and literature that echoes Hawthorne's stance:

> But it's all the same, and Lowell, like Winesburg Ohio or Asheville North Carolina or Fresno California or Hawthorne's Salem, is always the place where the darkness of the trees by the river, on a starry night, gives hint of that inscrutable *future* Americans are always longing and longing for. And when they find that future, not till then they begin looking *back* with sorrows, and an understanding of how man haunts the earth, pacing, prowling, circling in the shades, and the intelligence of the compass pointing to nothing in sight save starry passion [. . .]. (*Letters* 1: 221)

These declarations, be they Kerouac's, Hawthorne's, or of the literature to which Kerouac's city and state names allude, illuminate the Duluoz Legend as novel (it dare not swerve too far from the laws of identifiable human behavior), romance (it has license to embellish for purposes of rendering the truth of the human heart and passions), and history (it infuses the American past into the present to inform us about the future). In so doing, it foregrounds contemporary vestiges of the terrors of the early American wilderness experience that is inextricably bound with the bliss of enlightenment idealism, eliding the separation between ancient epics and the present and future.

Kerouac inherited the modernist turn away from social realism and naturalism to more abstract and ethereal forms of eighteenth- and nineteenth-century romanticism, a response to a zeitgeist in which certain ideologies had become distinctly suspect—for example, belief in the divine, human progress toward the good, free will, and the supremacy of males over females and whites over blacks. Within this tradition, the artist assumes the role of sage and prophet and becomes a secular speaker with the vision to not merely remain faithful to the physical perceptions of reality but to transform them into communiqués of universal truths. The Kerouacian truths that Duluoz conveys often go unspoken because they are projected indirectly through actions and mystical visions. But in general, installments of the Legend reiterate that human nature is fallible, suffering and death are inevitable, human connections and love (or the truth of the human heart) ameliorate suffering, America despite its flawed history remains the world's best hope, conventional forms of history thwart human knowledge and therefore must be overcome, the sole purpose of art is to teach others, individual free will while in part an illusion is the source of human salvation, and ultimately something greater than individual human life exists.

The above truths frequently emerge at a remove from more representational, didactic, or overtly political discourse. As Daniel Hoffman has argued, contemporary realities presented by romantic writers are often "disguised in the past of [the writer's] ancestors or in their childhoods or in the symbol-freighted voyages abstracted from economic and political life in their time" (353). Kerouac's narratives present a similar case. Their truths about human nature are not necessarily constructed to transparently speak for themselves or for an over-arching hegemonic ideology. As an American folk hero, Duluoz sometimes teaches, prophesizes, preaches, and helps others in the tradition of a Johnny Appleseed. But as a Jim Bridger, he creates tales that transmit truths through metaphor, allegory, multiple voices, stereotypes, dreams, visions, fantasy, humor, detailed portraits of his adventures, and his own brutally honest nature. On a macro scale, he exemplifies what Mikhail Bakhtin identified as the dynamics of stratifications and heteroglossia that "widen and deepen as long as language is alive and developing" (*Dialogic* 272). More specifically, Duluoz's American folk character corresponds with the distinction Bakhtin makes between the agenda of upper and lower social classes with respect to the form and function of language. The former, he contends, considers the task of literature, particularly poetry, to centralize "cultural, national and political" features "of the verbal-ideological world in the higher official socio-ideological levels" (*Dialogic* 273). The latter, or the lower levels of "local fairs, and . . . buffoon spectacles," allowed the heteroglossia of the clown to dominate, Bakhtin maintained. In this nether world, all languages and dialects are ridiculed; "the literature of the *fabliaux* and *Schwanke* of street songs, folksayings, anecdotes" develops; and no language center can be discerned among "a lively play with the 'languages' of the poets, scholars, monks, knights and others, where all 'languages' wear masks and where no language could claim to be authentic, incontestables face" (*Dialogic* 273). This parodic play is directed at the upper social level of unified literary voice, or "the verbal-ideological life of the nation and the epoch," and consequently operates in dialogic opposition to that centralizing effort (273).

American literary history, especially its romantic center, strongly suggests elements of both Bakhtinian centralization and dialogic opposition. Certainly a goal of the colonial and early postcolonial literary intelligentsia was to establish itself as worthy of its European ancestry, leading writers to draw upon and imitate classical as well as canonical European literary traditions and tropes. Simultaneously, the works of writers such as Melville, Hawthorne, and Thoreau evince the realization that citizens of the New World must address the character of that world, striking out against old forms to birth new voices and forms. In this process, their literature claims elements of the folk world, an attempt to legitimize heteroglossia as a device to deconstruct the still powerful ideological presence of their European heritage.

By the time Kerouac emerged on the post–World War II literary scene, a truly American literary intelligentsia was in place, represented by the Trillings and Van Dorens at Columbia, a powerful critical community that functioned in many respects to unify a twentieth-century literary voice that one can discern in writers such as Ernest Hemingway, William Faulkner, Norman Mailer, the early Saul Bellows, Carson McCullours, Sylvia Plath, Truman Capote, and others of the day. While certainly not ideologically or stylistically identical, works by writers such as these projected a kind of academic voice and experience, a sharp divide between those with experience within the literary academy or social class structure and those without, between those who spoke the language of the intelligentsia and those who did not. Kerouac as an American writer had his foot in the centralized world of language via his entrance into Columbia, which he briefly attended, and via his early studies of American writers considered canonical at the time he entered high school and college. However, as an inheritor of the early American romantic tradition, he also embraced forms and voices long associated with the folk, the illiterate, the unschooled, the maniacal, the terrifying, the spiritual, and the sectarian—all of which an American literary establishment, particularly in the twentieth century as the United States took secular leadership on the world stage, had tried to overcome in their most blatant forms. With the Duluoz Legend, then, one is left to read many conflicting interpretations of an America in which its mythology serves to eradicate iniquities and injustices while perpetuating the very same.[13]

GNOSTICISM

As descendents of a Puritan heritage, writers of early American romances found themselves deeply concerned about original sin, God, the myth of the land as both heaven and hell, human nature as "unfallen and demonic," and the discovery of the essential self, all themes that have long characterized American folklore, rituals, and myth. Out of this milieu they crafted variants on a hero presence with what Daniel Hoffman calls "preoccupations with the instinctual and passionatal forces of life, with pre-conscious and pre-Christian values, with sub-rational and often anti-rational formulations of meaning.

These values of course are almost invariably found in tandem with their opposites: full consciousness, directed will, reason, Christianity" (3). Kerouac shared these concerns, his consciousness formed within the Puritan sanctum of New England, a world that endowed him with the certainty that, as he wrote to Neal Cassady, "I was born, my damned sin began" (*Letters* 1: 250). In turn, like some of his romantic ancestors, he shaped a trope of ancient cross-cultural myths in which the hero, often cursed from birth, must leave his (rarely her) family on a quest to save himself, a nation, or a people.

This ancient story is a reflection of gnosticism, a spiritual practice rarely identified with American theology but one that, as Harold Bloom astutely contends, embodies a fundamental American religious temperament. Interestingly, Kerouac had some knowledge of gnosticism that extended beyond the level of recognizing this Bloomian quality of fundamentalism. Kerouac knew of the gnostic prophet Mani, the founder of Manichaeism, a world religion that synthesized elements of Zoroastrian, Hellenic, Jewish, Buddhist, and Christian mysticism. Manichaeism was also the religion that Augustine of Hippo practiced prior to his conversion to Catholicism. I stress here that I am not claiming an intentional causal link between early Christian gnostic sects such as the Manichaeans' and Kerouac's developing metaphysics, but that there is an important intellectual similarity. Kerouac's writing was not literally gnostic in the sense of a professed commitment to that faith system but rather gnosticlike in that gnostic myths and precepts implicitly provide a foundation for his literary interpretations of both Catholicism and Buddhism in the New World.

Bloom defines gnosticism as "a knowing, by and of an uncreated self, or self-within-the-self and the knowledge leads to freedom, a dangerous doom-eager freedom: from nature, time, history, community, other selves." Maintaining that if one has this temperament "and yet . . . cannot accept Jewish, Catholic, Protestant, or Muslim explanations as to why an omnipotent God permits the perpetual victory of evil and misfortune," Bloom concludes that "then [one] may be tempted by Gnosticism, even if [one] never quite knows just what Gnosticism is, or was" (49). Granted, knowing what gnosticism is or was is not easy. Many different gnostic sects flourished in the early centuries of the common era, some calling themselves gnostic, some not, so that "Gnosticism," "gnostics," and "gnosticism" defy coherent unification. With the discovery of the Nag Hamadi scrolls in 1947, however, a wealth of gnostic texts were resurrected, and the quality of scholarship devoted to the study of these early Christian communities is extremely high, enabling one to confidently generalize about what renders a belief system gnostic or gnosticlike.

The name "gnostic" comes from *gnosis,* the Greek word for "knowledge." As did Kerouac in the late forties, gnostic groups in general espoused mystical traditions that eschewed human or saintly mediation in favor of the search for personal knowledge (gnosis) of the divine as the way to salvation through reading and meditation (Barnstone and Meyer 1). This personal activity produces ecstatic information, which, as Willis Barnstone explains, feeds previously assimilated information into a revelatory instant that no matter how ineffable is "then translated back into speech, reason, or myth" for the world (798). Gnostic spiritual belief systems are usually syncretic, drawing from Jewish, Iranian, Egyptian, Syrian, Greek, and other sources. Platonism contributed the notion of dual theism: a transcendent divine that is separate and alien, called the Good, the One, the Alien, the Nameless, or the Father of Greatness (Barnstone and Meyer 15–16). A lower and evil power called the demiurge created the universe. In these traditions, humans exist in a state of alienation within the world and have a body and a soul created by the demiurge. Although the nature of the soul varies from sect to sect, the general belief is that the spirit lies encased within the soul, and that the spirit must be awakened through knowledge. The figure of Jesus acts as a messenger of the transcendent to awaken those held captive by the demiurge. But Jesus does not represent suffering or demand atonement for salvation (Jonas 127), and some gnostic sects maintained that he never assumed human form. As the historian Hans Jonas explains, salvation in the gnostic world is not the remission of sin but the product of knowledge— answers to questions of who we are, what we became, where we came from, and what is birth (32, 127). This knowledge awakens the spirit, propelling the soul toward the light of the transcendent and shedding vestiges of its human shroud until the pure spirit is merged with the transcendent.

Certain symbology, imagery, and themes characterizing these systems are relevant to Kerouac's quest, such as the following underscored set identified by Jonas. In his schema the concept of the "Alien Life" is central to gnostic thinking. This is the belief that not only is the transcendent, or original life, alien from the material universe, but that the human being, "thrown into this world," traps within itself something alien from that other world. The human endeavor is to find its "home" outside the universe itself with the transcendent. This home is associated with "light," while the mundane is the "dark"; however, the mundane is mixed with some light as well, the "foreign" and trapped element of the transcendent. In many gnostic writings, the body, as the product of a lowly and evil creator, is also evil, something to be shunned. The "Noise of the World," however, makes this difficult—humans are immersed in the sounds of vanity, sexual desire, or greed. One must seek the "Call from Without," which can arrive as a "voice," a "letter," or a "pearl," and is presented by the "Messenger," which can be "Jesus," or even the "serpent" that tempts Eve in the Garden of Eden. The Call directs humans away from the evil creator of the mundane: truth, love, hope, and faith are the reward, a return to the Alien All, rooted in unfathomable "Silence" existing beyond everything else.

Kerouac never to my knowledge adopted the distinction between the transcendent one and the demiurge (whether Platonic, Neoplatonic, or gnostic), but he yearned for a religion that could reconcile the apparently irreconcilable, especially what Bloom identifies in American folk culture as the distinction between the self and the soul, or in gnostic terms the soul and the spirit. Bloom speculates that these entered early in American history through the African American concept of the "little me within the big me," a "little self" that takes spiritual journeys while the big self remains with the body, and through the Orphic gnostic tradition inculcating Emersonian thought with the idea of the "potential divinity of the elitist self" (52). By the end of the twentieth century, both had become embodied in fundamentalism. What drives fundamentalism as "unwitting" gnosticism, Bloom argues, is the knowledge "that [humans] were no part of the Creation, but existed as spirits before it, and so are as old as God himself." The great wound that haunts this temperament, however, is the implication that humans "were never God, or part of God" (57). This is similar to what Deleuze and Guattari call the "fascisizing, moralizing, Puritan, and familialist territorialities" that constitute part of the destiny of American literature (277–78).[14] Elements of gnostic fundamentalism distinguish Kerouac's *Duluoz Legend*, which, while *by no means* fundamentalist or fascist in the sense of the antievolutionary, anti-individual, and patriarchal institution that Bloom critiques, reflects a deep desire to become part of God and insists upon primacy of the immediate experience, mistrust of the human body, desire for an intense interior journey, rejection of the fallacy that one can find self-fulfillment in family or church doctrine, and blessings for those who follow the solitary path of spiritual discipline toward the knowledge of universal truth.

Kerouac's quest was not unique at the century's midpoint. The United States had experienced dramatic social, economic, and political changes over the thirties, forties, and fifties that were discernible in average Americans' perceptions of their everyday lives. Fundamentally, the America in which Kerouac matured abandoned many nineteenth-century values and aimed for the twenty-first. In 1935–36, for instance, when Kerouac was a teenager, poll results pioneered by Frank Gallup only two years earlier revealed that Americans believed that the most important issues facing them were employment and governmental economic efficiency, and 82 percent thought a married woman should not earn money if her husband could support her. Forty-five percent thought the policies of the Roosevelt administration would lead to a dictatorship—in small-town New England where Kerouac grew up, this percentage was 52.[15] By 1944, Americans feared another depression after World War II, and 90 percent said that the amount of taxes they paid was fair. Ninety-six percent believed in God.

Twelve years later, however, money, domestic problems, war, the atomic bomb, and Communists in government had become Americans' greatest concerns, and their composite responses to questions about the importance of religion produced the highest number to this day, positioning religion as the primary vehicle to improve personal and national character. As the fifties' commodities culture ramped up to market the middle-class desire for more leisure time, the cultural upheavals that would tear apart the country in the last decade of Kerouac's life began to emerge as noteworthy. By the late fifties and into the early sixties, integration, race, peace, fear of Russia, and inflation were Americans' major concerns, and the issue of a woman's right to an abortion appeared for the first time in 1962—52 percent saying that the procedure was acceptable if the child would be born with extreme deformities.

It is also worth noting that the one name appearing most often in the top-ten list of most admired men during this time was the Reverend Billy Graham, who remained at the top of that list through 2003—forty-six out of the forty-nine times. The most admired woman was Queen Elizabeth, heading the list thirty-nine out of forty-nine times. Kerouac's America, then, was in the midst of invigorating yet unsettling, if not terrifying, transformations. Conditions and perceptions such as these challenged Americans, especially the white middle classes, to create what historian Elaine Tyler May calls "a home that would fulfill virtually all its members' personal needs through an energized and expressive personal life" (11). This "containment culture," Tyler May argues, was triggered by Americans' postwar need "to feel liberated from the past and secure in their future" (10).

Kerouac was not immune to these changes, especially to the need to find within the boundaries of family, whether biological and fraternal, an insight into the nature and purpose of life. Believing that a radically transformed world requires individuals to reconsider their place and purpose in terms other than personal security and material worth, he determined that postwar culture demanded a new kind of writing, which he called "New" or "Deep" form. In theory, this method privileged personal or essential experience, a reverence for the minutia of sensory perception, and a dialectical spiraling of narrative into the artist's mind and outward into the world, all channeled through the honest expression of language. But contrary to his public pronouncements, his fracturing of literary conventions in the service of spiritual devotion wedded to narrative and poetic expression did not constitute a linear advance in the sense of working against the grain of established form to develop an entirely new species. Rather, it is a recursive movement—metaphorically, a kind of Literary Darwinism—that "advances" the species by returning to, and strengthening by this return, more ancient forms that have presumably best served the species and therefore survived over time. In their contemporary guises, these often go unrecognized but resonate for many readers as authentic, thus distinguishing them from the conventional, known, and expected.

I contend that Kerouac's so-called new form was actually a contemporary version of *wisdom literature*. As such, it draws upon and manipulates the voice of the prophet, sage, teacher, and seer expressed as a classical pastiche of sermon, analogy, proverb, aphorism, song, parable, prayer, catechism, and confession to create a personal cosmology—that is, an explanation of the Beginning of All Things and the End of All Things. This cosmos—in effect Kerouac's *desire* for a single well-ordered and self-sustaining system enabling him to find meaning in life—follows not only structures of ancient texts such as the Old and New Testaments and the Buddhist sutras, but also the nineteenth-century wisdom literature of Carlyle, Ruskin, and Dostoyevsky, and is grounded in the texts of Montaigne, Blake, Wordsworth, Whitman, Melville, Thoreau, Rimbaud, and others. The myth of the rebel "Jack Kerouac," one can surmise, lives not as and because of a radical and unappreciated new school of literature, but as the continuing legacy of wisdom literature filtered through and by American culture.

All cultures have wisdom texts, whether oral or written. These are the transmitters of the truths upon which the culture and cosmos are based. Often seminal religious texts, such as the Bhagavad Gita, the I Ching, the Koran, the Torah, and the New Testament, they may also be the narratives of gods and goddesses, such as the tales of the ancient Greek, Roman, and Egyptian gods and the creation stories of Native American and African cultures. Religious confessions and autobiographies, including the confessions of Augustine of Hippo, the correspondence of Heloise and Abelard, and the spiritual memoir of St. Teresa de Avila, act similarly, as do texts that present knowledge systems explaining life and proper ways to live. Texts as disparate as the Socratic dialogues, Aristotle's *Nichomachian Ethics,* the U.S. *Declaration of Independence,* Sartre's *Being and Nothingness,* Simone de Beauvoir's *Second Sex,* and Karl Marx's *Communist Manifesto* function in this way.

Likewise, the creators of wisdom literature assume various forms. Some claim to be passive vehicles for the voice of the divine, others the divine incarnate, and still others human interpreters of the human. Over millennia the terms "prophet" and "seer" have developed to identify those with the gift to foretell the future, whereas "sage" has been used for the individual who is especially wise. Western industrialized cultures have adopted the name "writer" for those who fill these roles, so that, for instance, in more symbolic forms the romantic poetry of Rumi (1207–73), the meditations of the English Romantic poets, and the modernist mythopoetics of T. S. Eliot are the conveyors of crystalline truths about that life. So too do contemporary novelists, such as Saul Bellow, Ursula LeGuin, or Henry Miller, those whom writer Erica Jong describes as using fiction to cloak "philosophical truths about the human race and where it is heading" (Miller vi).

Some scholars of wisdom literature prefer to distinguish between knowledge and wisdom, seeing the former as the accumulation of facts through reasoned thinking and the latter as the acquisition of truth through more mystical processes, including the touch of the divine (e.g., the wisdom of the oracle of Delphi or Jesus Christ) or everyday experience (e.g., the wisdom of mother love). These categories, however, I find vexed and reductivistly unhelpful in the final analysis. Defining wisdom as knowledge about what is right or true seems more productive to me. Here I have found applicable George Landow's definition of such discourse as "the apprehension of that which lies out of the sphere of immediate knowledge; the seeing of which, to the natural sense of the seer, is invisible" (25). What remains central is that any author of literature claiming or deserving of the descriptor "wisdom" must apprehend and promulgate knowledge that lies beyond the purview of the average person and the so-called "natural" order.

Also helpful is Landow's division between the writings of the traditional sage, which he contends assume the received and accepted wisdom of the culture, and the words of the traditional prophet, predicated upon the belief that the traditional messages have been forgotten by and must be restored to the culture (23). Identifying the Old Testament prophets as the primary influence on much of Western wisdom literature, Landow singles out "the prophetic pattern of interpretation, [an] attack upon the audience (or those in authority), warning, and visionary promise" as the features most salient in more contemporary forms of the literature of sages and prophets (27). Kerouac's cosmological project reflects these traditions, speaking from a core of accepted cultural beliefs and from a set of what he presents as *lost* cultural values that must be restored for the well-being of humankind.

The Legend also represents the accuracy of Landow's paradigm for identifying the twentieth-century Jeremiah, seven rhetorical features in particular being relevant to Kerouac's literary production: (1) modulation of satiric and visionary statements; (2) attacks upon the audience and efforts to motivate it; (3) a focus on the interpretation of minute details of life; (4) a discontinuous, analogic form of discourse; (5) a tendency toward the grotesque; (6) idiosyncratic definitions; and (7) reliance upon the classical appeal to ethos, or the credibility of the author him- or herself (28–29). Kerouacian voice, diction, structural frames, and attitude or perspective toward himself and his audience all erect with considerable precision a correspondence with his ancient wisdom predecessors. Thus within the general categories of artist, Kerouac constructed the American sage ←→ prophet as a post–World War II dialectic embodied in the character of Jack Duluoz, a folk hero and archetypal representative speaking from, for, and to American culture.

Both the method and the assumption upon which the Duluoz narratives are based fit comfortably with post–World War II U.S. culture. In a nation that still holds fast to its enlightenment heritage of individual expression and free will as well as its belief in God (as recently as October 2005, 80 percent were convinced that God exists[16]), the transmission of wisdom through narratives of personal experience has become an effective mechanism to explore questions of human nature. However, one of the difficulties of reading wisdom literature written as first-person narrative fiction is the interpretation of authorial intent. It is not always as simple as reading a religious law such as "Thou shalt not kill" or even a maxim such as "No person can step in the same river twice." In Kerouac's case, the sage and the prophet frequently shun overt didacticism in favor of insights more subtly masked as the evolving and often contradictory portrait of the narrator-protagonist in relation with multiple characters, situations, and settings. The presentation and the reception of wisdom are less a top-down experience in which readers receive truth from an all-knowing source and more an egalitarian relationship in which readers are analogous to the author, actively constructing the wisdom presented in multilayered, ambiguous language. The author maintains a slight advantage as the speaker of wisdom, yet the reader moves into a relationship of fellow quester, following closely in the author's path, sometimes even hand in hand depending on the author's etiquette for addressing the reader. Wisdom texts of this kind are open fields in which readers tailor knowledge that can become commonly held depending on how others manipulate those same texts.

This method, and the Legend overall, resonates with unsystematically reconciled threads of Western philosophy regarding the place of reason, knowledge, nature, and the metaphysical. At one level, the Legend is grounded in Cartesian rubrics for following the natural operations of the mind, which since they are created by God, according to Descartes, are the most reasoned pathways to knowledge and are accessible to everyone (Lloyd 45). This Cartesian vision has split body and mind, a dualism that permeates the Legend, but Descartes' focus on the movement of the mind is similar to Kerouac's appropriation of Buddhist thinking that through meditative and other cognitive practices seeks to obliterate dualism. Also evident are threads of Scottish Enlightenment thinking, especially Hume's assurance that the humans are guided by reflective passions in the service of enlightened self-interest that builds civil society and the belief that morality comes from feeling and sentiment, not reasoned thinking. Equally if not more apparent is Rousseau's understanding that if the world is to become a better place, one must look back to nature to find the best and most natural selves and look forward to nature that provides rational principles emerging from the human hearts; it is upon these that the social order can be trained and nurtured (Lloyd 59–63).[17] All these beliefs filtered along with Catholicism and American mythologies and disseminated through Kerouac's primary, secondary, and postsecondary education were consequently reformulated by his personal experiences as a French-Canadian-American, an artist, and a student of Buddhism. The result is a complex set of texts in which reason, passion, the divine, the mundane, language, and sound construct truths about America and the world as processes of being and becoming.

Through metaphors drawn from religious and literary mythology, the following chapters advance the contention of writer John Clellon Holmes that writers such as Kerouac "were on a quest, and that the specific object of their quest was spiritual . . . their real journey was inward; and if they seemed to trespass most boundaries, legal and moral, it was only in the hope of finding a belief on the other side" (*Beat Soul* 229). I am not the first to recognize the Duluoz Legend as a spiritual quest. Ann Charters addresses it, as does Regina Weinreich, Warren French, Robert Holton, Ben Giamo, Omar Swartz, and John Lardas. Lardas, in fact, makes a strong case for the tradition of the spiritual Beat jeremiad as a text affirming an original covenant, advocating a communal ideal, warning a culture about its deviance from the ideal, and calling for renewal (28). What distinguishes my reading from others, however, is the identification of American folk culture and wisdom literature as central to the Legend. Working with interdisciplinary perspectives, a philosophical-literary exploration in a sense, I address Kerouac's adaptation of many forms of wisdom literature, ancient and more modern, to craft a spiritual and artistic life for his own and others' edification. I also address the reality that via a fusion of novelistic and autobiographical elements, Kerouac brought to literary life Jack Duluoz as a viable character related to but distinct from his historic creator.

The first chapter, titled "A Creation Story," explores in detail the methods with which Kerouac created Duluoz as a character and Duluoz in relationship to other figures in the Legend. This chapter relies upon a sampling of Kerouac's prose and poetry, including *Mexico City Blues, On the Road, Maggie Cassidy, Visions of Cody, The Subterraneans, Tristessa, Desolation Angels*, and unpublished manuscripts housed in the Berg Collection at the New York Public Library, to explicate Duluoz as the critical matrix around which Kerouac fashioned spiritual and literary motifs. "A Creation Story" is followed by "The Novitiate," which investigates Kerouac's early efforts to build and blend a life to serve human existence and art — in other words, the apprenticeship leading to the creation of Duluoz. This discussion draws on Kerouac's early letters, journals, and selections of his juvenilia to argue that Duluoz is the organic composite of Kerouac's literary probing of the

ontological and metaphysical. The next three chapters each address one of
Kerouac's mature works. "The Quest—Part I" focuses on *On the Road,* reading the seminal Beat novel as a modern variant of the gnostic text "Song of
the Pearl," a richly symbolic narrative of the quest for human knowledge.
"Cosmology" turns its attention to *Doctor Sax,* Kerouac's fantasy superhero
novel in which he allegorically uses the Shadow, the Great Snake, and Doctor
Sax to construct the history and operation of the universe. This is followed
by "The Quest—Part II," which investigates his spiritual and narrativistic
experiments through the study of Buddhism as presented in *Some of the
Dharma.* The penultimate chapter, "Songs and Prayers," addresses these
themes as Kerouac dealt with them in verse and prose poetry, particularly
Mexico City Blues and *Old Angel Midnight."* "The Story of the Fall" concludes the book, using *Desolation Angels* as a site from which to excavate
Kerouac's conclusions about the interstices of art and spirituality in the last
decade of his life. All chapters reveal threads of Kerouac's wisdom and warning that America, a land and people of capacious good will and the great
hope of the world's future, must recognize—sooner rather than later—their
Edenic folk roots if they are to fulfill the promises of the American dream.
By returning to this source, presented in the Legend as both a Buddhist Pure
Land and a Western utopia, America reclaims a vibrant, loving, and nonvio-
lent individualism grounded in one's innate godliness.

   To articulate this wisdom quest, I have not dealt with the entirety of
Kerouac's production, which is indeed voluminous. Doing so would have
given short shrift to texts that deserve a more critical eye and in some cases
replicated already existing scholarship. Even so, many of the texts that I discuss warrant considerably more interpretive attention. Nonetheless, this sub-
set will, I hope, aid in establishing Kerouac as a historical figure and literary
voice that reflects the philosophical and aesthetic tradition of American arts
and letters as the relentless search for the twin flames of spiritual wisdom and
literary expression. Both reside in the lived life and imagination of every individual, a cultural mythos explaining to some extent why Kerouac became
and remains a mythic figure in his own right.

A CREATION STORY

PART I: THE METHOD

The power of Kerouac's proclamations regarding the method of writing that he developed as he advanced the Duluoz Legend remains so great that it is virtually impossible to discuss the Legend and his wisdom quests without first addressing spontaneous prose. The method, as this chapter and others will illustrate, is highly relevant to the spiritual and artistic paths that Kerouac pursued, so that both its stated and unstated components must be elucidated to establish legitimate contexts for these quests. Kerouac never theorized extensively about genre or method, unlike Allen Ginsberg, who spoke, wrote, and taught at length regarding the theory and practice of literary production, but Kerouac did think somewhat systematically about the methods he employed to construct the Legend, and in 1953, at the request of Ginsberg and William Burroughs (*Letters* 1: 445), he wrote "Essentials of Spontaneous Prose," which was published in 1957 by the *Evergreen Review*. This short and exuberant text has become the standard upon which his work has been interpreted, and as public declaration, "Essentials" articulates some of what he considered necessary for artistic integrity and quality. In the following often-quoted passage, Kerouac instructs writers on appropriate rhetorical forms and their correlation to the author-reader relationship:

> Not "selectivity" of expression but following free deviation (association) of mind into limitless blow-on-subject seas of thought, swimming in sea of English with no discipline other than rhythms of rhetorical exhalation and expostulated statement, [. . .] satisfy yourself first, then reader cannot fail to receive telepathic shock and meaning-excitement by same laws operating in his own mind. (*Portable* 484)

This theory of spontaneity is governed by assumptions that in the aggregate ground Kerouac in the interstices of contradiction: a firmly held belief in the exclusivity of art as divine and an equally firmly held belief in the inclusivity of art as immigrant, populist expression. The manifesto disallows "slow measured inductive introspections sunk in anguished consultation about shoulds and shouldnots." In its place, he posited that the truest artistic emotions and ideas are expressed spontaneously (*Blonde* 89) like a "Running Proust" (*Letters* 1: 515) because the method triggers the subconscious to admit in its own language what consciously constructed language censors (Tytell 142). In effect, Kerouac reconstituted mid-twentieth-century writers as neoromantics who tap a collective unconscious linking all human minds: in other words, one may be unable to translate or paraphrase what the author is saying, but one will "know" intuitively what the text means.

Paradoxically, Kerouac's apparently narrow focus on self leads the author not into undecipherable narcissism but into the Berdyaevian limitless commune of human nature itself, which operates by laws transcending cultural codification. This idea is more than mimicry of Yeatsian trance writing or Freudian associative thinking. It more accurately represents a turn to Wordsworth's belief that all good writing is the production of powerful feelings. It also nods its head at Carl Jung's concept of archetypes, the innate prototypes that Jung identified as culturally and genetically transmitted in the creation of the unconscious, and at Emerson's oversoul, "the wise silence, the universal beauty, to which every part and particle is equally related: the eternal ONE" (281). Perhaps most importantly, Kerouac justified spontaneous composition with his religious beliefs, likening the method to the Christian tenet that the speaker who relinquishes control of language to God speaks unpremeditatedly the language of the Holy Ghost. The resultant work becomes what he described as a holiness or "Cathedral of Form" held together by "natural-speech and words" (*Letters* 1: 515).

Kerouac came upon this theory most directly by reading a 13,000-word document, now known as the "Cherry Mary" letter, from Neal Cassady in December 1950, only a few months before he completed the major restructuring of what became *On the Road* (*Letters* 1: 242). Responding enthusiastically to Cassady's prose, he declared that henceforth he would be embarking on a new kind of writing—an honest confession of his life story written directly to Cassady, who knew and understood him. Such writing, part of a new "little American Renaissance" that Kerouac envisioned, renounced both "fiction and fear" and swore allegiance to the truth that alone provides a legitimate reason to compose (*Letters* 1: 248). Kerouac told Cassady that since he, Cassady, had never sinned (a flagrant untruth perhaps created by Kerouac's epiphanic excitement), Kerouac's new voice would enable him to join Cassady in his "holy hole," a writer's underground to which he solemnly dedicated himself "as of this date, Dec. 28, 1950, holy night, snowy night" (*Letters* 1: 248). The allusion to Joseph Mohr and Franz Gruber's revered Christmas hymn "Silent Night, Holy Night," as well as Dostoyevsky's tortured underground man, welds Kerouac's conception of style and artistic mission into the creation story of Jesus Christ as the messiah, thus reconfiguring that savior as the writer who founds a new American renaissance of religion and literature. Duluoz as the primary creation of the creator is a literary figure in whom the holy truth resides. Subsequent Kerouac letters to Cassady illustrate that in accordance with this new-found directive, Kerouac began to reshape the Duluoz narrative as a fluid, confessional, and rhapsodic voice projecting full confidence in its mission, tone, and material as essential for the development of American literature and the spiritual welfare of its readers.[1]

In the process, the literary text and the means of its production became associated for Kerouac with a journey backward through cultural and personal time, a seeking of self-justification through the validation of his own first language, Quebecois or *joual,* which at the age of nineteen he described as "one of the most languagey languages in the world . . . the language of the tongue, and not of the pen" (*Atop* 151). This journey, one that preoccupied him his entire life, was an eschatological project—the search for the omnipresent primal poet, an "original kicker" (*Atop* 94), which he described in a letter to Ginsberg in 1952:

> Literature as you see it, using words like "verbal" and "images" etc. and things like, well all the "paraphernalia" of criticism etc. is no longer my concern, because the thing makes me say "shitty little beach in the reeds" is Pre-Literary, it happened to me to think that way before I learned the words the literateurs use to describe what they're doing. (*Letters* 1: 383)

What Kerouac espouses in this reflection is a process underlying the lyric mode itself, and more importantly the identity of the lyric poet, who, as Daniel Albright states, recognizes in that mode "some prelapsarian harmony" and " will tend to fall backward in his [or her] own sensibility . . . toward a consciousness more synthetic and indiscriminate than his own, toward someone almost prehuman" (55). For Kerouac, this poet was a writer like Shakespeare and Joyce, both of whom he greatly admired as geniuses who birthed new forms of language (*Portable* 488–90).

Kerouac sensed that what he called Shakespeare's and Joyce's Heraclitean genius—meaning, I am presuming, ever shifting and not time bound— enabled them to distinguish between noise, a social phenomenon, and sound, the timeless genesis of the word. "Shakespeare heard *sound* first," Kerouac wrote, "then the words were there in his QUICK HEAD" (*Blonde* 88). With respect to his own work, this sound may have been the French "oo" that permeates so much of his poetry, especially *Mexico City Blues*,[2] and is identified in conjunction with a drawing of a happy face ☺ as the "found" sound in the forty-fifth chorus of "Orlando Blues" (*Blues* 242). It may also be linked to the sound of the jazz horn, which, as Kerouac's friend and collaborator David Amram recalls, represented to Kerouac "some kind of ancient sound from the preconscious past of where he was trying to trace his roots way back to pre-christian Brittany" (55). In the hands of a writer such as Shakespeare, this sound, Kerouac concluded, emerged as a rave "in the great world night like the wild wind through an old Cathedral," and in Joyce, particularly *Finnegans Wake*, as "pure raving Shakespeare below, beneath, all over." (*Blonde* 86–87). In the ability to use sound to create language to rave at the world, Kerouac also linked Shakespeare and Joyce with his grandfather, a French-Canadian immigrant whose language empowered him to castigate and celebrate both nature and God, exemplifying the force of the oral human word to recognize its god while building its own world (*Atop* 151).

A related assumption grounding Kerouac's theory is that the method produces the richest and most *musical* words possible. Kerouac understood that the sound of spoken language, *parole,* has value in and of itself separate from the values associated with *langue,* the institutionalized and standardized meaning of words. This musical quality of literature, distinct from the primal sound of language, was crucial for him, who from his undergraduate days at Columbia identified strongly with jazz musicians, African American as well as Euro-American, such as Lenny Tristano, Bud Powell, Charlie Parker, Billie Holliday, Lester Young, and Lee Konitz. Just as a jazz musician begins with a chord or melody and weaves intricate improvisational works around what Kerouac called the "jewel point," the writer could start with an image and "blow-on subject seas of thought," freely creating musical sounds from the subject of the image (*Portable Beat* 57–58). This use of language, according to Ginsberg, led Kerouac toward a different kind of intelligence or modality of consciousness—"still conscious, still reasonable, but . . . a reason founded on conceptual associations" (Ball 160).

In the process, the Legend connects two essential features of human consciousness and the oral tradition. The first is sound, with or without linguistic meaning: as word, music, song, and metaphysical foundation. Ezra Pound referred to this as *melos;* Northrop Frye called it melopoiea, arising from babble, its subconscious or preliterate impulse. The term *babble* has appeared in critical discussions of Kerouac's idiomatic word production, the definition varying from meaningless chatter to a continuous murmuring sound like flowing water. Regina Weinreich, for instance, in her introduction to Kerouac's *Book of Haikus,* describes his method as having the capacity to *reduce* language to babble (xxiii, emphasis mine), the implication being that such language may be childish and thus inferior. Clark Coolidge uses the term in a more expansive and intentional way, identifying Kerouac's "Babble Flow" as "just letting it completely go on"—the result of the artist's desire to include everything in a poem or prose piece (48–49).

Kerouac disclosed in *Mexico City Blues* the limitations of these two perspectives when treated as mutually exclusive. The babblish baby talk in the lines "chinkly pinkly pink baby / Gleering . . .; He hugens to re-double / the image, in words" (100) enacts as a *simultaneous reality* the child's production of speech *and* the concept of letting all sounds flow out. It is a poetic gesture defining babble as the way the mind moves beyond and expands, that is, "re-doubles" that which is seen. Kerouac, too, used the term *babble*, particularly to capture those most productive yet dangerous moments when he found himself on "the edges of language." Reflecting on this precipice in "The First Word: Jack Kerouac Takes a Fresh Look at Jack Kerouac," an essay that *Escapade* magazine published in 1957, Kerouac described the point as "where the babble of the subconscious begins, because words 'come from the Holy Ghost' first in the form of babble which suddenly by its sound indicates the word truly intended" (*Portable* 487). Babble, then, with regard to Duluoz is the beginning of rhythmic and semantic imitation through sound associations—that with which all humans engage as they think and talk.

Sound's counterpart *and* twin is the image, or *opis* as Pound termed it, *phanopoeia* as Frye called it, or *doodle*, the playful association of images that humans use to learn to think, draw, and write. These terms do not reference the image as a literary device, which, as noted above, Kerouac repudiated in his correspondence with Ginsberg (although he often manipulated it effectively), but as a component of cognition. There is always something writers rely upon as the catalyst for literary production, a form that subsequently "hugens to re-double," or is transformed into and preserved as the literary image. Whether abstracted from the natural world (the perceived image) or memory (the mental image), it is always there: a psychological construct just as vital to creative and critical thought as are sound and other sense perceptions.[3] Kerouac intuited this knowledge that, first, compelled him to trust his memory as an indispensable source for poetic expression and, second, propelled him to practice sketching, a process mandating that words be applied like paint to capture the external or internal world—anything from a street corner, a riverbed, an old diner, to the memory of playing marbles could be sketched in words. When sketching, he wrote to Ginsberg in 1952, "everything activates in front of you in myriad profusion, you just have to purify your mind . . . and write with 100% personal honesty both psychic and social etc. and slap it all down" (*Letters* 1: 356). This process enabled him to explore the permutations of time/space continuums so as to enlarge or compress the visual world through the crucible of language.[4]

At the conscious and unconscious levels, babble and doodle ground thought and language and are essential tools of social human construction. One finds their fossil remains in the performative language of ancient societies that employ charms and chants to evoke the divine and to fuel communal and individual power through sound and rhythm and puns and riddles.[5] Of course, Kerouac was not raised in a preliterate world. His French-Canadian, working-class upbringing provided him with a rich experience in storytelling, sensitizing him to an organic connection between the trajectory of one's life and the texture of one's language (*Atop* 151). Kerouac spent his youth immersed in the printed word. His father operated a printing business, and Kerouac grew up fascinated with books and language, reading the Bobbsey Twins, the Shadow comics, Phantom detective magazines, Street and Smith's Star Western magazines, and newspaper sports reports (*Blonde* 93). As the collection of his juvenilia published in *Atop an Underwood* illustrates, the works of Albert Halper, William Saroyan, James Joyce, Thomas Wolfe, Ernest Hemingway, Orson Welles, Walt Whitman, and others nurtured his literary development. Thus, to grapple with Duluoz, one is obligated to situate Kerouac's pronouncements and practices of spontaneous method within the framework of oral *and* literate discourse.

It is easy for some—including Kerouac—to conclude that because he rejected socially contrived prescriptions and drew organically on his own internal processes to reach an essential consciousness, Duluoz is "more or less physiologically and/or psychically 'true form'" (Frank and Sayre xv)—that is, authentic form that grants the speaker its authority. It was this belief that Kerouac articulated so ecstatically to Cassady in December 1950 and reformulated for a larger public audience in his "Essentials" manifesto. While James Jones is correct to state that Kerouac's methodological intention was "to collapse the interval between inspiration and creation, to produce an immediate—not a mediate—version of reality to enact experience and emotions in language" (*Map* 142–43), this endeavor is ontologically impossible. All language emerges from not only individual consciousness but also the larger social contexts in which one has acquired language, from the very forms of discourse that create and mediate experience. Language and whatever authenticity and authority it has is always an immediate reality and a mediation of reality. Consequently, Duluoz as Kerouac's literary proxy combines socially constructed strategies of composition more complicated than his aesthetic statements suggest.

Kerouac's practice relied at times upon conventional processes of literary composition and revision to achieve a structure that best expressed his preconceived idea of what the novel, poem, confession, prayer, or letter should be. As Weinreich has noted, one way by which he accomplished this structure was through repetitive writing of various themes and stories (11).

Retelling or rehearsing stories, such as those of his birth, his father's death, his travels with Cassady, his brother Gerard, and his childhood in Lowell, reshaped and reinforced structural features of his autobiographical memories while enabling him to reshape the literary presentation of those memories. But verbal rehearsal was also complemented by revision and editing of large as well as small portions of spontaneously drafted texts. This latter practice, a secret reality undergirding his published manifestos, fueled his innovation predicated upon improvisation and spontaneity, allowing him, as Tim Hunt argues, to manipulate the page as a *space* in which and *place* upon which to work with the dual systems of writing—that is, script as oral analogue and as visual code.[6] In so doing, his writing foregrounds the speaker whose language is an act of mediation between the reader and the roiling world of babble, between thought and its artful expression. This system, while dominant, shares space with the page as a place upon which the poet demonstrates the complexities of human perception, the speaker, in Hunt's words, "dropping from the equation" as the reader enters the mind of the seeing, or doodling, eye. In the tension uniting these functions, Kerouac situated Duluoz squarely on the most powerful forms of melopoeia and phanopoeia. The result challenges and affirms language as experience itself and the intermediary of that experience.

By the time Kerouac made public his aesthetics of spontaneous prose, he was an accomplished writer with enough faith in himself to disseminate parts of the method most in line with the romantic persona that he and Duluoz had assumed. The strategy fueled his image as heroic American sage and prophet, the mythology of the spontaneous method fitting beautifully with the oversized, emotional image of a chosen people that to this day characterizes American consciousness. But the process, while engaging spontaneous production, was distinctly variegated, Kerouac contending that he required "solitude and a kind of 'do nothing' philosophy" allowing him "to dream all day and work out chapters in forgotten reveries that emerge years later in story form" (*Angels* 220). This statement may be the most direct that we have regarding how he composed mentally over long periods of time before transferring the ideas to paper, much of the story emerging whole cloth. The *manipulation* of memory was critical to his method.

As someone savvy about the nature of memory, Kerouac subtly threaded the Legend with the metanarrative of memory as reliable yet flawed. Of all the components of the Legend, *Desolation Angels* may be the most transparent in this respect. For instance, as the narrator of *Angels,* Duluoz reveals that a writer of autobiographical fiction at times must review photographs to recall past events and that the photographs record a self that no longer exists (240). Writing about his trips to Mexico, he admits that he always envisions the country as gay and exciting, with people rushing across glistening sidewalks, an image that dominates texts such as *On The Road* and *Lonesome Traveler.* "But I always get surprised," he confesses, "when I arrive in Mexico to see I'd forgotten a certain drear, even sad, darkness, like the sight of some old Indian man in a brown rust suit" (*Angels* 222). Contrapuntally, *Vanity of Duluoz* discloses that while Kerouac used his diaries to refresh his memory for purposes of storytelling, going so far as to quote from one, he realizes that sometimes these documents just do not suffice. "None of the adolescent scribblings of that time I kept in journals'll do us now," he admits (122)—in these moments, the writer's imagination has to take over. Such awareness signals that although Kerouac relied upon his experiences as well as documentation and verification of them, he was more interested in the act of telling stories than creating a historically accurate text. This secret he discloses in the last two installments of the Legend, *Vanity* and *Satori,* the most like conventional life writing of any of the books in that they focus on reporting facts (actions, dates, and names) rather than fictionalizing a story. *Vanity* includes asides in which he states that he will keep the action moving by skipping over parts that will bore readers, such as expositions of his development as a writer (100) and his memories of serving in the Merchant Marines (134). *Satori* admits that "it's hard to decide what to tell in a story, and I always seem to try to prove something, comma, about my sex. Let's forget it" (19). He thus implicitly acknowledges that using the public act of storytelling to prove something highly personal such as details regarding sexual orientation or masculinity, may be inappropriate. In concert, *Vanity* and *Satori* draw upon the capacity of life writing to make visible strategies by which authors selectively reconfigure their experiences to tell an engaging story.

Kerouac also lays bare the space separating historical fact and memoir, clarifying that when memory and language are used to recreate the real person or event, portraiture cannot overcome approximation; the reality of the past experience exists only in partial form in any postexperiential construct. *Angels* provides many well-defined examples of this pattern. To communicate the nature of his relationship with Irwin Garden, for instance, Duluoz falls back on what he admits are "sample attempts" of Irwin's language, using phrases such as "We'll wave our pants from stretchers!" and "We'll have assholes showing on the screens of Hollywood." (*Angels* 183)—not the real thing, but supposedly close enough. Parenthetical asides, such as "(or I guess she said, I don't remember)," confess that sometimes the presentation of an external referent's actual language is an illusion (*Angels* 263). The narrative also contains traces of the processes by which historicity and fiction merge and diverge. The pseudonyms of historical figures are occasionally replaced temporarily by the individuals' real names, as in the case of Raphael Urso who sometimes becomes Gregory Corso, his real-life template. What appear to be correct references to external sources also cannot always be trusted. For instance Duluoz's citing of

2 Corinthians 8:10, Paul's explanation of why he used letters to teach from a geographic distance, should be 2 Corinthians 13:10 (*Angels* 286). In a case like this, the appearance of a learned textual reference outside the imagination is not historical fact but becomes, for whatever reason, whether accident, sloppiness, or intent, an illusion of veracity and externality.

At other times, Duluoz's comments imply that he may be telling the story of *Angels* not as a first-person narrator with a limited perspective but as an omniscient persona. This device of narrative fiction, not life writing, is exemplified by Raphael's criticism of Duluoz's intellectualism: "Shelley didn't care about theories about how he was to write 'The Skylark.' Duluoz you're full of theories like an old college perfessor [*sic*], you think you know everything.' ('You think you're the only one,' he added to himself)" (280). How is a reader to understand Raphael's parenthetical comment? As an aside spoken under his breath and overheard by Duluoz, or as a silent thought privy only to an omniscient narrator? The phrase "he added to himself" is sufficiently ambiguous to encompass both possibilities. Therefore, any semblance to historic veracity must be predicated at least partially on imaginative reassemblege. This and other features of *Angels* confound the divisions between memoir as truth based and fiction as imagination based. In turn, Duluoz as a literary device allows Kerouac *the author* to remain attached to his spontaneous method and the legend of his miraculous memory, while it is his fictive representative Duluoz who undermines the myth of memoir as factual "tell all" with distinct artifacts of the literary imagination.

The elements of fiction and nonfiction revealed in *Angels* exist in other Duluoz narratives, although at times they are hidden if not seemingly nonexistent in the context of public awareness of Kerouac's spontaneous method. For example, the appearance of memoir threatens to subsume the artifice in *Maggie Cassidy*, a Duluoz text set in Lowell and constructed like a conventional bildungsroman. However, the "Maggie Cassidy" notebooks in which Kerouac drafted the narrative demonstrate that his first attempts to write about his teenage years began far differently than the published text. The latter opens with a scene of a group of teenage boys "staggering down the snowy road arm in arm," one of them sadly singing the song "Jack o' Diamonds" from a Western B-movie.[7] The first paragraph concludes with the trenchant statement "It was the New Year 1939, before the war, before anyone knew the intention of the world toward America" (5), a powerful articulation of the thrust of the narrative, which in the story of two New England teenagers' doomed love affair projects a nation's loss of innocence. A winter scene also introduces the notebooks, but it contains no overarching theme of American culture and politics, instead featuring an idyllic regional vision of people skating on a river. Mary is among the skaters, wearing white skates and a muff, described in angelic, saintly, and romantic language culminating in the narrator's identification of her as God's bride. The second page features a note penciled in the right column indicating that the narrative should actually begin at that point, which includes garbled descriptions of old Ireland followed by passages about Jack meeting Mary at a Lowell dance and erotic descriptions of her young flesh and their first kiss. This version rushes into the teenage relationship without establishing the romance as a metaphor for American history, one of the strengths of the published text.[8]

It was not until 1978, when *Visions of Cody* was published, that readers had the opportunity to witness Kerouac's keen exposition of the critical space separating the raw data of history from the artful representation of those data in the crucible of the writer's story-telling imagination. *Cody*, his most provocative and experimental novel, features "Frisco: The Tape," a transcript of conversations with Neal (Cody) and Carolyn (Evelyn) Cassady and a few others that is juxtaposed with "An Imitation of the Tape," Kerouac's rendering of free-flowing language parodically analogous to conversation. The contiguous texts argue for the distinct nature of the two acts. The taped conversations, at times funny and engaging, speak at points to Kerouac's process of re-membering that is necessary for the subsequent generation of imaginative stories. To develop knowledge of the time Cody spent in Texas with Hubbard, June, and Irwin, for instance, Duluoz prods him with the questions "What were you doing?" and "What he do?" When Cody responds with "I can't remember man, it's a terrible feeling not being able to remember what *I* was doing" (126), Duluoz intervenes with epistemological prompts: "[Irwin] said you kneeled in the road" and "why did [Hubbard] let go a blast of the shotgun at all?" (127).[9]

The transcript also demonstrates the performative nature of human speech, acting out characters or selves in a specific setting, in this case the Cassadys' home. For the actors and audience, the performances serve as both generators of knowledge regarding the actors and demonstrations of spontaneous collaboration. With respect to the latter, a passage in which Cody conducts himself, Jack, and a friend named Jimmy playing two piccolos and a sweet potato illustrates the scaffolding of improvisation. Cody takes the lead with "we gotta be like a string quartet, no beat and syncopation whatsoever, see," moving the performance along with phrases such as "slowly, children, slowly," "Now we trade," "come on go on," and "It's the piss hole [. . .] all hollow blowing" (150–51). These signal the movement and adjustments of the music they are playing as well as, at a metalevel, the nature of conversation itself: the sharing of instruments (language), the process of striving to create out of multiple voices a unified sound (prolonging the discourse or working toward points agreeable to all), and the open-ended, nonlinear nature of talk (fizzling out, ending as hollow air).

Despite these strengths, the transcription is often tediously obtuse and banal. Take the following excerpt from a conversation among Cody, Jimmy, Jack, and Pat that begins by discussing Gene Krupa's "Leave Us Leap":

JIMMY. (*playing with toy telephone*) Can you tell me why the manufacturer forgot to put a hole in the—the part where you hear through?

PAT. So it's so you can call your wife.

JIMMY. Ah . . . I was—

CODY. (*laughing*) So you can call your wife . . .

JIMMY. It doesn't fit on here . . . sounds better (*squeaking it*) that way

CODY. (*entering now*) Man . . . aww . . . Jimmy . . . is this different pot than what—

JIMMY. No . . . there's only one difference, there's about ten roaches mixed up, you know? (157)

The "aww's," truncated words, aborted phrases, digressions, and stutterings of human conversation represented in this passage only occasionally made somewhat intelligible to a reader via parenthetical descriptions, expose raw transcripted conversation as, according to Ginsberg in his epilogue to *Cody*, "interesting if you love or know the characters & want their reality" (410). But for those who do not, the degree of interest in the taped documentation can drop precipitously—as does the persuasiveness of Dadaist, Beat, and Personism arguments that any human act is art, that even the tape, again to quote Ginsberg, is "a spontaneous Ritual performed once & never repeated, in full consciousness that every yawn & syllable uttered would be eternal" (411). The tape of private conversation made public may appear to be a "democratic location for storytelling," as John Shapcott claims (237), as well as the mundane-as-eternal, as Ginsberg maintained, but more realistically it projects exclusivity, the inaccessible knowledge-beyond-language shared only by intimates.

In Kerouac's hand, however, features of human conversation when manipulated via literary mechanisms to satisfy the need to *approximate* human conversation can affect a democratic storytelling presence while simultaneously critiquing the problematic nature of taped conversation. "Imitation of the Tape," identified as a "COMPOSITION" written by Jackie Duluoz, was composed in the tradition of "Joyce, or e e cummings of EIMI," Kerouac informed Elbert Lenrow, a professor at the New School (*Letters* 2:103). The imitation of taped conversation artfully mimes oral conversation in lines such as "But no, wait in here, don't you know I'm serious? you think I'm—damn you, you made, you make, the most, m—I guess—but now wait a minute, till I!—but no I'll jump on in, I mean to say, w—about whatever—" (*Cody* 249–50).

The semblance of a multiparticipant discourse is projected through the continuous monologue of a single speaker, but instead of struggling to fill in the blanks of numerous discursive threads as one does with transcribed conversation, readers are supported by alliteration and dashes that render superfluous the discourse of the invisible conversant(s), sufficiently linking the speaker's phrases one to another. The technique eradicates the need to know what the conversants are saying and simultaneously accelerates the movement of the language, mimicking the musical quality of conversation semantically understood only by the performers in the moment of creation. The humorous nature of these passages, a literal parody of conversation, exposes two critical points: (1) the false belief that writing is a mere outer garment cloaking thought and speech, and (2) the technical and imaginative processes with which Kerouac as writer worked. Both illustrate that Duluoz is method and artifice, that speech and writing remain linked but essentially separate creative processes, and that the lived experience is ultimately unreachable through written or recorded discourse.

These points are underscored by Duluoz's turn to comic names for the speakers or characters in "Imitation," which employs dramatic form that looks like but is a far cry from identification of speakers in the transcription. Instead of Cody, Jack, Evelyn, Jimmy, and Pat, readers encounter Lady Godiva, who in Duluoz's voice tells stories about horse races, memory, and Lowell; a priest and an altar boy who mock Catholic Church ritual with Latinate puns such as "Tedoom te deum" (268); W. C. Fields, Gary Cooper, a man on a soapbox in Union Square, and a mountain skier who bawdily says only "By sooth and foreskin" (270); a reel of film that describes a brief scene with Charlie Chaplin and Two-Time Butch; the usherette Moldy Marie from the Rialto Theatre whose daughter Filthy Mary is gangbanged every night; and someone named Aderiande. This section, reflecting Joyce's hallucinatory sixteenth episode ostensibly set in a brothel (informally known as the "Circe" or "Nighttown" episode) in *Ulysses* that effects hyperreality to expose the hidden desires of author, character, and reader, relies on grotesque comic visions of human speech and actions to inversely bare both technology and writing as grand illusions.[10] The intimacy of human face-to-face interactions is driven into a bizarre Joycean sadomasochistic travesty: the tape recorder as a-synecdoche-of-technology and literature as a-synecdoche-of-human-reality are turned topsy-turvy. The point is not that the writer's treatment of oral material is superior to the primal form, but that the two are more like Siamese twins, sharing essential body organs but remaining distinct. The text thereby cautions that speech *and* writing are unreliable conveyors of lived experience or truth. It does acknowledge, though, that written signifiers of the oral have the capacity to disclose the limitations of technology. As such, "Imitation" hints at the possible downfall of a mechanomorphic American culture in which anthropocentric mythology has been replaced by narratives describing the world in terms of mythical machines (Toulmin 24).

Visions of Cody, more than any other chapter of the Legend, demonstrates that Kerouac's methods worked against the Aristotelian heritage of conventional narrative structure. Over time, this structure unraveled until he was working almost solely with forms of confession, autobiography, songs, poems, prayers, and meditations. These can appear to be slapped together but are nothing of the kind. Instead they constitute a recursive move to more essential texts of cultural wisdom and prophecy, ranging from the lyrical prayers and proverbs of the Jewish Old Testament to the parables of Jesus Christ in the Christian New Testament, to the lectures on causality and consequences contained in the Buddhist sutras, to the confessions of Christian saints, to the secular journals of Thoreau, the poetic sermons and lectures of Emerson, the Protestant liturgical rhythms of Emily Dickinson's poems and Melville's sermons, and to the epistolary genesis of both the Christian New Testament and the novel, all of which Kerouac knew well. The distance between the implied author and the first-person narrator diminishes as Duluoz approaches these ur-texts to achieve narrative authenticity, honesty, and credibility. Consequently, as American legend, Duluoz's story from *On the Road* through *Satori in Paris*, in which Kerouac finally replaces his literary proxy as narrator, situates America and its immigrant hero as consubstantial sites. Within these spaces, the nation and its fictional representative craft and predict the direction of American literature while performing essential American values to sustain the nation as mythic reality.

PART II: JACK DULUOZ AND COMPANY

Jack Duluoz first came to widespread public attention disguised as Sal Paradise in *On the Road* (1957), traversing North and Central America in search of ineffable truth. Dressed as an inferior folk hero and endowed with good-hearted, self-deprecating humor, he lopes after those whom he identifies as his own wisdom teachers until he achieves a relationship with the girl of his dreams and a life off the road. This character remains fundamentally stable as a subordinate, although individual segments of the Legend modify the role. *Visions of Gerard* (1963), for instance, focuses on how Duluoz learned life's seminal lessons from his parents, from the suffering of his older brother, Gerard, and from Buddhist sutras. *Doctor Sax* (1959) advances the chronology to reveal a young boy following the Shadow of comic book fame and his mother and father, whose folk wisdom teaches him to read human nature. In *Maggie Cassidy* (1959), Duluoz is a more outgoing teenager—a stature generated by romance, graduation from high school, and admittance to Columbia University. *The Dharma Bums* (1958), *Desolation Angels* (1965), and *Visions of Cody* (1972) feature Duluoz among his literary comrades, those whom he teaches and from whom he learns, and many of these voices waft through the prose poem *Old Angel Midnight* (1959). *The Subterraneans* (1958) and *Tristessa* (1960) record his middle-age relationships with women of color, both texts confessing his failure to learn from women's wisdom, and *Mexico City Blues* (1959) concludes with the apotheosis of the jazz legend Charlie Parker. In *Vanity of Duluoz: An Adventurous Education, 1935–46* (1968), Duluoz confesses that despite his efforts to follow well-meaning advice regarding "everything you're supposed to do in life," he has failed: "nothing ever came of it," he laments (268). *Satori in Paris* (1966) unveils the reality of Kerouac behind the fiction of Duluoz when the persona frustrates his efforts to write honestly about his adventurous genealogical search for the Breton Kerouacs (8). As end-of-life visions, then, *Satori* and *Vanity* suggest that Duluoz never fully develops as a figure that has achieved the American ideal of relentless progress toward material and spiritual perfection. He retains the identity of the neophyte who seeks the wisdom of others, fluctuating in his (dis)belief that he can save himself—let alone others.

However, elements of confidence color Kerouac's portrait of Duluoz as a gigantic and often misunderstood persona battling primal forces that threaten to quash the individual who seeks to control and unify all. His first attempt to write his autobiography in epistolary form to Cassady includes the revelation that even as an infant Kerouac sensed that some evil force, a snake, was pursuing him. In reflection, he told Cassady, "How proudly we American pipsqueaks play around with the pretentious ideas of Europe. Antichrist Kerouac, the SNAKE came for him alone, no one else. I now know, the SNAKE came for all of us and caught us all" (*Letters* 1: 251). By comparing himself as an American to European intellectuals, he reiterates beliefs that Americans have regarding their inferiority as the still-young descendants of revered European traditions. In Kerouac's vision, national angst generates false acts of hubris manifested as belief in the supremacy of the individual—and by extension, the supremacy of the United States. But the "SNAKE," Kerouac implies, favors no one: all who believe they are singled out by either good or evil are aping the hubris of the Antichrist, or Lucifer. The myth of American independence, exposed as only partial truth at best, bends to the realization of human impotence and frailty, returning both Kerouac and Duluoz time and again to the bosom of their family and friends.

As conveyor of these truths, Duluoz employs rhetorical techniques characteristic of romance and wisdom literature to convince readers that his words are reliable. First-person narration or the presentation of autobiographical, and especially intimate, information is perhaps the most effective device forging a historical rather than fictional impression, establishing veracity and believability. Then, too, his reliance on detailed sketches, or what art critics call word paintings, in effect, as Robert Stange writes, emphasize "a perceptual scheme, generally that of the moving eye . . . convey[ing] the immediate experience of discrete phenomena by means of image sequences, precise observation, dramatized acts of perception" (Landow 134). In passages such as the following portrait of St. Patrick's Cathedral from *Visions of Cody,* the technique fashions the illusion of immediacy:

> . . . most striking of the windows and I didn't expect strikingness at this late hour—is at upper front left—a lonely icy congealed blue with streaks of hot pink—little blue holes—painted with an immeasurable blue ink, *noir comme bleu,* black like blue, I was going to say three Apostles but there are only two, third slot is not figure, is three one-third-size endisced figures almost like holes in skating ice—but with a winter swamp water full of mill dyes and midnight—no sky has had the color of this glass, and I know skies—all other windows here now dimming except this—It faces East, must be amazing tomorrow morning—faces East like my poor hospital window—Lord, I scribbled hymns to you. (28)

The above passage reads as if it were written in the very moment of viewing the cathedral window, but the passage may well have drawn on Kerouac's previous visits to the cathedral, especially his January 9, 1951, visit, described in a letter to Cassady, as an attempt to escape the cold and find a quiet place to think (*Letters* 1. 285). That narrative situates the experience as mediated by memory and language, explicitly told at a remove of some hours and woven with cultural critique. But in *Cody,* Duluoz's moving eye framing parts of the window methodically emphasizes shapes and colors in quasi-scientific language; this conjoined with nongrammatical language and a self-assured but humble voice projects authentic immediacy rather than explicitly mediated occurrences or abstractions.

Duluoz also constructs an ethos or persona that situates him as a *Euro-American* sage and prophet, drawing upon many of the techniques that Landow identifies in nineteenth- and twentieth-century wisdom literature. The ethos rests upon his illuminating interpretations of unusual or inappropriate materials, the claims that he has unusual or mystical powers of perception (such as, on a small scale, the above claim that he knows skies), the contention that he has interpreted events and people accurately, quotations of and allusions to spiritual texts, and vast knowledge of many forms of American culture. All are founded on the assumption that readers deem most authentic, and therefore credible, the knowledge derived from personal experience (Landow 162, 166), a quality correlating with the American myth of independence and individuality.

However, the perception of credibility, or authority, is not the same as the thing itself, especially with respect to mystical knowledge on which the Legend frequently relies. From the Dickensian mother's vision that teaches Sal about his failure to honor love in *On the Road* to Leo's vision of St. Theresa of

Lisieux's showering of roses in *The Subterraneans,* which brings him momentary serenity, to Ray's sudden awareness that one "can't fall off a mountain" in *The Dharma Bums,* Duluoz's ethos centers on incommunicable mystical truths that correlate positively with the philosopher William James's description of such knowledge as "on the whole pantheistic and optimistic" as well as "antinaturalistic and harmoniz[ing] best with twice-bornness." These states correspond with sensation rather than conceptual thought, and while they have concrete epistemological veracity for the person who experiences them, others are in no way obligated "to accept their revelations uncritically," as James cautions (422). But reports of mystical knowledge can open nonreceivers to the possibility that forms of knowledge other than the rational exist (James 423–24). In this light, what Kerouac effects beautifully in the creation of Duluoz is to write out of absolute belief in mysticism as legitimate, if not superior to the rational. Consequently, even readers who do not value mysticism can find Duluoz credible within his own belief system.

Credibility is heightened by the fact that Duluoz embraces the confessional mode in the tradition of essayist Michel Montaigne—that is, he exposes his sins as well as his virtues. Blunt honesty, including comments about his tendency to drink too much and his belief that women are evil, contributes to a personality that, although unlikable at points, can be trusted because it knows and confronts its own strengths and weaknesses, even in the face of possible public ridicule. This feature aligns Duluoz with what Landow identifies as twentieth-century sage literature, in which writers "present themselves in terms of a far less elevated, less magisterial persona than their predecessors but also urge upon their readers their own flaws and weaknesses to an unprecedented degree" (172). Duluoz's de-elevated persona is enhanced by the emotional tone in which his wrinkles and warts are exposed, and the emphasis on emotion—for instance, the quick rush to judgment of himself and others and the ecstatic, blistering, or self-mortifying range of registers through which his voice travels—signifies an American proclivity toward the spontaneous, irrational, and natural rather than the planned, rational, and intellectual. The voice, while not as rhapsodic as Whitman's, as sonorous as Melville's, or as private as William Carlos Williams', resonates as a confession of common rather than magisterial proportions—the voice of a humble American *and* at heart a symbol of America's teeming polyphonic masses.

Representing the grandest of storytellers, Duluoz beguiles and bewitches with mastery of the word. To this end, he sustains a relatively close relationship with the reader through the informal, conversational voice of the teller of folktale, a legacy of not only authors such as Melville and Dostoyevsky but also Kerouac's childhood in Lowell, where he grew up listening to his parents and their friends swapping stories at home, parties, and social clubs. An amusing example of his early attentiveness to these voices is a brief sketch titled "Legends and Legends" that Paul Marion speculates may have been an English translation of Kerouac's mother or someone like her explaining the horrible history of the Kerouac clan. "Oh, your father's father! My how such a man could exist! Here! Let me tell you," she seems to gesticulate as she revs up her performance: "He used to stand on the porch of his house in the midst of thunderstorms and shout up to the heavens, to God, daring him to Strike!" (*Atop* 146). The tale loops around from descriptions of the father's mother to his brother to the narrator's family to her sister Alice, and back to the concluding statement that the Kerouacs were "a mad, mad lot"; all of these descriptions are bound by frequent direct addresses to her audience: "Little Dear" (147). Duluoz explicitly articulates facets of this heritage in *Desolation Angels*. In this text, one of Kerouac's most dialogic, Duluoz specifically links the folk speaker to his spontaneous method: "There's a certain amount of control going on," he claims, "like a man telling a story in a bar without interruptions or even a pause" (280).[11] *Angels* is not a tall tale about unbelievable scenarios such as the ten-foot blue gill that got away, nor is it a shaggy dog story, which is interminably long and often ends in a bad pun. Both of these might be heard at a bar or other informal community gatherings. But Duluoz is right in that his narrative replicates conventions of folktale construction and recitation perfected by the best storytellers over years of listening to their elders.

The folk tradition Duluoz follows, like the "Legends and Legends" snippet, is plot- and detail-driven—the "what happened next" and the "the life of it" (*Angels* 238, 220)—with the storyteller being the primary actor in a plausible setting with multiple characters. Moving from the bar to the page, Duluoz creates stories with markers of a local community's oral conversation. Readers find parenthetical asides; imperatives and rhetorical questions; restatement of the theme; vaguely associated digressions, often for personal aggrandizement; temporary loss of plot; insider commentary reflecting shared knowledge and values; self-deprecating commentary; profane, obscene, and scatological language; and rough or unexplained transitions. In folktales in general and the Legend in particular, these devices can maintain a bond or the sense of camaraderie between speaker and listener, build dramatic suspense, entertain through fear or laughter, preserve historical elements of the local culture, teach a lesson, and root speaker and audience in a recognizable world while providing temporary escape from the mundane. Folk techniques including repetition, loss of the narrative, and digressions also characterize Duluoz's stories, building a sense of the narrative's folding or looping back and around in time, which can sustain audience interest, solidify their understanding of the story's details, and foreground the teller's breadth of knowledge.

As he wields these techniques, Duluoz does just what master storytellers do. He ventriloquizes a range of voices, creating the illusion of being an entire nation, if not the world. Masterfully plying phonetic spellings to effect accents, Duluoz communicates essential features of other characters' histories and personalities. In *On the Road,* for instance, Sal recreates Neal Cassady's fast-paced, high-spirited speech in Dean's voice, such as "Man, wow, there's so many things to do, so many things to write! How to even begin to get it all down and without modified restraints and all hung-up on like literary inhibitions and grammatical fears" (4); Cassady as Cody Pomeroy is marked an authentic Western cowboy by "Why shuah," a classic slow Western drawl (*Angels* 213). Bona fide teenage voices ring throughout *Maggie Cassidy:* "'Hmmm. Isnt he dreamy?' / 'I don't know. He looks sleepy all the time.' / 'That's the way I like—' / 'Oh get away—how do you know how you like?'" (56). Even the thick accent of a German traveler in *Desolation Angels*—"I voud not take dat from a [Dutch] vaiter if I vere you! [. . .] Dis peoples vill get atrocious und unforgetting deir place!" (331)— comically reflects the speaker's country of origin and his judgmental attitude toward Europeans, alongside Duluoz's own tendencies to stereotype prejudiciously. Conversely, Duluoz's mother's pidginized English in response to a Mexican penitent in *Angels* simulates natural sincerity as Memere struggles to express feelings in a language still foreign to her: "Is she a penitente too? Dat little baby is a penitente? [. . .] But that poor young mother is only half way to the alter—She comes slow slow slow on her knees all quiet. Aw but these are good people the Indians you say?" (343). These voices ultimately illustrate Bakhtin's belief that such languages "lie on the same plane with the real language of the work" even as Duluoz "attempts to talk about his *own* world" in other languages (Bakhtin, *Dialogic* 287). Ventriloquizing in this manner centers Duluoz as the root of his narratives while continually decentering him in those moments when he assumes the vocal masks of others, this play configuring self as mediated processes.

Duluoz as speaker-for-all also demonstrates that his experiences have ranged widely across class and other social divisions. Master of many elements of high as well as low culture, he is a rugged sylvan breeze that easily traverses huge expanses of physical and mental space. Equally at ease in a 1950s Seattle burlesque house as in a conversation about Dostoyevsky's *Demons* (or *The Possessed*), a novel that Kerouac called "the greatest novel of all time" (*Letters* 2: 287), Duluoz is a Renaissance man shifting effortlessly from French to English to Hindi to patois, or, as in one of Sal's dreams, a young man on a white horse riding across the American continent felling telephone poles with his sword. Akin to the American romantic progenitors of the Legend, and as Duluoz's conflation of high and low culture illustrates, his is a story of light and dark, dichotomous elements that paradoxically resist autonomy. By the time Duluoz becomes the protagonist of *Big Sur* (1960/1961), a book that Kerouac described as written in the autumn of his life (*Letters* 2: 355), the darker elements of his and the American myth had begun to erupt full force in the Legend. The episodes unfold to reveal Duluoz's increasing disillusionment and his building frustration as well as impotent attempts to answer definitively essential questions about how to live peacefully and productively as an artist.

But even in its darkest moments (and many may find *Big Sur* to be one such moment), the Legend manages to project a fundamental sense of humor about Duluoz and the world. This attitude, characteristic of the American character in general, is reflected in Duluoz's persistent use of framework methods, coinage words, and rhetorical patterns indicative of American oral folk humor. Mody Boatright argues that American folk language patterns suggest that there was no reverence among the populace for language as precise or sacred. "To the freedom they already enjoyed they added" others, he contends, especially the freedom "to seek humor and vigor above purity and grace or elegance or ease; to prefer striking overstatement to exact statement; to choose rhetorical patterns upon which to hang a wealth of ludicrous imagery; and to engage in lawless coinage" (Boatright 146). One finds these qualities not only in folktales collected from the nineteenth century but also in nineteenth-century literature such as that of Kerouac's hero Melville, whose fondness for new words such as "uncapitulatable," "entangledly," and "instantaneousness" in *Pierre* offended the middle-class sensibilities of some then contemporary critics (Higgins and Parker 64–65). Kerouac also found these folk figures in the language of another of his heroes, Neal Cassady, whose diction in *Cody*'s taped transcription is sprinkled with linguistic irregularities, including "profoondified" (151), "kcwlminating" (204), "sonofabitch," (219), and "objects dee art" (243).

Boatright was not addressing Kerouac's writing, but his assertion regarding the character of American folk discourse, which corresponds succinctly with Bakhtin's notion of the dialogicized heteroglossia of the folk, may be one of the most accurate descriptions of Duluoz's language ever made. Take, for instance, the reliance upon the rhetorical pattern of ludicrous or exaggerated images. Duluoz shows no reluctance to tap this standard, beginning with *On the Road,* in which he exaggerates numerous mundane events, characters, and affectations as "the best" or "the greatest," especially laughs (*Road,* 21, 63). Others, relying upon more sophisticated language use, become emphatically folksy as the Legend progresses and as Kerouac assumed more editorial control over the publication process:

1. "the door of Johnnie's apartment knocks" (*Vanity* 198);
2. "I stand by that or stand by nothing but my toilet bowl" (*Vanity* 162);
3. "a Demonthenes pebble would have to drop way long down to hit that kind of bottom" (*Cody* 83);

4. "there's a moon as bright as a bucket of ice" (*Cody* 263);
5. "[regarding a horse Raphael bets on and comes in almost last] they'll be bringin him in by lamplight in my dreams" (*Angels* 163);
6. "not to grow up into a big bore rattling off the zoological or botanical or whatever names of butterflies, or telling Professor Flipplehead the entire history of the Thuringian Flagellants in Middle German on past midnight by the blackboard" (*Vanity* 41); and
7. "I'se ready as the fattest ribs in old Winn Dixie [a Southern-based supermarket]" (*Satori* 113).

Occasionally, the effects of exaggeration are enhanced by an outcome based on a condition impossible to fulfill, as in the case of no. 5 above, Raphael's horse crossing the finish line. Others depend on sheer illogicality—for example, a door knocking, every laugh being the greatest, and Duluoz as a rib in a supermarket meatcase.

Humor is often sustained through word choice as well, especially Duluoz's reliance on portmanteau words, or neologisms formed by blending two or more words. Portmanteaus can be easily confused with the fused or telescoped words such as *bebaseballhatted* and *lookingglass* (*Angels* 29, 31) that Kerouac liberally adopted, but the two are not the same. The following three portmanteaus are from *Vanity of Duluoz: cognizing,* a combination of recognizing and cognizant (206); *vestigitabbibles,* a combination of vestibules, tables, vegetables, and bibles (174); and *flagellents,* a combination of flagellant, flagellate, Plantagenets, and flatulence (41). Humor is produced by the strange sound of the word, the incongruent mixture of the echoes of source words, and the equally often incongruent juxtaposition of the semantic signifieds of those source words. For example, *flagellents* signifies a royal family of medieval England, self-mortification, and the expulsion of bodily gasses. Added to portmanteau words, one also finds unsanctioned endings to familiar roots of words, such as "NewYorkitis" (*Cody* 41), which relies on fusion as well as the unsanctioned "itis" to name a human condition, "stoppered" (*Vanity* 103), which transforms the noun "stopper" into a past participle with the unsanctioned "ed", and "whoopee-ing" (*On the Road* 16), which couples the unsanctioned present participial "ing" to the onomatopoetic "whoopee."

At the level of larger rhetorical framing devices, Duluoz crafts humor by drawing upon the folk standard of boosting the obvious incongruity between either realism and fantasy or the situation at the time the story is told and that described in the story itself. Kerouac recognized this device, writing under his own name in *Satori in Paris* that it was easy "to joke" about feeling scared when confronting possible muggers in Paris since he was writing about it "4500 miles away safe at home in old Florida with the doors locked and the Sheriff doin his best." The reader too is well aware of Kerouac's safety, so Kerouac can take advantage of humorous lines such as "No garrotes please, I have my armour on, my Reichian character armour that is" (75). There are many of these throughout the Legend, perhaps one of the most well-known being Duluoz in the guise of Sal Paradise telling the story of beginning his first road trip wearing huaraches and concluding it drenched with rain, riding back home on a school bus only a few hours later. Humor is forged by the incongruous juxtaposition of the images of a mature writer looking back at his naive youthful self: the former knows full well what the road requires; the other has only soggy childish dreams.

On an even larger scale, one sees incongruity in the whole of *Doctor Sax,* which again implies a mature narrator well established in life, in all good conscience and straight-faced telling the story of what happened to him as a child. That story is one of fantasy heroes, diabolical wizards, campy heretics, and a Great Snake, as well as realistic accounts of youthful male homosexual experimentation, a mentally challenged boy masturbating dogs, and a hor-rific flood that devastated Lowell in 1936. Humor emerges from the tempo-ral space that separates yet joins these moments. After all, recounted from such a distant and presumably placid point in time, how terrifying or dis-turbing can these tales be in terms of the narrator's and reader's immediate reality? The fantasy, then, is just that—a cartoonish childhood tale with no real bite. Even the grim stories of sexual development, perversion, and natu-ral disasters when told from a present-tense perspective of benign good-naturedness are transformed into innocent childhood play. Overall, the lightheartedness underscores the archetypal American condition as ever hopeful, grounded in the myth of new beginnings.

Often Kerouac's use of the frame is bolstered by secondary incongruities between realism and fantasy created between grammatical, highly rhetorical language of the framework narrative and the often profane, scatological, or "low-brow" language of the narrator himself and of other characters. *Dharma Bums,* as a case in point, opens with a narrative voice that is controlled and lyric as it describes Ray Smith meeting a saintly little bum. For approxi-mately the first four-and-a-half pages, the narrator presents only the smallest of deviations in registers as Smith recounts the night he and his temporary companion parted company:

> I bade farewell to the little bum of Saint Teresa at the crossing, where we jumped off, and went to sleep the night in the sand in my blankets, far down the beach at the foot of a cliff where cops wouldn't see me and drive me away. I cooked hot-dogs on freshly cut and sharpened sticks over the coals of a big wood fire, and heated a can of beans and a can of cheese macaroni in the red-hot hollows, and drank my newly bought wine, and exulted in one of the most pleasant nights of my life. (7)

The language is almost scientific in its peratactic precision except for the tiny echo of nineteenth-century formality in "I bade farewell." But even that rings consistent with the formal qualities of Duluoz's journalistic attention to accurately reporting his actions. However, the clean, Hemingwayesque objective recording of dialogue soon gives way to "'Well, Ray,' *sez* I, glad, 'only a few miles to go'" (7, emphasis mine)—the use of the nonstandard "sez" instead of "said" rupturing the narrative surface. This rupture rapidly widens as Duluoz abandons the reportorial voice of scientific journalism for a highly irregular register:

> All alone and free in the soft sands of the beach by the sigh of the sea out there, with the Ma-Wink fallopian virgin warm stars reflecting on the outer channel fluid belly waters. [. . .] Then the wine got to work on my taste buds and before long I had to pitch into those hotdogs, biting them right off the end of the stick spit, and chomp chomp, and dig down into the two tasty cans with the old pack spoon, spooning up rich bits of hot beans and pork, or of macaroni with sizzling hot sauce, and maybe a little sand thrown in. (7–8)

The narrative voice is now demarcated by hyphenated compounds ("Ma-Wink"), ludicrous imagery ("Ma-Wink fallopian virgin warm stars" and "outer channel fluid belly waters"), informal language ("got to," "right off," "dig down"), onomatopoeia ("chomp, chomp"), and nongrammatical structures ("and maybe a little sand thrown in"). The effect is a comic counter to the journalistic narrator who has been riven in two, his new half a grotesque carnivore devouring sand, meat, and cheap canned pasta. Frequently, the humor created by these shifts in register mocks Duluoz, illuminates the flaws in his character, and transforms him into a sympathetic, realistic figure whose travails in life—as well as his ability to laugh at himself—make him a worthy successor to the American folk hero who calls the nation back to its primal values. Viewed from this perspective, the humor of the Legend communicates a commitment to America as a geographical and imaginary locale now mature enough to generate and nurture its own narratives.

Interestingly, however, Kerouac at one point did experiment with an ancient, exotic, noncolonial and mythic setting for the Legend, drafting in April 1956 a narrative of Duluoz's origins as a peasant named Dawn True born in 15,000 BC in the land of Mominu in Atlantis. The narrative, included in one of Kerouac's notebooks of *Old Angel Midnight* reveals that Dawn True was an ancient soul certain about his karmic destiny of greatness in an idyllic Buddhist Pure Land named Honeyland. However, this garbled, first-person text of about 350 words, which implicitly argues that Dawn True is a compilation of Hellenic mythology, Buddhist realism, European fairy tales, Spenglerian fellaheenism, and American myths of the promised land— a syncretic ancient type, in other words—may not have seemed authentic to

Kerouac, since the story stops abruptly with a parenthetical statement that it will be completed elsewhere.[12] It never was, and we have no explanation of why he never finished the tale, but the abandonment of Dawn True suggests Kerouac's fundamental realization that the American writer is no longer forced to set his or her tales on foreign soil or at sea to achieve historical and moral credibility, as early American writers often did. Duluoz, a full-fledged son of the New World, yet one whose name reveals that he has not escaped or abandoned the Old World entirely, positions himself above, below, and among all those on American soil.

Kerouac's creation of Dawn True as a type of mythic rather than realistic and multidimensional figure is in keeping with Kerouac's general approach to America and his literary treatment of it. Ironically, while he was determined to create himself and Duluoz as an individual, he tended to perceive others as a "type" in a sort of grand historical play, similar to his visions of his French-Canadian grandfather striding forth like the Adamic man across a new celestial continent. Several years after Kerouac's death, Ginsberg made such an observation in an interview that he gave for a docu-drama on Kerouac's life (Antonelli), calling Kerouac's vision of the Beats archetypal. In fact, Kerouac's notes for an unpublished story titled "The American Night" that he was writing in the fifties contain a fascinating list of just such archetypal 159 types of Americans. The first few, exemplified by a rebellious girl from Lake Shore, Chicago, were annotated with names of acquaintances satisfying the type— Edie Parker, his first wife, in this case. Others, including intellectual novelists, alcoholic military men, Vassar lesbians, Yankee journalists, anti-Semitic German exiles, and Jesuit physicists, stand alone on the page, suggestive of readiness for an actor's name to be added to the playbill.[13] Generalizing in this manner correlates with Kerouac's belief in American lives as a unified whole an understanding that he used to justify linking his novels as the Legend.

On this grand stage he directed many characters, but their nature as types provides the unifying frame, which may partially explain why so many, especially secondary, characters tend toward either the sublime or the grotesque, which Duluoz appears to normalize. As sublimes, they embody elements of the Longinian notion of the spirit or the spark connecting the souls of both writer and reader. Many also project the eighteenth-century romantic concept of original genius. As grotesques, they constitute a linguistic structure that through the unresolved clash of incompatible forms alludes to worlds from which one is estranged, facilitating, as Bakhtin argued in *Rabelais and His World,* cultural reversal, rebellion, and release. Through disharmony, the grotesque critiques the strictures of the status quo, and in the world of the sage and prophet in particular, as Landow has shown, the grotesque exists as a sign through which one reads the current disorder of society. While the sublime functions as an ideal to be admired or modeled, the grotesque illustrates cultural deviance from the paths of virtue, frequently assuming comic or satiric form in this role. Kerouac's characters—often like flat comic book figures, stock elements from vaudeville and comic B-movies, or Cubist forms on canvas—expose the type or artifice rather than the multidimensional human originals.

The Legend is densely populated with types from simple jolly waitresses, angry middle-class housewives, pure peasant girls, and lonely young women looking for love to buffoonish young men, sweet Mexican boys, silent Buddhist poets, Negro jazz musicians, and hobos. Most seem to operate allegorically within the open episodic frame to direct readers toward a fuller understanding of Duluoz in the greater service of revealing the fallen state of American culture, the ramifications of this condition, and the path to atonement and rebirth in what is often depicted, especially in *The Dharma Bums*, as a jewel-like, external America that is a Buddhist Pure Land (Levering 15). Even minor figures carry this burden. Few, with the exceptions of Japhy Ryder (based on Gary Snyder) and Dean Moriarty/Cody Pomeroy, ever develop into credible simulations of psychological and social realism. This pattern is fairly easy to identify in Kerouac's minor characters, those such as Alyce Newman, based on writer Joyce Johnson, who is sketched as a Polish-looking blonde and "the first great woman writer of the world" in *Desolation Angels*. While Duluoz describes himself and Alyce as "wonderfully healthy lovers," giving her a considerable amount of dialogue compared with to his other girlfriends, she functions primarily to validate his need for heterosexual relationships and to enhance the diverse range of personalities with which he comports (293). Likewise, the "missing Beat," Lucien Carr, appears robustly as Julian in *Angels,* a loving family man with a steady job at the UPI in frequent competition with his impulse to carouse. But Duluoz's memory of a photograph of Julian at age fourteen fundamentally situates him as yet another angelic and exotic fantasy figure, "blond with an actual halo of light around his hair, strong hard features, those Oriental eyes," who by associating with Duluoz signifies Duluoz's privileged angelic nature (273).

Uniting these characters, no matter to what degree they attend to mimetic authority, is the quality signified by Julian's "Oriental eyes"—that of the exotic other. At times, as in the case of Julian, Duluoz feels privileged to associate with this other who distances him from the debauched bourgeoisie, or fallen America, that he abhors. Sometimes, though, the other fulfills the task of embodying terrifying aspects of an aging twentieth-century America. Often it is the female figure that shoulders both these burdens, particularly characters such as the destructive man-eater Mary Lou, the saintly and childlike mother Terry, Sal's aunt, and the fellaheen Mexican peasant girls of *On the Road;* the disembodied loving voice of Evelyn, who sustains the linguistic revelry of the boy gang in *Visions of Cody;* and the sweetly naive and sexual Princess of *Dharma Bums.* For the most part, these are either sublime goddesses or grotesque demons cloaked as mothers, poor peasants, or open-minded middle-class young women. As grotesques, they often illustrate the rapacious character of male-female relationships in America as well as Duluoz's fear of women, while exposing his inability to embrace both males and females according to the capacious Christian and Buddhist American principles that he espouses. Many other females are allegorical elements of American hopefulness, charity, and good humor or the immanent downfall of a country that has lost faith in youthful optimism. At times they are a mixture of both, as are Tristessa from the eponymously named book narrated by Jack Duluoz, and Mardou Fox from *The Subterraneans* narrated by Leo Percipied (based on the Mexican Esmerelda Tercedera and the African American Alene Lee, respectively). Their sublime qualities, such as sexual openness and otherworldly goodness born of abject poverty, disease, and female essence, are metonymized in their dark skin color, which projects the grotesque as well as the otherness of the oppressed and tabooed female body.

One might argue that Tristessa and Mardou illustrate the poststructuralist contention that the grotesque may really be a trope of the sublime, a parodic twist to disguise romantic sincerity and imagination as modern irony and cynicism (Russo 32). But since there is little of the latter qualities in the Legend, I find it more appropriate to identify them as "aerial sublimes," a term Mary Russo created to express "an embodiment of possibility and error" (29). From this perspective, the dark female bodies of Tristessa and Mardou are the locations upon which Duluoz situates his desire to escape (or fly from) bodily existence as a mortal white male, while implicitly exposing his inability to recognize his own privilege and the impossibility of transmundane release through apotheosizing the female body. The possibility of release is paradoxically founded on cultural and personal prejudices, in and of themselves errors that produce the desire to escape. There is little that is problematic with such constructions within the field of romance per se, but when these types become normalized, as they appear to be in the Legend, they undermine the vision of America as a land of promise for *all*—male and female—that is the foundation of the Legend itself.

Even individuals historically well known and associated with Beat culture appear as devices to communicate Duluoz's character and role as wisdom teacher. Little effort is made to ground them historically or explore them as psychological or material entities. Ginsberg, for instance, appears several times in fairly minimal form as a dark, rhapsodic mystic intent upon probing the human psyche. He emerges in his fullest form in *Angels* as Irwin Garden, the proverbial "wandering jew," openly homosexual, extremely wise and well traveled, "never without his own entourage" (230), serious about comprehending the smallest or most absurd of events and ideas in life (173), and a mystic who believes that his Blakean visions give him the authority to wield poetry for the betterment of the "Iron Hound of America" (253). But this portrait, charming as it is, by replicating Ginsberg's comic seriousness, hyper-active visionary politics, and simpatico with Kerouac that allowed the two to influence each other's aesthetic development so profoundly over the years, fails to elevate Garden as a credible *literary* persona divorced from his histor-ical template or as a viable historical record of that same template. Garden remains a composite of brief Duluozian word paintings that elevate language above the body and literary license above historical veracity—the grotesque and sublime as a rush of language exemplifying angelic America trying to reawaken its atavistic poetic consciousness and thus save itself. Duluoz, in his friendship with and knowledge of Garden-as-angel, reifies his own literary subjectivity as angelic visionary.

Neal Cassady most obviously typifies the grotesque-sublime construct undergirding the Legend, *On the Road* and *Visions of Cody* in particular con-figuring him as a tortured and impoverished yet exquisitely exuberant believer who marches through life with an egotistical smile and a humble swagger. The archetypal cinema cowboy who gets by on wits, charm, and luck, Cassady recreated as Dean Moriarty and Cody Pomeroy possesses a spirit so capacious and sweet that he never loses faith in his own abilities and natural right to exist and to tower above others. Cody is the bemused and beleaguered American dreamer, a rugged Westerner with little interest in writing and no ethnic heritage who professes wholehearted belief in the Christian god of salvation (*Angels* 138). But he too is flawed, a fallen angel who feels little for those weaker than he, gambles compulsively, cheats on his wife, and physically abuses his own daughter (363–64).

With memory, though, Duluoz discloses Cody's humble core of goodness that remains invisible to many, a characteristic enhanced by the literary twin-ning of Dean/Cody with W. C. Fields. Fields, born William Claude Dukenfield in 1880, got his start in burlesque and vaudeville and is remembered according to Nicholas Yanni for "the raffish cadence of [his] nasal drawl and his fleshy-nosed charlatan manner, the small wars he fought against a seemingly hostile world, and the precise manner in which he always drew a deadly bead on most middle-class values" (13). This is the character that Fields later transferred to Hollywood's B-movies, the cinematic fabula in which Kerouac saw vestiges of the childlike, ribald, and antiauthoritarian attitude of his father, Neal Cassady's father, Cassady himself, and an archetypal American. As Kerouac described Fields in an October 14, 1949, journal entry, Fields signified the downtrodden but diligent and self-effacing underdog:

> How I admire W. C. Fields!—What a great oldtimer he was [. . .] With his straw hat, his short steps, his belly, his wonderful face hid beneath a bulbous

puff of beaten flesh [. . .] his knowledge of American life, of women, of children, of fellow-barflies, and of death [. . .] His utter lovelessness in the world. Bumping into everything blindly. Making everybody laugh. The line he himself wrote, addressed to him: "You're as funny as a cry for help." [. . .] an Old Mad Murphy of time. (*WW* 236)

Kerouac concluded this description by calling Fields "a hounded old reprobate, a clown, a drunkard of eternity, and Man" (*WW* 236), the list of nominals moving from a description of the character that Fields portrayed on the screen to a universal name encompassing all of humanity, which Kerouac seems to have imagined himself playing in the role of Duluoz. This fatherly underdog and everyman appears in the Legend first as Dean Moriarty and then as Cody.[14] Certainly Duluoz"s fascination with Fields's lawless, cowboy, Anglicized language, such as "Ain't you got no Red Eye?" "Ain't you an old Follies girl?" and "I snookered that one" that Kerouac recorded in his journal (236), is manifested in the many portraits of Cody and Dean. Thus the Fields/Dean/Cody/Sal/Duluoz configuration suggests not only the emerging importance of celluloid Hollywood signifiers of American selfhood but also the centrality of historical memory and literary imagination in the project of self-formation as American salvation.

Granted, in *On the Road* the Fields/Dean/Cody twinning disintegrates when Dean returns as the tattered Shrouded Traveler whom Sal mourns as defeated and misspent youth. But in *Angels,* Cody remains Jack's friend and Fieldian confidant who reflects Duluoz's efforts to play Fields' twin—the self-deprecating, hopeful, maligned, but godly man who suffers through all and comes out a winner. With characteristic Kerouacian brevity, Duluoz indirectly links Cody to Fields by noting only that Cody's determination to recoup his racing losses was "like W. C. Fields" (157). The simile is slight in size but huge in connotative value, suggesting that Cody—like (1) Duluoz's father, (2) Duluoz's interpretation of Fields from Hollywood movies, and (3) Duluoz himself—is a man who is misunderstood, alone, good-natured, ever hopeful, accepting of what life provides, trusting in his own mind and heart, humble, proud, and ultimately godly. He is also a family man now, with a wife and children, and, like Fields's movie persona, the one put upon by that family, always working a scam that the women, children, and businessmen just cannot appreciate. At times he succeeds, but unlike his cinematic double, who in films such as *Never Give a Sucker an Even Break* triumphs over bourgeois blind foolishness, Cody struggles along, losing more often than winning. But he remains angelic in his determination to believe in something better, to face death daily, to laugh at his own absurdities, and to persevere when all seems bleak. He, like Fields—and as Duluoz imagines himself—creates a myth of many myths, be they literary, historical, or cinematic, of human beings as the source of their own salvation. Consequently, Dean/Cody as one of the more credible fictional persona in the Legend joins others to act on behalf of Duluoz. As the "King" to whom Duluoz bids adieu in *Visions of Cody*, he is the sublime ideal of individual potential, the very spark of transcendence that knows "IT" and "time." As "a frightening Angel" who pursues Sal across the continent in *On the Road*, he is a stark warning to Americans that they are on the verge of losing faith in a wild and innocent individualism that once recognized will be their strength and salvation. As "aerial sublime," Dean/Cody repeatedly encodes Duluozian fear of mortality, desire to become and dominate the other, and reluctance to admit one's innate goodness and potential divinity.

The Jack Duluoz who spins his Legend through personal and cultural narratives ultimately embraces a vast range of American culture, from folk and popular entertainment such as burlesque, baseball, horseracing, hopping freight trains, parables, proverbs, and tall tales to the most revered of Western culture's canonical writers and Eastern culture's moral leaders and poets. Speaking across cultural divides, he affects numerous voices, dialects, and accents to communicate humor, spiritual revelation, confession, and historical veracity. Contrary to many of his early American literary ancestors, he is not afraid to confront the legitimacy of America as a place where art can thrive. As he deals with relationships between history, memory, and linguistic representation, the novel as he manipulates it progressively disintegrates and coagulates until he is working with forms of confession, prophecy, and poetics that effect a recursive move to essential forms of cultural and individual wisdom. He is also an innocent—not that he has *not* engaged in transgressive activities—but in confession Duluoz's childlike innocence reifies belief in the supremacy and redemption of the human soul. Simultaneously, however, Duluoz depicts himself as small, insignificant, and typecast like all others. This persona paradoxically gives voice to the American tendency to desire connection to its generative cultures. In other words, the Old World is a haunt that remains connected to but beyond the reach of the New World, and in Duluoz the voices of the colonized and the colonizer cannot be erased. This quality becomes a rejection of the social realism of Duluoz's American and European forebearers, claiming instead a vision of himself and America grounded in mystical, Gothic, allegorical, and transcendental precursors (Hoffman, *Form and Fable* 354). As such, he projects good-natured, hearty humor but fosters darker visions as well. This duality is at least partially reconciled in his conviction that America writes neither a purely tragic nor a Christian resolution to its own stories. It writes itself. In all these respects, Kerouac's Jack Duluoz perpetuates America's master narrative while uncovering its flaws, inadequacies, and lacunae.

CHAPTER 2

THE NOVITIATE: JOURNALS, LETTERS, AND EARLY FICTION

History reiterates that questers spend the initial days of their journey study-ing the traditional texts and rituals of the communities they wish to join or have been raised in. Kerouac as novice was no different. His literary output during this time, from roughly 1941 to 1954, consisted of letters, journals, poetry, and prose that provide a stunning perspective on the life of a man who, while staring into the eye of global annihilation and his own demons, remained convinced that the greatest human endeavor is to know "thyself" and thus the universe. Fortunately for scholars and others interested in Kerouac, more of these documents are now being published by the Kerouac estate. Some of his early attempts to compose prose and poetry from 1936 to 1943 appeared posthumously as *Atop an Underwood*, edited by Paul Marion. His correspondence to friends, family, and literary associates is available in *Selected Letters 1940–1956* and *Selected Letters 1957–1969*, both edited by Ann Charters. The early collection, in particular, contains the fascinating dis-closure that Kerouac looked upon letter writing as a hybrid of pedagogical treatise, personal confession, and insurance policy to control his future rep-utation. To Neal Cassady, with whom he had established a prolific corre-spondence by 1948, he declared, "These are my views . . . (SILLY) (SELF-CONSCIOUS TOO) . . . and I'm not saying them for *your* benefit (don't have to) so much as for 'posterity' which might someday read this let-ter, all my letters (as Kerouac)" (*Letters* 1: 167). Most enlightening, however, are his journal entries from 1947 to 1954, published posthumously as *Windblown World*, edited by the historian Douglas Brinkley. In these, the

Kerouac who emerges on paper, especially during the late thirties and into the forties, resembles the persona that readers of *On the Road* were to encounter. His early sentences were more stilted and self-conscious than his later style—one can discern that the elevated vocabulary, syntax, and rhetorical forms of the scholars and writers whose words he was studying intrigued him—but the passionate, rambling, confessional voice of what was to become the *Road* is distinct as his meditations, teachings, argumentative essays, prayers, and personal reflections interrogate, consult, and lecture. It is almost as if he can do nothing else but rehearse and test his questions, confessions, and newly acquired wisdom. This novitiate is frequently predicated upon a continual dialogue with the tangible and the intangible, a "you" that shifts from figments of Kerouac himself and unrecognizable others to identifiable correspondents to representations of the divine and his demons. In toto, his private "scribblings," as he sometimes called them, while not a carefully reasoned or unified vision of self and world, create, record, and instruct others about confronting the complexities and paradoxes of life lived in service to identifying and teaching ultimate truths.

Kerouac was already recording this process in his teens. A short report of a dream intended for his Lowell friend George J. Apostolos (G.J.), written when Kerouac was only seventeen, announces that he was soon to make a "concerted study in religion" (*Atop* 20) and considered the Holy Bible to be his "first" bible. He was also dead earnest about achieving mastery and becoming an accepted member of the literary establishment (*WW* 26); to this end he assiduously read canonical works of the Western tradition, particularly Dostoyevsky, Shakespeare, Joyce, Wolfe, Hemingway, Saroyan, and others (*Vanity of Duluoz* 107). Even into the late forties, the issue of literary mastery concerned him as he queried himself in a November 1947 journal entry: "How do I know if I'm reaching mastery? [. . .] The thinking has got to be real now" (*WW* 26). Some of his earliest literary efforts reveal his philosophical and theological proclivities, as well as the voices and structures that became his literary standards. Indirectly touching on religious themes in a short, first-person narrative titled "Go Back" written in the summer of 1940, he focused his narrator's memories on a Lowell house in which he used to live, constructing a message of time and self: "Hold the present now because someday it will be very precious" (*Atop* 25). Another narrative, "Nothing," written that same summer, playfully begins as a comic text on "nothing to write about," but moves quickly into an imaginative cause-effect description of dust particles breaking down into smaller and smaller entities over millions of years. The narrator, marveling at the magnitude of this process, confesses that "I should kneel down and weep with joy at the marvelousness of such perfect nothingness," but then reasons that since it will take so long for everything to become nothing, "the earth will never quite completely be nothing" (27). Amateur logic reassuringly re-grounds him in the certainty of material reality.

The voice and content of much of his work from 1941 assume an elevated, sermonic quality. As a first-year student at Columbia University in 1941, Kerouac composed a first-person narrative simply titled "God," unveiling his spiritual revelation while sitting on a bench observing the New Jersey coast across the Hudson River. The preamble to his discussion of the revelation included the belief that artists must immerse themselves in the community of life (75). "Hermits make awful poets, I think" (75), he concluded before explaining that his new wisdom came upon him "calmly"— "I am not hit like St. Augustine" (75). After what he called "wide thinking," he realized that "God is consciousness. God is the perspective of the eye and ear and nose and mind. God is man; and man is God." Civilization and adulthood, he declared, lead human beings away from the wisdom of childhood, and "God is the thing, theological, pagan, or real" (78). While a poem titled "Observations" written that same year tempers the sermonic voice in lines such as "I am not a prophet, I am, like Whitman, a lover" (119), the speaker of the contemporaneous prose poem "I Am My Mother's Son" declares, "We have proven the earth's truth and meaning, which is, simply life and death," and he envisions himself as the grandson of the earth, placed here "to be her spokesman, in my chosen and natural way" (162). Others may think they know him, the speaker continues, but all he knows is that "I am my mother's son" (163).

In his later teens and early twenties, Kerouac was undoubtedly experimenting with genres and themes in the midst of doubts and questions that had begun to cloud his youthful certainty about his purpose in life. For instance, the theme of organic processes connecting all life forms presented in "I Am My Mother's Son" is countered in the 1941 poem "This I Do Know—," in which the speaker, a young writer, echoes the Americanist dictum that individual self-will is all there is: "We must make / (always have) our own design—" (169). "Sadness at Six," a touching autobiographical story written in 1942, records the narrator's first mystical recognition of himself as a human being who at age six walks home through the Centralville section of Lowell. Evoking feelings of sadness to denote the emergence of self-awareness and its antithesis, the story acknowledges the loss of childhood innocence and happiness, which conversely opens the youngster to music and "colors accentuated deeply, and the weird flutings as of Joyce could be heard emanating from my lips" (183)—in other words, on that day when he was but only six he was reborn to the life of the artist.

By 1943, his confidence had returned sufficiently to allow him to use the personal essay to proclaim knowledge of metaphysical truths. Confidently in "The Wound of Living" and exuberantly in "Beauty as a Lasting Truth," he declared art the great source of truth, explaining in the latter that literary expression projected "a beauty vast and deep enough to include all . . . transient entities," one that goes "beyond & above th[em] in a great circumveloping pall" (226). "Pall" in this context most likely refers not to a casket or a gloomy atmosphere but to a square, linen-covered board used to cover the communion chalice, implying that the great writer, Kerouac's prophesy of his own future, creates art to sanctify the world. He repeated this grandiose vision in "Beauty as a Lasting Truth," admitting that although he was no prophet, no moralist, he was intent on trying to make these sadly written beliefs comprehensible to the world, in a series of art works (227). In effect, he was establishing as his purpose in life the teaching of truth-as-beauty through art.

His youthful wish to educate and enlighten was initially realized by *The Town and the City*. Begun in 1946 after the death of his father and published in 1950 by Harcourt Brace, *The Town and the City*, a conventional third-person historical novel, draws upon many people from Kerouac's life in Lowell and New York City to produce a bildungsroman in the tradition of Galsworthy's *Forsythe Saga*, Goethe's *Werther*, and Thomas Wolfe's *Look Homeward, Angel*. Drafting, revising, editing, and retyping marked his writing regimen as he strove to render the novel worthy of the pantheon of writers who populated his literary imagination, as *Windblown World* reveals. With Hemingwayesque precision and endurance, Kerouac recorded the number of words he wrote each day. For instance, on June 15, 1947, he noted, "I give up after **500-words** of a preliminary nature"; the next day he wrote, "I write **2000-words** pertaining to the chapter, and things begin to break, or crumble & seethe"; on June 17, he recorded that "we hate original work, we human beings. Wrote **1800-words** pertaining" (8). After returning from his first road trip in November 1947, however, he noted ecstatically "2500-words today in a few hours. This may be it—freedom. And mastery!" (25). The result was a novel reviewed in *The New Yorker*, *Saturday Review of Literature*, and other publications as belonging in the venerable tradition of literary realism. By 1950, however, Kerouac had already moved in a direction far beyond his origins as the mainstream writer stabled in publishing houses the likes of Harcourt Brace. He had been cut loose—or more accurately, as his 1947 road trip intimates, he had cut himself loose.

It was during the 1940s that Kerouac left Columbia after quarreling with his football coach Lou Little, learned that Sebastian Sampas had died in the war, joined and was discharged from the Navy, served in the Merchant Marines, assisted Lucien Carr to cover up the killing of David Kammerer, married and divorced Edie Parker, and lost his beloved father to a long illness. Writing in 1945 to his sister, he found himself caught up in "a continuous blind circle," unable to "stick to jobs or to anything for that matter" (*Letters* 1: 87), and by 1947 he admitted in his journal that he was "undergoing an inner revolution"

(*WW* 25). To counter the downward spiral, he redirected his novitiate, constructing a liberal arts curriculum in the classical spirit of that nomenclature: the journey of a free man seeking personal growth. His courses emphasized action and the lived experience balanced with reading, writing, and deep personal reflection. These were the years during which he made his first road trips recorded in *On The Road* and *Visions of Cody*. They were also the years during which he became the spiritual descendent of Job, Jonah, and Ahab, wrestling with his god to forge a coherent philosophy embracing the concepts of selfhood, literature, and the soul. For instance, his correspondence with Sampas, which reads at times like scholarly prose, shows him formulating a poetics of self-definition. The poet, he wrote in March 1943, is an artist who respects beauty. Castigating his friend for not discarding "romantic 'outcast' notions," Kerouac advocated a more scientific Eliotic and Joycean process, although he did not identify it as such:

> But if I retain vision in myself by removing my own single identity in experience—that is to say, distill myself off until only the artist stands—and observe everything with an unbiased, studious, and discriminate eye, I do more good, as far as creation goes, than the Byronic youth . . . who identifies himself with the meaning of the world or if not that places himself in the center of its orbit and professes to know all about humanity when he has only taken pains to study himself. (*Letters* 1: 51)

"That's sheer adolescence!" he admonished. At the same time, he stated that the artist cannot remove himself from the world; no communally regimented utopias will suffice, and to avoid deadly ennui, "an artist *needs* life" (54). This certainty is reproduced a few weeks later in a letter to John MacDonald, in which Kerouac aligns himself with Hemingway's belief that those who are the strongest have been defeated.[1] Defeated by the world and himself, Kerouac at twenty-one was still sufficiently convinced about a purpose-driven life that he could pontificate about faith in his own artistic powers, and he remained convinced that his "debaucheries" were only "short-lived insurgence from the static conditions of [. . .] society" (56). However, a letter written in April 1943 to G.J. indicates that he deemed these rhetorical sureties untrustworthy, even his own, since "all persons wear a mask" (*Letters* 1: 59). A more intimate and less confident voice describes a duality of mind externalized by his friendships with Sebastian and G.J. The former he considered "the introverted, scholarly side"; the latter, the "half-back, whore-master, alemate [. . .]" side requiring "gutsy, redblooded associates" (*Letters* 1: 60). These two worlds he had tried unsuccessfully to reconcile, and while he appears confident that he finally achieved a synthesis by writing *The Sea Is My Brother*, he qualified his hope to G.J. that his letter will explain things: "*Maybe*," he says, but "*I don't know*" (*Letters* 1: 60–61, emphasis mine).[2]

1947–48

Much of the inner revolution and vast inner life that Kerouac revealed to his correspondents was primarily shaped and preserved in his voluminous journals, which testify to the difficult task he had set for himself and was made all the more challenging by depression that he struggled with in 1947 and 1948. He concluded, in a set of journal entries titled "mood log" for June 16 to 26, 1947, that his great task was to "reconcile *true Christianity* with *American life*" (*WW* 11). This was one way of naming the dualism that he detected within himself (17) and that he had earlier recognized in his friendships with Sebastian and G.J. It is also significant that in these entries he is not simply performing amateur depth psychology but is contemplating in more sweeping terms twentieth-century American culture, one in which he detected the Christian impulse manifested as critical consciousness, a perspective of "loneliness, morality, humility, [and] sternness." Its opposite is "charm, open-mindedness . . . humorousness, Faustian power and lust for experience," the latter, he joked, being good to help one get around (17). The journals illustrate that when Kerouac considered the meaning of his status as American, he focused on places and people who seemed most authentically American to him: Grant Wood's paintings should hang upon his walls, he wrote; Montana rather than Paris was the place he wanted to visit; and an all-night movie house on Times Square was much more appealing to him than the ballet (112). Being American also entailed living one's life for oneself, not living it "to be fulfilled, if at all, by [one's] children." Life was to be lived in his own way, and it was his father, Leo, whom he considered the model of the raw individualistic life in a country "too vast with people [. . .] to ever be degraded to the low level of a slave nation" (21).

This repudiation of a slave mentality was foreshadowed in a story titled "The Birth of a Socialist" which Kerouac wrote in 1941. Based on his experience working in a cookie factory in Lowell, it began with the bracketed caveat that the "story is an attempt to bring the reader the true meaning of slavery for others, in its most despised form [. . .] Though this story may be brushed off as a piece of Communist pamphleteering against the capitalists," he continued, it was intended to counter all forms of "slavery of the masses," including communism (*Atop* 85–86). The story ended with its narrator, after quitting the factory job, idyllically lounging in a pool of cool water and reading William Cullen Bryant's "Thanotoposis"—"the world was again fit for a man" (86). Carrying this transcendental image in the late forties, Kerouac found America's strength in cold war culture to be an anticommunist spirituality that promoted happiness, social humility, and decency (*WW* 142–43), a new world in which class boundaries could be breached without question. This vision led him to naively proclaim that all "exalted Americans"—and he uncritically identified Henry Ford, Mark Twain, and George Washington as exemplars—were "extremely humble and spiritual men" (142–43). At the same time, the journals intimate that Kerouac's concept of national unity was founded on a vision of America as "the pioneer country of pioneer disciplines strung on a rack and quivering—in quick transition to modern ideas" (112). The image of human meat strung on either a device of torture, commercialization, or preservation—all speeding into the future—captures dialectically the voracious American appetite for the new and the pain that accompanies such a grand break from the old.

At the same time, Kerouac approached his novitiate with a confidence grounded in Christian doctrine. A set of four psalms that were most likely written in 1948, when he was in his mid-twenties, directly addresses God, Kerouac pleading to see God because "I am tired, God, I cannot see your face in this *history*"; declaring that he will accept the will of the divine "as though I had asked You for [sorrows], and You had handed them to me, how I rejoice in these sorrows"; and finally thanking God for making him "like steel [. . .] Strike me and I will ring like a bell!" (*WW* 157–59). The journal had become for him a powerful vehicle to seriously address processes by which he and the larger culture could reconcile ideological polarities, and it was through the life and words of Jesus that he invested the most hope. "I know Jesus has the only answer," he proclaimed, later marveling that Jesus delivered "the most ringing sound of all human time" in the statement "My kingdom is not of this world" (John 18:36), confronting and confounding what Kerouac had considered "the terrible enigma of human life" (*WW* 12, 15–16). He considered this human condition analogous to his work as a writer: the source of each, human life and art, remains ineffable, beyond questions such as "*What* is it, *whence* does it come, where is it going, and why, and when, and *who* will know it?" (12). Any attempt to explain this vocation was analogous to asking questions about ontology and cosmology, the central concerns of metaphysical thought—ineffably full. But for that very reason, he deduced that these very questions, which express the great riddle of life, are the subject of great literature (11–13, 15), citing *The Brothers Karamazov, You Can't Go Home Again,* and *Moby-Dick* (16) as exemplars.

A month before he departed for his first cross-country road trip from Ozone Park, New York, where he was living with his mother, he ended the mood log with a lengthy exhortative passage claiming that human redemption is possible through one's recognition of the immediate present. Positing the possibility of a dead man's soul being allowed to return to earth, he concluded that "whatever this soul would *see* and *think,* that is for us now, the living now, that is the only truth" (*WW* 14). History and civilization are impermanent, "a glittering Babylon smoking under the sun"—Joycean nightmares from which we will eventually awake, he argued (13).[3] Humans will die and then return to earth, which is made by God, the only thing that "remain[s] the same." In effect, if not intention, this entry rewords Christ's message regarding the Christian kingdom as that which exists beyond the corporeal. Kerouac's vision of the universe includes the alpha and omega, the beginning and end of all things as God and earth, but by situating "god's permanency" on earth rather than on a metaphysical plain, Kerouac was implicitly attempting to refute the dualism of spirit and matter. At the least, by establishing the earth as a de facto heaven, his theory situated the spark of the divine within matter, moving him toward a kind of gnosticism or pantheism that defines all forces, laws, and manifestations as God.

Just a few days later, while in Kingston, North Carolina, visiting his sister with his mother, Kerouac rethought his theology. Still holding fast to the belief in the unimportance of personal achievements and in the existence of a transcendent "Father" or "All," he concluded that this "All," a distinctly more amorphous and nonhuman interpretation of the divine, is irreconcilable (*WW* 18). The reality that one cannot escape the perplexing fact of physical life as transitory and causally linked troubled him, especially the way the death of one creature causes the death of another, but he realized that one must kill the other in order to survive. How should one deal with this paradox, he wanted to know. Organic earth is really "unmoral," he determined, and acts according to its own laws that remain invisible to contemporary civilization, which operates according to American "Progress," a paradigm that had replaced religion as a guiding human force (18–19). Consequently, Kerouac found himself asking if any human being has the right to play God and mettle in the affairs of nature.

To solve the dilemma, he turned to parable. Implicitly imagining himself in league with the reader, he used the first-person plural to narrate the story of catching a fish that "we" name George, the act of personification suggesting an anthropomorphic common bond among all living creatures. "We" torture George with a cruel hook, then lock him away to suffocate while "we" pursue our lives oblivious to George's suffering. At this point, Kerouac shifts his perspective to confront God directly with the absurdity of this reality. "Oh God! — this [the fish] is all of us," fighting one another for space to breathe, dying a miserable death. "What shall we do?" he implored (19). His supplication elicits only silence, and as the energy of his address to God subsides, the only certainty remaining is the knowledge that since Christ and his Father made life hard, all must be blessed because it is all "God's whole works" (19).

This evolving interpretation of the Christ myth is highly sophisticated and certainly not one of which the Catholic Church would have approved, for Kerouac was eradicating its core beliefs in the afterlife; the concepts of heaven, evil, and original sin; and rebirth through baptism. Granted, Kerouac's emerging theology remained dualistic, preserving the concepts of a transcendental creator, the suffering of Jesus Christ, and the human soul. But it situated the concept of ever-lasting life, and thus Jesus and the soul, in the permanency of God's creation of earthly life and *in human action*. The individual, as he wrote to Cassady in August 1947, has the ability to perfect "doubt," that is, to ask questions and make choices, to not complacently accept any single conviction. Kerouac found it more laudable to seek a life "rich and full of loving—it's no good otherwise, no good at all, for anyone" (*Letters* 1: 117–18). Whether believing triumphantly in the innate beauty of life or in its inexplicable misery, he was crafting a theodicy consistent with his fervent need for a personal god to affirm goodness in the individual and the present.

After completing his road trip and returning home in October 1947, Kerouac resumed his contemplative practice, confiding in his journal that he disliked feeling "worldly" and knowledgeable, preferring instead the introspective stance of Thomas Carlyle[4] and eschewing indifference as the source of human difficulties. Whatever truths had been revealed to him on that trip, he elected to investigate their genesis and evolution. This tracing of truth's shadows, as he called them (*WW* 23–24), led him on an archeological trek with no easily discernible map in hand. From 1947 to 1948, as he composed *The Town and the City*, he pursued two major threads of thought. One questioned human nature and its relationship to the divine. The other questioned art as well as the nature, duties, and responsibilities of the artist. They formed a double helix of at least a single truth he had reaffirmed for himself: humans need to ascertain the relationship between the individual and others in this world.

Regarding human nature, love and beauty remained central for him—a deep desire for people to open their eyes to the mysteries among which they lived. In January 1948, he recorded a vision in which this desire appeared to him as gleeful little fairies who, because he had been open to the possibility of their existence, danced lovingly around him (*WW* 41). He had found a similar wonder in the wedding of the then Princess Elizabeth to the Duke of Edinburgh on November 20, 1947, an event symbolizing for him a healthy love to counter culture's preoccupation with the criminal and demonic (29). These passages are harmonious with Kerouac's professed belief in Christ's essential message that love is "the rule of human life" (135). But Kerouac also entertained two disparate and less ideal notions. One was that love and hate are fundamentally identical, merely constructed differently through the pride of individual personalities (33). The second was that hate is an "inversion of self-love," the genesis of which he recognized as the reality that self-love, like life, cannot last forever. He credited the recognition of mortality, combined with one's sense of self, as that which privileges material success over "ideal aspirations," leading "all religions" to incorporate the concept of immortality, or a "second chance," into their theologies (135).

In such moments, his theological writing strongly intimated a repudiation of the Christ story and an affirmation of the need to secure alternative explanations of the human condition. However, his compulsion to pursue knowledge of self and others continued to baffle him. Writing that he "tremble[d]" with the understanding that human concepts are separated only by extremely thin lines (*WW* 66), Kerouac confronted head-on as a fundamental component of human nature the difficulty of knowing oneself, let alone all humanity: "'truth' can only be the truth of myself, which I see inside me, and cannot be universalized and vaguely generalized into 'truth for all men' whose *insides* I of course cannot see—trusting, therefore, that the truth in me may be the same in them" (125). In other words, the human condition includes the ephemeral nature of human concepts, their malleable form as human constructs, and the fallibility of the human mind to acquire self-knowledge. This logic transformed the human condition from a matter of suffering that one must meekly accept as God's will into an approachable reality relative to the individual, who lives with only a dim hope of knowing the universal through self-knowledge—a much darker vision than the Berdyaev-Mannian mythic path that he would later follow.

Kerouac repeatedly rejected egoistic tendencies to seek knowledge, a perspective traced to a number of philosophical sources in his reading history. The most direct and best discussed in Beat studies is the German author Oswald Spengler, whose *Decline of the West* (1918), an aphoristic, rhapsodic, intuitive, and nonsystematic vision, furnished Kerouac with the term "Faustian." Spengler is a relatively obscure author today, but in the mid-twentieth century his works were well known to many Western intellectuals. In *Decline,* he depicted the character of human cultures as individually distinct yet governed by identical histories generated by inexplicable forces moving as endless formations and transformations of organic forms, specifically birth, development, decay, and death. All human cultures, which he distinguished from smaller nation states existing within the larger culture, are born with a religious impulse. Spengler, however, did not present religion as a mark of cultural sophistication, but rather as a life-generating impulse in all cultures that runs its course, as does the analogous principle in other organic forms.[5] Revealing through direct quotation his Goethian heritage, he concluded that as cultures move through their organic cycle, "the Godhead is effective in the living and not in the dead, in the becoming and the changing, not in the become and the set-fast'" (49). History, then, is to be judged by the degree to which it propels the life cycle. In the wake of World War I, he determined that the Faustian Western world was no longer capable of significant achievements. Atheistic, ego driven, pacifistic, and a slave to destructive technologies, it was immersed in the impotence of decay (40).

Kerouac read and discussed *Decline* with Sebastian Sampas as well as Burroughs and Ginsberg (Nicosia 87, 134), and he was also familiar with Goethe's version of the Faust myth, thus incorporating the concept of failed Faustian striving into his interpretation of modernity as anti-individualism speeding toward global annihilation.[5] His reading of Christian texts, including Carlyle's autobiographical writings, Paul's epistles, Augustine's *Confessions,* and Thomas Aquinas's *Summa Theologica,* no doubt firmed up his conviction that striving for knowledge, rather than living by faith, was a doomed process. However, he kept returning to the belief that all humans must nevertheless strive for knowledge of the human condition, an idea for which he sought expression in a mix of psychological and literary forms. At one point, he explained destructive dualism as the result of intellect unreconciled with feelings (*WW* 103). Another time, humans appeared to him to conceal the image of a "paranoiac cougar," and he clung to the need to see in the world an organic morality, or "real manly gentleness, a manly calm among dangers," to save one from one's violent psychosis (66–67). During this same period (1947–48), he called this feature the "inevitable cretin" in the human soul (136–37). Human nature as a duality also meant distinguishing between the physical body and the soul, the latter, however, *not* being the conventional ghostlike substance subject to a life after death, but one's ability to perceive the poetic mysteries of life, those "fairy glees" living in one's own heart (41). This reconstruction of the body-soul dichotomy, in effect, corresponded with his persistent efforts to unify that very dualism.

The barrier to unification he repeatedly identified as pride. As with dualism, his definitions of pride ranged quixotically from the slavish condition of all peoples (whether one worked for the state or for personal gain) to the need to overcome others, to the crime of knowing "that something is necessary, yet not need it for oneself" (*WW* 138). He speculated that pride could be human nature, that which gives life, but that conversely it was human death (48–49). In August 1948, he even experienced pride as a truth revealed to him in a vision of a tiny organism palpitating like a beating heart on the front of the human brain. It is difficult to discern from the journal the exact sequence of events that constituted his mystical experience. What seems obvious, though, is that he temporarily resolved his conflict between his need to understand denaturalized truth and his belief in one's limited ability to reach beyond the self. He did so by implicitly denouncing ratiocinative processes and propositional thinking as false, replacing them with the mystical production of knowledge. The palpitating brain of pride was universal knowledge because, he noted, it came as "thoughts [. . .] unannounced, unplanned, unforced, vividly *true* in their dazzling light" (125). Although he stated that he saw these truths *inside himself,* the language of the entry suggests that the ability to see "unannounced, unplanned, [and] unforced" was the gift of something greater or unknowable. The entry intimates, as do many others, that his resolutions bear an otherworldly mark.

Once he had solved that dilemma, he could construct a list of truths about himself. The eleven truths that he identified are a conglomeration of contradictions, coalescing around a celebration of self as the center of all knowledge. He instructs himself, for example, to not love others because it wastes time and he is "better" anyhow; to justify himself only to himself, so that he may hide his faults from others; to accept death as natural and nonhuman and thus of no concern; to realize that he can admit his weaknesses without being despised by others; to reject the belief that speaking self-truth is masochism; to refuse to seek truth, an act of "vicious pridefulness"; and to accept no forgiveness unless it is genuinely offered. The "I" that dominates the list signals Kerouac's intention to limit such knowledge to himself, but his use of the declarative, as in "truth #4," "Greed is pride, vice is pride, morality is pride," creates aphoristic statements directing these truths to others as well.

Kerouac's theological turn at this point presents fascinating consistencies of thought as well as new directions. He remained life focused, while rejecting the secular wisdom of science, especially as represented by Freud. However, his vision of a palpitating brain as "all life" and "spirit" indicates a turn away from the notion of a personal god, especially one who is human incarnate. The absence of a rhetoric focused on evil, sin, and faith and the predominance of the rhetoric of wisdom and knowledge suggests a movement toward beliefs regarding human nature now recognizable as belonging to or compatible with Platonism, early Christian gnosticism, and nineteenth- and twentieth-century existentialism. This turn makes sense, since Kerouac had been reading many wisdom texts, both sectarian and secular, and his early fiction, letters, and journals evince his practice of blending diverse theological and nontheological perspectives as a central method of his quest to understand human nature. That Kerouac's journey should reveal the bundling of gnostic and existential strands of discourse also should not be entirely surprising, since the two movements, despite the almost 2,000 years separating them, share key elements, including the focus on the individual, the concept of alienation, and the rejection of the idea of any natural order dictating the essence of the human being.

Kerouac never followed any identifiable school of existentialism. Existential elements in his writing, such as his description of nature as "*merely Nature, nature unchangeable, uninteresting, unhuman*" (*WW* 127), more accurately represent his personal insights rather than adherence to any particular philosophical system. This image of nature implicitly places humans in a setting that cannot provide an essential purpose; the universe merely revolves with alien indifference. Additionally, Kerouac references

Nietzsche significantly enough to hint that he fundamentally understood Nietzsche's declaration regarding the death of God. Granted, Kerouac scoffed at Nietzsche, calling him jealous of God (*Letters* 1: 251) and rebuking Nietzsche's claim that God is dead (*Vanity of Duluoz* 171). But the Legend as a whole allies Kerouac with the Nietzschian call for a Dionysian approach to life—that is, transforming the classical figure into a metaphor for the creative act. It is probable that Kerouac rebuked Nietzsche's Dionysius as the raw and recurring "will to power," and he may also have misunderstood Nietzsche's coupling of the Dionysian principle with Ariadne, the human complement tempering the eternal life force. However, a telling passage in *Visions of Cody* includes the character Aderiande, a parodic facsimile of the classical Greek character, who in a state of Olympian hyperreality counsels others to think pragmatically. Her caution that "this thing [apparently a human battle of some kind] is going to get us down unless we do something about it immediately don't you think" suggests that Kerouac had some knowledge of the Nietzschian counter to unrestrained human power (269).

In the face of such power, Kerouac staunchly maintained an allegiance to Jesus, although vacillating between viewing him as a godly man and as a manly god. By the late forties, Kerouac was describing Christ consistently as a wise human rather than as a divine presence, and, in a 1948 journal entry, apologizing for being anti-Christian, he called Christ "the first man" to realize the rule of love (*WW* 135). This use of "man" rather than "god" is an important signal of the diminishing viability of Christian tenets in Kerouac's thinking. Even more convincing is an undated philosophical statement titled "God as the Should-be (THE HUGE GUILT)" from this same period in which Kerouac laid out an atheistic explanation of the concept of God. Finding the "most beautiful" of ideas to be a child's notion of its father as all-knowing, Kerouac describes as angst-filled that moment when one realizes that no human has such knowledge: "God," he concludes, is really our desire or belief that "there must be a way, an authority, a great knowledge, a vision, a view of life, a proper manner, a 'seemlisness' [*sic*] in all the disorder and sorrow of the world." The notion that there "should-be" is God, which renders humans "*guilty* thereby" (143–44). In other words, humans desperately want to believe in the omniscient other, but it is not there, and they are left on the brink of despair or madness.

Kerouac did not elaborate on the idea of guilt, but by disconnecting it from a creation narrative such as the two Adam and Eve stories in Genesis that ground guilt in human sin against God, he situated the desire for a meaningful universe within the human condition. By implication, he was making two prevalent twentieth-century philosophical claims. The first is the deconstructivist precept that the signifier-signified complex "God" is predicated on its binary component "no god." God cannot exist without the invisible and necessary desire for something to fill the void of no-God. Second is an existentialist position that the greatest "sin" of any human being, which is guilt, comes from a human's inability to see itself as the only source of knowledge. In accordance with these ideas, by looking inward, Kerouac chose a path to create himself as he wanted to be, thus modeling what others should do as well. "I take the position morally," he wrote, "that psychology is a hesitation-in-analysis and not an action-in-the world. Knowledge has it place, but the work of *life* needs to get done" (*WW* 149). This aphoristic private writing implies that one acts on behalf of others by first making choices for oneself.

In language and belief, Kerouac was positioning himself in philosophical harmony with a major tenet of Jean-Paul Sartre's atheistic argument that existentialism is a humanistic rather than nihilistic endeavor. "Existentialism is a Humanism," Sartre's lecture on the subject, delivered in 1946 and published in French in 1948, may have been familiar to Kerouac. There is no evidence now available to definitely claim that he had read the essay, but Kerouac acknowledges French existentialism in his journal of 1947–48, grouping it with Reichians, organists, gays, marijuana users, and others who he believed had begun "to recognize the existence of an 'atomic disease' of sorts [. . .] and were 'enemies' of 'Bourgeois culture'" (*WW* 141–42). Clearly these ideas, along with communism and socialism, were circulating in Kerouac's intellectual world, so it is logical that he would have assimilated some of them, although he seems to have viewed them skeptically if not ambivalently. They were there in 1948, when Kerouac identified the battle against one's fears as an essential component of existential action—that is, the need to challenge the despair and unsolvable problems that "the modern thinking man" recognizes through self-knowledge. While admiring these "thinking" men (147), he expressed disdain for their condescending admiration for the folk:

> They see "patterns" instead of tableaus among the people; they notice their vigor as a kind of anthropological-economics phenomena—in other words, their admiration is partly an admiration of themselves for being so observant of the people and their "ways." Think of all the terms—"folkways," "working-classes," "lower economic groups," and so on, all the braintrust terms which never take blood, music, and grace into account. (*WW* 147)

Lecturing himself that "their understanding is strictly Olympian, naturalistic, aloof, academic, sparse, [and] 'factually objective'" (147), Kerouac concluded that this modern man, unable or reluctant to really live, ironically loves defeat, consequently giving up hope and riding "like a chip on the river and prefers not to plod in a line of his own" (148).

Reflecting on his desire to lead an agrarian life of solitude in order to write, he carefully rectified that vision with his argument about what authentic thinking and living should be: "Literature doesn't necessarily mean neurotic laceration of things. It might also mean knowledge of all men's lives, and knowledge of men's sense of themselves everywhere" (*WW* 148–49). The secular wisdom that Kerouac was advocating at this juncture in his novitiate justifies the removal of oneself from the vortex of life to create art and philosophy if the knowledge communicated by that art extends beyond the self. In this respect, his distrustful take on existentialism ironically adhered fairly harmoniously to Sartre's belief (articulated in 1948 in *What is Literature?*) that "to write is thus both to disclose the world and to offer it as a task to the generosity of the reader. It is to have recourse to the consciousness of others in order to make one's self be recognized as *essential* to the totality of being" (1347). In other words, Kerouac implied a conscious realization that his own freedom to seek solitude in which to create is predicated upon human freedom, the essential condition of the Sartrean individual. Separating his view of human nature from Sartrean existentialism, however, was Kerouac's belief in the dualistic nature of spirit and matter—if not acquired, then affirmed via his vision of the palpitating brain. "Pride," as mystically presented to him, while the source of human trouble, actually throbbed with a wild beauty and was all of life itself, including vanity. This "Pride," which exists in all humans and could not kill, he implied, because it was "*all* spirit," is one of the concepts that reconfigure certain features of Kerouac's thinking and writing during this time as gnostic.

In the late forties, Kerouac's journals suggest that he did not harbor the gnostic, particularly Manichaean, repulsion for human and other forms of flesh, although he came to do so later in life. As one entry clarifies, he considered fleshly pleasures a panacea for twentieth-century depersonalization: "Everybody is deeply sane because of their flesh. Thank God for flesh! Thank God for the sanity of wine and flesh in the midst of all those I.B.M.'s and prisons and diplomats and neurotics and schools and [. . .] suburban homes where children are taught to despise themselves" (*WW* 163). But after his initial road trip, he distanced himself from monotheism and a personal god, and his quest for truth relied heavily on the mystical and the intuitive. Kerouac's gnostic move during this period was his rejection of a personal, anthropomorphized supreme other, which he replaced with his nascent understanding of the transcendent All. Like gnostics before him, Kerouac considered life to hold both light (love) and darkness (human anguish). Darkness was not the Augustinian guilt of original sin, that is, the sin of *having* knowledge, but rather the *lack* of knowledge about the self and the world, particularly as pride filled.

This complex process of seeking the truth of human nature relentlessly compelled him to question the nature of art and the nature of the artist. His humanity remained deeply rooted in his artistic inclinations, as his journals from 1947 to 1948 passionately reveal. He wrote in his "Town and the City" journal that "when a man presents the world with its own details, and lights them with his celestial visions of unworldly love, that is the highest genius" (*WW* 42). The maxim suggests that the genius of the artist rests not in understanding externally imposed laws of writing, which Kerouac said eluded him the more he consciously examined them (52–53), but in the act of serving as messenger, using otherworldly visions to cut through the noise of worldly love to expose something greater.

Kerouac's stance resounds with Platonic terminology, especially the Good, the Beautiful, and the Soul, concepts that he had often unsystematically applied to his writing, as his early fiction and essays in *Atop an Underwood* illustrate. He even went so far in his journal as to redefine the novel as "soul-work," a term that he deemed somewhat "fancy" and "laughable," yet indicative of someone "writing all-out for the sake of earnestness and salvation" (*WW* 94). This precept demanded that the artist gladly accept the reality of beauty and love in the world, that he love himself and others, and that by retiring from life he can better see life's beauty and convey this reality to those still in the anguish of living (139). Kerouac maneuvered himself into an articulation of this philosophy in the following passage:

> The world is a neutral place in the unspoken state of itself until some "little thing" of a human being artist comes along and thinks on it, and *speaks,* and turns neutrality into *positiveness,* of any kind, stupid, crass, simple, complex, or otherwise. This itself is greater than the "degree of awareness" man can have, the mere amiability of human art is a great thing in itself. This is vague, except for one undeniable thing; art should not be used as a cosmic "gripe" at everything, it should be a sincerity in its deepest sense. (*WW* 140)

At the time he wrote the entry, he was immersed in Dostoyevsky's *Raw Youth* (1875), a novel about a contentious father-son relationship exposing the contrast between the Russian ideologies in the 1840s and the youthful Russian nihilism in the 1860s. Kerouac admired Dostoyevsky's sincere effort to probe the human condition, and *Raw Youth* he interpreted not as a cosmic gripe but as Dostoyevsky's sincere and relentless effort to speak *for* life (140). Kerouac was also rejecting various metaphysical propositions grounding his heritage as Western and Christian. Foremost, the notion of the world as "a neutral place" contradicts a Catholic view of nature as both God's creation and as sinful because of man's fall. Secondly, Kerouac's view of the relationship between nature and the artist repudiated the Platonic view that the artist is a deceiver who cannot improve upon nature, itself an inferior copy of a separate and eternal Form. Thirdly, it counters the Aristotelian view of nature as both inorganic and organic, elevating the artist and including a god as the prime mover with the power to make mute forms speak.

Kerouac's artist is a force of positive change, and his literature seemed destined to combine both American pragmatism colored with humility and decency and Russian brotherhood, a new kind of wisdom for life at mid-century. Life and art are one and the same for the "true" artist who, he wrote, "entered the house of doubt—and [. . .] explored all the rooms and left the way he came in" (*WW* 144). The true artist, unafraid to confront human doubts, remains fundamentally unchanged, sacrificing nothing for art but instead writing and living according to his own dictates, Kerouac ascertained (*WW* 140–50; *Letters* 1: 168). Eschewing the demands of university writing classes to pursue "a close study of the science of writing" if one hopes "to successfully probe and analyze and dissect the human foibles and social surfaces" (*WW* 143), Kerouac embraced poetry, lyric joy, "Dostoyevskyan moral fury, . . . emotional grandeur, . . . sweep and architectural earnestness" (143)—the voices of *human* wisdom called forth in a world wrecked by its own pride.

1949–50

By the end of 1948, Kerouac was completing *The Town and the City* as well as attempting to start *Doctor Sax* and *On the Road*. His thinking life as recorded in his journals begins a new phase, subtly moving him toward his intense and serious study of Buddhism, which probably began in 1951, before he composed the scroll version of *On the Road* (Nicosia 451). This period can appear confusing and contradictory—many times he seems hopelessly lost or naively blissful—but threaded intricately amongst the dross are intimations of a maturing personality ready to break loose into a life that makes no distinction between itself and its art. There was, as he wrote, "an evergrowing tree in [his] breast" (*WW* 243).

One aspect of this internality was a more confidently focused articulation of the function of his writing. Journal entries from this period show that he sought writing that was action centered and confessional, that dealt with real people's lives, and that reflected his belief in human sexual energy grounding and connecting people, this last a partial result of his reading of Wilhelm Reich (*WW* 62). His writing also demanded a search for individuality free from "the great interruption of ephemeral civilization" (163), coupled with a sense of the sprawling unity of American life. Electing to use his journal to find his true voice, which he theorized would become a universal sound (159), he had already come to realize that writing was an extension of teaching, and he compared his unpublished work to "An Oral History of the World" by the Greenwich Village legendary bohemian Joe Gould (165), also known as "Professor Sea Gull" because he claimed to speak seagullese. Gould's reported nine-million-word tome, composed as he sat in restaurants and subways recording the voices he heard, had gone unrecognized,[6] and Kerouac saw himself as a Gouldian eccentric and out-sider, actually fearing that he would die old, ugly, and alone like Gould (86).[7] But Kerouac aimed his art much higher than Gould did, describing his teachings as a vehicle for a source beyond the human; his muse was the Truth: "*IT'S NOT THE WORDS THAT COUNT BUT THE RUSH OF TRUTH WHICH USES WORDS FOR ITS PURPOSES" (252). His role had become that of the earthly prophet who channels the message of truth through language.

Realizing that such a project required a new form of writing, he elected a structure much like ancient wisdom texts, especially the Old and New Testaments with short chapters and verselike headings. An October 1949 journal entry reveals that he envisioned this form as "a narrative poem, an epos in mosaic, a kind of Arabesque preoccupation . . . free to wander from the laws of the 'novel' as laid down by Austens & Fieldings into an area of great spiritual pith" (WW 241–42). In an earlier entry from August, he had singled out categories of individuals worthy to create such texts: "Is this the way the world is going to end,—in indifference? [. . .] Where are the old prophets and scriveners of the Scriptures? Where is the Lamb? Where are the little ones? What happened to parable?—to the Word?—Even to mere tales and seriousness?" (205). The allusion to the statement of the speaker of Eliot's "Hollow Men" ("This is the way the world ends / Not with a bang but a whimper") suggests that Kerouac believed writers must battle against the indifference of the human world, but his was a battle that did not take place on Arnoldian darkling plains or the fields of Armageddon. Instead, it was waged in the language of prophets and the authors of scriptures—their words sculpted as parables and tales, as his also would be.

In the process, Kerouac toyed with more postmodern philosophies of writ-ing and reality as discursive entities. The following passage, while referencing no particular philosophical text, collects strands of what are now recognized as postmodernist questioning and erasing of monolithic reality:

It may even be true, by God, that all of us make myths continually and that therefore . . . there is no reality. I am not no dashing mad Kerouac, I'm a sad wondering guy [. . .] and similarly, my pictures of others have been equally untrue and absurd: but since we even have pictures of ourselves, there must be no reality anywhere, or, that is, reality is a sum total of our myths, a canvas out of which everything shows (as in Dostoevsky) with little left out, a cross-section of individual phantasmal creations (in the sense that the daydream is a creation, a whole production.) The energy of this creation [. . .] is the energy of life and art. Yet the watch-repairer has no illusions; I repaired a watch-bracelet Saturday, no illusions about it, [. . .] The reality is there [. . .] Our fantastic creatures *are* our relationships—that is, the mere fact of fantasy is the focal point of communication. And this is all words, words,—another music. (*WW* 176)

His speculation that we are "the sum total of our myths" situates reality as Mannian succession stories and also relative to the writer who manipulate the language. The self as a stable entity is replaced by many selves (phantasms or fantasies) seen most lucidly through the art of a writer such as Dostoyevsky. This all echoes in content, if not intent, the postmodern undertaking of replacing the human project of metaphysics with the centrality of language and textuality as well as the slippages and contradictions of meanings with language systems. Kerouac's conclusion that these fantastic creatures constitute human relationships, the point of all communication, also corresponds with contemporary epistemic and phenomenological theories, such as those of the philosopher Richard Rorty and the Russian psychologist Lev Vygotsky, which posit the construction of the self to be a discursive social practice. Of course, as the above passage also makes clear, Kerouac was not ready to live in a world of mercurial word-people or in a reality that was all illusion. Metaphorically playing Samuel Johnson refuting Bishop Berkeley by kicking his foot at a stone, Kerouac was confident that the watch-bracelet he had repaired was a physical reality.

By November 1948, Kerouac was experimenting with more free-flowing methods of writing early drafts of *On the Road,* leading him to consider the metaphor of the balloon or bubble to explain the connections between art, self, and life. He and Ginsberg had discussed this image, which Ginsberg called writing that "floats lightly over an abyss, like a balloon, like reality" (*WW* 169). Kerouac extended the metaphor, morphing the balloon into pink bubbles misting all human eyes with a life-loving vision (169–71). Analogous and yet counter to his vision of the "palpitating brain of pride," the bubble metaphor represents the fusion of art, human nature, and natural goodness in more positive form for Kerouac, becoming a leitmotif of the Legend, especially in *Mexico City Blues.*[8]

During this time, Kerouac also felt himself growing more mystical—that is, believing more firmly in knowledge derived from intuition, contemplation, and meditation (*WW* 201). Likewise, calling himself an "anachronistic Catholic" (175), his dualism intensified. In the face of an ugly, nasty world that he acknowledged could simply be naturalism at its worst—"Fellaheen flesh sweating and food for maggots" (212), his version of Tennyson's "red in tooth and claw"—he returned to more direct references to Jesus as the son of God, reminding himself that

> my own interpretation of Christ I will write soon: essentially the same, that he was the first, perhaps the last, to recognize the facing-up of a man to life final enigma as the only important activity on earth. Although times have changed since then, and "Christianity" is actually Christian in method by now (social-ism), still, the time has yet to come for a true "accounting," a true Christlike world. The King who comes on an Ass, meek. (199)

Rejecting brutishness and pleading for passionate belief in greater powers, he invoked a personal god who knows and loves him despite his pettiness, shal-lowness, and other human foibles (273–74). Simultaneously, he probed human nature and the divine in a gnostic manner, pursuing the large and small facts of human existence as well as its great sweeping truths. In one of the most beautiful passages in the journals, he reflects on the process, calling his life "a river of meditations" in which he wanders through his mind "as one picking berries and packing them in proper boxes, all for 'later consumption' of some kind, or pressing in the wine-vats of more formful thought such as accompanies artwork. Poosh!" (238–39). As this entry intimates, his understanding of a god pursued meditatively was beginning to coalesce around the concept of the distant, unknowable transcendent coupled with a life-generating force that permeates the natural and human world.

In early form, *On the Road* itself was intended to reveal this mark, Kerouac envisioning one of the primary characters, Smitty, as an innocent who seeks pure knowledge because "he wants God to *come down*" to earth "only for reasons of pure knowledge and the essence of knowledge. The essences in his brainpan are not there for nothing, the swirls in his won-dering soul and about his head are not there for nothing. He is not demanding *power,* only love, which is pure knowledge of the unknown" (*WW* 231). *On the Road,* then, in its early manifestations was a human quest for love and an exploration of the gnosticlike quest to "stare at God's face, his 'reality' of a streetcorner [*sic*] or a tree, or anything," to answer "the Why of Whys," as Kerouac called God (231–32). But at times, his concept of God was the more amorphous "continuum of living across pre-ordained spaces, followed by the continuum of the Mystery of Death" that never ends (198), a view allowing him to embrace more Eastern prebirth states of existence through which humans move. To the latter, he linked the belief that he could communicate with the dead, including his father and Sebastian Sampas (230–31), a desire later reflected in his writing that repeatedly resurrected many of those closest to him, especially his father and his brother Gerard.

For the most part, though, none of these ideas dominated his novitiate. While he remained steadfast in his belief in a kind of holy humanism or life itself as the seat of holiness, encouraging humans to love one another (or at least they *should,* he repeatedly sermonized), the idea of God-among-us-as-love seemed insufficient. Other possibilities were threatened by the allure of another world, which he imagined in various forms, including God waiting for humans "in bleak eternity," a Platonic Whole Form, an apocalyptic Holy Final Whirlwind, "the grace of the Mysterious God" that will eventually reveal itself, and an uncaring mystery that demands human submission (*WW* 210–11, 233). Christ and Dostoyevsky remained the primary emissaries of this unknowable other for him, and Kerouac saw himself as a "Celestial Tongue" inheriting that lineage (322, 325).

One manifestation of the process whereby he solidified his vocation as literary sage is the presence in his journals of elements of a personal cosmology. This cosmology, which was to find its most fantastic expression in *Doctor Sax,* contained a set of literary motifs that populates much of his prose and poetry as teaching devices—stories that he repeats, names that resonate throughout his work to evoke a core of themes, emotions, and truth for those who have come to know his theology. The one that dominates the 1949–50 journals is the image of the Shrouded Traveler, a figure that aligns Kerouac's spirituality more firmly with a gnostic Christianity than with Catholic orthodoxy, intimating his imminent turn to Buddhism.

In an early reference to this figure, an entry dated May 2, 1948, Kerouac embedded structures of Christian mysticism and Buddhist legend to speak of his journey as writer and spiritual quester: "But my soul it is not water: it is Milk, it is Milk. For I saw the Shrouded Angel standing in the Hooded Tree, and Golden Firmaments on High, and Gold, and Gold. And the Dusky Rose that glows in Golden Rain, and Rain, and Rain" (188). This highly coded description resonated with romantic Christian language, such as the milk of the Virgin Mary and Christ, the sustenance of salvation. The Shrouded Angel, unlike Gabriel, remains an anonymous emissary of the divine positioned under a living tree. Above all is a golden firmament, symbolic perhaps of heaven or wisdom. The Dusky Rose in the rain may point to Theresa of Lisieux, whom Kerouac long revered, showers of roses being the primary sign of her saintliness. This meditation introduces the Shrouded form as an ambiguous figure of both earthly and other worldly origin, a strange and portent-filled gnosis conveying signs of both darkness ("Shrouded") and light ("Angel"). It is the mystery around which all other elements in the tableau are stationed, the messenger and the call.

This mystery is explicated in a later entry in which Kerouac discussed his theory of life as a series of deflections from forgotten goals leading to circles of despair, which whirled around "one dark haunting *thing,*" which he called "the Shrouded Stranger that I dreamt once." He imagined this "thing" as the ever "unnameable" central to human existence, comparing it to "Wolfe's 'brother Loneliness,' Melville's 'inscrutable thing,' Blake's 'gate of Wrath,' Emily Dickinson's 'third event,' Shakespeare's 'nature'?" It could also be God, he surmised, and it was unequivocally "every man's 'mystery' and deepest being." He even thought it "as plaint may be a song as well. Ecclesiasticus" (249). The great mystery of life that can never be solved, the Shrouded Stranger connected by juxtaposition to the last Book of Wisdom in the New Jerusalem Bible is motif of both the transmission of truths about human conduct and also humankind's greatest sadness or grief, a message connoted through the archaic literary meaning of *plaint*, which is a lamentation (249).

This particular reading of Kerouac's conjectures is relatively positive in terms of his artistic life and perception of human existence. Other efforts to make sense of the image as a cosmological figure produced darker visions. Even when asking if the figure could be God, Kerouac concluded that it was really one's damnable fate (*WW* 251). In later journal entries, the stranger became a mean and hellish entity living in a world where only insanity and falseness exist (321). As the result of a later experience with trancelike meditation, Kerouac transformed the stranger into existence itself, finding in the Shrouded Existence the awful ambiguity into which each person is born. Humans are rooted, he declaimed, in a Shrouded Existence or Dream, which is hell; although we are born into heaven—a distinctly nongnostic or nonorthodox Christian belief—he maintained that we are haunted by the hell from which we come (321–23). It is the Shrouded Traveler, a vestige of the knowledge that we are connected to a horrific otherworld, that comes among us as an alien form of ourselves—"pursuing us *on* to heaven which is great life on earth; and if we lag, he may catch us and cast us down in the darkness again," he concluded (323–24).

Kerouac's explication of the Shrouded figure alludes to a cosmology in which humans are created in a loathsome otherworld but cannot avoid being cast onto earth where they must learn to understand the dualism of dark and light and to seek the light ever after. Hell, in both an antignostic and anti-Catholic move, is not the material world of earth; nor is it a secondary netherworld. It remains an inexplicable entity unto itself. Humans are inevitably part of it and struggle constantly during their lives on earth to remain free of it. A multifaceted sign embodying this cosmology narrative, the Shrouded Stranger is the alienated light within the dark (humans on earth and the transcendent's emissaries of knowledge) and the alienated dark within the light (the evil part of humans and the material universe itself that exists within the unnamable All). As knowledge of humans' origins in darkness and the human inheritance of the light, the Shrouded Stranger signifies human beings as their doom and their savior—knowledge that one must shed and must seek. In other words, he is "the Immemorial Pearl" (*WW* 324) of wisdom in both gnostic and orthodox Christianity, the goal of the human search for knowledge that paradoxically curses and blesses.

This paradox is made visible in two short, undeveloped narratives that Kerouac apparently wrote in 1950. Concluding *Windblown World,* "The Saint's Thoughts" and "Made by the Sky" each project a unique voice and perspective on the question of human nature. Together they illustrate Kerouac's patient journey away from orthodox Catholic and Protestant Christianity toward a gnosticlike and Buddhist vision of the universe that afforded him a method to teach spirituality while avoiding separating art from other aspects of his life. In "The Saint's Thoughts," the first-person narrator assumes the extreme Christian position (both Catholic and gnostic) of finding the mortal, vegetable world that is sinister and without love. Humans are bereaved and alienated within this place created by a cruel divinity. Knowing that he never sought such a life but was thrown into it and must suffer in it, the narrator denies it any allegiance: "This world is not mine and I owe it nothing" (*WW* 367). Believing that goodness exists only in the otherworld, he calls the earth "a gallstone" that "weighs heavily in my patience and makes me cry, and seek, in vain" (368). His future is an "ecstasy" that "will only come much later after much sweat and useless hankering," and he believes the Second Coming to be near at hand (367–68).

A strikingly different tone characterizes the narrator of "Made by the Sky." Indulging in metaphoric language engendering calm and hope, this narrator is far removed from the belligerent and long-suffering narrator of "Saint's." The "Sky" narrator begins by separating himself from those he loves, stating that for them, contrary to himself, it is a sin to have been created by the sky. But as a poet, he is "a spright," an emissary sent to the vegetable world by the creator to watch its movements, work hard, avoid the pleasures of "lettuce nature," remain joyful, and return to "the Heavenly Wheel," which is detached from or alienated from the natural world. His mission is "to bring back [his] knowledge to the angels of the rack, the poll of the Universe" (*WW* 370–71). Both narrators, then, perceive themselves as alien forms placed in a corrupt material world, and therefore they must seek transcendence.

But the "Saint's" narrator is made by the divine as part of the worthless natural world and has no knowledge of why he has been put on earth; he knows only that nature has instilled in him the will to live and that his reward will come in the afterlife. The Saint's life is one of submission to an anthropomorphic god, a cruel Yahweh that expects suffering and obedience from his earthly creations. "Saint's" can be read as a narrative of the Judeo-Christian orthodoxy that grounds Kerouac's thinking about human nature and the divine but brings him no pleasure, since in this worldview humans can only suffer in blind ignorance; transcendence remains but a possibility.

In contrast, the "Sky" narrator knows that his place of origin is wholly the otherworld and that he has been sent to perform a special mission on earth. His life is one of purposeful observation and action in a universe of many worlds, leading him not to "God" but to heaven, where he will find infinite joy and knowledge of the on-going principle of life: the Heavenly or Eternal Wheel. The "Sky" narrative as myth accepts the corruption of the material world but promises hope through the poet who arrives as a chosen messenger from the transcendent, imaged not as a cruel god but as natural phenomenon: movement (the wheel) and light (the sky). As both, the transcendent as Heavenly Wheel suggests the condition of immanence that "transfigures time into Eternity . . . total presence in the present," as theologian Huston Smith maintains (*Beyond* 4). "Sky," however, ultimately remains more a narrative of becoming rather than being. But because it *suggests* the *possibility* of immanence, it portends the path toward which Kerouac was heading as the mature writer and spiritualist who would create the Duluoz Legend.

CHAPTER 3

THE QUEST—PART I: ON THE ROAD

By the conclusion of the *Windblown World* journals, Kerouac was immersed in what is now recognized as his most productive period as a writer. The end of 1950, when he was twenty-eight years old, saw him embarked on a serious study of Buddhism, using Dwight Goddard's *A Buddhist Bible* as his most cherished collection of Buddhist primary sources, which as he told Ginsberg in 1954 "is by far the best book because it contains the Surangama Sutra and the Lankavatra Sutra, not to mention the eleven-page Diamond Sutra which is the last word" (*Letters* 1: 415). In addition, he had typed the "scroll" version of *On the Road*, a project that he began on April 2, 1951, radically transforming the third-person narrative of Ray and Smitty into a lyrical, bop-driven vision of America embodied by Cassady, the model for Smitty. Over the next several years, as Tim Hunt has meticulously documented, this process involved revisions, consultations with editors, and much anguish on Kerouac's part as he struggled to reconcile "the symbolic truth of the inner world of the child and the realistic truth of the outer world of the adult" (117). Kerouac called the book a meditation "on problems of the soul" (*WW* 206), and as such *On the Road,* despite the editorial changes that Kerouac later denigrated and the extent of which readers still remain unaware, was the first major teaching of Kerouac as paraclete, a critical transition in his journey. Significantly, it is not a text that directly addresses Duluoz's vocation as a writer, one of the key elements that had guided his novitiate; only brief asides identify the narrator as a professional writer. The text that propelled him and the Beat generation into the national spotlight constitutes instead his efforts to articulate a blend of Christian and Buddhist truths about the human condition that can educate and forewarn others.

Implicitly, the narrative models the sources of human truth in a binary of contemplation and action: adventure, fellowship, self-abnegation, excess, family, love—and ultimately story itself.

On the surface, the book seems little like many ancient or conventional wisdom texts. It is not a litany of commandments setting forth how to live a godly life; nor is it a visionary tale of the end of the world, a collection of wise sayings, or a myth of divine origin, suffering, and salvation. Nor is it the life story of a saintly or godly individual who has achieved great wisdom. Rather, it is the first-person narrative of Sal Paradise, a disillusioned American writer living in the late forties, and his friend Dean Moriarty, an exuberant Western con man and autodidact. Sal's opening statement, "I first met Dean not long after my wife and I split up," signals that his relationship with Dean portends the quest for a new life: (3). Through his relationship with Dean, a student-teacher and younger-older brother bond filling the void of the lost heterosexual relationship, Sal seeks the amelioration of his "feeling that everything [is] dead" (3). This new life crystallizes around four themes of the American character, the first being social consciousness, or the active repudiation of many middle-class American social values. The second is an Emersonian and Whitmanian individualism by which one aligns oneself with the marginalized and self-reliant. The third is psychic wholeness, the search for answers about why one feels empty and alienated. Finally, the fourth is spiritual enlightenment, the engagement in activities to transcend the corporeal and temporal spheres. Within this four-part dynamic, Sal adheres to Ihab H. Hassan's definition of the rebel-victim, an iconic figure in American cultural lore who "create[s] those values whose absence from our society is the cause of [their] predicament and ours" (30).

The success of Sal as narrator is due in part to Kerouac's creation of him as an "everyman" who manages to cross routinized boundaries of self while maintaining their sanctity. One of the most important but underrecognized strategies to this end is Sal's status as comic fool. He is someone with whom the reader can initially identify yet feel a bit superior. Particularly in the early stages of the journey, Sal is self-deprecating and somewhat of a dense bumbler. Perhaps nowhere is this dramatized as artfully as in the end of the second chapter of part 1, when Sal realizes that his initial efforts to hitchhike a single route across America have been thwarted by a literal dead end only a few miles west of New York City. His naivete about traveling leaves him stranded in the rain and forced to seek rides from fellow travelers: "I stepped right up and gestured in the rain; [. . .] I looked like a maniac, of course, with my hair all wet, my shoes sopping. My shoes, damn fool that I am, were Mexican huaraches, plantlike sieves not fit for the rainy night of America and the raw road night" (13). Sal realizes that his "stupid hearthside idea" of hitchhiking has failed him, and by making himself the butt of the joke through caricature, Sal allows the reader to laugh at and with him, to feel somewhat superior and yet akin to him. Sal ends the fiasco by buying a bus ticket home, juxtaposing his memory of his disheveled self with his travel mates, a "delegation of schoolteachers coming back from a weekend in the mountains—*chatter-chatter blah-blah,* and me swearing for all the time and the money I'd wasted" (13, emphasis mine). Mocking himself as the odd man out, preoccupied with silly things such as swearing and worrying about money, Sal is contrasted to the teachers, whom he also mocks with the derogatory "blah-blah" but elevates above himself: after all, they are having fun and he is not. This method constructs Sal as a trustworthy narrator, one wise enough to laugh at himself, to see himself as once worse off than readers who most likely wish not to be thought of as a clownish Falstaff or W. C. Fields but as a mature adult with the equanimity to acknowledge the comic missteps of one's past.

Alongside the introduction of Sal as an everyman, chapter 1 introduces Dean, who is clearly *not* part of that mainstream. "Dean," Sal reports, "is the perfect guy for the road because he actually was born on the road, when his parents were passing through Salt Lake City in 1926, in a jalopy, on their way to Los Angeles" (3). Dean's birth story projects a faint echo of the Christ story, that of a great spiritual soul born in the humblest of conditions in a place apart from any conventional home. A combination of holiness and its human emissary, Dean arrives in Sal's life as a mysterious shower of glory from the promised land of the West to deliver the ancient call to regenerate his life. Unequivocally, this figure represents the manifestation of the basic life force. It is a half-naked Dean (wearing only shorts), interrupted in what Sal calls the holy act of lovemaking, who first greets Sal (4). An inheritor of the innocence of the Adamic man, Dean embodies in Sal's mind the original American character that had by the twentieth-century been rendered impotent. Just as clearly, however, he repudiates the traditional American spiritual leader. He is no evangelical Billy Graham, the country's most admired male figure at midcentury, and in this iconoclastic guise, Dean risks alienating many readers, which the character did as early publications demonstrate, including Norman Poderertz's "No Nothing Bohemians," published in 1958, and Paul O'Neill's "The Only Rebellion Around," published in 1959.

The first chapter of *On the Road,* however, lays a foundation that can enable the reader to question Dean's viability as guide while retaining trust in Sal's choice. This is a delicate rhetorical maneuver, and it is a popular culture figure, rather obscure today but well known to Kerouac's contemporaries, that takes on this task. "My first impression of Dean," Sal states, "was of a young Gene Autry—trim, thin-hipped, blue-eyed, with a real Oklahoma accent—a sideburned hero of the snowy West" (5). The comparison to Autry is central to an understanding of *On the Road*'s quest and to Kerouac's vision of America. One of the world's most popular entertainers and starring in dozens of Western B-movies throughout the thirties and forties, Autry was not the Hollywood gunslinger who, as dramatized by an actor such as Gary Cooper in *The Virginian, The Gunfighter,* and *High Noon,* represented elegant dark repose and wielded the gun as a metonym of America's maturing moral center (a mechanical site through which American values are still contested). Known as the "Singing Cowboy," riding his horse Champion while crooning ballads such as "Don't Fence Me In," "Tumbling Tumbleweeds," "You Are My Sunshine," and "Back in the Saddle Again,"[1] Autry was much better known for the guitar he played than the gun he carried. Millions of adults and children perceived the American west through Autry, who did *not* have a real Oklahoma ascent like Dean and whose version of the cowboy life was filtered by the Hollywood entertainment industry to promote the wrangler as a clean-cut gentleman who with his Pepsodent-white smile was as comfortable wearing a gray flannel suit in Manhattan as his cowboy gear on the range. Following inexplicable and wooden transitions, Autry the cinematic cowboy would one moment quell a fight with stern rhetoric while the next break into a tune that his fans could dance to at the Starlight Ballroom or on "The Lawrence Welk Show," a sanitized vision promoting cultural harmony and patriarchy.[2] Autry's west was a Disneyland fantasy far removed from the early twenty-first-century's realistically gritty video games or television programs like today's "Deadwood" populated with grotesque deviants killing for personal retribution, oblivious to social law and order. Dean as avatar of Autry signifies Sal's perception of Dean as sweet, gentle, and fundamental American goodness—a respectable role model for children and an image complementing Dean's unsophisticated brilliance, his genuine desire to better himself. Dean as Autry also underscores the American belief in its manifest destiny to move westward across the continent. The promised land is literally land itself, the natural terrain that one navigates, lives within, and eventually consumes—but by art (life) instead of guns (death). Less directly and subversively, Dean as an Autry crooner speaks to Kerouac's emerging tendency subsequent to his novitiate to adopt a nondualistic philosophy of human nature that does not separate body and soul, constructing in Sal a *false* and thus unreliable vision of human nature that locates American goodness in a sanitized transcendent image.

The Dean of *On The Road,* however, also embodies the contrary of Gene Autry's bowdlerized Americana, espousing William Blake's voice from hell that predicates the palace of wisdom on the road of excess.[3] That is, Dean intuitively, even mystically, understands that holiness resides in the life force itself performed in the Dionysian pleasures of the natural body and of human beings in life-affirming communication with one another and the world. As hero and savior, Dean appears to be an antinomian libertine who has achieved freedom from human moral laws by removing the locus of moral suasion from institutional authority and relocating it within the immediacy of the body itself. As such, he engages without fear in what many mistakenly, from Sal's perspective, consider evil carnality. Sal's reference to Dean as "the Natural Tailor of Natural Joy" (10) suggests that the object of Sal's quest will be found in the natural world of sensory pleasure and the youthful world of existential exuberance. In other words, one need not suffer on earth, awaiting one's reward in a nonexistent heaven: heaven resides in individual agency and America itself. But this insight also carries the subterranean implication that Dean's carnality, his mad race through life, is a repudiation of the natural world: he recognizes its dangers and attempts to defy them (ultimately unsuccessfully) by reveling in them. Consequently, Sal's presentation of Dean and nature becomes an ambivalent binary of lightness and dark, morality and immorality, antinature and pronature.

Both sites of salvation—sanitized Autry and antinomian Dionysius—are manifested in Dean's history as a petty thief who has done jail time, distinct deviations from the Autry legend but signs that Sal interprets as saintly suffering caused by the inability of the less godly to recognize Dean's holiness. Sal's vision endows him with the ability to forgive and to welcome all into his life. With this attitude toward the world, Sal assumes a position of moral superiority to Dean, which thus lends credence to Sal's ability to perceive in Dean lightness ("the shining mind") and darkness (the "con-man"), the apparent harmonious blending of which creates a "holy wrangler" whose "Call" Sal hears and vows to follow.

There is in Sal's opening portrait of Dean a tone of sweetness and tenderness that becomes the overarching voice of the text, augmenting Sal's character as a trustworthy narrator. While strongly resembling the voices Kerouac used in his correspondence and journals, Sal's voice carries little of the strident didactic tone that often emerges in his letters to Ginsberg, the polished businesslike voice of Kerouac's letters to his editors, or the analytical voice of many of his journals. Sal's voice is constructed of complex syntactic forms, not the least of which is a reliance on adjectives characterized as utilitarian or feminine, primarily "little," "cute," "pretty," "sweet," and "tender." As a variant, Sal often adds a "y" or an "ly," in the plural and singular, to convert nouns into feminine-sounding descriptors, such as "childly," "dewy," "grapy," "cobwebby," "raggedy," and "shroudy" (Grace, *Feminized* 153–54). The overall effect is a voice that projects qualities stereotypically associated with the child and the feminine.[4] Sal, then, as speaker of wisdom and prophecy is not a muscular Jeremiah or John the Baptist, but is more akin to the Virgin Mary and Child, two of the essential divine components of Catholic orthodoxy. The pairing paves the way for Sal's narrative of salvation. When taken together, these rhetorical structures validate Sal as a prescient speaker, one who with passivity and childlike exuberance predicts at the end of chapter 1 that "the things that were to come are too *fantastic* not to tell" and "somewhere along the line I knew there'd be girls, visions, everything; somewhere along the line the *pearl* would be handed to me" (11, emphasis mine).

The key words to my reading of *On the Road* are *fantastic* and *pearl.* The latter is frequently referenced, since many *On the Road* readers are familiar with the general significance of the pearl as a symbol of wealth and wisdom. Kerouac's expression of that significance is so beautifully worded and strategically placed in the narrative that it demands quotability. But the image of the pearl extends beyond both the realm of universal symbol and the confines of *On the Road* itself. Playing a major role in the wisdom texts of Mesopotamia, Judea, and Greece,[5] it is honored in the gnostic tale known as the "Song of the Pearl," alternatively titled the "Hymn of the Soul," its oldest version possibly dating back to 247 BCE–224 CE (Layton 371). This symbol-rich tale, found in the Manichaean "Acts of Thomas," can be read as a morality tale or a quest myth populated by fantastic creatures participating in high adventure. In both cases, the anthropological and literary associations provide an intertextual foundation to establish *On the Road* as a contemporary variant of ancient wisdom literature. The discussion that follows makes no claim that Kerouac modeled *On the Road* after the pearl tale. It is much more likely that he drew upon the pearl image as a general cultural reference. He did, however, find it significant enough that it became a leitmotif in *On The Road,* thus suggesting that the pearl tale as an interpretive template is relevant as a source of an expression that even today holds significance and power. By examining *On the Road* as a variation of that much older story, one can see how particular features of mythic plot and characterization remain viable long after a culture has lost track of their original form.

The "Pearl Song" recounts the story of a young prince, whose father sends him to Egypt to recover a pearl guarded by a sea serpent. Once in Egypt, the young man falls asleep under the spell of the local populace, but his parents, on learning of his condition, send him a letter delivered in the form of an eagle to awaken him. Once awake, he charms the serpent to sleep and seizes the pearl. The letter subsequently assumes the disembodied voice of a woman encouraging him on his journey home. En route, he discovers a glorious robe, which becomes a mirror revealing visions of self-knowledge. Motivated by love to accept the robe of gnosis, he returns home with the pearl, prepared to meet and adore his father, who promises that they will soon travel "to the gate of the king of kings" (Barnstone and Meyer 394).

The song invites the singer and the listener to take pleasure in its opulent fantasy, which conveys many teachings through the multifaceted image of the pearl, including salvation in light, self-knowledge, the soul, gifts of worship, maturation, or the self that adores the highest power—the "king of kings." Foregrounded is a two-pronged message stressing the necessity of the quest and the need for all to return home filled with both love for others and self-knowledge that leads to greater glory. Whether this is in the natural world or somewhere else, the song does not say; its silence suggests both. The journey to capture the pearl is grounded in recognition of human fallibility and the power of human relationships to save the individual and the community. It also integrates the visionary and the fantastic in the form of the bird letter, the female voice, and the magical robe of knowledge to suggest that the path to the "king of kings" is not solitary or antimaterialistic. Those who take the journey must be open to messengers of wisdom and the support of others. When they are, great riches sublimely descend upon them. In this respect, the tale features a doubling or twin element: the one in whom others place their trust for salvation must himself be saved by them—father truth and mother wisdom (Barnstone and Meyer 392).

On the Road tells a similar story, Sal and Dean reveling in adventures that turn the mundane inside out and upside down. As artist, adventurer, and mystic seer, Sal reveals to readers how the journey can be taken and what is encountered along the way, exhorting them to appreciate why the journey is necessary and foretelling what may happen if the status quo is merely maintained. Sal's narrative, however, is not as plot driven as "Song of the Pearl," his American spiritual narrative a structurally more discontinuous text, one that stops and starts such that it emerges as more episodic and picaresque than deeply plotted (Holton, On the Road 31). On June 1, 1949, Kerouac had written in his journal that On the Road should assume the form of his "rain-and-river" meditations—that is, like these natural occurrences, the story of the human soul does not include "a real goldstrike, or a real scientific advance," but revelations from day to day, the "ever-moving" stability of the continuum of life across time into the mystery of death (WW 198). However, on October 30, he revised this plan, electing to construct the new novel to resemble an epic poem with short chapters and a fast pace forming a "string of pearls" (242). The novel that he eventually revised and was published combines these two approaches woven tightly together with plotlike catharsis and denouement. Chapter length and pace, the speed of the latter created by the alternating of short and long sentences coupled with the piling on of serial descriptors like small pearl necklaces themselves, create an episodic quality in which a preponderance of language is devoted to describing what happens rather than to the analysis of the actions, although reflective discourse is present.

The short, fast-paced form also emphasizes what some readers have interpreted as lack of physical and psychological progress—the sense that nothing ever really happens in the story, that Sal is not going anywhere. Such a reading is not entirely inaccurate. The composition of the cross-continental trips creates repetition, which is just as much like rain and rivers as it is like pearls, a continuum of motion through time and space with some moments more intense than others, but the whole a repetition of action and thought. Yes, Sal meets the same people; he keeps looking for love; he repeatedly makes mistakes; his dreams keep falling apart; and he keeps returning home to his aunt. But this approach, which is not the spiraling psychological realism of Joyce, Faulkner, Woolf, or James or the painterly social realism/naturalism of Dickens, Austen, London, or Hemingway, makes sense as a manifestation of Kerouac's thinking in the late forties and early fifties that wisdom is an ever-changing reality acquired slowly through repetition, just as plant life and geological formations change over time in the presence of rain and rivers, the "continuum of living across preordained spaces" (*WW* 198). The only difference appears to be that for humans this is not the repetition of rain showers or shifting riverbeds. It is a practice, spiritual or mundane, such as saying the rosary, listening each Sunday to a preacher delivering a homily, meditating under a tree, praying daily, going about one's daily duties, and reading specific texts, just as Kerouac immersed himself, especially through-out midcentury, in Christian and Buddhist scriptures until they became seamlessly integrated elements of his thinking and writing.[6] The doing, whether that of the illiterate penitent or the literate scholar, guides one toward truth. It is always a process of knowing and reknowing, which in Sal's literary expression of his own practices is manifested as the horizontal and identical, movement not up or down but back and forth, form not mercurial but open ended, parallel, mirrorlike. Marco Abel has argued that by introducing this element of repetition into the narrative, Kerouac "invents not only a new poetics but also a new map of the American landscape" (237). More likely, however, Kerouac's articulations about the continuum of human wisdom, the ways in which it is and is not, all contextualized in his personal mission of calling readers back to their historic roots while shaping a new world, argue not for the new alone but for a revisioning of the alpha and the omega of both the old and the new.

Sal's story is one of living this kind of life. He does not didactically pre-scribe this knowledge but instead acts it out, in a sense following the natural progressions of his mind and the worlds in which he finds himself. Each time he hears the greatest laugh in the world, eats the best apple pie ever made, rides the fastest ever with Dean, meets the most tender person alive, discov-ers the best woman ever, finally understands what "IT" is, feels the beatest ever, or sees his dreams collapsing around him, he is accepting the present for what it offers and accepting the recursive character of human life. Sometimes those moments bring him feelings of euphoria and at other times misery. But the key is that he does not dwell extensively on them or read too much into them, instead moving on, willing to take the next adventure that calls to him, just as the prince in the "Song of the Pearl" willingly obeys the call of family, enemy, bird, disembodied feminine, or bejeweled robe.

At the same time that Sal embodies life as both pearl and rain/rivers, his narrative integrates a distinct plot demonstrating life as the slow accretion of the same kind of matter (be it the pearl or water) and as a process of recognizable change, the metaphoric mountain or ladder that one must climb to reach God. This thread begins with Sal setting out alone on the road to follow Dean in hopes of being "handed" the pearl. He does not perceive the journey as a quest myth in which he will face great trials—at this point, there is no hint of serpents lurking in his American dream, which postdivorce is instead a warm, cozy, and easy "hearthside" map-derived vision. The Route 6 incident quickly teaches him differently, but it does not deter his hearthside reverie, which is validated at several points during this first trip. For example, he finds the depths of human tenderness in Mississippi Gene's care of a sixteen-year-old boy hitchhiking across the plains; his B-movie fantasy of cowboys in Omaha, Nebraska; the top of the world in Denver; and the love of a true woman of the earth with Terry, a Mexican single mother. However, the destruction of these dreams, analogous to the continuum of life's contraries, repeatedly confronts him, this first trip challenging his notions of what the "pearl" is and whether he must grab it himself or rely on someone else to hand it to him.

The first significant sign of this challenge is the red-sunset experience set in Des Moines, Iowa, a beatific passage that confirms Sal's belief that he is on the spiritual path. Alone and tired in a cheap hotel room near the railroad tracks, Sal, who has slept most of the day, awakens at sunset to hissing and creaking sounds permeating the cracked walls of the room. In this eerie space at the middle of the continent, his identity momentarily vanishes so that he becomes "just somebody else, some stranger, [. . .] the life of a ghost" (17). This other self does not scare him, and in true episodic fashion, he immediately pushes on to the next adventure, happily eating apple pie and ice cream and watching beautiful Des Moines girls. Only briefly reflecting on what the vision may mean, from hindsight he speculates that the geographical setting for the experience may represent the transition from his youth into his future (17), an unbalanced rhetorical figure and fairly simplistic interpretation. A secular humanist would say that Sal merely experienced the common human event of cognitive disorientation caused by lack of sleep, irregular diet, and a new environment, but in the literary context of the wisdom quest, the red-sunset experience portends Sal's openness to or passivity necessary for entrance into a transcendental realm where hidden knowledge awaits. In this respect, the vision mirrors the ancient robe of knowledge in the "Song of the Pearl," the robe of the Gnostic tale transformed as the strange face into which Sal stares, a twin self viewed from the perspective of life's amorphous moving

continuum oblivious to the individual human presence. From this standpoint, Sal receives an intimation of the self as an illusion, a concept that will
be reiterated during his subsequent adventures.

Significantly, the red-sunset experience does not terrify Sal. He simply and
speedily moves on to erotica and gluttony. It is just as simple and speedy to
interpret this sequence of actions as evidence of Sal's and Kerouac's immatu-
rity, his inability to reflect on monumental moments in his life and to convey their import to others through powerful language. This would be a
mistake, however. Sal's narrative of a particular, although never named, wisdom quest establishes his psychic state in opposition to that of venerated
Catholic mystics such as St. John of the Cross, the Spanish ascetic and poet
(1542–92), whose personal experience taught that the ascetic must accept
multiple stages of terror, including the "dark night of the sense," in order to
receive divine love and wisdom. In terms of the Catholic Christian quester,
Sal's response to the vision places him more congruently within what I call
the more progressive mystic tradition, which, as represented by St. Teresa of
Avila, encourages tolerance for human discretion and playful mocking of the
human ego. For instance, in the thirteenth chapter of her autobiography, the
founder of the Carmelite order counsels beginners to aim "to feel happy and
free. There are some people who think that devotion will slip away from
them if they relax a little . . . Yet there are many circumstances in which, as
I have said, it is permissible for us to take some recreation." Sal's actions also
align him with the libertine gnostic Christian belief in returning to mundane
pleasures after a revelatory experience (Jonas 228–29), so by reflecting elements of esoteric gnosticism and Teresian discretion, the sunset passage
implies that Sal already possesses the requisite wisdom to continue the journey, which he acts on intuitively, a signifier of a preexisting life of spiritual
practice.

At the conclusion of part 1, the role of visionary is filled by as the trope of
the Shrouded Traveler, whom Sal meets near Harrisburg, Pennsylvania. The
little old man, identified as the Ghost of the Susquehanna, says that he will
lead Sal to a bridge and tells him stories nonstop as they walk along the river
in the dead of night. Sal describes this experience much as he did the red-
sunset episode, as spooky and somewhat hellish, "a terrifying river" flanked
with "bushy cliffs [. . .] that lean like hairy ghosts over the unknown waters.
Inky night covers all" (104). They never find the bridge, and Sal, again
exhausted and starving, eventually parts company with the man. But his
image as lost, forlorn, and ghostly in the wilderness of America lingers as the
shadowy presence of an alienated kinsman propelling Sal toward home. He
eventually returns to New York City, where his aunt has woven him a rich
rag rug from the material of their family clothing—material confirmation of
family love. This is the quest and pearl myth in miniature, and Sal, who has

heeded the vision of the Shrouded Traveler, now receives the gift of family history, analogous to the gilded robe of knowledge, and settles in to "figure the losses and figure the gain" (106) of his experiences.

Interestingly, on July 25, 1948, Kerouac had composed an entry for his journal in which he used the rug as an icon of romantic, heterosexual love: "Someday my wife and I shall go to the rug in the bedroom, every night, and kneel, facing each other, and embrace and kiss, and she shall say, 'Because we'll never part,' and I will say 'Because we'll never part.'—and then we'll get up and resume. This is a frenzy, this love. Every night the rug, or all is lost" (*WW* 107). His later interpolation of the rug for narrative purposes—it is not the exotic pearl Sal has sought, and he is soon on the road again—removes the sharp focus on Dionysian matrimonial fidelity but retains its signification of home and heterosexual family life as part of the American and heavenly goal of Sal's quest.

The Shrouded Traveler haunts Sal's second journey as well, although this time it is Dean who assumes the tropic mantel. Although younger than Sal, Dean functions as a mystical older brother. He is the one who knows "IT" or "time," code words for ultimate knowledge, and he is certain that God exists, a reality that he refuses to explain, simply living by faith that God directs the course of life. In Dean's extravagant wake, Sal with renewed hope in his joy for America again references the pearl quest: "[Dean] and I suddenly saw the whole country like an oyster for us to open; and the pearl was there, the pearl was there" (138). At this stage, Sal has begun to realize that he will have to take action if he wishes to seize the elusive treasure—neither others nor the oyster itself will deliver him the pearl. But as Sal follows Dean, Sal's sense of elation is continually haunted by his sense of America as an antiquated repressive police state (136) and by the Shrouded Traveler's human mortality, each contributing to his confusion about why he is traveling and for what he is searching. These misgivings are realized when they arrive in San Francisco, where Sal finds himself confronted with his first great test: his teacher and savior, Dean, leaves him starving and broke, stranded with Dean's ex-girlfriend, Marylou. Significantly, at this dire moment, Sal tells Marylou the story of the evil "big snake of the world" that will be destroyed by the saintly Doctor Sax. The snake may be the devil, he explains, or it may be "a husk of doves" (172), an image that may have originated in a conversation Kerouac had with Ginsberg in the early fifties about a Great Bird. "I participated in the conception that it should be a husk of doves," Ginsberg stated to Gerald Nicosia in an interview for *Memory Babe*, Nicosia' biography of Kerouac. "It should be opened up to, the bird should be a papier-mâché thing with a lot of doves inside" (Nicosia, Ginsberg interview). This is the image that in tandem with the Great Snake became the cosmological centerpiece of the Legend in Doctor Sax.

For many readers of *On the Road,* the snake story makes sense in the context of Jewish and Christian creation myths, and for those familiar with gnostic traditions, it will resonate as the inversion of the snake as a symbol of good rather than evil. When Sal posits that the snake may enclose doves, an ancient symbol of Christ, he unknowingly evokes gnostic myths celebrating the snake as that which frees Adam and Eve from the destructive power of the creator God by bringing knowledge to the earth. There is also a way in which the serpent as the "husk of doves" allegorizes the gnostic understanding of the human condition: the soul (the doves) trapped in corrupt material form (the serpent's body) from which it must be freed or awakened by the messenger and the call, a variant of which "The Pearl Song" encodes as the sea serpent who holes the pearl. Dean, then, may be likened to the evil snake coiled within the earth, preparing to strike and devour all, or he may represent the pure human soul trapped within evil matter, waiting to be released by the great messenger, Doctor Sax. In both interpretations, the tale within a tale signifies Sal's perception, explicitly and allegorically, of Dean's fallibility as savior. Enveloping gnostic and orthodox possibilities, it presages Sal's abandonment by Marylou and the next fantastic event in his psychic and spiritual life: the Dickensian mother vision.

Kerouac wrote about this vision in a letter to Cassady on January 8, 1951 (*Letters* 1: 277–78). This letter appears to be a compositional draft of the powerful epiphanic passage in *On the Road,* a pivotal point in Sal's quest for self-identity and authenticity. In Kerouac's narration to Cassady, he described strolling by a San Francisco fish 'n chips shop in February 1949 and seeing "a woman, a proprietress, staring at me with a kind of fear; why, I don't know" (277). In his imagination, as he told Cassady, she was transformed into a Londoner who looked "like the frightened women in Charles Dickens movies, and mother of David Copperfield, anything you wish" (277). Suddenly, he realized that the woman was his mother who feared him because "here was her awful Jack-son returned from the shadow of the gallows, her wandering blackguard of a son, her pimp-child, her thief, returned to cheat her" (279). Kerouac told Cassady that in a state of ecstasy he then tried to determine what had happened to connect him in 1949 to that nineteenth-century self: "This is not only a fleeting glimpse of possible reincarnation," he stated, "but a definite sensation of the presence of God, and like the short-wave radio, it's all in the air and is still there for me to grasp another day" (280–81). As fictionalized in *On the Road,* this experience highlights a grimy and hungry Sal who stares at the proprietress of a fish 'n chips shop, who he imagines fears that he will rob her. Transmogrified into his "Dickensian mother," the allegorical figure castigates him as a selfish and lost soul, berates him for his sins, and demands that he never visit her again. Kerouac's portraiture of this moment, more richly detailed than his letter to Cassady, presents the experience as "the complete step across chronological time into timeless shadows, and wonderment in the bleakness of the mortal realm, and the sensation of death kicking at my heels to move on, with a phantom dogging its own heels, and myself hurrying to a plank where all the angels dove off and flew into the holy void of uncreated emptiness" (173). In this mixture of "void," "angels," "timeless shadows" and "uncreated emptiness"—a mosaic of Christian and Buddhist language and symbology—Sal comes to know himself as a flawed person, knowledge that, since it resides beyond human time, identifies his own condition as the eternal human condition.

Sal's experiences at the Des Moines hotel and with the Ghost of the Susquehana in Pennsylvania had made known to him the mundane human condition as lost and alone. The Dickensian mother vision repeats and expands on this message, her voice, like that of the letter in the gnostic pearl song, effectively reifying the female as transcendent wisdom separate from the mundane. In the realm, divorced from but necessary to male growth in the greater social sphere, she opens up to Sal his sinful and unworthy nature. Such knowledge is necessary in the Christian tradition for atonement, but Sal's transport as he recalls it is more akin to the Buddhist world of rain and rivers, a continuum that he knows exists because of "the stability of the intrinsic Mind that these ripples of birth and death [take] place, like the action of wind on a sheet or pure, serene, mirror-like water" (173). In his reading of *On the Road*, Eric Mortenson likens this state to Merleau-Ponty's concept of temporality: "There is only one single time which is self-confirmatory, which can bring nothing into existence unless it has already laid that thing's foundations as present and eventual past, and which establishes itself at a stroke" (Mortenson 63). Merleau-Ponty provides a helpful gloss of Kerouac's literary use of Buddhist wisdom in *On the Road*, knowledge gained through his reading of Lin Yutang, Spenger, Emerson, and Thoreau prior to completing the scroll. The experience demystifies death: it is no longer an unknown future to be feared, which explains why Sal, in this night dark, literally and figuratively, senses his death but can, again, walk away, eventually finding his way to Marylou's hotel room and reuniting with Dean, who now deems him "worth saving" (173–74). This last element of the plot is distinct revision of Kerouac's conclusion of the experience in his letter to Neal Cassady in which he reminds Cassady that "that was the night you had gotten the pots-and-pans job and when I came in you began the joyous talk," no mention being made of the abandonment (280). It is not clear whether Kerouac actually felt abandoned at that time, but significantly Sal does. His Dickensian mother vision replaces, at least temporarily, the male voice and real-time presence of salvation with the female as aerial sublime, a grotesque vision that does not negate the dark world but allows him to see more clearly within it. New visions that she generates within him guide him to safety within the real world, demonstrating acceptance of his own devices and desires as authentic and reliable.

In parts 3 and 4, Sal's character matures within the light-within-the-dark, although his efforts to follow a savior exemplify the wisdom that brightness can also obscure one's vision. This is a common feature in spiritual narratives, the neophyte traveler often misidentifying as truth that which is not, succumbing to false prophets or allies, and often experiencing more doubts and pain as the journey progresses. Sal's solo trip to establish himself as a patriarch in Denver, an extremely idealistic and flawed venture that ends miserably, mirrors this feature of quest literature. He also continues to have ecstatic moments of "IT" followed by the world falling apart around him, vacillating between the ecstasy of believing that he has achieved ultimate knowledge, whether secular or divine, and the horror of realizing that he is corrupt, inept, and unworthy. At heart, Sal seems to struggle to choose one of three paths: the familiar and prescribed American line of individuality grounded in belief in a Christian god; the secular humanist belief in the pleasures of the natural world, imagination, and reason; and the Buddhist understanding of the illusionary quality of humanistic individualism.

Sal's relationship with Dean externalizes the internal difficulties of this struggle. Part 3, for instance, presents scattered images of Sal's fluctuating perceptions of Dean. At one point, Sal sees Dean as others see him, particularly the women in his life, who have legitimate reasons to feel abandoned and lonely when their husbands and boyfriends take off on male-only road trips (186–87). Sal's imagination also transforms Dean into the grotesque Holy Goof who tries desperately and comically, with a broken thumb flagging the air, to share his wisdom with others who refuse or simply cannot understand the sublime nature of his message (194). This state renders Dean the status of Beat, which Sal defines as "the soul of Beatific" (195), and with this knowledge, Sal takes care of Dean, defending him, offering to take him to Italy, and mothering him in his time of need (195). Dean is now the one who must become passive in the face of Sal's power, but Sal remains reluctant to perceive his knowledge as equal to Dean's, to which he still turns to make life easier and more fun. Despite his visions, Sal longs for his teacher and savior to hand him the pearl (206).

The narrative, however, progressively reveals Dean's boisterous will-to-live as a dangerous, Dionysian will-to-power untempered by any stable Ariadnian complement. After all, his broken thumb, which Sal interprets as a sign of growing holiness, comes as a result of hitting Marylou, an act of domestic violence that Sal acknowledges (185). While no means violent himself, Sal does not chastise Dean for this act, but Dean's aggression toward women paradoxically coupled with benign mysticism portends the cracks that begin to develop in their relationship. These become apparent as Sal rides east toward Chicago and Detroit with Dean in 1949. Sal's evolving awareness of his savior as flawed is revealed in one of the book's most famous passages, Sal's reference to Dean as a "mad Ahab at the wheel" (234), a Melvillian combination of dark hubris and angry nature pursuing the undefeatable that elucidates Sal's evolving awareness of his savior as flawed. Sal, like Ishmael and St. John's Christian ascetic, passively resigns himself to the ride, telling himself that he cannot escape the fury and the trip (234). But Sal is not trapped on the Pequod, and like the ascetic, he has chosen to ride along, using his sense of inferiority to avoid taking action once on board. Perhaps within the context of Sal's quest for the pearl of knowledge, he intuits a conflict between passivity and action. Whatever it is, something within him recognizes the destructive nature of the choices he has made, this reality appearing to him in another mystical vision. This one, a "horrible osmotic experience" (244), takes place in a Detroit Skid Row all-night movie house. Sal falls asleep, snoring to the echoes of Peter Lorre, George Raft, Syndey Greenstreet, and Eddie Dean[7] filling the theater, a bizarre swirl of gangster voices (Lorre, Raft, Greenstreet) and a singing cowboy (Dean) perpetuating the ambivalent conflation of American antinomian toughness and gentle individuality, the gun and song battling for supremacy as Sal dreams of shooting Indians, a trope of Anglo-Euro supremacy in and right to own the "new" world. He awakens to Dean's report that theater attendants created around him a pile of garbage so high that it almost reached his nose and he barely escaped being swept away.

The scene is ultimately humorous, since Sal is obviously unharmed and Dean's language is comically exaggerated, so Sal could easily slough it off as inconsequential. But instead the grotesque vision compels Sal to picture himself as "embryonically convoluted among the rubbishes of [his] life" (244). Imagining what he would say to Dean, analogous to the way the Dickensian mother spoke to him, Sal tells the phantom Dean to leave him alone, since he has no right to disturb a man in the pukish place where he is truly happy (244–45). He connects this scene to his memory of being a seaman in 1942, having fallen asleep around a toilet used by hundreds of drunken seamen throwing up. Shaking off these "sentient debouchments" as inconsequential, the wiser Sal asks himself, "What difference does it make after all?— anonymity in the world of men is better than fame in heaven, for what's heaven? what's earth? All in the mind" (245). The two visions, Dean's comic report and Sal's horrific yet humble self-study, introduce rational conscious thought into the mystical experience, revealing Sal's process of resolving his personal sense of inferiority and guilt through Buddhist reasoning that any belief in self and heaven is illusion. Rejecting material fame and spiritual fame, Sal has also rejected, or is at least seriously questioning, core American beliefs such as faith in capitalism, individual recognition, progress, and the Christian concepts of salvation and an afterlife. In their place, he asserts, one's rubbish life is just as preferable, if not more so.

At this stage, Sal as wise narrator reveals that during that particular point in his past he had begun to see clearly enough to recognize Dean's destructive nature and through his relationship with Dean something about the nature of the universe. As Sal and two other friends, Tim Gray and Stan Sheppard, plan to travel to Mexico, Sal unexpectedly learns of Dean's imminent arrival, and the Dean that he now envisions is no longer a realistic figure of human hubris (Ahab) but a fantastic two-headed embodiment of historically antithetical schools of thought that Kerouac sought to reconcile: Christianity and secular humanism. As the former, Dean is pictured as a terrifying image of godly vengeance—the Shrouded Traveler garbed like a "frightening Angel," the prophet of doom incarnate with wings, a chariot, and shooting flames. The latter is contained in a solitary word, the name "Gargantua" (259), the legendary representation of humanistic philosophy created by Francois Rabelais in his novel *Gargantua and Pantegruel*. By likening Dean's arrival to that of the sixteenth-century argument for secular wisdoms and pleasures, Sal situates Dean as the father and himself as Pantagruel, the son. He is also intimating that Dean, himself a son, is also the earthly embodiment of the father. In this respect, consistent with Bakhtin's interpretation of Gargantua, Dean does not "immortalize one's own 'I'" [or] "selfhood" but rather the growth or perpetuation "of his beast desires and strivings" (*Dialogic* 204).

Analogous to Kerouac's Snake of the World, this two-headed presence thunders across the continent destroying all in its path. Sal recognizes Dean's madness but does not run from it. While frightening, Dean's two-headed madness is a grotesque that augurs inner and spiritual wisdom, escape from the horrors of the body, the apocalyptic realization of the liberating nature of the metaphysical sublime, and the affirmation of human life itself as one's immortality. In turn, Sal elects to accommodate the world for this bizarre creature. This section of the novel can be read as repetition of Sal's acquiescence to Dean as Ahab, but it is fundamentally different. Sal is not giving in to human egotism as he did when he saw Dean as Ahab. Figuratively he is preparing the way for both the Judeo-Christian prophetic messenger such as Ezekiel or Christ and the intellectual humanist father, each of whom offers his own version of the promised land. Within these salvation narratives, Sal's actions reflect belief in both Buddhism and Christianity, but particularly the medieval Catholic dictum that one must endure the destructive powers of the divine, which are intended to purge one of all that prohibits the revelation of ultimate knowledge. In other words, the wrath and the words of the father, or the older brother or the hidden twin, be he or they human or transcendent other, must be obeyed if one desires salvation.

It is prudent to say at this juncture that Sal, the one who goes on the road, believes that America with its coplike cultural soul is the entity that has fallen short and failed to deliver on its promise to actualize the myth of the New World. Capitalism, individualism, progress, and institutional Christianity are clearly revealed as bankrupt. By removing himself from the continental United States in favor of traveling into a fellahin land "rockribbing clear down to Tierra del Fuego" (265), Sal uses his life story to subtly identify flaws in American culture and the problems that will accrue if they are not addressed. As several critics have noted,[8] Sal's turn to Mexico reflects Kerouac's interpretation and incorporation of Spengler's concept of the fellahin, the detritus of dying civilizations moving unaffected through time. Unlike Spengler, however, Kerouac idealized the abject and illiterate fellahin as living vestiges of Christ's wisdom and the indomitable human spirit. As symbolic prophecy, Sal's journey into Mexico then rejects the Christian roles of proselytizer and social activist to claim two more holy missions. One is the personal search for wisdom. The other is the honoring of God incarnate in the poor above all things.

By not addressing socioeconomic and political problems at home through direct political action, Sal and Dean can both appear extremely narcissistic. But as they continue the journey, even though frequently unable to articulate why, each exhibits the force of will to shield them from the criticism of not acting, of only waiting passively and solipsistically for the pearl to be given them. Their hedonistic adventures as Sal reimagines them dramatizes their two holy missions as an analogue of what theologian Paul Tillich, describes as a "holy waste" growing out of an abundant heart. Those with such hearts are not afraid of "accepting the waste of an uncalculated self-surrender nor from wasting [them]selves beyond the limits of law and rationality," Tillich wrote (47), interpreting Jesus's words in the Gospel of Mark to his disciples when they question his decision to allow a woman to anoint his feet with costly oil. "She has done a beautiful thing to me," he tells them. "For you always have the poor with you, and whenever you will, you can do good to them; but you will not always have me" (Mark 14:3–9). Likewise, Sal, especially in his willingness to prepare the way for Dean, chooses to honor and to venture forth into the dark path of the dark god in human form. Through his journey, and his narrative construction of it as wisdom and prophecy, he sets in motion a series of events that serve as models for the kind of moral and spiritual human behavior that Tillich advocated.

In many respects, the Mexico that Sal finds provides what he seeks. The people he encounters in the company of Dean, his "revelatory genius" who looks "like God" (285), are without suspicion, giving freely of their material possessions, enjoying simple pleasures such as dance, sex, and marijuana. Magically they personify for Sal the eradication of laws restricting human desires (276–80), assuming archetypal significance as "the source of mankind," in contrast to Sal and Dean themselves who stand out as self-impressed American carpetbaggers (281). His narrative voice unabashedly takes on a prophetic tenor and cadence as he considers himself in relationship to them:

> For when destruction comes to the world of "history" and the Apocalypse of the Fellahin returns once more as so many times before, people will still stare with the same eyes from the caves of Mexico as well as from the caves of Bali, where it all began and where Adam was suckled and taught to know. (281)

Sal's prophecy is a fascinating synthesis of secular, theological, and literary tropes holding forth a twentieth-century statement on etiology and eschatology. Robert Holton argues that Kerouac's fellahin is a "sign of the real, a device which allows him, a white male, a means of reflecting on himself . . . more than it provides insight into the experience of the marginalized other" (274), and this interpretation makes sense within Sal's quest, which is much more about conflating images of Mexico with the Asian "caves of Bali" to find a vision of himself and his god in the world than it is about the socioeconomic realities of post–World War II Central America. Sal claims that this prophecy about the fellahin came as he drove through Mexico, but the narrative perspective shifts in this passage so the "For when" functions not solely as a memory of his thoughts but also as a directive to the reader, presenting a vision of the inevitable destruction of civilization in accordance with both Spengler's Hegelian vision and the prophet John's Christian revelations. In accordance with *Revelation,* the world itself will not end (the final battle of Armageddon never happens) and in accordance with Spengler and the four Christian Gospels, the downtrodden and meek progeny of Adam who were "taught to know" will continue. The prophecy then ironically calls forth in an age of linear progress the ancient symbol of life as an unbroken circle, and its emphasis on Adam as the source of human life implies a gnosticlike understanding that attributes human endurance to human knowledge rather than obedience to and faith in God. The prophecy is also generated by a flawed human source—Sal—not from an involuntary instrument of a divine speaker or a divinity incarnate, and it is just this flawed source, a biblical Doubting Thomas who values scientific observation, that lends credence to prophetic words directed at a contemporary audience.

The culmination of the Mexico trip again presents Sal with loss of self-identity or detachment, although, unlike the previous ones, not occasioned by circumstances of hunger, despair, loneliness, alienation, or a desire for salvation. In fact, Sal, Dean, and Stan, still high from marijuana, sex, music, and dancing, drive into the stifling hot Mexican jungle feeling euphoric, at peace, and in harmony with each other and their environment. This natural setting is critical to what follows, because until this point in the narrative Sal has not dwelled extensively on the natural world. There is a decidedly narrower focus on nature writing in *On the Road* than there is, say, in *The Dharma Bums* and *Desolation Angels,* but the jungle in *Road,* while not described in minute detail, vividly comes alive with insect and animal energies. The combination of pitch black sky and heavy velvet air lead Sal to realize that he and the atmosphere are one, a negation of corporeal dualism allowing him to sleep unafraid as an infinite number of bugs shower down upon him, the whole like a continuum of rain and river (296). In this state, he sees an apparition of a wild white horse running toward Dean, whom it benevolently skirts (296). When they later awake, neither Sal nor Dean knows what the white ghost horse means, but Dean too has a slight memory of dreaming of the horse, another signifier of the connectedness of their human existence in opposition to belief in the sovereignty of the self or transcendent.

The trio then drives higher into the mountains, a setting easily interpreted as a veiled reference to enlightenment. It is here that they encounter Indian girls selling rock crystals, whom they associate with the Virgin Mary as a child, Sal reading in the girls' eyes the message of the "tender and forgiving gaze of Jesus" (298). Significantly, however, Dean is the one who gets out of the car to exchange gifts with the girls, expressing in Sal's mind reverence and sadness as he gazes upon them. For all of the purgative and apocalyptic allegorical garb that he has worn to this point, Dean now emerges as a more truly Christ-like person than at any other time in the narrative, the only one willing to walk among and deal equitably with those whose holiness is manifested in their abject condition. Granted, one can argue that Dean is so ego-filled and sex-obsessed that he must have the adoration of little illiterate girls who "coo" and "ah" over him, so that Sal's interpretation is false. However, Sal does not describe Dean as acting with any self-enhancing motives, only out of simple tenderness and sadness. Consequently as a vehicle of Sal's regeneration, Dean is more accurately read at this stage as a genuine Christ figure for Sal.

Dean's elevation, like the mountains, serves to validate Sal's trust and faith in Dean as well as the reader's perception of Sal as also trustworthy. Structurally, Dean's elevation is also necessary for the act that follows: his abandonment of Sal, whom he leaves in a fever-induced delirium while he, Dean, drives back to New York to a new girlfriend (302). Dean's action can be read in at least two ways within the spiritual quest paradigm. First, if one accepts the Catholic position of a St. John of the Cross or St. Teresa de Avila, the savior chooses when to draw closer to and when to draw away from those who seek ultimate knowledge. The one abandoned, as was Christ on the cross when he cried out "My God, my God, Why hast thou forsaken me?," cannot understand why the divine is so uncaring as to desert the less powerful but must accept this reality knowing that the act is committed out of love to enable the tyro to grow stronger. Sal admits that this is what he did when Dean deserted him: "I had to understand the impossible complexity of his life." With blind faith, he writes, "Okay, old Dean, I'll say nothing" (303). Reflecting on the incident, however, Sal writes that he later came to realize that Dean was a rat, plain and simple. This knowledge replicates the narratives of many religious traditions including Buddhism and Christianity, as well as the philosophies and narratives of secular humanism such as Joyce's *Portrait of the Artist as a Young Man* and Rabelais's *Gargantua and Pantegruel* warning readers to guard against false prophets. *On the Road* consistently iterates that recognition of the false prophet is dependent on the loving prophet who comforts through changing degrees of spiritual proximity and vice versa. In other words, one cannot know the falseness of abandonment if one does not know the truthfulness of love and acceptance. Neither one can exist without the other. Mexico, then, like Egypt in the "Song of the Pearl," is the land that misdirects and anesthetizes one in ignorance, but as part of the New World, also awakens one to clarity of vision. Sal gains wisdom over the course of his relationship with Dean through Dean's pattern of unannounced arrivals and departures, and Sal's Mexican jungle experience suggests that the greatest lesson learned is that a relationship with such a person can be beneficial, as long as one comes to recognize and rent the veil of Maya.

Part 5, the conclusion of *On The Road,* suggests as much in its narration of Sal's last trip home and his final meeting with Dean. During this trip, he once again encounters the Shrouded Traveler, this time an old deathly Jeremiah with flowing white hair carrying a backpack who tells him to "Go moan for man" (306). Uncertain what the prophecy means, Sal uses the old man's appearance as does the young man in "The Song of Pearl" who listens to the female voice of the letter—to spur him on toward home. Sal, like the "Pearl's" hero, returns home with the knowledge that humans can deceive: Dean had been a rat, a false friend, an inattentive teacher, and failed savior. He also returns to home as the place where he discovers even greater treasure. For Sal, it is the life he has sought: not a life with Dean on the road but true love with the "pure and innocent" (306) girl of his dreams, a reincarnation of Kerouac's vision of himself and his love kneeling on a shared rag rug to pledge their lives to each other. Dean eventually returns to Sal's life, but this time as a ragged, forlorn, and almost inarticulate soul who pathetically wants to hitch a ride with Sal and Remi Boncouer who are headed to a Duke Ellington concert at the Metropolitan Opera. Remi refuses and Sal concurs, the mingled world of high (opera) and low (jazz) city culture coupled with home and heterosexual fidelity overpowering nature, the road, brotherhood, any potential figments of homoeroticism, and the narcissistic self.

Sal's last sad memory of Dean is of him walking alone into the freezing night. As the penultimate version of the trope of the Shrouded Traveler,

Dean no longer signals hope, knowledge, wisdom, and life, but a dark
hopeless attachment to the falsity of what-could-have-been or what-should-be
instead of the truth of what-is in a mundane world. Equipped with this
knowledge, Sal concludes that God is Pooh Bear, a playful phrase that
Kerouac took from one of Neal Cassady's children.[9] Within the wisdom
quest context, the cryptic expression signals that God, and thus religion, may
be just that, a playful creation of the child's imagination, something lovely to
think about but as the "last thing" something one cannot reach. Ironically,
this truth Sal knew almost from the beginning of his travels but had to come
to learn all over again: "Nobody can get to that thing," he had told Carlo
Marx before ever taking his first road trip, "[but] we keep on living in hopes
of catching it once and for all" (48). What exists, expressed in sweeping,
sonorous tones, is a *literary vision* of nature and America that echoes F. Scott
Fitzgerald's conclusion to *The Great Gatsby:* the rolling continent and the
stars above as a place in which we can meditate upon "the father we never
found" (310), but which finally reveals and is revealed as pure benevolent yet
mute darkness. Ironically the land itself, like the female voice of the letter in
the "Song of the Pearl," is a disembodied reality, a guiding metaphysical force
that resists codification as time and space. In its velvety linguistic miasmas,
an imaginative world connected to but far removed from its mythic origins,
a final version of the Shrouded Traveler transformed into the amorphous and
unknowable all, this is the knowledge each of us must come to accept, the
ineluctable fact of death.

Sal's quest for the pearl is a highly complex set of actions, events, and
actors that deliver an almost equally complex configuration of treasures.
Cradled in the knowledge of death, there resides the eternal need to recognize that which is both possible and not possible. Friendships, for example,
do not remain stable. Ever-expanding circles of friends give way to conventional happiness at home in a monogamous heterosexual relationship.
Eschatological knowledge eludes the human effort to find it. Belief in consistent human progress through time is unattainable. The palace of wisdom
does not exist on the road of excess. Conversely, knowledge of self and other,
to some extent, can be made visible. Love for another human being connects
and sustains humanity. The individual is a tenacious and worthy creature
who can survive the death of civilization. The journey to wisdom, whether
spiritual or secular, produces teachings and prophecies to guide others. The
road of excess can lead to the palace of wisdom. And it is not easy but possible to achieve the knowledge of death as all that can be known.

As modern-day wisdom literature, then, *On the Road* instructs and warns a
nation, not just a generation, through the perspective of an ordinary person
telling his fantastic and thus entertaining story. Its very telling is the use of
performative language to reify the abstract and intangible. It is also rhetorical

language designed to promote thought and action, to enable others to find a moral path to self-knowledge, to contemplate how to make one's life and one's world better, despite its inevitable end. It is also spiritual literature of the most symbolic and metaphoric kind that, like ancient narratives, demands the act of interpretation. Finally, *On the Road* reminds one that in song and in narrative, in mystical visions and in the literary imagination, hope remains sheltered in the darkness and light of everyone's story.

CHAPTER 4

THE COSMOLOGY: DOCTOR SAX

It was July 1949 when Kerouac wrote in his journal that *On the Road* dealt with problems of the soul, while *Doctor Sax—Faust Part 3*, which he was writing simultaneously, was "mere language and mystery" (*WW* 206). The derogatory "mere" clarifies his belief that literature claiming an immense metaphysical theme such as the soul warranted greater merit than other literary endeavors. However, Kerouac later came to look much more fondly on *Doctor Sax*, which he completed in 1952 after he had developed his method of spontaneous prose through the drafting of *On the Road* and *Visions of Cody*. The book is a tour de force of language and genre—rich religious symbolism, camera shots, poetry, myths, parodies, and, as Gerald Nicosia observes, "a mixture of modern American idioms, traditional Yankeeisms, and Shakespearean grandiloquence, of neologisms and puns" (410). In the service of the soul as the supreme theme of art and as breathtaking polyglot fused with visionary and cinematic fabula, *Doctor Sax* wields the guise of comic-book fiction, East European mythology, and autobiography to create a mid-twentieth-century cosmology—the story of how the universe came to be and how it functions.

Kerouac almost certainly had no intention of using *Doctor Sax* to create a cosmology like those of the ancient Jewish writers, Plato, Plotinus, and others. His journals and letters indicate that he wanted to continue working within the sweeping, cyclical approach to history that he had found in Spengler, Joyce, the Old and New Testaments, his Buddhist readings, Dostoyevsky, and Goethe. The project also drew indirectly upon the modernist position articulated by T. S. Eliot that writers should work within the greater scope of their cultural literary tradition, tapping a sense of history that compels them to write with knowledge that their literary traditions have "a simultaneous existence and compose a simultaneous order." It is this historical sense, according to Eliot, that makes a work both of its time and timeless—and its writer "acutely conscious of . . . his [or her] own contemporaneity (Leitch et al. 1093). In *Doctor Sax,* Kerouac's deeply held sense of Euro-American literary and cultural traditions results in a play of self-visions creating a panorama of American cultures, in combination both a personal mythopoeia and a modern syncretistic explication of the universe.

As a cosmology, *Doctor Sax* begins backward. By this I mean that it reverses chronological form by withholding until the end discussion of proto-entelechy, or the first cause—that is, how the universe was created. Instead, the narrative concentrates on the universe's infrastructure—its major components and their relationships with each other. In its boldest form, these devices feature the figure of Doctor Sax, who is a composite of characters from Faust myths, the Shadow comics, and Kerouac's inner circle of friends, especially William S. Burroughs. Other characters in the tale include the Great Snake; Count Condu, a campy Dracula-like figure who lives in Snake Castle on Snake Hill; the Wizard, a demonic figure who also lives in the castle; the Dovists, a heretical cult; Jack Duluoz, a young French-Canadian boy nicknamed Ti Jean or Jacky; and the narrator, the older Jack Duluoz who has long left Lowell, which is the setting of the story based on Kerouac's childhood. Around this core cavort numerous family members, boyhood friends, townspeople, and fantasy characters such as a Contessa and a Baron.

The admixture of mythic, fantastic, and autobiographical figures populates an analogous admixture of settings to mirror the materials with which Duluoz constructs his tale: "Memory and dream are intermixed in this mad universe," he states (5). Suggesting that the mixture is process as well as product, Duluoz assembles memories and dreams as the engine of life. The narrative enacts this thesis, but Duluoz addresses it directly in a passage about two childhood friends, Bert Desjardins and Cy Landeau, whom he is trying to remember but who seem to elude him,

> denoting the cessation of its operation in my memory and *therefore the world's*—a time about to become extinct—except that now it can never be, because it happened, it—which led to further levels—as time unveiled her ugly old cold mouth of death to the worst hopes—fears—Bert Desjardins and Cy Landeau like any prescience of a dream are unerasable. (74–75, emphasis mine)

Memories and dreams become prophecies that trigger subsequent events or "levels," and this process leads to an awareness of one's temporal, finite existence. It is not Father Time that activates memory and dream but Mother

Time portrayed as a grotesque generator of knowledge, and it is her ugly mouth of death that fuels the world by preserving human identity and connection.

Some of this admixture introduces the novel. Working with memories, dreams, nightmares, and fantasies combined with those of Goethe and William Gibson, creator of the Shadow, Kerouac constructed layers of self/other representations that distance him from his persona as the adult writer. For instance, Duluoz explains that the book began as a dream in which he instructed himself to use his skill as a word crafter to paint a Lowell neighborhood seen through his childhood eyes. "Let your mind off yourself in this work," he remembers his dream-self saying (3). Subsequently, little is revealed about Duluoz's present-state existence, especially compared with *On the Road's* Sal Paradise. However, two brief passages tucked among the fantasy provide insight into Duluoz's mental state and his interpretation of the dream function. Separation and loneliness plague him, in essence a primal rift occurring at birth (111), and efforts to rid himself of these have led to dreams that he defines as the nonillusionary plane of life in which "participants in a drama recognize one another's death" (112). This insight calls into question common interpretations of perception and memory as infallible and, conversely, dream and fantasy as fallible. The resultant cosmology presents history not as the recording and rearrangement of bits of information (systemic signifiers of credulity), but as the creation and discovery of recurring signs linking the personal, cultural, and universal. In combination, these signs shape a web of being over millennia, leading to a unified, coherent, and grandiose story of how worlds are born and how humans live within them.

Like memories and dreams, Ti Jean's story does not flow linearly, although an overarching structure of the first fourteen years of his life frames the text. Ti Jean's world is in part filled with domestic details of Depression-era Lowell—the names and even a map of the streets on which he lived, descriptions of the social club that his father belonged to, memories of his brother Gerard's death, snapshots of French-Canadian Catholic rituals, narratives of horse-racing games that he played with marbles, dialogues with his mother and sister, trips to the library, and the great flood of 1936 that ravaged the town. Much of this material accurately records elements of Kerouac's own past. Documentable and personal, this world is another grotesque/sublime, one in which a mentally retarded friend masturbates dogs on the porch, mothers fix luscious meals of porkball stew and hot cherry pie, visions of the turning head of St. Theresa haunt the church, and little boys run freely through the streets. Complementing the domestic is Ti Jean's fantasy life, a romantic and mythological Lowell that is a composite of the prehistoric, the medieval, and Hollywood. Horses gallop where the waters of the Merrimac River flow, a castle sits atop a hill, superheroes and evil demons fly through the skies, and poetry rings from the bell towers. This world is traceable to fantasies of other fantasies, the narrative compelling one to simultaneously suspend disbelief and yet disbelieve strongly as Ti Jean and Duluoz repeatedly collapse and reopen time, the twin selves often merging as one. "Ti Jean/Duluoz" as protagonist is a believable little boy struggling to comprehend a dualistic world filled with death/horror and life/laughter, as well as a visionary adult who claims deep knowledge of why that world exists. The product of Kerouac's sketching method, the narrative spirals rapidly through time and space, often so quickly that a reader can easily lose hold of the literary semblance of chronology and verisimilitude.

The cosmology that *Doctor Sax* reveals characterizes humans as thrown into the universe as infants *without sin*. This experience, which Duluoz explains as "a universal sad lost redness of mortal damnation," is symbolized by a snake "coiled in the hill not [one's] heart" (17). Damnation, then, is not the Augustinian concept of original sin or a gnostic belief in the evil material body trapping the pure soul, but a feeling or an awareness that one acquires of something external, yet related, to all perceivers (a universal condition). Some as they move through adolescence seek to learn more about this mystery, receiving a call, mystic or otherwise, to understand the contrary nature of human existence. Duluoz presents Ti Jean's emergence into this world as a "strange" occurrence—"all eyes [h]e came hearing the river's red"—and Ti Jean's call is an instantaneous synesthetic awareness at birth of his ability to hear the color of damnation (17).

Many in Ti Jean's community seem unconcerned with such metaphysical pursuits. Some like his friend Joe remain rooted in the mundane, haunted only by the phantoms of "work and earn money, fix your knife, straighten the screw, figure for tomorrow" (60). In this life, the spiritual, if it is even recognized, is segregated and dealt with through routine practices and surrogates. The priests, and to some extent the nuns, are the authorities on questions of the afterlife as well as good and evil, and they are the ones who prescribe punishment or absolution for those who fail to abide by church law. Community members follow their dictates, praying at the Stations of the Cross by the schoolyard to ward off evil and the possibility of spending eternity in hell. Simultaneously, some, such as Ti Jean's mother, father, and their friends—self-named *La Maudite Gang* ("the damned gang" or "gang of the damned")—deal with damnation by engaging in working-class defiance of authority. They routinely hold wild parties and play tricks on the local parish priest. Their Rabelaisian, carnivalesque gnostic mocking that flouts damnation and those who claim privileged knowledge of it gives little Ti Jean some comfort in the face of Catholic gloom: "At least I had the satisfaction of knowing that no real shades would come to get me in the midst of such strong adult mockery and racket—Gad, that was a gang" (61). But still,

Ti Jean knows that he does not belong to their gang or to the community of the church. The knowledge seeker in this cosmology is alienated among his peers. In these concerns, Ti Jean stands alone.

As the alienated central figures in Kerouac's extension of the Faust myth, Ti Jean and Duluoz embody a fascinating complex of reality and fantasy associated with Christian scripture, medieval history, and enlightenment literature. Most directly, Ti Jean and Duluoz can be traced to Spengler's use of Goethe's *Faust,* the two-part story of a medieval scholar who in his obsession for knowledge of good and evil discards the intellectual world of books in favor of a pact with Mephistopheles. Spengler transformed Faust into an all-purpose label for Western civilizations characterized by ego, the desire for immortality, and a fascination with the full biographical life of the individual. But in Goethe, Faust's story of unrestrained egotism culminates in a battle between angels of goodness and Mephistopheles, a struggle won by the angels who beguile the devil with flaming roses and subsequently bear Faust's soul up to God. Goethe's Faust was indebted to Christopher Marlowe's poem about the same character, which is most likely connected to the historical Faust, a sixteenth-century magician who became the scandalous hero of a German text published in 1787, fifty years after his death. In this version, contrary to the two later ones, Faust meets a horrific end: the devil claims his soul, leaving behind a mutilated body with eyeballs smashed on the wall and Faust's torso tossed on a rubbish pile. This Faust lived in Nittlingen, Germany, a location that Kerouac used in *Doctor Sax* and that links his narrative with the German folk tale (Paton 138).

The character of Faust, however, stretches back even further to Faustus, Augustine of Hippo's Manichaean teacher. Predating both Faustus and Augustine but linked to them is yet another Faustus, this one a historical figure named Simon, also known as Simon Magus, who appears in the New Testament story of the apostle Phillip's proselytizing in Samaria. Simon is reported to have used magic to trick the Samarians into believing that he had "the great power of God" but was later converted to Christianity and followed Phillip (Acts 8:10–13, 895). Simon is most often, however, associated with gnosticism. Using the name Faustus, "the favored one" in Latin, he is identified by heresiologists as a gnostic founder accompanied by a former prostitute whom he claimed to be the reincarnation of Helen of Troy and the fallen knowledge of God trapped in the evil material world (Jonas 111).

In *Sax* these Faustian elements are blended with memories of Lowell and Duluoz's experiences as spiritual quester. As such, he is compelled to look inward, to listen to the twin of himself, the dream self that directs him to resurrect Ti Jean through the magic of language. Of course, Ti Jean is not a corporeal reality resurrected from the grave but the creation of imagination, a being akin to the homunculus that Wagner, Faust's servant, creates in the second part of Goethe's drama—an artificial manikin that appears superior to Mephistopheles and has been interpreted to be an expression of Goethe's beliefs in beauty and "promotive activity" (Taylor 473). Goethe's manikin was probably based on the alchemist Paracelsus's homunculus, a human created without the female womb, a fabrication of human nature and human art for which he supplied explicit directions in *De Generatione Rerum*. Paracelsus wrote that such creatures are by art born, and "therefore Art is in them incarnate and self-existing" (Taylor 472), a statement that speaks less to alchemical magic than it does to literary and other artistic processes. With respect to Kerouac, his literary magic situates himself and Duluoz as Faustians who trust their own intuition and artful powers (the destructive forces of evil in Christian terms) rather than an all-powerful external divinity. These powers enable Kerouac to bring to life a homunculus of action and beauty—Duluoz, who then magically calls forth another human form, Ti Jean, a typical boy from the American interwar years. As a manikin of the manikin, Ti Jean speaks like a wonder-struck witness who in his blessed state of resurrection must narrate his adventures as a little Faust. This is a process that, like a set of Chinese boxes or Russian nesting dolls, mysteriously creates the human complex via the inward-turning eye, one shape magically opening itself to reveal an identical yet smaller version. The Paracelsusian homunculus, then, serves as an ideal metaphor for the construction of the literary self.

As a little Faust, Ti Jean believes with childhood intensity that he has the power to discover truth and beauty. One of the most engaging examples of his quest for power as a little boy is his Black Thief Game. As the Black Thief, a form of the Shadow and other pulp fiction superheroes and villains, he steals his friend's favored possessions and hides them in his basement, leaving behind notes warning that the Thief will strike again or attributing the fait accompli to the Thief. Eventually caught, he is chastised by the friend's mother and his own mother, who threatens to confiscate his thriller magazines, which she believes to be the cause of his transgressions (49–50). The Black Thief antics, harmful to others and himself, are a form of play introducing a child to the adult world in which one exercises power, manipulating others for one's own sadomasochistic pleasure. The narrative hints that Ti Jean recognizes the danger in playing this Faustian game: "'What foolish power had I discovered and been possessed by?' I asts meself" (49). The subtle use of the present tense ("asts") in this passage creates a voice that speaks for Ti Jean *and* Duluoz, the latter's marked by sophisticated vocabulary and syntax as well as the playful Irish accent in the attribution phrase. The former's surfaces in the greater context of the scene itself. Immediately preceding his question is a description of Ti Jean returning the stolen items to his little victim, Dicky, who "was wiping his red wet eyes with a handkerchief" (49). The correspondence of the boys and the use of the past progressive tense ("was wiping") produces an immediacy that, when directly followed by the rhetorical question regarding power, connects that awareness, nascent as it may be, with the child. The adult can rationally proclaim that the childhood power was foolish, but the child *feels* it, which in Ti Jean's Catholic worlds leads to a sense of guilt and the implied threat of having to spend eternity in hell.

The quest for power, however, leads neither Duluoz nor Ti Jean to make a pact with the devil. There is no possession of the soul, a narrative element separating Kerouac's characters from the Fausts and Faustuses of past legends. In fact, one learns in the sixth and last section of *Doctor Sax* that Ti Jean has a profound love for books, which Goethe's Faust disdainfully discards. Ti Jean's passion is similar to that of Goethe's Wagner, who attempts to temper Faust's lust for ultimate power: "My need / Is all for books," he declares, "from page to page to read. / Ah, what a different joy sweet reading yields! / . . . / For when we spread a precious scroll or missal / the joy of heaven itself comes down to earth" (67). The power of books is rendered in similar rhapsodic language in *Doctor Sax,* although without reference to the transcendent, as Duluoz remembers the intoxicating feeling of seeing "rows of glazed brown books" on the Lowell library shelves. In response, "[his] soul thrills to touch the soft used meaty pages covered with avidities of reading—at last, at last, [he's] opening the magic brown book [. . . to] see the great curlicued print, the immense candelabra first letters at the beginnings of chapters—and Ah!" (183). Duluoz, unlike Faust, does not disparage this magic, which does no harm but instead opens Ti Jean to a glittering world of immense imaginative possibility—a key to his ability to successfully find wisdom. Ti Jean and Duluoz, then, embody features of Faust, the heretical and flawed superman, but *Doctor Sax* also decenters and fragments the Faustian nature of Ti Jean and Duluoz to reference the more mundane and subordinate yet artful Wagner equipped with a bookish literary vision and the power to actualize that vision.

Interestingly, in contrast to much of the Legend, Duluoz's cosmology features the devil more predominantly than it does Christ. As in *On the Road,* evil is represented by the devilish Great Snake, an ancient symbol recognizable as a version of the Old Testament snake responsible for tempting Eve to eat of the tree of knowledge, leading to the primal couple's expulsion from Eden. Kerouac's snake is equally, if not more, evil—huge in form, living deep within the earth, a masculine body rumbling and slithering beneath the surface of everyday life. He is, however, not only a sign of Judeo-Christian evil, but "the enigma of the New World—[. . .] whose home is in the deeps of Ecuador and Amazonian jungle" (28). From this perspective, the Great Snake reconfigures the allegorical figure of masculine evil into a construction signifying the recursive nature of human historical traditions and the possibility of new beginnings.

This theme is played out in several ways. First, as a creature whose home is the southern American continents, the Great Snake is directly connected to Quetzalcoatl, the primary god of the Toltec and later Aztec cultures of Mesoamerica. This god, whose name means "feathered serpent," was considered the god of civilization, goodness, and light as well as the focus of a violent culture of human sacrifice. As a contemporary version of this deity, the Great Snake embodies human destruction and human salvation. In this form, the Snake as signifier loops eastward again to the ancient cultures of the Israelites and the Christian gnostics—especially the Peratae, a gnostic-era tradition that drew on Assyrian and Egyptian serpent mythology.[1]

The Peratae considered the snake symbolic of unearthly perfection and the power that guided Moses out of Egypt. According to their leader, Peratic, it was the serpent that gifted Eve with true wisdom. In this fascinating cosmology of a tripartite universe consisting of the Father, Son, and Matter, heaven is crowned with "the beauteous *image of the serpent, turning itself,*" according to Hippolytus of Rome in his *Refutation of All Heresies.* Eve, the wise primal mother, directs life toward heaven, from which all life emanates as motion through the serpent. This radical reinterpretation of Judaic cosmology is carried even further by the Peratae, who concluded that Jesus as the Son of the Father leads human beings away from the evil of matter (there are evil serpents in this cosmology as well) to transcendental goodness: "No one, then, [Peratic says] can be saved or return (into heaven) without the Son, and the Son is the *Serpent,*" wrote Hippolytus. Jesus then is clearly, and most heretically according to Judeo-Christian orthodox traditions, aligned with Eve and the Serpent as a triumvirate of goodness and light (Jonas 93).

The Peratae tradition, as well as many other religious traditions, including orthodox Christianity, also connected Eve and Eden with rivers—the waters of life that nurture human life and carry it toward the transcendent. Duluoz interprets his Great Snake within this pantheistic and deistic frame, associating the Snake with the Merrimac River, whose history he attributes to "some snakelike source with maws approach and wide, welled from the hidden dank" (7–8). The Merrimac, as code for all rivers as well as the one that churns through Lowell, mirrors the snake, the perpetual motion of life, transforming a sign of evil into cosmic harmony—a twinning or masking that emerges as a motif fundamental to the narrative. In this sense, Kerouac's Great Snake stands as a contemporary representation of the snakelike yin-yang symbol described in the I Ching and of the Uroborus, the snake that eats its own tail, an ancient Egyptian sign conventionally interpreted as the self-renewing universe or the union of the chthonic with the celestial. The Great Snake also shares a subtle link with Mecalinda, the Serpent King in Buddhist mythology, who used his coiled body and hooded head to protect Buddha from the evil tempter Mara.

Rhetorically, then, the Great Snake in its many manifestations as primeval enigma in the New World disguises a multiplicity of historical traditions, including Mesoamerican, Judeo-Christian, Mesopotamian, Mediterranean, Middle Eastern, and Asian. Among these rich cultural antiquities one finds the agnostic, Spenglerian natural cycle of civilizations, ancient goddess-worshipping cultures, the split among early Christian sects over the power of the feminine, a gnostic understanding of the material world as the creation of an evil source distinct from any transcendent benevolent power, the belief in the serpent as a positive sign of power and redemption, and the fusion of Jewish and Christian traditions into orthodoxy. In compilation, they blunt historicity, particularly elements of Judeo-Christian patriarchy, so that a new people can be generated, all while refusing to erase those traditions entirely.

As with any religious tradition, Kerouac's Great Snake has his followers, demonic and otherwise. The most developed is Count Condu, a campy vampire with a Nazi-like demeanor who likes his religion blood-red rare (23). His parodic and comic-book outline critiques the diminished but still prevalent belief systems based on genuine disregard for human life, including in the most veiled of symbolic form a condemnation of the passion of Christ. This reading is not the stretch that it may at first seem when one considers the following conversation that the Count and his companion, La Contessa, have about the Snake:

"You think it will live?" [Contessa]

"Who's going to kill it to revive it?" [Count]

"Who'll want to kill it to survive?"

"The Parisacs and Priests—find them something they have to contend with face to face with the possibility of horror and bloodshed and they'll be satisfied with wooden crosses and go home." (24–25)

The Count indicates that the Snake (evil) must die in order for others to live, an allusion to the Christian story of God's sacrifice and the resurrection of his only son so that all who believe in him can be saved—a defeat of evil (John 3:16). But the dialogue's Socratic dialectic and Steinian repetition create a powerful chantlike rhythm that echoes and mocks Christian beliefs dictating salvation through Christ and the destruction of evil. Condu and the Contessa have mastered the rhetoric of their enemy, the church, but Condu also knows that those who represent the church, the "Parisacs and Priests," are hollow men who hide behind impotent, false symbology, such as the cross. In their campy arrogance, the Count and the Contessa, representing elements of the snaky Faust figure spouting knowledge of those they disdain, undercut the foundation of Christology.

A figure closely aligned with the Snake is the Wizard, who lives in the Castle with the Count and is described as a grotesque named Faustus. With a "moveable jaw-bird beak and front teeth missing" (50), the Wizard bears the mark of the devil: scars on his neck of the evil one's attempt in the thirteenth century to kill him by strangulation. He is also depicted as a scholar fiddling with papers and quill pens late into the night. Morphing into "a martinet with books, cardinals and gnomes at his spidery behest" (50) is the Master of Earthly Evil. Although a minor figure compared to the Count, Faustus in comic form is fairly complex. Obviously, he represents the human tendency to seek knowledge by going into league with the devil. His magical powers—he is after all hundreds of years old!—are so great that he has many minions at his beck and call, and in this respect he caricatures historical church hierarchy (cardinals) and folk fantasies (gnomes)—superstitions mocked as ironically powerless since they exist to serve him. But while Faustus functions as an allegory for the human attraction to evil, the narrative does not clarify the extent to which his allegiance is free will or slavery. His enthusiastic worship of the Snake suggests the former, but the scars on his neck signal a union made under duress, implying that he is flawed in his ability to fight evil but has the will to survive, thus exemplifying an element of free will with the potential to overcome evil. This portrait endows human beings with both the weakness to practice evil and the power to recognize and combat evil—in effect, Duluoz's attempt to define human nature and salvation.

With equal ambiguity, beings known as Dovists flit in and out of the narrative as allegorical shape-shifters. Also associated with the Count and the Wizard, these minor characters possess no systematic logic for their belief in goodness, love, and freedom, and have been called a parody of the then current hipsters and a representation of Beat spirituality (Nicosia 400). But a more significant interpretation of them may exist in a more obvious reading. One is hard pressed to miss the fact that the very name "Dovists" is a blunt reference to Christianity, the dove having long been a symbol of the interpretation of Christ as gentle, peaceful, and feminine. In this respect, the Count shows them little respect, employing the renaissance rhetorical tradition of elaborate invective to distinguish Dovism from his own bloody, masculine form of worship: "they can act up with their ashes and urns and oily incense . . . bloodless theosophists of the moonlight—excalibur dull bottards in a frantic hinch, cock-waddlers on pones and pothosts, rattle-bead bonehead splentiginous bollyongs" (26). The Count's allusions to the "bells and smells" of ritual Catholic practice and to theosophical beliefs[2] transforms the Dovists into a bizarre, cultish hybrid of mystic Catholicism, Buddhism, high Protestantism, and Blavatskian spiritualism. They are obviously not manly enough for the Count's evil tastes—too foppishly romantic, and within the context of mocking Catholic orthodoxy in *Doctor Sax* and in the Duluoz Legend overall, the Dovists' cultish hybridity leaves them vulnerable to Duluoz's disdain. However, in opposition to the Count as evil, their very hybridity situates them somewhat more positively. Their association with theosophy, Christianity, and a long history of doves as symbols of peace and love distinguishes them historically from orthodox Christianity in that the symbol of the dove, well before and after the consolidation of the Catholic Church, represented in gnostic and other religious traditions the goodness of human nature encased in evil corporality.

This theology as revealed in a Dovist poem read mockingly by one of the Count's evil subordinates, Baroque, reifies the above duality while portending the repudiation of dualism that concludes the novel. The poem prophesizes that on Judgment Day the Great Snake will collapse in defeat as gray doves fly from its mouth and the cry of "Twas but a husk of doves!" will fill the golden air (109)—a repetition of the tale that Sal Paradise tells Marylou in *On The Road* although Sal conveys, his version with sincerity rather than ridicule. When Baroque, as the messenger of the Count, who represents evil trapped within the body, uses mockery to repudiate the Dovists, he enacts the foundational Augustinian Catholic position calling heretical the gnostic belief in the essential goodness of the human soul and the evil of the material world in which it is encased. Simultaneously he manifests Catholic and Protestant doctrine denigrating the theosophical belief in the presence of life, consciousness, and God in all matter.[3] In relationship to the Count, then, the Dovists embody a dialectical binary refusing to negate either belief in the natural world as malevolent or belief in that world as divine, and no theological or metaphysical system appears to supersede any other in the establishment of teleological clarity. Mockery repeatedly undermined by mockery leads to a dialectic that propels a cosmos in which neither pole is true north. Neither can operate apart from the other, and as the novel eventually demonstrates, this a process, erases the reality of good versus evil.

In no other figure is the concept of dialectic reality anthropomorphized as it is in Doctor Sax. Based on a fantasy figure that Kerouac created as a young boy, Sax is a complex representation of modern-day and ancient beliefs and desires. Associated with death and fear, Sax is a version of Kerouac's Shrouded Traveler, but little in his brief introductory portrait indicates that Sax is not flesh and blood. He is introduced as a credible, living although mysterious human being, "the dark figure in the corner when you look at the dead man coffin in the dolorous parlor of the open house with a horrible purple wreath on the door," as Duluoz describes him (4). He is introduced as palpably real as in the eyes of an impressionable child who has not yet learned to differentiate fact from fancy, and palpably real as a product of human imagination in the eyes of the adult writer. However, the possibility of Doctor Sax being a verifiable Lowell character is soon dispelled. One learns, for instance, that Sax, as does the Snake, springs like a rhizome from multiple sources, originating from the ancient rivers of South America *and* from Butte, Montana (29). An alchemist who lives in the woods of Lowell's Pawtucketville neighborhood, he glides through the sickly brown night, maniacally screeching "Mwee, hee ha ha ha" (21). His presence is also manifested in the gleeful sound of children playing at night (57–58). Paradoxically, he can see all that they do, including masturbation, bestiality, and other forms of sexual experimentation (68–69). He looks somewhat avuncular, like Carl Sandburg (23), yet hawkish, like the Snake and Bull Hubbard (an imaginative representation of William Burroughs), and he has spent his life seeking the Great Snake of Evil (28–29). The narrative also reveals that he has found the home of the Snake through the reading of nature, or in other words through the process of natural correspondence—for instance, seeking the perfect dove, "a white jungle variety," or a bat with a "snaky beak" that looks like a bird, and deducing from this creature that part of the Snake can be found in the South American jungle (28–29). We also learn that Doctor Sax has great moral courage. Instead of using a gun as does the Shadow, a variant of the gunslinger and mobster images of American popular culture, he has spent years learning to recognize "good and evil and intelligence" (32) and seeking the rarest of herbs to create a potion to annihilate evil through his telepathic powers of light, distantly akin to those singing cowboys such as Gene Autry and Eddie Dean who tamed a lawless America with their guitars and tender voices (31). He is Ti Jean's great friend and protector (33–34), a figure whom the little boy learns not to fear—in other words, he is Kerouac's Shrouded Traveler transformed as the angel of good.

Doctor Sax reverberates as a constellation of contradictions, which seems logical as the invention of a child's imagination. The constellation operates effectively as cosmological symbology in a narrative in which the major elements seem to twin or mirror each other, revealing and concealing elements of each other as the narrative progresses. For instance, Sax suggests the interrelatedness of these symbolic and natural forms in his association with the Great Snake's origin in South America, his ghostly form reflecting the Count and the Wizard, and the linking of the bat and the dove for which he searches. So too does his characterization, about which Duluoz is nothing short of blunt, calling Sax a Faustian man, a label justified by Sax's human desire to know and conquer evil and thus save (or control) the world.

The cosmology incorporates textual traces of the history of this superego, actually providing itself with the illusion of credibility through historic documentation. The vehicle upon which the novel relies to document itself is a fantastic twentieth-century autobiographical adventure tale written by Sax himself, set in New England in March 1922 (the month and year of Kerouac's birth), and inserted into Duluoz's narrative. The document, a set of yellowed sheets of paper blown in the winter wind, is found by a Lowell mill worker, who picks it up because, as Duluoz speculates, what else "would anybody do seeing this thing, it was though it *talked and begged* to be picked up the way it sidled to him like a scorpion" (134, emphasis mine). The comparison to a talking scorpion, a creature most others are unlikely to pick up, hints at the extraordinary power of this talking book, which announces that it was written by Adolphus Asher Ghoulens, the pseudonym Sax uses to tell in the third person his tale of terrorizing a group of humans partying in a castle called Transcendta. The manuscript is presented in full. Sax as the implied narrator creates himself as a malevolent messenger delivering "private knowledge of the world" (142) to the assembled types, such as drama students, young women in slacks, an interpretive dancer, a composer, and other "gay barbarians"[4] and bohemians burlesqued by Sax. Their host, Emilia St. Claire, wants them all to be "frightfully mad," a cliché of bohemia since the days of Henri Murger's *Bohemians of the Latin Quarter* (1848), and in clichéd voices—"Really, do you study engineering? I mean *really?*" (138)—they unwittingly flaunt their vacuity. Many at the party, especially the women, faint at the sight of Sax whose purple lips spout his message, which is revealed not explicitly or rationally but mystically and intuitively, rather osmotically, through his noxious caped form. Laughing in mockery of them all, Sax concludes his tale by gliding into the night, leaving the false artists and intellectuals to begin to regain consciousness. Described as "a stirring of stunned minds," their awakening signals a burgeoning, new self-awareness (143).

This tale-within-a tale provokes many intriguing questions and interpretations, not the least of which is what to make of an author assuming the guise of a fictional character creating its own history through a decentered omniscient perspective. What are we to make of a Kerouac who creates Duluoz, who creates Sax, who creates Ghoulens, who then recreates Sax? "Ghoulishly" disguised, Sax acknowledges his superhuman powers as "reptilian" and asks if Sax is truly a man (142), which is just the question we must ask of Sax and Duluoz as well as of their significance as nonhuman. The layering and fun-house twinning of narrators reveals that the dark, primal quest for knowledge is situated deep within the human imagination and is born of a prehuman source where it may remain invisible for millennia. It also suggests that this human quest is one that can only be told "at a slant," to use Emily Dickinson's language, since to look at one's self or to speak the truth directly is either too dangerous or ineffective; someone else must craft the words for us. One's reptilian search for knowledge (it is a most ancient impulse) can only be recognized through the mythic retelling of stories.

However, Sax, whose ego is so huge that he dares to report his adventures as dark prophet, is humble enough to question his humanity, and it must be acknowledged that he never knows that his adventure tale has been discovered or read by anyone else. So in a sense, Ghoulens/Sax is, like Kerouac/Duluoz, both the private, humble writer of his memoir and the public, ego-filled dramaturge of his own life.

The Ghoulens/Sax adventure story functions as a component or installment in the long lineage of the trope of the talking text in spiritual and theistic literature. Certainly it corresponds with the letter and the female voice from the gnostic "Song of the Pearl," which itself is a progenitor of not only the Anglo-African slave narrative trope of the talking book that Henry Louis Gates brought to critical attention but also the romantic American Renaissance version exemplified by *Pierre*. Melville, much like Kerouac, had inserted into his autobiographical fiction a text titled "Chronometricals and Horologicals," identified as part of a series of lectures called "EI" by Plotinus Plinlimmon. The lecture fragment—contrary to *Sax*, we are not privy to the fiction of a full text in Pierre—relies upon the conceit of a chronometer keeping Greenwich mean time and satirically counters Plotinian wisdom that humans have to work diligently to align their moral and intellectual virtues with those of the God of Absolute Unity (Stumpf 138). Plinlimmon reasons that since the laws of the Christian god are contradictory to human nature, the divine chronometer can never be aligned with that of the horologe, and he concludes that "the only great original moral doctrine of Christianity," which is the doctrine of salvation, "has been found a false one" (Melville 239). While Pierre discovers and reads the document, the narrator, much as does Duluoz, presents the text for readers to do with as they wish ("each person can skip, or read and rail for himself" [234]). Also, much like the Ghoulens/Sax tale, the Plinlimmon lecture reveals in the disguise of double-voiced discourse the implied author's judgments and beliefs. This is most obvious in Plinlimmon's lecture, a point underscored by the fact that Pierre fails to heed Plinlimmon's logic and, in his effort to act according to the Christian virtue of self-sacrifice, kills others and himself. In like fashion, Ghoulens' biographical account conveys Kerouac/Duluoz's dislike of false American intellectualism and equally false individuality—a point that, as this chapter will later elucidate, is reinforced by Duluoz going into league with Sax, an act leading to a triumphant rather than tragic quest.

All of the above versions of the talking book trope rely upon double-voiced discourse, which exposes the shifting functions of orality and literacy in epistemological projects over centuries. In the Pearl song, for instance, the patriarchal wisdom text *speaks* in a disembodied female voice. In Gates's model, the white-written wisdom text, usually the Bible, sometimes *speaks* with the black slave voice (*Signifying Monkey* 131). In the Plinlimmon lecture, the classical Neoplatonic wisdom text is *rewritten* as a masculine satire of Christian doctrine. In the Ghoulens/Sax adventure, the voice of ethnic childhood and adolescent wisdom *is written* as adult history. The inversions of the tension between oral and written discourse is critical in this quadrangle. For instance, the gnostic pearl story illustrates a world in which female orality exists, but only as a transcendent rather than corporeal presence. Her voice is acknowledged but negated as having real power in the mundane world. Thus she resides as only the remnant or possibility of female agency subordinated to the reality of male domination and male fantasy. In the Anglo-African slave narrative, the book, while at times speaking in a black voice, is often muted or seems to speak only to white readers—a representation of the black slave's recognition that "objects can only reflect the subjectivity of the subject, like a mirror does," as Gates explains. The black voice is deprived of literacy (156).

In Plinlimmon's text, an exemplar of enlightenment literacy, the oral voice is muted, or at least diminished, and is replaced by the nineteenth-century lecture, which is written before it is delivered orally. This case, the writing of a then modern American man (Plinlimmon), assumes white male supremacy and brings to the fore certain inadequacies of the classical and Judeo-Christian traditions (Plotinus), in which the New World still seeks to ground itself. The oral reclaims some of its power in the Ghoulens/Sax tale, Sax's fantastic story resembling children's fairy tales that can be traced back to oral European traditions. However, it also functions like Melville's in its assumption of white male literacy and in its doubling of voices from written texts. For it is not only the wisdom of the child that double-speaks but it is also the very genre of wisdom literature itself, which, like the letter in the Pearl song and other textual forms of divine revelation, is satirically rewritten as the voice of twentieth-century gothic adventure, a tale depicting contemporary American culture as imaginatively and introspectively inadequate. Thus the Ghoulens/Sax tale reintroduces orality and gothic fantasy back into the American character, affirming its patriarchal heritage through the double-voiced male narrators, each of which prophetically calls for a return to American romanticism.

But Sax, like Ti Jean and Duluoz, has not made a pact with the devil, a twist of the Goethean conceit effected, first, through associating Sax with benign Christ symbology, the antithesis of Faust, and, second, by extending the definition of the *true* Faustian as one who is by nature a fellaheen. As a Spenglerian survivor of the cycles of history, Sax has come to know death and therefore does not fear the dark, which Duluoz describes as "Skull, Blood, Dust, Iron, Rain burrowing into earth to snake antique" (43), the uppercase initial for each word performing like emblematic titles of material existence complicating the description as medieval or Blakean prophecy. Within the

Legend, as one sees in *On the Road, fellaheen* signifies Christ-like goodness within suffering, the true loving nature of humans revealed through abject and mystical marginalization. Framed as such, Sax exists as a rejection of Faust as a categorically distinct allegory of the devil's power, of God's power, of the natural and the supernatural as mutually exclusive, of materiality as evil and spirituality as good, and of light as goodness and darkness as evil. Granted, one can construct a convincing reading of *Doctor Sax* by pursuing any one of these threads as well as the critical position that a dominant interpretation depends on the existence of a subordinate and oppressed binary opposite. But within Kerouac's theological and philosophical schemata, the character of Sax exists more convincingly as a sign that binaries, whether explicit or masked scriptions, are ultimately illusion.

This precept one can attribute in part to Kerouac's reading of Buddhist texts such as the Diamond and Surangama sutras during these years, although unlike *On the Road, Doctor Sax* features few allusions to Buddhism. Instead, the negation of binaries is performed by the narrative structure itself, specifically through Kerouac's skillful manipulation of plot, setting, and point of view to fuse autobiography or memoir with fantasy and myth. Essential to the project's success is setting, which is as complex as the character of Sax himself. The opening scene takes place in an unidentified location in present time that dissolves almost immediately into Duluoz's memory of dreaming that he is in Lowell. As this imaginative space unfolds, incorporating his memories as well as those of his younger self, the setting is indirectly explained as bipartite through the voices of the Count and Duluoz: "'Has my box arrived from Budapest?' *queries* the Count (a mile away Joe Plouffe *makes* the Riverside corner before a gust of rain)" (24, emphasis mine). Duluoz's parenthetical aside illustrates the material world operating simultaneously with the metaphysical, magical world, each as a present-tense reality. In other words, history is happening all around us; the dead are all the time living all around us.

A narrative that posits such a dual vision of reality could continue in this vein, relying on the juxtaposition of these coexisting worlds, which is what Kerouac does with the interplay of English and French-Canadian languages throughout much of the text. The language of his family and friends is often presented first in patois, and the English translation then appears parenthetically. Structurally, this technique signifies the separation of worlds that like languages are similar, but in translation always slightly different. The technique also unifies the text in its consistent message that multiple social systems exist synchronically. Kerouac, as is his pattern throughout the Legend, affirms this epistemology while undermining it. Discrete realms exist in his cosmology, but they are also revealed to be philosophical patina replaced by a vision of the world in which barriers between natural and supernatural are so permeable that they may not even exist. Time and self, like the rivers and the rain, flow back and forth, merging, collapsing, separating, expanding, and then merging again, so that *Sax* becomes a holistic surface in which the imaginary must be seen as real, the real as imaginary, and all of it as a continuum.

The narrative accomplishes this vision through at least two mechanisms: Duluoz's belief in history as the repetition of forms through time and his use of the cinema trope. With respect to the former, in part 1, for example, his description of a site where he once lived uses popular culture imagery to effect this view of time: "On Beaulieu St. our house was built over an ancient cemetery—(Good God the Yankees and Indians beneath, the World Series of old dry dusts)" (35). The reference to the rivalry between the New York Yankees and the Cleveland Indians as the two most dominant major league baseball teams during the late forties to mid fifties is a humorous device not only to illustrate the repetition of historical events (baseball battles are but new forms of an old rivalry or new forms disguised as old rivalries) but also to erase the artifacts used to divide and thus control time (the past remains with us no matter how deeply buried or disguised it may be). *Sax's* Talking Book trope also reifies this point, the memoir as adventure tale surfacing unexpectedly as it floats through time and the narrative voices, written no matter how long ago, becoming disembodied present-tense experiences.

However, it is the cinema as a structural and thematic trope that even more explicitly communicates the notion of a holistic world in which the real and imaginary are constantly affirmed and negated. Book 2 carries the subtitle "A Gloomy Bookmovie" and consists of twenty-five scenes, something like Kerouac's journal concept of the new American novel formed by passages strung together like pearls on a string (*WW* 241). These scenes are not constructed as an actual screenplay, but nonetheless each is identified as a sequenced unit, and some feature directorial-like language. Scene One, for instance, begins with the time and brief description of the setting: "TWO O'CLOCK—strange—thunder and the yellow walls of my mother's kitchen [. . .] (81)". Scene Seven presents a ground-level shot of a fallen branch that, because of the camera angle, looks "enormous and demented," as it might to a worm (83); Scene Nine opens with a description of two characters framed for the opening shot: "Both our faces peer fondly out the window at the rain" (83). Scene Eleven references the viewer and synchronic sound, the source of which is identified by the film's image: "Thunder again, now you see my room, my bedroom with the green desk [. . .] You hear my footsteps unmistakably pounding up the stairs on the run" (85). Scene Sixteen calls for a "flash shot" of two of Ti Jean's marbles racing across the floor (87); Scene Seventeen consists entirely of a sentence fragment seemingly directed at the film editor: "The marbles crashing into wall" (88), which appears to cue a point-of-view shot representing the character's line of sight rather than some other. Dialogue is included as well, although not in script form; long paragraph blocks incorporate conversation in Quebecois with parenthetical English translations, which could in a film appear as subtitles.

Most of the scenes, however, are lengthy narratives, some parenthetically spliced into the script, based on memories of his childhood fantasy games using marbles to replicate horse races and visits to his father's local social club. The second-person and the imperative voice appear occasionally to remind one that this section of *Sax* is a blended genre—the bookmovie is memoir or first-person narrative reflection integrated with screenplay directions to actors, editors, cinematographers, and the audience. Even though the past tense is used to plausibly represent time as a categorical imperative, the narrative voice remains a present-tense experience for the reader. Likewise, the screenplay cues to actors, audience, and filmmaking personnel locate the construction of the scenes in a distinctly remote point in time. Yet the reading, or viewing, of that language positions the experience as a present moment in the mind of the reader/viewer who creates it even while being guided by it. This, as Louise Rosenblatt has argued regarding reading and textual interpretation in general is a transactional process in which the reader/viewer's attention pulsates between the text and one's responses to it. The bookmovie does call special attention to the collaborative nature of all textual creation, especially film, while simultaneously foregrounding the "I" as central to the creation. This paradoxical hybrid also situates the constructed nature of time and the self in a setting that presents both as stable, a priori realities. Neither position is negated, but neither is supreme. History and self as historical constructs float as disembodied signifiers into the ken of the present.

The bookmovie as an epistemological device is complemented by Duluoz's memories of a single film, the 1931 adventure film *Trader Horn,* directed by W. S. Van Wyke, that was a precursor of the Johnnie Weismuller Tarzan films. *Trader Horn* serves as harbinger of the 1936 flood that becomes the theme of book 5 and a catalyst for the mythic adventures Sax and Ti Jean share as the climax of the narrative. Set on the African savannah, the film portrays two "New World" males, Aloyshius "Trader" Horn and his sidekick, Peru, rescuing a young white girl who has been abducted by the natives. Duluoz's noncritical summary of Ti Jean's interpretation of the film is collaged with, or abruptly spliced into, a vision of ancient Mexican priests cutting out the heart of a sacrificial victim to placate the sun and the snake god. The image of an innocent victim at the mercy of a brutal force sets up, beautifully and distastefully, Ti Jean's extremely racist image of hordes of "horrible black Fuzzy Wuzzies of the bush" with hair like "Blake Snake halos" that convince him that the world is coming to an end—the New World, or white civilization, is at the mercy of the "buggywuggies [. . .] like so many cockroaches" (149–50). Demonized and dehumanized, the Africans as constructed by Van Wyke and magnified in the child's mind argue that Ti Jean's understanding of the story, like the film and the actions of the ancient Mexican priests that introduce it, is a cruel worldview that distorts, terrifies, and misdirects. The histories of both Aztec and African cultures appear as legitimate present-day realities—that is, one lives with these stereotypes as reified truths repeated in various guises throughout time. But what binds them is their reality as artifice, the emptiness beneath, the lack of any a priori essence. The process and products of history, demonization and false truth, surface as illusionary constructs in illusionary time, but all clothed as material reality.

Kerouac reveals the illusion of material reality most consistently through narrative point of view, working at such a fine level of distinction between Duluoz's and Ti Jean's selves, memories, and fantasies that the two often become one. The vision of the brutal Mexican priests noted above is a prime example. The passage in which the vision appears begins with Doctor Sax in Teotihuacàn, Mexico, researching the snake and eagle religious cultures, his journey presented as if he were a person in real time. This is followed by a parenthetical aside, in which an introductory modifier suggests that the "I" speaks from the top of the Pyramid of the Sun and simultaneously from a ground-level Mexican neighborhood. The grammatical construction creates temporal and spatial confusion. Is the "I" a present-tense Duluoz whose imaginary self resides at the top of the pyramid and composes much of the text while in Mexico, or is it possibly Doctor Sax, who is part priest himself? Both potentialities exist in the literary reality of the vision. The connection linking time, self, Sax, and the narrators is even more clearly activated in the following supplication from Duluoz that concludes book 1:

> Doctor Sax, whirl me no Shrouds—open up your heart and talk to me—in those days he was silent, sardonic, laughed in tall darkness.
>
> Now I hear him scream from the bed of the brim—
>
> "The Snake is Rising Inch and Hour to destroy us [like the flood] [. . .] Snake's a Horror—only birds are good—murderous birds are good, murderous snakes, no good." (77)

Who, one has to ask, says, "Now I hear him scream . . ."? The speaker can be Ti Jean asking for Sax's blessing but also the older Duluoz, who, in the very act of writing about his own past, lives again in the presence of Sax. This blurring of speakers blurs past and present, not to collapse time, but to transform and enlarge it, the text suggesting that in the world as continuum (a world altogether other than a duality of the natural and the supernatural) the universe is ever expanding.

Passages such as these, and in fact the entire cosmological cast that populates *Doctor Sax,* question the morphological structure of life. Kerouac, again, does not pursue this topic as would a systematic philosopher, but his cosmology, by incorporating elements of Spengler's use of the mineralogical term *pseudomorphosis,* works as a critique of structuralism. Pseudomorphosis refers to the process whereby a crystalline substance moves into a hollow left by the disintegration of a previous and different crystalline substance, assuming the form, although not the molecular composition, of the older substance. Spengler and others (Jonas 36–37) have used the process as an analogy for the cycling of civilizations or institutions within particular cultures. Spengler applied it to the process by which older cultures oppress newer cultures arising within, stifling them so severely that they are forced into the mold of the dominant older culture. For instance, one can (although Spengler did not) see the present-day United States as an example, its Puritan and fundamentalist character an artifact of the European colonial mold into which it grew. The idea of substances masked as older, more dominant forms is particularly salient to *Doctor Sax.* Kerouac's fusion of older selves within new forms, such as Ti Jean in the memory of Duluoz, mid-twentieth-century baseball players in the shape of warring primeval peoples, and fictional characters including Faust and the Great Snake in the cast of older versions from folk literature and theology, proposes not that the dominant forms are necessarily harmful, as Spengler's theory suggests, but that one must question the unique nature of any subject or object within the universe. Do these forms, whether recognizable because we have seen or read about them many times before, possess a distinct structure, or does the die into which they have been cast point to the illusion of human subjectivity and natural objectivity? Is the morphing that one observes a structural change or epistemological wizardry?

One way in which *Doctor Sax* answers these questions is to construct simultaneous pseudomorphisms by which, one, fantasy and religious narratives are molded to the shapes of modern memoir and the superhero tale and, two, the modern superhero narrative and memoir are molded to ancient religious narratives and fantasy. As the integrity of each form is masked and thus questioned, a space of consubstantiality, or liminality, develops. Within this space, the cosmological plot of *Doctor Sax* is played out: human beings alienated from birth strive for knowledge of good and evil by seeking a sage who will deliver them the truth. In keeping with the typology of cosmology narratives, *Doctor Sax* employs two cataclysmic events to trigger this search: the surreal death of the watermelon man and the romantic Great Flood of 1936, both based on actual events in Kerouac's life. Prior to these events, Ti Jean has been aware of Doctor Sax's presence and had imitated him by playing the Black Thief Game, but the two have not communicated. With these two events, however, Ti Jean is thrown into a new realm of awareness, a hypersensitivity to death itself.

The death of the watermelon man recounts an experience Ti Jean and his mother have while returning home one evening from praying at the Lowell Grotto, a Catholic shrine of the Six Stations of the Cross that culminates with a large statue of the crucified Christ atop a small hill. "Everything there was to remind of Death, and nothing in praise of life—except the roar of the humpbacked Merrimac passing over rocks," Duluoz remembers; "I always liked to get out of there" (125–26). But Ti Jean, a thirteen-year-old who is happy to have escaped the Grotto, suddenly has his world ripped apart by the inexplicable sight of a man carrying a watermelon collapsing in death as he crosses the Moody Street Bridge. While utterly terrified, he still cannot restrain himself from looking: "I feel the profound pull and turn to see what he is staring at so deadly-earnest with his froth stiffness—I look down with him and there is the moon on shiny froth and rocks, there is the long eternity we have been seeking" (128). Ti Jean knows that it is "something private" that is carrying the man away, and while others on the scene think it worthwhile to call an ambulance, Ti Jean's mother knows differently: "*Non, sti'homme la est fini* [no, that man there is finished]" (128), and the stain on his pants, urination, the sign of his final act of life, convinces Ti Jean that the man is truly dead. Duluoz recognizes in his mother's wisdom something that the little boy does not: she does not prophesy death but rather possesses the "secret snaky knowledge about death," which he compares to fellaheen Mexican dogs, whose prescient barks signal death somewhere (129). Ti Jean, however, can only respond viscerally, shuddering, shivering, and hallucinating white flowers, the mystic sign of death (129). They head home, where he remains so afraid that he sleeps with his mother that night, "huddled against [her] great warm back [. . .] she wasn't afraid of any shade" (148). Angie Duluoz, a mother who has lost her first-born son to death, is herself a fellaheen like Doctor Sax—she knows and does not fear death.

As the plot builds toward the union of Ti Jean and Doctor Sax, this episode foreshadows several critical features in the cosmology. By sequencing the death of the man immediately after the frightening trip to the Grotto, the narrative implies that while the church teaches human beings to follow specific rituals of prayer to Christ for salvation, death itself cannot be thwarted and remains unfathomable. The church sends forth only empty rhetoric based on fallacious doctrines impotent to match the wisdom of fellaheen animal nature—that "secret snaky knowledge" to read the natural world with which Ti Jean's mother is gifted. In effect, the material world is a giant revolving talking book that speaks to her and other fellaheens.

Linking the snake of knowledge to his mother, Duluoz evokes the prehistoric chthonic power of the female and feminine symbolized by the snake, a feature of goddess-worshipping Neolithic cultures integrated into Mediterranean cultures as, for instance, the Minoan Snake Goddess, the

Oracle of Delphi, and the Greek goddess Hygeia, the latter being the patroness of healing and midwifery symbolized by the snake and still visible in the caduceus used as a logo for various medical associations.[5] Later Greek-influenced gnostic groups reconstructed this chthonic female power as Pista Sophia, representing the concept of "faith wisdom" or mysterious intellect. A few sects, such as the Ophites, retained within the Hebraic genesis story this interpretation of the serpent as the messenger of goodness who brings to Eve knowledge of the spurious nature of the Jewish god Yahweh. Others, African as well as Caribbean, still exhibit vestiges of the snake/female cosign of wisdom. Interestingly, the guiding principle that concludes Goethe's *Faust: Part 2* also conveys this ancient symbol. It is the eternal feminine or woman-soul ("*[D]as Ewig-Weibliche*") that signals the end after Gretchen and Faust have ascended into heaven; the lines "Woman Eternal / Draws us on high" embrace and inspire all human action. As Duluoz's modern reincarnation of the female wisdom principle, his mother embodies the long history of institutionalized knowledge seeking, first through religious practice and then through the scientific method. In this history, which long ago eradicated most credible signs of women's wisdom and power in the material world, she humbly reclaims that lost past by employing threads of history that converge in her ability both to read logically the physical evidence of the human body itself and to read prophetically the numinous signs of nature.

And it is her fellaheen folk wisdom that prophesizes even greater tragedy. "*Regard, la face de skalette dans la lune!*" (129), she cries as she and her son leave the dead watermelon man—language that figures imminent death. It is the moon that mirrors the death-masked face, and only a few days later, on March 12, Duluoz's fourteenth birthday, Lowell is struck by the worst flood to hit the town in more the twenty years, closing schools, leaving hundreds homeless, and causing damages of over $100,000. As the *Lowell Sun,* reported in an extra front-page story headlined "River Runs Wild," "Lowell shuddered to the drive of a mighty ice-strewn river tonight, as a raging Merrimack thundered down from the hills with the greatest water flowage to be recorded here since 1896." At first Ti Jean associates this tragedy with the death of the watermelon man and his mother's reading of the moon. However, Duluoz later identifies Doctor Sax as the prophet of the flood coming in the form of the Great Snake (151, 155). Thus Sax's supernatural powers are merged with female power, Ti Jean's fantasies of magic flying doves, and the Great Snake that like a giant sea monster is churning through town (an image not unlike those used by *Lowell Sun* reporters). Provocatively, however, the flood is not introduced through realistic Depression-era childhood memories entwined with comic-book fantasy. Rather, a collage of prose and poems that evokes medieval and Renaissance literature and myth incorporating haiku and the American vernacular disrupts the historically focused narrative to present Ti Jean's internal world, in which the flood signifies immanent physical manhood, high romance, lost love, literary quests, and secrets of the universe.

This rupture is established by a brief sentimental narrative of a young boy mourning the loss of his lover as he stares into the "fairyplace" source of the Merrimac River (156). The story within the story, punctuated with crude sexual descriptions that humanize it, turns Goethe's Faust into a defeated lover without the magic to hold his Gretchen, who, instead of dying tragically because he has seduced her, has stood him up for a more masculine beau, Rolfo Butcho. In despair, the lad throws into the river a rose that he had intended for her. A medieval symbol of romantic love and sexual passion as well as the pure love of Christ and Kerouac's St. Theresa, the rose travels downstream and through time, pulled by waters transformed into the power of language, or "the poems of night." Time in this metaphoric realm becomes a product of human linguistics, and it is this imaginative ability to see roses in rivers that reshapes the prose of courtly romance into two poems (156).

A result of this conversion of prose to poetry is the abandonment of Ti Jean Duluoz as narrator(s) in favor of "anonymous"—the unidentified although distinctly Kerouacian—speaker who presents the two poems as a kind of Goethean Walpurgisnacht, a magical space that eludes verifiable observation and certification as material reality. Thematically, the poems speak not to natural disaster as the work of God or mundane human activities, but rather to the interpretation of such disasters. This becomes the common thread that erases false markers in the name of history. In tandem, the poems reside within the full narrative as conspicuously secularized visions—sublimely lofty and comically grotesque—of the nature and impact of human activity. In this sense, the poem interlude mirrors Doctor Sax's talking book, envisions the conclusion of the narrative, and unmasks the entire novel as poetic wisdom literature.

In this service, the first poem, titled "The Poems of the Night," portrays the rose flowing through the waters of time in language that combines styl ized romantic vocabulary (e.g., "harp," "golden hero," "heavens," "Golden Rose," "adamantine," "so doth"), nonsense words (e.g. "froosures," "ang," "mam-mon,"), onomatopoeia (e.g., "ringalaree," "rang a dang"), colloquialisms (e.g., "chaw," "crud," "fritters") and actual historical place and group names (e.g., "Manchester," "Pittsburgh Pirates"). Sometimes structured as free verse, the poem has a wonderful Goethean quality projected through crude rhymes or doggerel, such as "Dabbely doo, dabbely dey, / The ring has got the crey," (157), which can be read as rough equivalents of Goethe's verse, in German called *knuttelvers,* that emphasize the feeling and sound of the lines rather than the poet's mastery or any didactic, prophetic, or other such theme. The first six stanzas establish an ethereal watery world, in which Sax and a Mr. Rain shroud the earth. These are followed by ten haikulike poems arranged in two columns of five each. Featuring highly symbolic language, these poems in shape and theme reveal the texture of the universe in flood: golden rose, lark, lute, mist, rain, ice floes, falls, eyes of eagles, angels with wet wings, the whistle of an Arcadian fluke, all concluding with the pronouncement "Flaws in Heaven / Are no Pain" (158), a promise that human suffering does not exist in the afterlife. The next eight stanzas, each only two to three lines long, focus on Sax and Beelzabadoes (a neologism for Beelzebub) comically dancing the polka as the floodwaters rise. The last six assume a more serious tone, although the unpatterned rhymes sustain an innocent singsong quality as the lyric voice watches the discarded rose riding the Merrimac like a knight on horseback until the flood is swallowed by eternity, leaving behind only rain and rainbow and heaven.

The message of the survival of the natural world in the face of cataclysmic events is repeated in "The Song of the Myth of the Rainy Night," which contains eleven stanzas, ten of which are each two to four lines long; the third-to-last stanza consists of twelve lines. The speaker also employs doggerel, singing the words of what one can interpret as multiple voices. Kerouac's placement of quotation marks creates considerable ambiguity, so the poem appears to incorporate the voice of the rose itself that takes responsibility for the flood and the voice of someone that could be again the rose, or either Doctor Sax or an unidentified speaker from beyond. In this choral construct, a voice sings a Dovist song claiming that the snake is merely a husk of doves and bursts into pronouncements regarding "poor life" as "paranoid gain / hassel, hassel, hassel / man in the rain / 'Mix with the bone melt! / Lute with the cry! / So doth the rain blow down / From all heaven's fantasy.'" (162). These stanzas ring as disembodied artifice, the source and name of which remains ineffable, although *hassel* may be word play alluding to the Times Square junkie Herbert Huncke who appears in *On the Road* as Elmo Hassel, a macabre ghost of Beat despair, victimization, freedom, and endurance that Sal and Dean pursue. This intertextual link intimates that the "man in the rain" is a further troping of the Shrouded Traveler as wisdom teacher. What remains certain, however, is the human belief in heaven and the futility of human perception of life as progress, that is, "gain."

With the same abruptness that launched the poetic interlude, the narrative reverts to more realistic accounts of Ti Jean's memories of the flood, setting the scene for Duluoz's explication of the cosmos's first cause. Initially, he and his friends consider the flood extremely good fortune, gleefully watching the river rise and hoping that the dreary world of adult routine will be destroyed (171). After the flood destroys his father's printing shop, though, he sees it as an evil monster that acts gratuitously. But from hindsight Duluoz applies a more complicated, although not necessarily more accurate, Spenglerian interpretation of the event, describing it as "hopeless, gray, dreary, nineteen-thirty-ish, lostish [. . .] that can't possibly come back again in America and history, the gloom of the unaccomplished mudheap civilization when it gets caught with its pants down from a source it long lost contact with" (180). This source in Spengler's philosophy is the deep-seated need for freedom that exists in all that is a microcosm, which he identified as "beat and direction," "being," or that which separates "itself from the All and can define its position with respect to the All" (vol. 2, 4). In humans as microcosms, this desire is combined with "waking consciousness" or "tension and extension," the forces creating a conflict between existence and consciousness, misleading humans to believe they control history (vol. 2, 7). In *Doctor Sax*'s cosmology, the modern American man-in-the-gray-flannel-suit, "the City Hall golf politicians and clerks," believe they control All (180). Without the imagination to see the universe as it is, they find nature a mere inconvenience and are thus caught in its swirling web.

The falsity of this egotistical gray-flannel belief is revealed in the last section of *Doctor Sax,* which begins with the lull after the flood, a prelude to the climactic event of the cosmology: the great battle between Doctor Sax and the Snake. The prelude focuses on idyllic trips that Ti Jean and his sister take to the library and the movies, as well as their fantasies of food. It is a celebration of life that in the larger cosmological scheme suggests that mortal pleasures must be acknowledged and used if the imagination is to lead one toward greater wisdom. And indeed it does for Ti Jean, who, while a happy boy, lives with memories of impending doom, which serve as catalysts for his meeting with his sage and divine protector, Doctor Sax, who holds the key to personal and universal knowledge. Ti Jean does not question the source of his supernatural power to call forth Sax (27), and it is the wiser Duluoz who describes Ti Jean's powers as the seduction of personal pleasure: "something secretively wild and baleful in the glares of the child soul, the masturbatory surging triumph of the knowledge of reality," for which he searches (102).

As the liminal mind constructed by the fusion of the two, Ti Jean Duluoz configures knowledge somewhat differently: it is the fusion of the egotistical belief that one can acquire knowledge of reality and the humble realization that acquiring such knowledge is an ontological impossibility, a literary device that portends the denouement of the tale. For instance, once Ti Jean and Sax finally meet, the shadowy hero in Faustian fashion says he will explain "the mysteries" (194) to the boy. The two then depart on fantastic rides through the night sky of Lowell. Equipped with knowledge of all that is happening in the town, they encounter fantasy creatures and humans, including a "great dark eagle" and Ti Jean's friend Gene Plouffe, who is lying in bed reading. Ti Jean senses that the world is turned upside down, that he and Doctor Sax have "lost all contact with irresponsibility," a rewording of the common expression implying that the oddity of their imaginative state is a responsible way to proceed toward wisdom (195). In a swirl of night and day magically dissolving into and out of each other, Ti Jean listens as Doctor Sax counsels him on the future, predicting that the boy will come to know death in a world ruled by human time that is the creator of civilization. His prophetic voice maps out Ti Jean's life, warning that he will never be as happy as his fourteen-year-old "quilt-ish innocent book-devouring immortal night" self (202–03). The passage also again emphasizes the difference between Sax and other Faustian figures that disparage book learning. Sax presents the practice of literacy as the center and the best time of a young boy's life—a place apart in which one experiences the transformational power of language.

Moreover, Sax declares that the Snake and the Dovists will be destroyed on this night, explaining to the perplexed Ti Jean that he must approach all similar ventures in life with an innocence rooted in the wisdom of one's inner voice. "Listen to your *own* self—it ain't got nothing to do with what's around you," says Sax using the vernacular and metaphoric to make his point. "It's what you do inside at the controls of that locomotive crashing through your life" (211). In Sax's presence, Ti Jean begins to shed the hubris that has convinced him that he has supernatural powers and becomes more objectively humble as he observes the people of Lowell going about their lives, particularly his mother and sister reveling in mundane activities of shopping and chitchatting. Now armed with humility and affirmation of self, Ti Jean next follows Sax to Snake Hill and the Castle, where the two traverse layers of Dantesque worlds filled with centipedes, spiders, slithering snakes, and a phantasm of other grotesqueries. Even the landscape sheds its lamblike mask to emerge as the Great Snake of evil. These are unmistakably boyhood demons, though, and not the contemporary grotesque specters of human nature, such as those Burroughs created in Interzone totalitarianism or even those Kerouac conveyed through Dean Moriarty in *On the Road* or Mardou Fox in *The Subterraneans*. The demons in this castle, symbolizing the human mind and material world, remain terrifying only to the adolescent—the characterization of Sax as a whimsical parody of pop culture heroes ameliorating any resemblance the creatures have to contemporary human life. When consolidated, these highly didactic passages reify and situate within the natural rather than supernatural human subject Kerouac's belief in the fundamental goodness of human beings, the natural world as *not* malevolent, and the supremacy of the individual self—the last point being a contradiction that Kerouac's nondualistic construction of the universe persistently undermines.

The remainder of the narrative synthesizes elements of biblical, Mesoamerican, Faustian, and Spenglerian fantasy and philosophy to establish childlike innocence and imagination as the source of wisdom and truth. The cosmic battle between good and evil is endowed with some of Spengler's evidence signifying the crumbling of civilization, or a kind of apocalypse: the rise of dictators, coups, and civil wars. The Wizard's minions attempt a coup, the Dovists declare that the Snake will not destroy the world, one of the Count's subordinates recognizes the evil of those who believe in the devil, and Ti Jean is gifted with the vision to see within the Castle layers of people living in ignorance of the horror taking place around them. Judgment Day is here, Sax decrees, and Ti Jean recoils in fear.

At this critical juncture, Sax turns his sights on religion, yelling "God offers man in the palm of his hand dove-like seminal love, embowered" (237). The Dovists view him joyfully as their liberator, and Ti Jean, no longer worried about his own safety, expresses distress for the people of Lowell (237–38). Additionally armed now with concern for others, Ti Jean faces the Snake, and in the novel's most important passage narrated through the wisdom of the older Duluoz, he learns that the Snake is neither nature nor a huge cosmological force distinct from himself but, in a Neoplatonic-and-Buddhist-influenced lexicon, "the void [. . .] the Dark [. . .] IT," the all beyond the illusion of thingness. "IT" is his "mad-face demon mirror of [him]self." Now he knows that the Snake is indeed coming for him—in other words, an individual subject's subjectivity is *un*avoidable, and it is that very self that creates its fear of death (238; Johnson 24).

In effect, this logic, which is the certainty that the self is its own creator, the one who brings into being the myth of the dualistic universe itself, means that Sax's efforts to destroy the Snake must ultimately fail, because if he succeeded, he would be destroying all human life. Thus with equanimity and humility, stripped of his superhero clothing, Sax materializes as an elder W. C. Fields/Gary Cooper/Old Bull Hubbard type, an intellectual, clown, and cowboy actor wrinkled with humor and resigned to death and living with the presence of evil. Young Ti Jean, however, remains ego-bound and persists in wanting to know why humans have to live this way. As if in answer to his dogged childhood perseverance, he and all others are spared final annihilation thanks to the descent of a large black bird with hooded beak surrounded by hordes of white doves, little Italian *pippiones* with gorgeous feathers of Heaven called Bird of Paradise, that scoop up the Snake and carry it up into the clouds. "I'll be damned [. . .] The Universe disposes of its own evil!" Sax marvels (245). Ti Jean, blissfully carrying within him the seeds of knowledge that Duluoz will later come to know in more rational terms, happily walks home, finding and discovering two roses that he puts in his hair. Duluoz also notes that several times since that day he has seen Doctor Sax, whom he now associates with the happiness of children playing in the idyllic autumn dusk.

This imagery of the novel's conclusion is baroque in its lushness and medieval in its symbolism—a fecund text for a multiplicity of readings. But it cannot be stressed enough that in this cataclysmic ending *no one dies*. Sax and Ti Jean survive, the Wizard survives, the Dovists survive, and even the Snake itself survives, kicking and screaming but alive as it is transported into the "bedazzling blue hole of heaven" (244), a site where theistic mythologies contend that no one dies. In this deathless world, a set of readings resides compatibly with Kerouac's evolving concept of human nature and the universe. First, as already noted, the cosmology disturbs the conventional dichotomy of good and evil. All the major figures, including human beings, incorporate vestiges of both. Even the Snake, portrayed most consistently as the incarnation of evil, possesses elements of the good, initially through the Dovist/gnostic belief that the Snake will not destroy the world but will instead give metaphoric birth to thousands of doves, and secondly through its transcendence into heaven. There is even a third indicator of the Snake's hidden goodness, in that his apocalyptic disturbance of earth is accompanied by doves and the great black bird. As they ferry him away, he is fused with them into a feathered serpent akin to the Toltecan and Aztecan symbol of goodness and civilization as well as the Christian symbol of peace and everlasting life. In the composite structure of a feathered serpent of goodness, the Great Snake of the World refutes orthodox Christian dualism, the Mesoamerican and Christian barbarism of human sacrifice, and the passivity inherent in Spengler's vision of the cycles of history. These can be stripped of their power if the universe is understood in its holistic process of permanent impermanence, the circular, repetitive nature of life. The conflation of bird and serpent transforms the serpent from a masculine signifier of evil into an ancient symbol (gnostic and classical) of female fertility, positive knowledge, and the continuity of life. The lineage allows one to understand the Snake as an ancient object of life-generating salvation. The Snake's quasi resurrection and salvation (it assumes a likeness to both Jesus and Faust in its ascent into heaven) consequently signal triumph over the devil's best efforts, but neither the power of a god nor the sacrifice of God's son effects this victory. Human salvation resides instead within the human mind, a great, all-encompassing unity.

Kerouac relied only on "heaven" with a lowercase "h" to name this unity in the conclusion of *Doctor Sax,* but terms such as "One," "All," "Void," "Eternity," "World Soul," and "God" appear frequently enough, with or without the initial uppercase, in Kerouac's private journals and literary publications to validate an interpretation of "heaven" as a signifier of the universe's blended nature. But even without this label, *Sax* directs itself toward such a conclusion. Textual signifiers eluding stable signification through twinning and retwinning of characters and imagery undermine the notion of the universe as discrete, firm, and knowable Spenglerian microcosms. Contrarily, the text shifts and reshifts to blend component parts into holistic union, most overtly effecting this end through the Faust trope. Faust as superman, for instance, slips in and out of Sax as a character, to Ti Jean, to Duluoz, to the Snake, to the Count, to Emil and Angie Duluoz; from an evil, flawed character to a paragon of tenacity, a model of childhood fantasy, adult wisdom, humble resignation, and defeat. The Castle is a site of slippage as well, vacillating among childhood fantasy, home of historical Lowell personages, center of the universe, salvation, Kerouac's personal dream, a common metonymy of monarchical rule, and a symbol of the universe as multilayered.

The instability of these forms blends Mesoamerican, Neoplatonic, gnostic, Buddhist, and Judeo-Christian folk myth and religious doctrines, making it impossible to claim that Sax supports any one tradition more strongly than another. For instance, one can argue that Sax revises the orthodox Christ myth, but the absence of a personal, masculine transcendent god who sacrifices his son does not simply revise but nullifies that myth. The omission of human sacrifice in the Toltecan and Aztecan myth undermines the heart of that tradition as well. The belief in salvation as separate from human efforts, signified by the sudden appearance of the dark bird, contends the Buddhist understanding of human effort and practice as central to release from false human desires. The Christian belief in grace, another version of faith in the universe and a personal god, is itself undermined by the narrative's concentration on the individual human imagination as the source of final wisdom. The Buddhist concept of samsara (the endless repetition of birth, life, death, and rebirth) is negated by fantasy, comedy, and parody that dominate the text. Feminine elements of gnostic and goddess cultures are evident but not strong enough to overcome the pervasive masculine character of the tale. The gnostic repudiation of church doctrine and the sanctity of Jewish scripture are critiqued by the text's final testimony to faith in the material universe overall rather than an individual's quest for knowledge. Likewise the gnostic, Jewish, and Christian beliefs in the evil or flawed nature of corporality are negated by the way the cosmology situates such doctrinal notions as falsities created and perpetuated by human intellect. Christian and Judaism are negated by the absence of any kind of real heaven, hell, or purgatory to which the human soul eventually goes.

Perhaps the philosophy that comes closest in some respects to the Sax cosmology is that of Plotinus (ca. 204–70 CE), whose philosophical theology, now known as the Enneads, bridges Platonic thought and Augustinian Christianity and whose work Raymond Weaver recommended that Kerouac and Ginsberg read while attending Columbia (Nicosia 139). Plotinus's vision of God, the unchangeable Absolute Unity that produces the Soul of the World, from which emanates the human soul and subsequently the human body, resonates with Kerouac's notion of a philosophy that nullifies the duality of heaven and human. Evil according to Plotinus cannot come

from the perfect and unchangeable One but is explained as either a subjective interpretation of human actions or the absence of order as matter moves
farther from the principle of rationality (Stumpf 132–38). Plotinus did not
consider matter evil per se, nor does *Sax*, but *Sax* makes no claim that
rationality is the good. Plotinus was also concerned about the salvation of
the human spirit, which he believed developed slowly through the
Aristotelian virtue of moderation guiding the moral and the intellectual:
right thinking and right conduct. In *Sax*, the righteousness of this path is
dispelled by the conclusion that the universe takes care of itself, with or
without human intervention.

Ultimately, *Sax* is a cosmology story in which the universe is an optical
illusion, and not the "illusion" of Buddhist definition. Rather, *Sax* renders
the universe complexly as a fixed optical construction that, because of its
composite parts, the brain recognizes as an ever-shifting phenomenon of
multiple shapes. The best example is the well-known Necker cube from
gestalt psychology, depicted below,

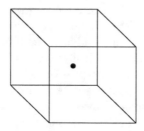

that, no matter how long one looks at it, continuously shifts orientation.
This is exactly what *Sax* does, cradling and foregrounding one form—the
self-regulating universe as blended oneness, in which everything emanates in
illusionary form—and then another—the universe as the sole creation of the
solitary human mind. In this literary "Necker cube," neither the supremacy
of the individual nor the ineluctable unity is negated completely and perma-
nently. In fact, the text concludes with two cryptic bylines that encode this
message of a pulsating universe. The first reads "By God," and the second
"Written in Mexico City, / Tenochtitlan, 1952 / Ancient Capital / Of Azteca"
(245). The former states that a supreme being has created the entire published narrative and the cosmology. The second, a passive voice construction
that does not identify the author, alludes to a human rather than metaphysical presence through the specificity of compositional location—the exact
city, year, and history of the geographical site all markers of human presence
and human civilization based on time, as Sax prophesied. The second, then,
directs one to Sax, Ti Jean, Duluoz, and finally Kerouac.

The "God" reference, however, can also be a construction of human imagination, so within that phrase the individual also resides. Likewise, the absence of attribution in the last passage signals an unknown or mysterious author, a force of life connecting all things through, and thus negating, time. The two passages constitute a dialectical polarity *and* the very obliteration of that polarity, within which resides the message that the universe is a flickering reality of the A/all and the O/one, in which the subject must die and the subject must live. The narrative assures one that this knowledge is attainable through belief in the imagination and the life force itself. Duluoz himself states it more poetically and mystically: those who enter eternity "without me—my end is as far from his as eternity—Eternity hears hollow voices in a rock? Eternity hears ordinary voices in the parlor. On a bone the ant descends" (105). With the medieval "bone," also meaning prayer, Duluoz announces that there is no mystery to eternity. It is the material world into which one descends—on the bone of the body or the bone of imagination. Once this is known, life can be claimed for all the joys and sorrows it offers.[6]

CHAPTER 5

THE QUEST—PART II:
SOME OF THE DHARMA

Some of the Dharma, posthumously published in 1997, records Kerouac's intense study of Buddhism from 1953 through 1956. The collection of over 400 pages, which began in December 1953 as notes Kerouac constructed to introduce Ginsberg to the topic (*Dharma* x), evolved from an eclectic mix of bibliography and translations into the working out of aesthetic and spiritual theories. Kerouac completed *Dharma* on March 15, 1956, but since *Dharma* is such a newly available—and odd—text in comparison with most of his literary production, Kerouac scholars have yet to devote much attention to it, and while some reviewers praised the book for its beautiful narrative of a young man's quest—Tom Clark, in particular, highlighting its "bones of real suffering" and "a mercurial mimesis . . . in the emotional colors of the writing"—its postmodern form has drawn negative evaluations ranging from too impenetrable to "ersatz Buddhism from postwar America's most overrated author."[1] As with much of Kerouac's work, some reviewers also tended to emphasize passages in which he comments on his drinking and distrust of women.[2] But *Dharma* provides a rich source of material regarding Kerouac's vision of himself as writer, scholar, and spiritual leader at the height of his writing powers. Perhaps more importantly, it is a fascinating example of the artistic vision through which twentieth-century wisdom can be forged and disseminated, and it represents, as does *Doctor Sax,* Kerouac's syncretic vision. Granted, *Dharma* includes the proviso that Kerouac intended to eschew even Buddha and Jesus as he probed the ultimate mystery himself, to avoid a "syncretically re-developed" religion, and to find an answer that embraces truth as Emptiness "without Tathagatas or Holy Ghosts of any kind" (178). Despite the disclaimer, *Dharma* reads as the attempted reconciliation of contradictory principles from a number of religious and other traditions, the whole consistent with the metaphysical and ontological beliefs Kerouac had been developing.

To craft *Dharma,* Kerouac worked with an eclectic set of materials as diverse as *Summa Theologica,* the Surangama Sutra, *Ecclesiastes,* and passages from Thomas Wolfe, Frank Sinatra, Edgar Cayce, and his own journals. The result is perhaps the closest he came to creating a truly rhizomatic text, one with hundreds of starting points exposing its many sources through circles, swerves, and truncated paths. Its ultimate message constitutes a literary echo of the Buddha, who is reported in the Surangama Sutra to have proclaimed, "To attain wisdom, you must practice mindfulness and concentration of mind in *Dhyana* [Sanskrit for "meditation"] for many, many *kalpas*" (Goddard 196). Since a *kalpa* in ancient Indian traditions is a period of some hundreds of millions of years, the prospect of a quick fix in Buddhism is a moot point, particularly when compared to the immediacy of Christian conversion, baptism, and life after death. The conclusion of *Dharma* itself suggests this teaching. No great "truth" saves its author; no grand epiphany or teleological finale of surcease triumphs. Unlike the narratives of Jesus's crucifixion and resurrection, Paul's conversion experience on the road to Damascus, or St. Augustine's confessions, *Dharma* spins more like a wheel, returning again and again to declarations of the All, the existence of reality as "dream," and the unspeakable reality beyond language and dualism. It repeats, as do Buddhist sutras, lessons of cause and conditions, which are the basic tenets of the belief system. In a sense, *Dharma* can do little else since the Buddhist truth is knowable only through daily practice and long devotion to it—not simply through human desire or the reading of scripture. This approach may frustrate readers, but if one is willing to trust Kerouac's fusion of form, content, method, practice, and belief, reading *Dharma* can be a pleasurable experience and affirmation that his Buddhism was more than Beat whim.

Identifying *Dharma* by conventional literary genres is nearly impossible. It fits neatly into few singularly recognizable categories, thus confounding the distinction between its author and narrators which at times appear clearly as Kerouac and at other times Duluoz. At first glance, *Dharma* appears to be Kerouac's religious studies notebook, an apprehension that is not altogether incorrect. Like many students, Kerouac used the notebooks to preserve important ideas from primary and secondary sources, recording passages of significance from Goddard's *Bible* and texts from the Harvard Oriental Series and the Pali Text Society. He defined key terms, which were accompanied with his annotations, interpretations, and comments. For example, *epiphany* he parsed as "(from EPI, upon, PHAINO, I appear) means manifestations"; "gnosis" he defined and annotated as "metaphysical introversion, apocalyptic certainty, which Jesus, Allah and all the Tathagatas have" (43). He also made concerted efforts to reconcile Catholic precepts with his own spiritual and physical needs, while refuting those precepts in accord with arguments he was reading. An etymological history of the Indian word *karuna* (translated as "compassion") and the Greek work *agape* (meaning "selfless love" or "unconditional love") achieves this end, in minute detail splitting and suturing the definitions to identify their similarities and differences (130). To distinguish Buddhism from Christianity, he reworded the first line of the Gospel of John to transform a declarative sentence into the rhetorical question, "In the beginning was the word, and the word was made 'God' but as to essence what can you say of it?" He thus undercut Christian belief in monotheism by implicitly discriminating between the One and the false "god" who made earth (184).

This stance, cradling both gnostic and Buddhist potentiality, is exemplified in a short, lopsided pyramid-shaped text that plays with the notions of reality as both illusion and Aquinian proofs. Much like Aquinas's efforts to prove the existence of God, Kerouac began with what appears to be precise mathematical logic ("43 x, equals 392 means x, equals 9.11"), deducing that "to prove my existence you have first to prove proof, which is just what it sounds like—POOF!"—an illusion (235). The exercise is a humorous and literary exercise in logic that reveals the false nature of human sign systems. A textually unusual variant of this method, at least for Kerouac, is his treatment of the Buddhist concept of the Five Defilements: individuation of form, false views of form, desire for form, grasping at form, and imagining conflicts between forms. To apply this teaching, he created "FIVE DEFILE-MENTS OF TIGER AND ME," a two-column text, much like a reader-response notebook in which one copies a passage in one column and then comments on it in the other. In the left-hand column, he applied the concept of arbitrary conception to the tiger, and in the right-hand column, to himself, the composite demonstrating that all sentient beings live equally according to the principle of the perceiving mind (104).

But *Dharma* is more than a notebook for a course in comparative religions or Buddhist philosophy. It is also a writer's notebook, and as such, Kerouac used it to experiment with different voices and genres, writing his own proverbs and maxims, such as "Vest made for flea will not fit elephant" (344) and "But we use words to get free from words until we reach the pure wordless Essence" (330), as well as numerous stories and poems, some of which he labels "great" (128), some critiqued in detail, and many standing alone as interpretations of Buddhist wisdom. As a writer's notebook, *Dharma* also evaluates other writers in relationship to Kerouac himself as a Buddhist writer—an identity eventually compelling him to reject authoring literature itself, the "awful abstract 'I' of writing," as he called it, which produces nothing but continual egoistic suffering (221). Giving voice to inner conflicts regarding writing, however, did not stop him from defining his own literary genres, including tics, pops, and bookmovies, and the notebooks routinely served as a crucible to generate and store material, such as "found" poems and wisdom sayings, especially from Neal and Carolyn Cassady's children.

A writer's notebook is usually an exceedingly private artifact, a meditation or diary intended for the author only (Hunt, "Jack Kerouac" 233). The *Dharma* notebooks seemed to have functioned similarly: Kerouac as the primary reader carried on a dialogue with himself, displaying his fears, misdeeds, flaws, and desires as one does in a personal journal. In staunch Yankee fashion he regarded, like a Benjamin Franklin or a Jay Gatsby, the notebooks as commonplace books in which to record notes on daily events. Resolutions such as "One meal a day / No drinking of intoxicants / No maintaining of friendships" (127) are repeated throughout. Many, as this one exemplifies, draw on standard novice monastic precepts (e.g., don't eat past noon and non intoxicants), while deviating with personalization to fit his own needs (e.g., no friendships). Dominant themes encompass his unfathomable love for his mother, arguments with his friends, difficulties understanding women, a determination to teach others, and struggles to find peace and wisdom. The poems, prayers, and more standard dated journal entries record the story of his three-year labor to attain Buddhist ideals: his gut-wrenching practice of trying to live according to the Buddha's Eightfold Path and his sincere efforts to meditate to achieve enlightenment. Analogous to the sanctity of the confessional in a Catholic church, his writing lays bare the emotional journey he took to modify his egoistic needs within the parameters of Buddhist teachings. The private world created in the journal is inhabited by a young American man who had chosen not only the Yankee approach to journal writing but also what Alan Watts called the "Yankee" approach to Buddhism, electing to go full force along the hardest of roads, thus making the process alienatingly difficult for himself. As both private journal and common daybook, *Dharma* becomes, as Kathleen Fraser describes the genres, "a private receptacle for distilled observation something not so finished and official as a poem, yet a site for close reading of the subject (the shifting self . . .)" (152–74.)

Finally, and here is where the discursive character of *Dharma* becomes most problematic (or intriguing, depending on one's inclinations), the notebooks are public discourse, but not the kind most easily recognizable or accessible to contemporary Americans. Since Kerouac was set upon the mission of creating a new kind of writing "for the sake of an American Dharma," presumably the spread of Buddhism in the United States that would "not kowtow to established cupidities nor at the same time be a piddling Notebook" (255), conventional forms of literary communication had to be replaced by American versions of the sutras, origin stories, and wisdom sayings. These he would compile in "[a] large loose book, built as solidly as a Bronze Statue of the Seated Champion of Samadhi and yet containing images & ideas as ethereal and magical as the jewel in the lotus" (255). As a uniquely structured spiritual communiqué to America, *Dharma* is filled with pronouncements about the meaning of life and human activity. These are often brief declarations, such as "Happiness won't come from coddling the senses but from cultivating the mind" (93), or imperatives, sometimes rather witty, such as "Noxzema and Peanut Butter are of the same intrinsic nature, but for the purposes of life on earth dont go tasting them to compare; leave that to non-discriminating infants fresh from eternity" (35). However, many lengthier texts, often titled to address a "you" other than Kerouac himself, constitute much of the teacherly voice, by relying on a hypostatized omniscient point of view stripping Kerouac of his conversational, spontaneous garb to clothe him in the robes of the Buddhist sage, Christian prophet, or existential philosopher. For example, "AREMIDEIA AND THE PARACLETE: Religious Fancies for Western Believers" and "LETTER TO BEVERLY: A Buddhist Letter," while pertaining to Kerouac's personal quest, evoke the presence of silent others, the former through the subtitle "For Western Believers" aimed at the masses and the latter through its title and its greeting, "Dear Bev, " a most personal of devotees.

"AREMIDEIA," the text that introduces this volume, draws extensively on the first- and second-person perspectives to discuss the question "Am I or am I not God?" the "I" signifying not only Kerouac but also any "Western believer," whom the narrator lectures using biblical language that resonates, as does the following, with prophetic tones created by repetition, parallelism, inversion, and coordinated syntax: "But that you will fear about death, this is a grief; that you will die of pain, that is the truth" (44). The "I" and "you" incorporating both Kerouac and the reader are appropriate for the lesson's conclusion that there is no distinction between "I" and "you," both of which are Paraclete the Comforter—God and the All (45). The "Letter to Beverly" also uses "I" and "you," but the discursive structure directs readers to interpret the "I" as the historical "Jack Kerouac" and the "you" as his real friend Beverly Burford, with whom he had a relationship in 1950. Interestingly, though, the letter lacks a signature, suggesting that one cannot assume the author to be Kerouac but that it might be his fictional persona Duluoz. Kerouac's language in "Letter" is also more intimate and conversational than in "AREMIDEIA," the "I" that attempts "to explain the Teaching of the Buddhas of Old to you [Bev]" (205) drifting in and out of relational proximity to his audience and at times effecting the persona of distinguished teacher but also reassuring Bev that he is her equal, sensing the difficulty of the lessons he presents. At one point, he confesses that if his ideas confuse her it is because the material itself is "the highest and final TEACHING" and the narrator himself is still "very profound[ly] ignoran[t]" (209). The search for one's divinity, he implies, is a long, long journey grounded in the practice of attempting to teach others.

Dharma's narrative voices and the readers addressed by these voices extend the narrative personas that fill the pages of earlier texts, such as the *Windblown World* journals and Kerouac's private correspondence—an "I" in dialogue with a "you" sometimes imagined, sometimes a shadow of Kerouac, sometimes his critics, and sometimes recognizable friends and family. The mercurial or unstable presence of signifieds and signifiers confounds the consistent construction of an author-reader relationship. The public nature of the text, existing along with private discourse, contributes to *Dharma's* perplexing constitution, making it difficult to negotiate one's relationship to it. Should, for instance, one approach it like a standard collection of private letters and journals that most readers conventionally consider primary documents not to be enjoyed for their imaginative capacities but for the information they reveal regarding persons of note? If so, then the narrator can be considered Jack Kerouac, and the narrative distance between himself and the narrative voices shrinks dramatically. But should readers assume that they are the ones Kerouac intends to teach and thus pay close attention to his argument and conclusions? If so, narrative credibility resides more precisely in a reader's efforts to construct momentarily stable understandings of who narrates, to whom, and why.

The ostensibly precarious apparatus bridging the private and the public in *Dharma* is not merely a rhetorical chimera generated by posthumous publication but exists in the history of the book, which substantiates its artistic integrity, the constructed nature of the artifact. The published version of *Dharma* is not the Beat publication of primary materials—that is, the personal letters, spontaneously crafted poetry, or the personal journals that have become through these writers' own efforts a signature of the Beat ethos.[3] Nor is it the result of estates and publishers posthumously bringing into print unshaped materials that the author deemed unready for publication or that the publisher reshaped via a ghost editor, as in the still controversial case of Ernest Hemingway's *The Garden of Eden*. Kerouac's correspondence with Ginsberg and Gary Snyder clarifies that he intended *Dharma* to be a teaching tool (*Letters* 1: 461, 551), and the published text is in almost all respects a facsimile of the text that he intended to publish.

The book began within eleven breast-pocket notebooks, in which he composed and recorded Buddhist texts and thoughts. However, the early draft differs dramatically from the typescript, which he created by carefully typing each of the discrete texts, with all of their visual idiosyncrasies onto standard ($8 \times 11\frac{1}{2}$) sheets of bond paper.[4] The texts included in the typescript are not simply a retyping of what he composed in his notebooks, but rather a carefully constructed reformation of them. In the most general sense, the typescript contains pencil outlines, lines of demarcation made with asterisks and other typewriter symbols, squiggles, and images, including a dove on the last page drawn with what appears to be a black felt marker of some kind. Few of these marks characterize the notebooks. More specifically, when Kerouac composed the typescript he narrowed the focus, so that the book clearly begins with the Buddha's essential message: the Four Noble Truths and the Eightfold Path. On the contrary, the first *Dharma* notebook begins with an entry titled "MEMORY BABE Dec 9, 53," which sketches a memory of a black dice cup from a Parcheesi set that Kerouac played with as a child, the tiny cardboard cup functioning like a magic crystal ball in which his past materializes. In the haze of language, he concludes that "the Wheel of Life is riddled with the mystery of objects like these, that rise to memory like shiverings in the chest" (Dharma 1 Notebook 4). The "Memory Babe" passages are beautifully written, but one can assume that Kerouac might have rejected them as the introduction for *Dharma* because as memoir they are thematically only tangentially related to his Buddhist work—they appear nowhere in the typescript.

As this example illustrates, Kerouac culled material from the notebooks and other sources, rearranging the pieces to build a coherent text. He even revised material as he selected and retyped it, as is the case with "IMLADA THE SAGE: A Little Tale by Jean-Louis," which appears in book 1 of the published text. The composition history of this story exemplifies extensive revision resulting in a published story that more precisely reflects Kerouac's personal and Western expectations for Buddhism than does its original version. In *Dharma,* "IMLADA" is preceded by a three-line platitude on the sadness of clinging to arbitrary conceptions of selfhood. The notebook version of "IMLADA" has no such title, emerging instead from a longer prescriptive entry about kindness and preceded by a formal introduction in which the speaker self-consciously announces that he is a man who has just begun his book of religious visions with a sentence of kindness. This sentence is followed by the opening line of the story, "In the honey-scented land of Mominu [. . .]" (37), which also introduces the subsequent typescript and published versions. In all three versions, the sage Imlada imparts the wisdom of kindness "to a former self of his, John Kerouac of America," who is struggling with despair (36). Kerouac, the former self, comprehends the message and achieves happiness. The "future" self, Imlada, perhaps a pseudonym for Duluoz, continues on his journey, begging for food, preaching, and meeting a companion named the Big Saint. The notebook version of the story, however, also features a figure named Carnee, a descendent of a race of huge, massive peoples, who is Imlada's wise teacher and the dominant character. Carnee was replaced in the typescript by the Big Saint to serve as Imlada's companion and subordinate.

The elimination of Carnee effects a radical reconstruction of the tale's conclusion, with the typescript and published versions culminating in the following closed rather than an open ending passage: "And the moon rose high, white, bright, and bats cried in the tree above Imlada's sleep, and little mice breathed and snored in the depths of the cactus grove" (37). All is harmony and peace in the brightness of night, but not so in the notebook, which features a more postmodern—and Buddhist—twist on the artifice of fictional and metaphysical closure. In this version, Imlada tells Carnee about crafting an idol and finding a cave bequeathed to him by a man whose name he cannot remember. Carnee replies with the Buddhist wisdom that such details need not be remembered since there is ultimately only one name, with isolated names and figures being interchangeable. The narrator then declares the story ended. However, this pronouncement is immediately followed by a metaphysical conundrum:

"The story is ended before it is begun, because the story is not in perfect, free, intrinsic, mysterious realization of everything at the same time everywhere forever, wrapt in the circle of Emptiness like as the circle around the moon, the hymn of the rim of the ride of the rain in the translucent jewel clear night permeated by crystals and snow blossoms and milky veins of the lotus and illuminated by the golden waterfall of the Lute of Heaven showering us in kindness."

Symbols of enlightenment, such as the jewel and the lotus, situate the narrative as an imperfect representation of cosmic unity—an illusion of "thingness" that is not the realization of "everything at the same time." The story must end "before it is begun" since it cannot by its very status as an illusion of the whole ever succeed in communicating the nature of the whole.

As with much ancient wisdom literature, it is unclear who authors this cryptic speech, but the quotation marks suggest that the source of the voice is closely connected to the omniscient narrator who serves as a mouthpiece for a transcendent font of truth. At this point, Carnee begins his own story about ignorantly trying to maintain power over his daughter, his gold, and his wine cellar. Imlada listens and simply thanks Carnee for what he has said. The Imlada story ends here at a subtle point in a circular process of teaching and listening, listening and teaching, which by inference never stops. This conclusion diverges philosophically from the typescript and published versions, in which Kerouac, through his multiple personas of author, narrator, and temporal forms of himself (past [John Kerouac the American] / present [Jean-Louis/Duluoz] / future [Imlada/Duluoz]), projects the desire for certitude onto a Buddhist tale.

The certitude expressed in the conclusion of the Imlada tale, however, is insufficient for a reader fond of or reliant upon such literary conventions. Blank spaces and the juxtaposition of thematically divergent texts repeatedly rupture the experience of imposing or discovering narrative or argumentative coherence between and among *Dharma* elements. Efforts to discern literary messages are thus stymied, and consequently readers may be tempted to skim *Dharma*, fishing for tidbits that strike them as readable, or they may read with tunnel vision—that is, the narrowed purpose of isolating particular themes, historical information, or other data relevant to Kerouac's personal and Beat history. In the process, *Dharma* can lose artistic integrity, becoming more like an encyclopedia or a scientific journal article from which we cull items for pragmatic purposes. But even so, what Kerouac accomplished by reconstructing his raw notebook materials was to force reconsideration of the form and function of conventional literary, philosophical, and spiritual paradigms.

This process is aided by a collection of visual forms that push readers to relinquish attachments to traditional and, as the text suggests, illusionary signifiers of truth. Tim Hunt has argued that Kerouac's dominant visual element was the style of the typewriter, Kerouac creating visual designs to "evoke the immediacy of the spoken voice" through "various juxtapositions and simultaneities" ("Jack Kerouac" 233). Hunt's theory well represents the whole of the Duluoz Legend, and granted, the typewriter is the major visual element in *Dharma*. But Kerouac's typewriterly constructions, while functioning as Hunt maintains, lead more directly in *Dharma* to the static presentation of intellectual and emotional content that has long characterized the studio arts, especially the modernist urge to reinvolve viewers in the visual media through the element of shock. Within this tradition, the visual quality of *Dharma* bridges and blurs popular or lowbrow culture and academic or highbrow culture, nodding toward the signature of spoken discourse (an intimate relationship between reader and author) but *embracing* the framed and distant objectified form of the sculpted word.

As a popular culture artifact, *Dharma*'s visual discourse most resembles the scrapbook, a mode of recording personal and family memorabilia that historians have traced back to the early 1800s in Germany and England.[5] A hybrid of artistic expression and recorded history, the scrapbook is a dominant popular form of amateur artistic expression, with nineteenth- and twentieth-century technologies making even the most artistically inept capable of snapping photographs, snipping greeting cards, writing annotations, and inexpensively preserving personal data. The design of the scrapbook is open-ended enough to provide flexible individual expression and yet is structured enough (e.g., preset spaces for photographs) for more mundane record keeping. One can paste and arrange items according to strict chronology or idiosyncratic whim.

Dharma appears to follow both. Kerouac's construction of many differently shaped texts; italics, asterisks, and dashes to set off texts from one another; amateurishly hand-drawn shapes; the seemingly baffling placement of dates (there is no discernible pattern to determine why certain entries are dated); and the equally nonsystematic attention to documentation all suggest the personal scrapbook meant for an audience of one or for only a few close confidants. The scrapbook quality of *Dharma* as popular art also connects it with memoir, the scrapbook being a kind of autobiography to preserve individual and community histories. As a viable companion of life writing, the scrapbook complements structural features of the Duluoz Legend overall.

Conversely, *Dharma* as high art most resembles collage. Collage fundamentally refers to a constructed form using various objects such as paper, fabric, and wood pasted onto a surface to create an aesthetic shape. All collages, including those made entirely of paper, are characterized by three-dimensionality, an extension out from the surface itself. The medium of collage extends back centuries to Japan, examples of it existing in the Middle East, Europe, and the United States from the mid-seventeenth century on. It took the modernists, however, to elevate collage, Georges Braques (1882–1963) and Pablo Picasso (1881–1973) most often receiving credit for legitimizing it as Western art, and by the early to mid fifties, collage was well integrated in U.S. visual and literary arts communities, including the Beat movement. Kerouac, for instance, is known to have collaged newspaper clippings of words and pictures into some of his texts, such as his notebook for *Book of Dreams,* and Burroughs also experimented extensively with collage on paper and film.[6]

What renders *Dharma* the character of collage is its intense focus on the visual form itself, directing attention to the book as architectural form and to the hand that constructed it. One can spend hours simply scanning the text as a linear construction of 420 canvases (pages) on which hieroglyphic shapes are organized in lines, columns, trapezoids, and other geometric shapes juxtaposed with blank spaces, typewriter insignia, or handwritten annotations. In this sense, *Dharma* is discourse that dissolves into and out of visual patterns.[7] The reading or decoding of these images can legitimately take place as purely visual signifieds that demand interpretation within the boundaries of the canvases itself. Each canvas (or single page) is viewed within its own frame, but each is also double framed with the overarching frame of the individual book (composed of eleven sections) in which the page appears, as well as tripled-framed by the construct of the book's front and back covers. Quadruple, quintuplet, and other such framings appear as individual pages visually move out of and from others. The multiplicity of frames extends the text outward from the page, like collage, creating new vanishing points in front of and around the flat surface itself.

Of course, the fact that *Dharma* is composed primarily of words con-structed as comprehensible phrases and sentences, the canvases segmented into eleven sections unequivocally titled "Books," foregrounds its essential literary nature. As such, *Dharma* can be likened to contemporary concrete poetry or medieval emblems, the former shaping words as recognizable images to highlight the message of the discourse and the latter emphasizing a highly symbolic and often intricate image accompanied by a proverb or maxim. These heritages render *Dharma* the character of a high, modernist text intended for a small, exclusive audience capable of interpreting its intri-cate coding. Simultaneously, however, the openness of the collage/scrapbook hybridity unlocks the text to a democratic multiplicity of readings. Consequently, *Dharma* paradoxically invites and rebuffs interpretations that privilege authorial intentionality and biography, as well as those that privi-lege reader-response or poststructuralist methodologies.

Perhaps the one overarching concept lending credence to the form and content of *Dharma*—other than the Buddhist materials that will keep scholars occupied for decades—is Kerouac's belief in the supremacy of the moving mind: language, images, and other perceptional data flowing organ-ically into, out of, and through each other following a logic of association. Kerouac described this thinking in "Essentials of Spontaneous Prose," but *Dharma*, too, speaks directly to this notion. An undated text titled "NOTE ON WRITING" theorizes that writing should proceed like the creation of a dream, instantaneously, spontaneously, and completely without plot, external planning, or editing. Explaining that this "inner form of writing" emphasizes the present moment as a scene and then moves on to another scene, much like the "Bookmovie" section of *Doctor Sax*, the text also notes that the method applies "only to Non-Teaching writing. For if you want to write about Things, write *like* Things, spontaneously & purely" (106).

This method may sound contradictory to *Dharma*'s original purpose as a teaching text, but as a jagged, disrupted assemblage *Dharma* argues more profoundly than modernist stream of consciousness for the nonlinear nature of thought and the capability of the visual artifact to replicate the dimen-sionality of an individual's interior life. "Truth," the Buddha says to his dis-ciple Subhuti in the Diamond Sutra, one of Kerouac's favorites, "can not be cut up into pieces and arranged into a system. The words can only be used as a figure of speech" (Goddard 104)—a prescription to which *Dharma* adheres. It is *not* a systematic argument or narrative, and in terms of a liter-ary heritage it is more like Gertrude Stein's genre-defying experimental style, to which Kerouac was familiar, than Joyce's, Woolf's, or Faulkner's. Like Stein, whose writing the poet Anne Waldman describes as Buddhist in its egoless tracking of all thoughts as equal, *Dharma*'s concentration on words, phrases, and sentences as discrete visual objects creates a sense of "looking down at a landscape from a plane . . . [where]," as Waldman says, "every-thing is equal" (Grace and Johnson 273). There is no static or unified future perspective from which *Dharma* is narrated—no omniscient authorial perspective, no backward-turning personal eye. The linguistic and visual artifacts are held in place by the negativity of white space, the very void, in which they are nestled, an open-ended plane that concurrently highlights and obliterates their nature as things.

Kerouac invests ego more explicitly in language than did Stein—his narratives exhorting the "I," hers muffling it—but in Stein's work, as in *Dharma*, the narrative self(s) appears fragmented and disengaged. Both Stein's *Tender Buttons*, for example, and Kerouac's *Dharma* strip away the mask of historical veracity and narrative mendacity to expose objects of per-ception that constitute the naked continuum of memories, knowledge, his-tory, self-understanding, art, and finally dreams and desires—all realities by which one identifies the individuated self. *Dharma*, then, is not the "real" story of the "real" Jack Kerouac, since signifiers are interchangeable and illu-sions. Instead, by revealing the swirling wheel of perceptional material that humans manipulate to create selfhood, *Dharma* destabilizes the notion of authorial integrity and intent to expose the universe as neither linear nor personal.

This belief is relayed structurally through the scrapbooking/collaging of nonattributed, appropriated passages. One of the most frequently used is the Surangama Sutra. Book 4, for example, includes a small picture of a disem-bodied arm with its hand pointing down; directly opposite is a short text stating the hand is neither pointing up nor down. "Why?" is typed below the hand, and underneath that, the drawing of a tiny man facing left; behind him another short text claims the man can be facing in any of the four direc-tions of the compass. These are actually Kerouac's notes or paraphrases of a lesson from the sutra itself in *A Buddhist Bible*, but *Dharma* does not cite the external referent. Unless one is familiar with this sutra, it appears to be Kerouac's creation of a Buddhist teaching. In other instances, passages like these are captured within quotation marks, signaling that the text is authored by someone other than Kerouac or Duluoz but not revealing by whom. To discern this pattern, one needs some knowledge of the sutras and other texts Kerouac studied. For such a reader, the text, or at least portions of it, can be read as untethered to its human origins in either Kerouac's intelligence (some unattributed quotes could be his own words) or the other authors from whom he borrowed.

However, the effect of nondiscriminated sound created by scrapbooking/collaging is undercut by the very unattributed quotations and paraphrases that constitute it. The quotations, in particular, call attention to the concept of ideas and words as private property, and at times Kerouac does supply details about his sources. The combination of minimal, nonexistent, and more enhanced citations and documentation reinforces the belief that a single author has created the work and that he duly understands to some degree his academic and legal obligations to credit the others upon whose work he depends. Within the tension of these two polarities—one, the erasing of a verifiable authorial agency; two, the reification of the notion of a verifiable author with precise ethical and legal intensions and obligations—*Dharma* engineers the complexities and contradictions of human existence. This is not in a noumenal nether world, although the heritage of that belief permeates the text, but in the somatic individual who follows that path. *Dharma*'s blending of life, art, and the self approximates the nondualistic reality that Buddhism teaches and the dualistic reality of the Judeo-Christian tradition, synthesizing both as illusionary dream and concrete reality.

Consistent with this overarching philosophy, *Dharma* contains only minimal references to sin, evil, hell, or purgatory, and little rhetoric pleads for salvation or favors from God. "Stop being angry and you wont have to repent (unlike Christian repentance)," Kerouac wrote in book 3, repudiating contrite orthodoxy (126). By the time Kerouac began *Dharma*, he had long since become disillusioned with institutional forms of religion, especially Catholicism, which in general appears in *Dharma* as a boogeyman of false dualism responsible for the warring technocratic nations of Western civilization (66). Applying Spengler's concept of pseudomorphosis in *Dharma*, Kerouac determined that the Catholic Church of Aquinas and the papal hierarchy were the pseudomorphosed forms of a primitive religion, what he called "Apocalyptic Christianity" transformed through Pauline theology. This confusion and suppression of forms, particularly the primitive disguised as the civilized, he determined, explained why Faustian individuals, those who believe in the supremacy of the self, could still hold fast to the notion of a devil (99). At the same time, *Dharma* repudiates much of Spengler's mindset as "The Climax of German Thought" preoccupied with a falsely detailed view of history (100). Spengler, he concluded, failed to understand Eastern thought or the nature of the universe.

Nor was America spared his criticism. Retreating from his earlier praise of American progressivism that characterizes *Windblown World* and is discernible in *On the Road* and *Doctor Sax*, *Dharma* interpreted that same robust individual "know-how" as a curse upon one's efforts to escape suffering (54). What one needed, *Dharma* argues, is not Christianity defined as a theodicy, an argument in defense of God's goodness, or a misleading, wishful dream religion about God (81, 319–20), but the realization that religion is more accurately "an insight into reality" (319). Thus he turned to a cosmodicy, Buddhism, a nontheistic religion based on the universe, rather than an anthropomorphized, personal god in order to preach a Pure Land, further for the nation.

Buddhism in two respects well suited Kerouac's need for a new, postapoc-
alyptic vision to "wake-up" the world to its own potential. Buddhas' virtues of
compassion (*Karuna*) and loving kindness (*maitri* in Sanskrit) rang harmoniously with Kerouac's belief in kindness and tenderness, a legacy of his
Catholic up bringing and moral lessons learned in the aftermath of World
War II, as did Buddhist tenets of independence and rationalism. However, he
found little evidence that America provided a fertile ground for these teachings. Even today, while Buddhism has grown in the United States to the point
where between two to three million Americans are thought to be Buddhists,
the practice has not developed a broad-based following: approximately only
800,000 of those practitioners identify themselves as Euro-American con-
verts.[8] Kerouac correctly acknowledged in *Dharma* that the American character does not interpret all life as loss or sorrow (61), and it holds fervently to
the belief in a personal god. While Americans champion change, this change
remains rather than Buddhist impermanence, the kind of change necessary
for American ideals of material and spiritual progress, the latter exemplified
by the recurrence of political efforts to eradicate the separation of church and
state—not the wisdom that cuts through the deception of the ego to the
knowledge of a world without soul and afterlife (319–20).

From almost the opening page, however, Kerouac constructed *Dharma* to
include Jesus Christ, explicitly signaling the competing and compatible
human representatives of these two religious traditions and the one great
"other" upon which his version of Buddhism rested. Book 1 reflects his efforts
to situate both Buddha and Jesus within metaphysical and physical contexts
to eradicate in his own thinking the Christian dualisms of human/God,
life/death, and good/evil. For instance, based on personal, Benzedrine-
induced visions of Christ's heaven filled with anxiety, he decided that Buddha
exists beyond fate and the Christian concept of heaven and thus is superior to
Christ (3), an idea that he repeats in slightly different language in book 9:
"The truth that is realizable / in a dead man's bones is / beyond Jesus and his
Cross / o o o o o /—it is Prajna" (376). The five *o*'s identified as the Sanskrit
word *prajna*, meaning "wisdom" or "insight" and juxtaposed with the word
cross speak to the eternal movement of the whole, negating the stark and
exclusive image of the Constantinian cross, the vehicle of individual hatred,
sacrifice, and salvation upon which most Christian sects rest their doctrines of
resurrection. While Kerouac considered Jesus inferior to Buddha, he also
called him a Buddha, although one who failed to teach about the final and
absolute truth, instead "gild[ing] the lily with [. . .] humantalk, of *fathers* in
heaven" (389). He preferred the "bare fatherless Truth" of Buddhism (389).

Despite his preference for a world of priceless emptiness, Kerouac's
Christian-American, literary can-do heritage refused to be obliterated. Jesus,
the Buddha, and Kerouac's fantasy of himself as a grandiose writer coexist at

times. Some passages suggest and others outrightly declare his co-opting of the notion of reincarnation for purposes of egoistic gratification. In one instance, he wrote that he was "Buddha come back in the form of Shakespeare for the sake of poor Jesus Christ and Nietzsche" (41), situating himself as an icon of Western literature and Eastern religion, greater even than Jesus, on a mission to save Western religion and philosophy. In moments such as these, the earthly and selfless teachings of Buddha and Jesus retreat in the face of his belief in his own fabula as the last Buddha: Kerouac, a divine conveyor of salvation. At another point, *Dharma* contends that Jesus and Buddha are of equal magnitude, both Paraclete the Comforter (43) and human teachers who, as the typewriter visually shouts in uppercase to the reader, successfully free "THEMSELVES OF THE SUBCONSCIOUS DREAMFLOOD WHICH IS THE SOURCE OF 'RELIGIOUS VISION' AND AVAILABLE TO ANY DOZING MAN" (9). This insight, psychologically and historically accurate, suggests that Buddha and Jesus were able to disassociate from older, hierarchical religious institutions—Buddha from what *Dharma* describes as "Vedic clutter" (8), and Jesus from Judaism. They instead chose paths leading to what each considered true wisdom rather than false religious visions. The vision *Dharma* develops most consistently of Jesus, then, is more of a human being and wise sage than a god incarnate. Buddha too is configured as a human being and wise sage as well as a concept of continuity and change—a conflagration of the principle of enlightenment within the present, a Buddhist position that Kerouac identified as Hinayanistic, and the principle of the divine life force emanating from all human beings, a Mahayanistic Buddhist position.

HINAYANA AND MAHAYANA

The issue of Kerouac's Buddhism as either Hinayanistic or Mahayanistic is intriguing. While Kerouac is often presented as a Mahayana, some even erroneously contending that he was a Zen Buddhist,[9] *Dharma* offers considerable evidence illuminating his presumed allegiance to one or the other tradition as something more complicated. No doubt this complication can be traced in part to Kerouac's major introduction to Buddhism through Dwight Goddard's *Buddhist Bible,* an anthology of primary texts from various Eastern religions that Kerouac found at the San Jose library while staying with Neal and Carolyn Cassady in early 1954 (Nicosia 457).

Also complicating the issue is Kerouac's association with Gray Snyder, who practiced Zen Buddhism. Further confounding readers is the fact that the name Hinayana that Kerouac used is now considered a derogatory or degrading term bestowed by the Mahayanists to separate the two appraches. More often, at least currently, those practicing what is known as Hinayanism call themselves Theravadins and consider themselves adherents of a Buddhism that most closely reflects that of Gautama himself. Kerouac rarely if ever used the name Theravada, so for purposes of this discussion I will use Hinayana, as he did to identify himself and particular Buddhist practices. No matter whether Hinayana or Mahayana, *Dharma* begins with the most fundamental of Buddhist teachings, the Four Noble Truths. These foundation blocks maintain that all life is loss or suffering, that is, the process of birth, life, decay, and death; that all humans experience suffering because of ignorance caused by the belief in the self or ego; that the ego can be overcome; and that one eradicates the ego by following the Eightfold Path regarding "right" words, thoughts, and actions — also often presented as wisdom, morality, and meditation. Bearing in mind that Buddhism is a capacious tradition embracing the magical and the mundane, the recognition of the Four Noble Truths leads to an understanding of "thingness" as illusion or appearance. All things, particularly the notion of the self, are impermanent and arbitrary conceptions of the egoistic belief in a self. The neophyte is taught to practice meditation, the purification of one's mind aimed toward the experience of nonattachment to "thingness" or "appearance"; in other words, to strive to see through the appearance of the *atman* (self) to realize the *anatta* (nonself) in "nothingness" or the "no thing" of that which is immanent *and* beyond. This is often referred to in Kerouac's and Ginsberg's works as the Universal Mind, a signifier not of physical phenomena but a formless, ever-changing continuum separate from the appearance of the body and individual human consciousness. The latter dissolves into the greater continuum when the physical body decays into death.

Kerouac labored over these teachings, seeking to make the rhetorical illusion of Buddhist wisdom an integral component of daily life, at the level of rational thinking (remaining ever-conscious of the anatta) as well as at the level of full enlightenment (achieving the absolute cessation of attachments and cravings). The process pulled him in counterintuitive directions, another version of the dualism that he had been seeking to reconcile, only this time Buddhist rather than Catholic. Therefore, the Buddhism that he appears to favor most consistently as expressed in *Dharma* is the subtle dualism and individualism of the Hinayana, not the more radical, nondualistic, and group-oriented Mahayana.

The Hinayana sphere, or the "Lesser Vehicle," of Buddhism refers to Buddhism's origins in India, later spreading to countries such as Burma (now Myanmar), Sri Lanka, and Thailand. Although many layers of the Mahayana and Hinayana schools of Buddhism overlap (so many that even gross distinctions quickly become tangled), Hinayanists generally concentrate on the moral principles and behaviors of the Eightfold Path that one should follow, stressing an individual's strict observance of behaviors prescribed through the sutras to achieve personal enlightenment or Buddhahood in this lifetime. They do not consider Buddha a divine being and they do not worship divine beings. Those who through their own efforts have reached enlightenment are often referred to as *arahats* or *arhats,* one in whom greed, delusion, and anger have been extinguished (Ross 47).

Mayahana, or the "Greater Vehicle," is the Buddhism that spread through Northern India, Nepal, Mongolia, China, Korea, and Japan. It does not reject Hinayanistic principles, but augments them. Mahayana Buddhism, as Nancy Wilson Ross explains, generally posits the tapping of "an intuitive wisdom to achieve the realization that one already possesses the Buddha-nature; it has simply to be 'recovered' or uncovered" (44). Mahayanism tends to be more democratic, opening up the practice to individuals and emphasizing not only the Eightfold Path but also the six paramitas (perfections): generosity, morality, patience, vigor, meditation, and wisdom. Additionally, Mahayana Buddhism places more importance on the process of an enlightened one helping others to reach that same state, analogous to the Buddha's decision to postpone parinirvana, the final release from the physical world, by incorporating into the vow of monks and nuns the chant "Sentient beings are numberless; / I vow to save them all" (Ross 48). In these traditions, which believe in many Buddhas preceding and following Gautama, the term *bodhisattva,* or being of wisdom and compassion, refers to someone who has all but achieved the englightenment of a Buddha, is on the path to becoming a Buddha him- or herself, and unlike the arhat can be reborn to assist others (Epstein 42). Mahayanism, however, also embraces interpretations of Buddhism that consider the Buddha to be divine and that allow for other divinities to whom one can offer petitionary prayers, although in general these traditions still do not consider Buddha to be a divine savior but one whose teachings aid others to achieve enlightenment.

Considering Kerouac's proclivities for the mystical, intuitive, and worldly, his declaration in the 1968 *Paris Review* interview that he was most influenced by Mahayana Buddhism makes sense. It is well known that he favored the Diamond Sutra, a Mahayanistic sutra that as interpreted by Goddard, openly criticizes Hinayanists as individuals unable to free themselves from arbitrary conceptions and the belief in a universal self (Goddard 97). Additionally, Kerouac's favorite Buddhist saint, who appears in *Dharma,* was Avalokitesvara, one of the most important figures in the Mahayana tradition, a "merciful lord" who had vowed to listen to the petitions of any sentient being (Sojun Roshi). But *Dharma* illustrates that Kerouac was more of a Hinayanist than has been acknowledged. At the very least, he confused the two forms, or did not care to follow one more faithfully than the other, evidenced by his tendency in *Dharma* to refer to himself as both an arhat and a bodhisattva, using the two terms interchangeably and most often to acknowledge his advanced yet uncompleted state of Buddhahood. More telling, however, he included texts, presumably his own, that blatantly criticize Mahayana Buddhism as a "later Puritan-like super-addition, or

Protestant overlay, or New Vision, of original primitive *non-political* Buddhism" (97), a "polite whitewash" of Hinayanism (319), and Mahayana practitioners as "Fairy talers" of "continual compromise" (175, 351) whose belief in reincarnation was a way to cling to "eternal Ego-life" (175). Finding the Hinayana tradition to be his "Ecclesiastes" (175), the reference to one of the Old Testament's most revered books of wisdom establishing a strong affirmation of the Lesser Vehicle, he confessed that he remained an "ignorant Hinayana disciple" seeking "Nirvana-for-Self" (319). Kerouac's biographies as well as the Legend also construct a man fundamentally more sympathetic to the single-mindedness of Hinayana Buddhism than to the community-mindedness of Mahayana, an insight articulated in book 1 of *Dharma:* "By living in solitude you will accomplish everything that there is in social life and more" (30), a maxim that appears to be not only addressed to unknown others but also to Duluoz, the "you" he desired to become.[10]

Kerouac, however, paid more than lip service in *Dharma* to the charitable and other-directed features of Mayahana Buddhism. One sees this most consistently in his thinking about his life as a writer. Unquestionably, Buddhism led him to doubt the ethical stance of his writerly life: the extent to which ego drove him to write and the repercussions of attachment to that activity. The farther Kerouac traveled across Buddhist terrain, the more he began to believe that he must abandon writing if he was to free himself from egotistical cravings (159). Numerous entries contain apologies for wanting to write and self-admonitions to take to heart the truth "that the greatest things in the world is not writing but realizing—Self Realization of Noble Wisdom that cannot be written——From *Writer* I'll go to *Realizer*" (253; see also 55 and 380). These passages connect most directly with "The Lankavatara Scripture: Self-Realization of Noble Wisdom" in Goddard's *Buddhist Bible* and read as a deduction from Buddha's teachings that the verbal assertion of anything, even Noble Wisdom itself, means that it participates in phenomenal nature. As such, it is part of the cycle of birth and death (samsara) and therefore not truth (302). This teaching must have been extremely difficult for Kerouac to accept, and while he earnestly tried to believe that language always falls short of the goal of truth (55, 405), he could not relinquish language altogether. Emerging as a more tenable position is his renunciation of one form of writing, that is, literature, in favor of another, teaching the dharma to others (12, 32, 160, 220, 388).

Kerouac was deadly serious about writing as a teaching to aid others, and in 1954, contemporaneously with his work on *Dharma,* he composed a text that he intended for just this purpose. "Buddha Tells Us—or Wake Up," which he described to Ginsberg as "a Lake of Light, really great . . . a real simple explanation guaranteed to explain the inside secret of emptiness" (*Letters* 1: 485), was published posthumously in the Buddhist magazine *Tricycle.* It is a fairly faithful paraphrase of the Surangama Sutra, but lacks the great clarity and American character that Kerouac thought would "convert many" (*Letters* 1: 498). But its existence testifies to Kerouac's genuine intent to use Buddhist wisdom to teach. In *Dharma,* he announced these intentions, coupling them with an extravagant explanation of why they were necessary. Naming himself the "Writing Buddha," he declares that there is no reason to write except to emancipate others from attachments and cravings (312). Pronouncements such as this envision the Mahayanist determined to "safely carry all seekers to the other shore of Enlightenment," according to the Great Heart Sutra (Goddard 86). They also support those elements of *Dharma* that emphasize the more autobiographical and didactic, rather than the imaginative and artificial, nature of the text.

Kerouac's self-appointment as the Writing Buddha positions him figuratively as a secular Great Emancipator—one who through the verifiable and the imaginary crafts didactic texts to improve the American character, both individual and corporate. In this role, Kerouac connects himself with the nation's most revered emancipator, Abraham Lincoln, who actually appears in *Dharma* reincarnated as a tiny doll-like figure who is clothed in black and begs for food. The text, simply titled "FANTASY," implies that Lincoln is reborn as a diminished figure of emancipation "because he read Life of Buddha but tolerated War" (10). In other words, Lincoln is a Faustian who failed to emancipate people through kindness and charity, but Kerouac, now the Writing Buddha and a self-proclaimed "dedicated world-lover teaching the end of all things," will use writing like "a big unasked building of a Cathedral" to save all (140). This is not the salvation of the Union or of enslaved African Americans, but instead the salvation of the entire human race through wisdom of the nature of the universe.

Imaginatively replacing Lincoln as the true emancipator, Kerouac sets his sights on Southerners, those whom Lincoln did not live long enough to rescue from carpetbaggers and Jim Crow. In a rather funny but condescending lesson plan on how to proceed, the speaker of the syllabus states that Southerners would better understand Buddhist wisdom if he simply substituted the phrase "Mind Essence" for their expression "Mind of God" (198–99). Of course, this simple substitution fails completely: the American vision of "God," Southern or otherwise, is far removed from the Buddhist understanding of that which is impersonal, immanent, and beyond, and while American Christianity and Eastern Buddhism share a long history of appropriation, the doctrines do not mirror each other. However, Kerouac's fantasies of saving the South from Christianity, no matter how uninformed, manifest the Buddhist precept that there is no difference between Buddha and other people. Kerouac's playful imaginings evince his willingness to relinquish his identity as a great literary figure to exemplify Gautama, who taught that all are capable of enlightenment and of helping others.

Not surprisingly, however, Kerouac's efforts to use writing to teach and save must also be read in the contexts of other rhetorical strategies he employs to justify a more egotistical pursuit of the literary life. In one instance, for example, he argues that his Buddhist teachings will draw more respect from his pupils if he succeeds as a writer prior to beginning life as a Buddhist sage (164). In another instance, the Buddhist concept of reincarnation offers him a rationale to create past lives that blend his Buddhism and his literary interests: in addition to having been "Avalokitesvara the bhikku, Asvhaghosha the desert monk, [. . .] a Chinese wandering Buddhist, [and] a Mexican Indian in Azteca," he claims he was Shakespeare and Balzac (380). In this case, as with all his references to reincarnation, it is difficult to determine whether he understood the term in the Buddhist sense of impersonal vital energy that flows into rebirth or in the non-Buddhist sense of the rebirth of a permanent, individual soul. Considering his Judeo-Christian heritage, coupled with his reading of the spiritualist Edgar Cayce, whose teachings Neal and Carolyn Cassady advocated during the early fifties,[11] it is reasonable to conclude that he had more of a proclivity for the Christian concept of the transmigration of a permanent soul, as Christians conceive of it, which he interpreted as reincarnation, a neat theory to justify his fervent belief in his own literary genius. Consequently, as genuine as it may have been, Kerouac's Mahayanistic plans to aid others are eventually undercut by the ego he strives to overcome.

The distinctions between nirvana and samsara espoused by the two schools additionally situate Kerouac more firmly in the Hinayana camp. Again, it has to be noted that disentangling interpretive differences among the many sects can be vexing, as with any tradition whose primary texts are highly poetic, symbolic, and first orally transmitted. Indisputable demarcations often confound both scholars and practitioners, which is the case with nirvana and samsara. But as Edward Conze maintains, Hinayana Buddhism generally defines nirvana as the "permanent, stable, imperishable, immovable, ageless, deathless, unborn, and unbecome, . . . the place of unassailable safety; that it is the real Truth and the supreme Reality" (Conze 40). Nirvana is contrasted with everything that is impermanent or unstable, particularly the individual, who can attain nirvana by only achieving the not-self (anatta), or awareness that the self never existed (Armstrong 113). Nirvana, however, as Karen Armstrong clarifies, is not the same as personal extinction; rather, it is "the fires of greed, hatred, and delusion" that are replaced by "a profound peace of mind in the midst of suffering" (85–86).

The development of Mahayana doctrine effected a transformation of Buddhahood from the human principle of Gautama the *human teacher* into a transcendent spiritual presence that in some quarters came to encompass everything, *including* the samsara of birth, life, decay, and death.

The figure of Mucalinda the Serpent King who saved Buddha from the temptations of Mara is sometimes cited as a sign that nature itself participates in the Buddha spirit. This notion of nirvana as a working principle in all particulars contrasts with the Hinayanistic nirvana, which is a more static, indifferent, and dispassionate reality with no intimate connection to the world of "birth-and-death" (Paraskevopoulos 1). In fact, in *Desolation Angels,* Duluoz notes this distinction between the two schools, favoring the Hinayanist to the Mahayanist position (237). Kerouac's deep need to escape the condition of human suffering seems to be a more Hinayanistic position than living with the belief in Buddhahood as part of the nature. Kerouac, at about midpoint in *Dharma,* actually flatly announces that nature is the cause of all suffering (175)—a blatant misreading of Buddhism, which is not against nature, as Armstrong notes—but considers nature a condition, not the cause, of suffering that one can remedy but never totally obliterate. Kerouac's statement, though, strongly suggests that by the time he began working on *Dharma* he had developed grave misgivings about living in the natural world and was searching for a practice affording him a clean break from anything connected with human life as he had known it. Buddhism in its most comprehensive form, which he described as "all the way out" with "no intermediary stops such as the imaginary judgments of Jesus' Path with its decisive conceptions of self, other selves, living beings to be delivered, and a universal God self existing eternally" (417), provided this for him, and it was Hinayana Buddhism in particular toward which he seems to have gravitated.

Perhaps, however, the Hinayana-Mahayana question is answered most accurately in Kerouac's literary self-representation as Ray Smith, the first-person narrator of *The Dharma Bums,* who tells his mentor, Japhy Ryder, that he is "an oldfashioned dreamy Hinayana coward of later Mahayanism" (13). The placement of the derogatory nominal *coward* in this phrase creates a double reading, *coward* describing the proper noun *Hinayana* and the prepositional phrase "of later Mahayanism." This zeugma, or yoking, presents Kerouac as a mixture of both the more starkly atheistic, dualistic, and monastic Hinayana and the more metaphysical, community-minded, and nondualistic Mahayana. His intentions fixed him between the "Greater" and "Lesser," where he had the desire but neither the strength to follow the prescriptive and solitary life of the Hinayana nor the selfless perseverance to give himself to others that the Mahayana asked. Within these polarities, Kerouac negotiated his identities of writer, teacher, Buddhist, and Christian. Knowing that Buddhism teaches one to live within the dream of arbitrary conceptions and to understand nirvana as found within oneself and thus possible for all in the present, he reminded himself that he had "to walk the path in life—I'm stuck in the dream" (*Dharma* 273).

BUDDHIST CHRISTIANITY

In this thinking life, Kerouac reveals the difficulty of a Western mind understanding Buddhist concepts, the no-self being the one he apparently found most difficult. Many passages in *Dharma* expose his efforts to rationally clarify the idea, and he applied a variety of techniques to this end. One is the following sermonic analogy, in which he compares himself as a distinct personality to a river in a valley:

> The water is like Mind Essence, the shores Jack Kerouac—as soon as it gets "out to sea" there is no more river and my realization of essence of mind restored unshackled to shoreless void—but mind will continue to suffer down other rivers after my river runs out of its banks, so "I'll suffer again," because I'm mind, my realization of suffering is due not first to my personality-shores but due and informed by the mind essence "waters" that stream through—So as long as ignorance exists I'll, as mind, suffer—consciously, too—The mistake of ignorance is in my own mind now. (183)

In the image of the river, the universe becomes an illusion of interrelated parts: the flowing continuum, the illusion of selfhood, and the source of suffering, in effect a Kerouacian translation and interpretation of the Mahayana Buddhist concept of Universal Mind according to the doctrine of the Three Images or what is more commonly known as the three bodies of Buddha. These are *dharma kaya*—unmanifested, unqualified, and pure potentiality that has not exercised itself yet; *sambhoga kaya*—the heavens, where the celestial Buddhas and bodhisattvas are manifested; and *nirmana kaya*—the lower levels, where earthly Buddhas, bodhisattvas, and everything else is manifested. Kerouac's version, like many ancient Buddhist stories, relies on elements of nature and a student's observable experiences, thus serving as an excellent teaching tool.

But even excellent pedagogies do not guarantee success. While the tone of the river lesson projects calm and confidence, *Dharma* tells a story of such moments balanced with extreme frustration and self-doubt. Repeatedly in *Dharma*, Kerouac writes that he has achieved enlightenment, as he did, for example, in a passage dated December 25, 1954, in which he recorded that he had attained "at last to a measure of enlightenment.—Perhaps a touch of Annuttara-Samyak-Sambodhi [. . .] That I am at last in touch with the 'eternality' beyond death and life and so 'never die'" (189). But only a few weeks earlier, he had been at "the lowest beatest ebb" of his life, lonely, cheated by his friends, drinking too much, and abusing himself by burning his hands and taking Benzedrine. In the midst of this despair, he determined to apply Buddhist intelligence to save himself (185). This cycle of ecstasy followed by despair characterizes the exchange of voices throughout *Dharma*, elation sliding into gloom that is countered with American pull-yourself-up-by-the-bootstraps determination suggesting that the more one asserts what one wants to believe, the more likely the belief will come true.

Simultaneously, *Dharma* repeatedly affirms the Buddhist notion of assertion as the destruction of truth, The Kerouacian/Duluozian "T" at times modulated with more self-reflexive discourse, such as this passage from book 6:

> Here's what I've been doing:- I come to crucial lapses in faith, I pray to Avalokitesvara to instill faith in me—he does—then, feeling secure, I indulge myself in worldly thoughts, thinking I'm safe from contamination—but slowly I lapse and become entangled & sick again . . . Fallible human nature! (280)

The "I" sees into its own past, gaining insight about why progress toward enlightenment is so slow, a perception that he attributes to his false feelings of security that are a product of flawed human nature. The "I" also at times decides how to remedy the mistake. In one of *Dharma's* most illuminating passages, he achieves this capability through the analogy of his first wife, Edie Parker. Admitting that he had mistakenly assumed that one could sit inside Mind Essence as in a bright room, he determines that he can live with it but not *in* it, like his wife Edie, who "used to want to live inside my body but all she could do was live with my body—'I wanta crawl in you and curl up'" (186). How, he asks, can one curl up in nothingness? The question is likely rhetorical, for he knows that Mind Essence is not like a mother's womb, no matter how much he may wish it to be.

Some mistakes in the "I's" journey to enlightenment, as the room/womb analogy illustrates, are caught by the practitioner, but *Dharma* acknowledges that it would be humanly impossible to catch all the missteps, the "I" occasionally tripping on errors that it cannot see. The above confession about his crucial lapses in faith exemplifies this tendency. What he fails to or cannot recognize in this case is the falsity of his belief in a transcendent other that he petitions for salvation. In this sense, he has slipped back into a dualistic mode of thinking, which fails him once again. This I-other dichotomy leads him astray many times, especially in a text about his sister Nin that suggests a degree of unreliability on Kerouac's part countered by the wisdom of others. It is her comment "Where'd this trash come from?" when she finds him writing in her backyard amid garbage scattered by dogs that upsets him, prompting the written retort "For all she sees is a trash-remover not a Poet-Shakespeare" (380). But what illudes him is the realization that Nin is speaking Buddhist wisdom, for is not trash removing as important as Shakespeare's writing? Should not one work to see the daily routines of one's life as significant instead of egoistically striving for fame and immortality? In her unintentional, unstudied, and matronly way, Nin materializes in this tiny domestic drama as more Buddhist than her brother.

Such slips and errors as these disclose the difficulties Kerouac had relinquishing muscular American Christianity, and indeed he never fully did. It is not surprising that the Buddhism Kerouac constructed in *Dharma* is deeply infused with Christian terminology and doctrines, but does not resemble orthodox forms of Christianity. In effect, the essence of the synthesis of Buddhism and various orthodox and heretical strands of Christianity in his own words is "THE BUDDHA NIRMANAKAYA and the Messiah made flesh, to re-teach again among the Defiled and Fallen, promising purity and Grace again [. . .] God is Mind Essence, the Father of the Universe, the Manifesting Womb—Atman is Soul and only appears to exist and transmigrate, like physical body, which is but spectral Heaven Stuff all of it" (297). Here, he combines Buddhist and Christian concepts, respectively, of life as decay and sin-filled, of purity of mind (nirvana) and the grace of God (life ever after in heaven), and of the body as transitory and of the soul as eternal. As in Buddhism, the concept of the individual self (atman) is obliterated, but replaced with the concept of "soul," which does not exist in Buddhism. As in Buddhism, the individual physical body is impermanent and thus "defiled," although Kerouac's version perceives the physical body to have fallen, presumably from the grace of God, and thus is sin-filled, a Christian concept. God is personified as the creator of the universe, another Christian-like belief. The soul, which the text implies is part of human existence, is heavenly material moving through the physical domain, a gnostic-like interpretation of the soul trapped in the tainted body until saved by the individual's will to acquire knowledge.

There are many ways in which Kerouac's retention of Christianity establishes *Dharma* as a sutra of American Christian Buddhism, not the least of which is his belief in conversion, especially his own power to convert others to Buddhism by personal example, a conviction redolent with tones of Christian proselytizing. Likewise, he maintained a belief in mystical healing powers, recording, for example, his ability to cure his mother of a painful cough by interpreting the symbolic language of a self-induced vision, implicitly following a method like that of spiritualist Edgar Cayce by hypnotizing himself "to investigate cure and cause" of his mother's illness (419). This event he later revised as a miracle in *The Dharma Bums*. While the concept of the miracle is not alien to Buddhism, ancient Buddhist sutras do not interpret such acts as the result of divine intervention, instead calling them practical, human behaviors indicative of individuals who have achieved an advanced state of samadhi (meditation). For instance the actions of bad individuals deciding to reform themselves, much like Kerouac's self-improvement efforts, can be considered miracles in the Buddhist sense. Buddha also warned individuals against the solipsistic trap of considering oneself capable of performing such extraordinary feats prior to enlightenment. The *Dharma* version of the healing of Memere suggests a Buddhist approach: a reliance not on divine intervention but on one's intellectual powers as more expansive than everyday logic posits. This position Kerouac reifies in *The Dharma Bums* by having Ray Smith remember that a nurse said the cough was most likely an allergic reaction to flowers in the house (148). However, Kerouac's revision of that act as a miracle in *The Dharma Bums* still maintains the Christian patina glossing much of his life.

Then, too, *Dharma* projects Kerouac's felt sense of being an alien other— "a visitor from the other world, invisible (angel) world"—who, like Jesus and other messenger figures of heavenly origin, performs visitations and observes that humans are basically good (366). The identification with angels, dominant throughout his life, remains far removed from the Surangama and Diamond sutras that teach the logic of human impermanence in Mind Emptiness. Even some of Kerouac's attempts to explain away the belief in God using Buddhist reasoning often return him to a dualistic Christian ethos. Take his discussion of a cat's will to live as "God, in a cup-form-body, temporarily regnant there" (12). He reasons that this trapped "will," which is proof of God who reigns over all, is released as the body is reborn in another earthly form, punctuating the discourse with the declaration that "'God' is a Faustian, false concept" (12). The logic of the passage is terribly tangled but manages to illustrate a belief in all humans as natural forms that carry within the spark of the heavenly source. Consequently, the Faustian coda reads unconvincingly.

Kerouac continued to read Christian theologians and mystics simultaneously with Buddhists texts as he refined *Dharma*, seemingly seeking points of intersection between the two. One can speculate that in a passage such as the following from the *Mystical Theology* of Dionysius the Pseudo-Areopagite, Kerouac found a Christian voice expressing the godhead compatibly with Buddhism: "the Darkness of Unknowing wherein (the true initiate) *renounces all the apprehensions of his understanding and is enwrapped* in that which is wholly intangible and invisible" (*Dharma* 129). No commentary accompanies the excerpt by Dionysius an obscure writer, whom historians place in the second half of the fifth century, although the passage that follows Dionysius's is a telling diatribe against Dante's mystical hierarchy, which Kerouac likened to the ignorant Faustian desire to measure the properties of angels (129). Perhaps Kerouac responded similarly to the Pseudo-Areopagite's hierarchical discourse but found comforting the Buddhist-like message of surrendering false distinctions through a contemplative life that strives for the intangible darkness to which all belongs beyond the light.

Likewise, Kerouac's commentary and reflections on the wisdom of Anicius Boethius (480–524 CE), a Roman statesman and philosopher widely considered to have died a Christian martyr, make explicit his interest in identifying sites of Buddist and Christian commonality. *Dharma* devotes almost three pages to his Consolations of Philosophy or Theological Tractates that Kerouac was apparently reading in early March 1955. He does not identify the specific volume by title, but copied numerous passages from it, critiquing each in the context of Buddhist wisdom. *Ignorant* is the term most prevalent in his evaluations of Boethius's conclusions that God can be anthropomorphized, endowed humans with reason and freedom of choice so they can struggle toward perfection in heaven, and did not use divine substance to create them because he did not want them considered divine. Kerouac found more palatable Boethius's elevation of baptism as the "saving truth" of Christianity, writing that "here Buddhism and Christianity almost kiss" in that each stresses a life of purity (275). Similarly, Kerouac reacted favorably toward Boethius's linkage of the Christian Cross and the Bodhi tree, under which Buddha attained enlightenment—each symbol signifying, in Boethius's words, "the bliss that is to be" (*Dharma* 276) as the natural world decays and passes into another form.

A Duluozian interpolation of this sentiment took the following poetic form in *Dharma*, illustrating that equating Buddha and Jesus afforded Kerouac a mechanism to deal with the perplexities of the human condition:

BUDDHA UNDER THE PRINCE'S SWORDS

and Christ on the Cross *had* to

subdue their discriminative

thoughts and craving desires

and see the light—it's the

eventual meaning, *awakening* . . .

awakening to PERFECT TRANQUILLITY

OF MIND

. . . to the empty light . . . (413)

The fusion of religious iconography and doctrine that Kerouac effected in this poem—a taking literally of the Buddha's last words to work out one's faith for oneself—fabricates a religion in which an individual values one's own gifts and talents, believes in the inherent goodness of life, frees oneself from dogmatic dualism, seeks a better life, and retains faith in the words of the sage. As such, Kerouac's Christian Buddhism is distinctly American, the human presence embodied in the words "Jesus" and "Buddha" rooting wisdom, progress, and divinity in the individual who resides in a New World where the vision of human goodness flourishes and seeds itself.

However, despite the surety that I have just conveyed, an argument imply-ing that *Dharma* resolves Kerouac's wisdom guests in Christian Buddhism, Kerouac concluded *Dharma* exactly where he began—at a point of departure and doubt as well as certainty and stasis. Like the snake eating its own tail, the end of the book and the beginning exist as distinct entities and a unified whole. The last passage of the book illustrates this principle in both words and images. Simply dated March 15, it takes the form of a catechism or les-son, asking if the three-year project had all been preparation for an epic novel on the Tathagata, the name meaning "thus come and thus gone" for Buddha after he achieved enlightenment. The answer is a handwritten and emphatic "NO (next page): —" ("NO" is underscored twice,) and Kerouac's signature *doveangel* (my term for his fusion of the angel and dove) inhabits the space underneath. Here, one encounters Kerouac as the single author of the entire book as well as Kerouac the teacher who addresses his question to himself as both student and sage. The answer, especially the image of the doveangel, connotes the Buddha's story, and by implication all human stories, as open-ended and beyond language. It matters not whether they are categorized as fiction or nonfiction, philosophy or religion, autobiography or novel; names are but illusions of the All in which Jesus and the Buddha reside. In this respect, *Dharma*'s conclusion recourses back, like *Finnegans Wake*, to its ini-tial presentation of the Four Noble Truths. *Dharma,* then, seems to resist efforts to make it fit neatly within the Duluoz Legend as a literary, historical artifact. But fit it does as a redoubtable expression of Kerouac's persistent endeavor to know art, God, and the self.

CHAPTER 6

SONGS AND PRAYERS: MEXICO CITY BLUES AND OTHER POEMS

As so much of Kerouac's private and published works attest, his pursuit of a literary life devoted to probing the metaphysical and ontological was predicated upon few if any concrete distinctions between poetry and prose. Neither the debate about the nature of genre nor the consistent exercise of precise literary terminology appears to have much interested him. Consequently, the historical record presents contradictory claims on his part. As *Dharma* illustrates, he could fastidiously create and define genres or subgenres, such as haiku, blues choruses, tics, dreams, and bookmovies, some adhering to more standard generic conventions, others flagrantly violating them. Yet prose was either "an endless one-line poem," as he wrote in a poetic statement for Donald Allen's anthology *New American Poetry* (*Blonde* 76), or a series of poems called "paragraphs," as he told Ted Berrigan (Plimpton 114). *Mexico City Blues,* easily recognizable as free verse, he identified as blues poems, while *Old Angel Midnight,* distinctly proselike in form, he defined for Lawrence Ferlinghetti in 1958 as "not prose, it's really a long one-line poem" (*Letters* 2: 98). While he identified narrative as the primary function of prose as opposed to the wide-open imaginative and confessional impulse of poetry (Plimpton 104–05), the Legend effects a critique of genre as hermetic, suggesting that all language is legitimate as long as it serves a higher purpose.

What he considered most integral to his writing was the writer's commitment to the most honest form of expression, which he persistently called "the true blue song of man" (*Blonde* 74) or the "eternal search for truth"

(*Atop* 122). It is safe to say that while Kerouac never composed a systematic theory of genre, in this equation the element of song acts as a portal of human discovery. Poetry such as *Mexico City Blues, Old Angel Midnight,* and other poems that this chapter will address, was meant to be sung, and it could not escape its fundamental musical nature. For Kerouac, the new American poets of the 1950s represented "childlike graybeard Homers singing in the street," telling the story of America. Their new poetry was to be experienced by anyone who could sing (or swing), and within this timeless universe, Kerouac intended to rescue poetry from the rigid, elitist depersonalization of "gray faced Academic quibbling" (*Scattered Poems,* unnumbered). His practice meant to return poetry to its origins in the bardic oral tradition and, through the singing of stories, to reawaken the ancient, lyric, visionary voice of truth.

Connecting the musical concepts of the bard and the lyric, much of Kerouac's writing also attempted to create with pencil and typewriter what jazz musicians created with horns, pianos, drums, and voices. The bardic/jazz-inspired product, as he often described it, was antiformalistic, unpremeditated, and unrevised, grounded in improvisation and spontaneity. Writing to his editor Malcolm Cowley in 1955, he declared, "The requirements for prose & verse are the same, i.e. *blow*—what a man most wishes to hide, revise, and unsay, is precisely what Literature is waiting and bleeding for—Every doctor knows, every *Prophet* knows the convulsion of *truth*" (*Letters* 1: 516, emphasis mine). Kerouac's evoking of *prophet* and *truth* in the Cowley correspondence ostensibly configures the poet as one who rejects socially contrived prescriptions and draws instead on cognitive processes to reach an essential form of consciousness rendering authenticity from which the poet as sage and sayer derives both the power to transcend human consciousness and the authority to speak that universal truth. The result is *spontaneous bop prosody* equating essentialist truth with personal honesty through free, unpremeditated flow of sound—a construct that, rightly or wrongly, still dominates definitions of Beat literature. In effect, Kerouac's composition method redefined twentieth-century poetry as a recombinant power in which the poet's relationship with the audience was that of public performer (the bard/musician) and solitary speaker (the lyric, visionary voice). The method situates him as a bridge between modernism and postmodernism, his poetry existing in dynamic tension as (1) the voice of the human soul communing with the metaphysical, recognizing the symbolic transparency of language, and (2) an "intellectual and sonic construction" privileging technique and the materiality of language (Hoover xxxv).

"E BOP SHE BAM"[1]

Kerouac declared in the author note to *Mexico City Blues* that he wanted "to be considered a jazz poet blowing a long blues in an afternoon jam session on Sunday." Jazz, a complex form of social and individual expression with visible connections to both preliterate and literate vocal and instrumental musical production, also guided much of his thinking about his writing. The distinctions between musical and literary composition are sometimes not easy to delineate, primarily because the cultural and psychological histories of both are rooted to some degree symbiotically in the same materials and processes. Since music and literature have always drawn on many of the same devices, any discussion of jazz as a literary influence will be somewhat vexed, particularly if the goal is to separate the distinctly musical from the distinctly literary. My intent is not to identify a set of practices and forms that are uniquely jazz oriented to argue their place in Kerouac's literary and spiritual life. Rather, my discussion will explicate particular devices associated with but not necessarily unique to jazz that function as analogues for the sui generis forms of cognition on which Kerouac drew and the complicated, socially derived structures that he manipulated. Dipping into and out of jazz and literary production, he wrote *with and against* these art forms.

Like Western European music, jazz has a history of musical notation,[2] but it was not this particular feature of jazz that captivated Kerouac. He remained uninterested in pursuing the page to score lyrics or create a poetic version of musical composition, as, for example, Anne Waldman does in "skin Meat BONES," in which the three titular words are placed on the page as notes on a scale. However, Kerouac's poems occasionally feature elements alluding to the composer's page. One sometimes encounters broken words that read as if scored to accompany notes in a song, the common pronunciation of a word distorted by the linking of phonemes and syllables with musical phrases, such as "Of o cean wave" and "Ra diance!" from "Bowery Blues" (*Blues* 98, 99); "Ai   la   ra   la / la   rai   la   ra" and "M'c'r y o cking" from *Mexico City Blues* (8th, 26th choruses); and"A—mer—ri—kay" and "ho / o / ome" from "San Francisco Blues" (*Blues* 34th, 38th choruses). He also used large blank spaces to represent the pause or rest that a musician takes (138th Chorus *MCB*) or parenthetically included words such as *pause* (143rd Chorus *MCB*).[3] Sometimes he worked with the standard three-line A-A-B form of the blues song, and when he wanted to leave no doubt that his poetry depicted conventional singing, he told the reader outright, as he does in the 84th Chorus of *Mexico City Blues,* which begins with "SINGING:—" directing the reader to sing the stanza, which plays with lyrics from the early twentieth-century popular ballad "By the Light of the Silvery Moon."

However, there is no heavy reliance on these devices. As heuristics, they seem to have proven somewhat inflexible for Kerouac. Instead, the jazz form that he directly acknowledged and used routinely was the set number of musical bars. Many of his most successful poems, those that he called blues choruses, loosely mimicked the twelve-bar form of blues/jazz composition. As he stated in the introduction to *Book of Blues,* his jazzlike method limited each poem, often titled a "Chorus," to the size of the page of the small breast-pocket notebook in which he wrote them. For a poet like Kerouac who relied on aleatory procedures, a lot could happen within those bars, that is, the approximately twenty lines per page, but when he came to the final bar—the end of the page, the composition was complete. This method enables the carryover of, repetition of, or the variation on themes, sounds, and images from chorus to chorus, analogous to the carryover of musical phrases from measure to measure.

For instance, choruses 79 through 84 from *Mexico City Blues* flow smoothly into one another, a movement produced primarily by the carryover of key phrases. "Goofing at the table" in the 79th Chorus becomes the opening line of the 80th, which introduces the theme of ham, bacon, and eggs. In the 81th Chorus, this trio is transformed into "Mr. Beggar and Mrs. Davy," otherwise known as "Looney and CRUNEY," which are transformed into "dem eggs & dem dem / Dere bacons, baby." Using Beat black jazz lingo, the singer then calls on a "brother" to continue the riff on eggs, bacon, and so on, only now with the sounds of his trumpet instead of the singer's spoken/written words. "'Lay that down / solid [. . .]" he directs, "'Bout all dem / bacon & eggs[. . .] All that luney / & fruney." "Fracons, acons, and beggs" begin the 82nd Chorus, which concludes with "Looney & Booney / Juner and Mooner / Moon, Spoon, and June." The 83rd Chorus returns to a directive to the trumpeter to "lay it down"—the sequence ending in the 84th with "Croon— / Love— / June—." The dominant aesthetic foregrounds continuation, or time, rather than structure, or space—in other words, how long can the jazz musician/poet spin the musical invention. The resemblance to a musical composition is fashioned by recurring rhythms, recurring phrases, and the linking of sound units from line to line and chorus to chorus. The language of this set of choruses in particular exemplifies Ginsberg's analysis that Kerouac was highly sensitive to the way "black speech influences the breath of the music which influences the breath of Kerouac's [written] speech" (Nicosia, "Interview"). The semantic links, integrating the song element into the work, suggest surrealistic metamorphosing, as a breakfast meal is transformed into a man and a woman, who through their nicknames become, ironically, the very words they sing from "By the Light of the Silvery Moon."

This structure emphasizes the performance of continuation while employing a structuralist approach to achieve that prolongation. The small notebook pages, instead of inhibiting the progression of his ideas, as one might expect, became a template for expression. For instance, in *Mexico City Blues,* a supermajority of the poems, 186, or 76 percent of the choruses, are highly similar in length, ranging from nineteen to twenty-five lines, thirty-five having twenty-two, thirty-five having twenty-four, and thirty-one having twenty-three lines. The shortest chorus is seven lines long and the longest contains thirty-one lines. This commonality makes sense if one accepts Kerouac's claim that each chorus was composed within the parameters of the breast-pocket notebook pages. Rarely do these choruses end midsentence or midthought—that is, at semantic points that fail to bring closure to the chorus. Kerouac seems to have developed a felt sense for the form imposed by the size of the page and learned how to compress his subject into that tiny space. With *Mexico City Blues,* of the 244 choruses (the 216th Chorus contains parts A, B, and C), only the 164th ends midsentence: "and suddenly there's a guy," which continues as "under the table" in the first line of the 165th. However, because the speaker is describing a dream in the 164th Chorus, the illogical introduction of "a guy" to conclude the poem fits the surreal quality of the chorus, rendering it a textual whole. Likewise, the phrase "under the table" in the subsequent chorus situates the reader in *media res,* a fairly conventional introduction for lyric verse. In this respect, each chorus, while thematically a constituent part of a whole, carries formal integrity. The notebook page, then, simultaneously provides the expansion of space necessary for the poet to improvise while arbitrarily establishing a form as tightly prescribed as for a sonnet or sestina.

Improvisation is the characteristic most often associated with jazz composition, a process that Kerouac addressed in "Essentials," stating that continual and unrestrained movement of words was imperative. In *Book of Blues* he even instructed readers to aim for "non stop ad libbing within each chorus, or the gig is shot" (1). At one level these statements affirm a lay understanding of improvisation as naive and uninformed. They also allude to something that happens on the spot, and in this regard his method corresponds with real musical performance: in the act of performance a musician rarely has the luxury of stopping to correct a mistake or improve expression—what comes out comes out. Kerouac's practice reflected the application of this point as well. The four breast-pocket notebooks in which he penciled *Mexico City Blues,* within a week, according to his correspondence with Sterling Lord (*Letters* 1: 510), shows that 155 of the 244 choruses were published exactly as they were originally composed. In the entire set of 244 poems, only two words appear to have been erased: the last line of the third stanza of the 26th Chorus contains a space between the words "pale light" where another word had once stood, and the second line of the 45th Chorus clearly shows erasure marks and the word *softened* written over them.[4] Similarly, most of the published sections of *Old Angel Midnight* were composed without revision, except substituting "Old Angel" for "Lucien" and a tiny revision related to Ginsberg and Burroughs' relationship, presumably to avoid libel.[5]

This textual evidence reinforces and validates the myth that Kerouac wrote quickly and on the spot.

Impressive as all this may be, a more productive approach to understanding how Kerouac's poetic sound relied on spontaneous improvisation is to consider the nature of improvisation as practiced by jazz musicians, a process not wholly unlike that of a writer. Jazz improvisation is usually a community activity, not a solitary performance, and as such, improvisation has several meanings. It can refer to war or battle (i.e., "cutting") as the musicians try to outplay each other, or it can mean a conversation, or dialogue, as the musicians congenially exchange musical talk with each other. It can also denote composition and revision, the restructuring of existing themes and tunes. With all three definitions, the improvisation depends upon the skill of the participants. In the hands of the best jazz musicians, improvisation is built on broad expertise transforming the most disparate of materials into the extraordinary. One need not be able to read music to compose this way, but rather to have a studied ear for the techniques and processes. In jazz, the musician is required to have a knowledge of many standard tunes and be capable of playing them on demand, of being able to take a well-known tune and give it new sound, of knowing how to reshape its chord structure, and of having a set of motifs (or clichés) to draw upon to reshape those tunes or chords, such as once-repeated notes, sequences, long silences, or a "teetering" pattern related to a trill. For instance, Charlie Parker, the jazz musician whom Kerouac most admired, used roughly one hundred "motifs," or fragments of phrases, to create his unique sound.[6] These motifs, in rhetorical terms something akin to Aristotle's rhetorical *topoi,* provided a rich assortment of materials with which to improvise— that is, to respond to particular meters or harmonic progressions. Wynton Marsalis describes this process as "improvising within a form. You challenge that form with rhythms, with harmonies [....] You set parameters and then you mess with them" (*American Heritage* Oct. 1995). In practice, this can mean that the musician will start with a set form of some kind—Parker, for instance, frequently used other musician's tunes rather than creating them from scratch—and then rework it. The musician revises the structure within any single performance or from one performance to the next. Each time the music is performed, the result is a different product.

Revision can be so extensive from performance to performance that one may not recognize the catalyst piece, as in the case of Parker's improvisations on Ray Noble's tune "Cherokee," which produced the innovative and autonomous "Koko." As Charles Hartman contends, jazz improvisation "centers not on escape, but on the liberation of certain aspects of the music from rule-governed regularity, so as to make them variable, and so potentially expressive" (70); the composition "is unplanned, but not entirely unprepared. Some of the mediating influences on it favor a highly organized, even rigorously architectonic sense of structure"(21). The better one is, the more one's finished product, which often seems to be or is knocked off quickly and without premeditation, will be grounded in training, expertise, external influences, and, yes, natural talent. Kerouac may well have been adlibbing—or "not thinking," as he told John Clellon Holmes—when he wrote poetry, but his compositions were anything but naive, uniformed, and chaotic. His spontaneous improvisation with words mirrored jazz practices, in that it was predicated upon, and often hid, his knowledge of oral and literary forms—vast structures undergirding what can appear disconnected, uncanny assemblages. He used many motifs, but the following appear as the most prominent.

The expository statement underscored with "the rhythm of rhetorical exhalation" so dominates that one can speculate it was Kerouac's favorite motif. The form produces an accumulation of rhythms, many driven by the phonological phrase that through stress prominence creates distinctly American speech, carrying the speaker to the poem's conclusion. The space dash complements the expository statement, accelerating and decelerating the rhythms. Kerouac also believed that the dash avoided the artificial pause of conventional punctuation and accurately "measured pauses which are the essentials of our speech" (*Portable Beat* 484). The power of the dash can be seen in this passage from his long poem "Sea," which blends motifs to capture the sounds of the Pacific Ocean:

Shaw———Shoo———Oh soft sigh
   we wait hair twined like
Larks———Pissit———Rest not
———Plottit, bisp tesh, cashes,
   re tav, plo, aravow,
shirsh,———Who's whispering over
there———the silly earthen creek!
(*BS* 222)

The voices in this passage, expository statement (e.g. "the silly earthen creek!") and onomatopoeia twined like the human hair (or its oceanic analogue the seaweed), to which the speaker alludes, oscillate languidly, pushed into and away from each other like water and sand or voices sung in choral call and response. The rhythmic communication between two life forms, a human and the sea, is sustained through the dashes, a concise, confident sign of the pull of earth and lunar gravity that keeps the sea in motion.

Kerouac varied the expository statement to create the tic, or a sudden vision of a memory. As he explained in *Some of the Dharma,* ideally the tic "is one short and one longer sentence, generally about fifty words in all, the intro sentence and the explaining sentences" (342). To exemplify, or perhaps to aid his memory, he included with his definition a tic titled "Cold Fall mornings":

> Cold Fall mornings with the sun shining
> in the yard of the St. Louis school, the
> pebbles—the pure vision of world beginning
> in my childhood brain then, so that even the
> black nuns with their fleshwhite faces and
> rimless glasses & weepy redrimmed eyes looked
> fresh and ever delightful . . . .
>
> (341)

The first "sentence" of this tic is in fact a noun phrase ("Cold Fall mornings"), followed by three prepositional phrases ("with the sun," "in the yard," "of the St. Louis school"), one participial phrase ("shining . . ."), and an appositive ("the pebbles"). The explanatory passage that follows the dash includes a noun phrase ("the pure beginning . . . then"), a conjunction ("so"), and a relative clause ("that even . . . delightful"), delineating the memory of the schoolyard as an ever-hopeful sign of the genesis of life.

Kerouac consistently alternated the expository statement and the tic motifs with an expansive yet relatively fixed set of structures. For instance, during the early fifties when composing *Mexico City Blues,* he was intent upon using his writing to teach Buddhist wisdom, so *Mexico City Blues,* as well as much of his later poetry, reflects his immersion in Buddhist literary form fused with Catholicism. He favored proverbs, parables, and fablelike passages, such as:

> Knew all along
> That when chicken is eaten
> Rooster aint worried
> And when Rooster is eaten
> Chicken aint worried
> (*MCB* 26)

As "aint" in this poem suggests, the elevated speech in which these forms have been historically preserved is often rejected in Kerouac's poetry. Haiku, or haikulike structures such as the lovely "Like kissing my kitten in the belly / The softness of our reward" (230th Chorus), contribute a humble sermonic tone, as do aphorisms exemplified by the following—"The sea don't tell——— / The sea don't murder———" (*BS* 240), which relies on an informal variant of standard edited English.

The sutra in various forms is also prominent, the 111th Chorus of *Mexico City Blues* presenting one of the finest examples. This chorus begins with the vernacular—"I didn't attain nothin"—moving smoothly into laconic Zen speech crafted with repetition, anaphoria, simple description, and Buddhist terminology:

> I attained absolutely nothing,
> Nothing came over me,
>   nothing was realizable—
>
> . . . .
> People asked me questions
> about tomatos [*sic*] robbing the vine
> and rotting on the vine
> and I had no idea
> what I was thinking about
>
>
>   and abided
>   in blank ecstasy
>
>   (111)

The anaphoria of hymn construction is also evident in poems such as the 228th Chorus of *Mexico City Blues*, which echoes the Christian Doxology in its repetition of "Praised be" to introduce the list of items worthy of celebration, including man, delusion, I, and the singer's "fellow man / For dwelling in milk" (230). Prayer, too, finds its way into many of the poems, sometimes as highly dramatic supplications, as in the 192nd and 193rd choruses of *Mexico City Blues:*

> "O thou who holdest the seal
>   of power, raise thy diamond
>   hand, bring to naught, destroy,
>   exterminate.
> . . . .
> All these words
> Of mystery,
> Svaha,
> So be it,
> Amen." (192–93)

These motifs, literary genres in their own right, complement and are complemented by personal narrative, the most extended example being what James Jones calls the Lowell Cantos section of *Mexico City Blues:* seventeen choruses (87–103) activating the heart of poetry as " a great story and confession" of Duluoz's childhood (87).

Conjoined is a set of rhetorical figures that function as linking, emphatic, or signifying devices. Kerouac loved puns or double entendres and not only applied them to familiar phrases but also used them to link stanzas or choruses.

"Mission of mercy," for example, the standard upon which Kerouac improvised "Mersion of Missy" in the first chorus of *Mexico City Blues,* is revised as "Mercy on Mission" in the concluding line of the 128th Chorus. Through word inversion, a variant on the pun, linguistically improvised, Kerouac shifts meaning without changing the basic sonic structures of the phrase, as in "The pool of clear rocks . . . . Clear the pool" (*MCB* 4) and "Man's Made Essence / Essence's Made Man" (7). Kerouac also had a particular aptitude for punning on names by splitting the name with a short preposition or pronoun, as in "Brigham Me Young" (71). English vocabulary pidginized with French, Spanish, Latinate, and other phonemes occurs frequently as well, often creating a humorous, childlike commentary, as in "Simplificus? Ricidulous? / Immensicus? Marvailovous!" (95). This improvisation on Latin suffixes effects an emotional simplicity enhancing the theme of the chorus: a vision of the speaker's childhood in Lowell, which in the turn to the French-like *marvailovous* expresses childlike joy through his native tongue.

Phonetic spellings to replicate the vernacular texture all the poems. In *Old Angel Midnight,* some of the most dramatic abound: "but d y aver read a story" for "but did you ever read a story" (1); "reacht" and "fixt" for "reached" and "fixed" (8–9); and "lottawords foir nathing" for "a lot of words for nothing" (20). As "lottawords" illustrates, Kerouac's poetry took advantage of fused or telescoped words, such as "hooftrompled," "boommusic," and "redpanting," (*OAM* 17, 54, 38), many of them artfully accentuating the synesthesic nature of linguistic concepts. The stringing or tombstoning of nominals as adjectivals is the last and perhaps most distinctly Kerouacian syntactic technique, illustrated by this line from *Old Angel Midnight:* "Mike Mike milkcan Ashcan Lower Eastside Dreams" (17). Threads such as this stitch together many components of his poetry and fiction.

These elements are not simply filler to be plugged in when Beat imagination ran dry. In other words, they are not predominantly the detritus of free association or automatic surrealism. Instead, they are compact forms consistently repeated, spliced, and rearranged within phrases, stanzas, paragraphs, and choruses, creating a double compositional movement that progresses and repeats (5).[7] Take, for instance, the following sentence from *Old Angel Midnight:* "The Berber types that hang fardels on their woman back wd as lief Erick some son with blady matter I guess as whup a mule in singsong pathetic mulejump field by quiet fluff smoke North Carolina (near Weldon) (Railroad Bridge) Roanoke Millionaire High-Ridge hi-party Hi-Fi million-dollar findriver skinfish Rod Tong Apple Finder John Sun Ford goodby Paw mule American Song—" (56). The sentence, readily identifiable as Kerouac's prosodic voice, follows a standard subject-predicate structure. *Types* is the subject, and the predicate features a compound verb: "wd . . . lief . . . whup" linked with the correlative conjunctions "as. . . as." The predicate embraces

Kerouac's playful improvisation: phonetic spellings and puns (unified and split). The word *Erick,* part of the pun on the Viking explorer Lief Erikson, holds multiple grammatical spaces in the sentence. It can be part of a phrasal verb ("lief Erick"), the object of the verb "lief," or an adjective describing the object ("son"—the last element in the split pun "Erick some son"). The sentence is also textured with a diminutive "y" adjective ("blady"), fused words, and nominal strings as modifiers.

The nominal string that lies adjacent to the "pathetic mulejump field" leads the reader on a long journey to the noun *Song.* Flat and elongated, the string mirrors a river or a road, either one of which could run alongside the vision of a real or imagined field. With respect to the Legend overall, the nominal string effects a Buddhist and American sense of equality, the discrete parts all on the same hypotactic plain. This sameness, or the eradication of the uniqueness of each word, is augmented by the demands the device makes on the reader's cognition. Comprehension of a long, unbroken list of words, most of them nouns acting as adjectives (as in the above twenty-nine-word string), requires that each modifier be interpreted in the context of the previous. This act becomes more strenuous the farther away one moves from the string's initiator, especially without conventional adjectival forms or the hierarchical structure that subordination or paratactic syntax provides, both of which greatly facilitate comprehension. In effect, the nominal string frustrates signification, causing the reader to lose track of the expanding semantic space. Repeatedly retreating and reconstructing, the reader may discover that the nominal string discloses discrete and interchangeable parts while morphing into nonsemantic sound. Consequently, the *Song* under consideration here is not just music, but a specified place, a party, a man named John, economic currency, a patriarch, a fruit, and a fish. Eventually it is America, in which the many become the all and brutality is negated in the unity of being.

Less complex than nominal strings, quotes are another linking device critical to Kerouac's poetic motifs. Frequently, like quotes in conventional narrative fiction, they designate the speech or dialogue of certain characters. In this capacity, the quote provides the Lowell Canto section of *Mexico City Blues* with tonal and historical dimension, the voices of Duluoz's father and friends mingled with lovingly humorous versions of his childhood voice. Equally conventional, the quotation marks in "Sea" demarcate the sea as personified, a natural phenomenon through which the speaker recognizes romantic correspondences enabling him to read himself. At other times, however, quotes mirror the way Parker and other jazz musicians inserted snippets of well-known songs into their elaborate improvisations, the musical standard signifying, or mocking, other artistic forms and artists. For instance, Kerouac occasionally integrated lines from widely recognized pop lyrics and improvised on them, as in the opening stanza of the 53rd Chorus of *Mexico City Blues:* "Merrily we roll along / Dee de lee dee doo doo doo / Merrily merrily all the day" (53). At one level, the lyrics call serious attention to the connection between poetry and song, which the chorus subsequently makes explicit: "Life woulda been / a mistake without music." But "Merrily we roll along" is spliced into the poem much the way Charlie Parker spliced the clarinet descant of "High Society" or Percy Grainger's "Country Gardens" into his improvs, the quotations signifying the bebopper's insult or contempt for anyone who thinks the bourgeois melody better music than Parker's intricate harmonic manipulations.[8] Likewise, in *Mexico City Blues,* the seemingly naive voice singing a nursery rhyme as prologue to a philo-sophical statement about the importance of music in human culture mocks the bourgeois need for fallacious categorizations distinguishing "good" or "high" music from "bad" or "low."

Quotation marks also link nonattributed speech to other passages, fre-quently without signifiers of the external source, just as is found in *Some of the Dharma.* Snippets of speech of Kerouac's friend Bill Garver appear nonat-tributed in *Mexico City Blues,* but many others remain unidentified. Even when a quoted passage is attributed, the free-floating passages often merge with the verbal material surrounding them, especially those marked only with opening quotes, reminiscent of the poet Charles Olson's open paren-theses. Much like voices singing or instruments playing in unison, they are recognized as discrete sources of sound, but the cumulative effect signals blended presentation. Consequently, with or without attribution, the voices lose authority: as the pattern repeatedly shifts from solo to group expression, aural illusion resists efforts to identify individual voices. Is it the voice of Jack Kerouac, Jack Duluoz, or someone else being quoted? The cumulative effect of the quotes, coupled with the dash, loosely mimics jazz cutting. The lines swing into metrical verse, then conversational speech, then didactic forms, such as sutras and aphorisms—sometimes aggressively, sometimes collea-gially. The rhythms shift awkwardly and unexpectedly, opening out as new forms are cued to enter. In poem cycles such as *Mexico City Blues, Old Angel Midnight,* or "San Francisco Blues," this shift disrupts the sense of where or when the performance commenced, each new voice entering, each stop and start signaling another beginning—a recursive movement producing the illu-sion of multiple entrances and exits.

In any discussion of Kerouac's jazz motifs, his well-known reverence for Charlie Parker renders it difficult *not* to seek compositional links between the two. We should be careful not to push the correspondence unproductively, but there is one motif that deserves studied attention—and my insertion of it here is only the briefest of introductions. I am referring to the stacked stanza—short lines layered one on top of the other—the vertical twin of the horizontal nominal string. The form may reflect Kerouac's reading of

William Carlos Williams, as Jones speculates, but it also acts much like Parker's scalar descent, which Thomas Owens describes as phrases and groups of choruses arranged with the goal of arriving "on a final note that lies at the end of a lengthy stepwise descent" (35). Parker, it is believed, introduced this figure to jazz, according to Owens (35), and while there's no evidence that Kerouac intentionally appropriated Parker's descending scales, the stacked stanzas create a heavy beat sweeping many of the poems downward to a point of exhaustion or rest. For example, the trochee-driven "Maynard / Mainline / Mountain / Merudvhaga" in the 1st Chorus of *Mexico City Blues* accelerates the poem downward to and sets up the last line, "Mersion of Missy," the little punning tongue twister summarizing the spiritual journey on which the singer and the reader have embarked.

"No Revisions (Except Obvious Rational Mistakes)"[9]

Through intense reading and writing, coupled with a natural ear for music and voices, Kerouac prepared himself so well that he became adept at the jazz manipulation of motifs, so much so that he could, as I have already noted, compose poetry quickly and with little conventional revising. However, his prosodic style also owed a great deal to his years as a wordsmith—those discordant yet euphonic years illuminated in Kerouac's *Windblown World* journals. In fact, the composition history of some of his most successful poetry, *Mexico City Blues* in particular, reveals that his spontaneous bop prosody in actual practice *integrated* jazz improv with more conventional writing strategies. The manuscripts and typescripts of these texts also suggest that traditional writing processes, the often tedious acts of drafting and revising, were most likely undertaken at his own initiative rather than being imposed by an editor.[10]

Mexico City Blues provides a dramatic example of this approach. Despite the fact that many of the poems remained unchanged from penciled notebook to published book, the compilation underwent revisions in several distinct stages after its initial composition. This resulted in a poem cycle that, somewhat like Charlie Parker's alchemical metamorphosis of "Cherokee" into "Koko," transformed an inchoate collection of prayers, dreams, stories, and tics into an autobiographical poem of spiritual awakening and atonement—paradoxically deconstructing the standard forms it challenged and re-imposing these forms on itself, effectively masking the artifacts of its heritage. Although it is not known exactly when, sometime after Kerouac composed the four *Mexico City Blues* breast-pocket holograph notebooks, he determined that a poem cycle would be culled from these entries, which were not written in the order of the published cycle and were not originally numbered. What became *Mexico City Blues* was interspersed throughout the notebooks with passages from *Tristessa, Book of Dreams,* and other unpublished or untitled musings. The notebooks reveal that Kerouac reviewed the collection, determined which poems to keep, and numbered them to create 242 distinct choruses. He even noted where new poems should be added: for instance, at the top of what became the 166th Chorus, he wrote in pencil "INSERT G's 3 DREAMS," referring to dreams of his friend Bill Garver. These became choruses 161–65 but are not part of the notebook materials.

The first five poems in the notebooks remained as the first five choruses of *Mexico City Blues,* but from there on reordering dramatically altered the text. The most significant result is that the poem cycle assumes the form of a linear contemplative narrative culminating in a declaration of aesthetic, spiritual, and personal truths. The rigid imposition of numerical sequencing (the title of each poem is its number, or place, in the sequence) illustrates that Kerouac intentionally worked against rhizomic improvisation and toward a specific teleology. For example, it is by no means insignificant that the last archived notebook ends with what became the 221st Chorus, a poem about the African American blues musician Huddy Leadbetter (1889–1949), known as Leadbelly. This chorus concludes with the lines "Old Man Mose is Dead / But Deadbelly get ahead / Ha ha ha." The play on "Leadbelly" as "Deadbelly" and the slightly demonic laughter that closes this chorus suggest that the jazz musician/poet is a tricksterlike figure transmogrified from "the furtive madman / of old sane times" into a self-serving modern hipster. In contrast, the published text concludes with a penultimate three-chorus set eulogizing and beatifying Charlie Parker. Instead of foregrounding a blues trickster/hipster figure who undermines the spiritual quest, *Mexico City Blues* positions Parker as a human being who transcends the corporeal: "No longer Charley [*sic*] Parker / But the secret unsayable name" to whom the speaker prays for personal and universal forgiveness. Parker, a metonymic signifier of Christ's messianic power (Parker died on Kerouac's birthday, March 12, 1955), is recognized as both authentic human subject and the secret site of the poet's fantasy life. As poetic device, Parker becomes a complicated set of psychic constructions that encompass recognition, compassion, and empathy for Parker's colonized existence in American culture while splitting him into a second self that, in a fetishlike way, provides the speaker with a subterranean, epiphanic realm of liberation in which to perpetuate difference.[11] This constellation of contradictory beliefs augers the speaker's declaration on the nature of human thought: "The sound in your mind / is the first sound / that you sing," the primeval and heavenly lyric voice, which invests the poet with visionary power to prophesy about the thieflike character of death. The singer of the chorus can then counsel others to follow his vision of benevolent life: "Stop the murder and suicide!" he cries, "All's well! / I am the Guard." Through discursive interaction with an imaginary rendering of Charlie Parker, the great master of human sound, Duluoz the bardic singer becomes the "other"—in this case, the prophetic and to some unrecognized or despised keeper of the world.

However, Kerouac, did not always faithfully follow his twelve-bar format, that is, limiting the individual choruses to one notebook page.[12] For instance, he penciled the 11th Chorus on the same page as the twelfth, separating the two with the end mark. As published, the 11th Chorus contains a large blank space and a parenthetical describing it as the momentary silent brooding of the musician, but these jazz elements were revisions that only appeared later in the typescript. Ten of the choruses also conclude at different points in the holograph than in the published version.[13] When Kerouac numbered the poems, he chose to end them at the bottom of the page rather than at their original conclusion, which carries over to the next page and is clearly marked with a squiggly line (〰). Thus the idea of improvising within an established parameter was imposed on some of the language through revision. Shortened by revision, these choruses as published carry over thematically to the next chorus, whereas the first drafts had no such "hold" of a "note" from one bar to the next.

The holographs suggest, however, that Kerouac clearly wanted to follow his method, even when he seemed to know that the chorus was incomplete but he had reached the end of the page. He would sometimes squeeze two or more lines onto the last line of the page, write up the margins, or insert phrases between lines. Nonetheless, several choruses are also the combination of disparate poems that most likely, on Kerouac's second thought, appeared to belong together. Take for instance the 86th Chorus, which is a composite of three separate holograph poems; the first two lines, "Take your pick, / If you wanta commit suicide." are clearly the end of the preceding five poems, which became choruses 81–85, and complete the playful riffing on the phrase "luney and cruney." In the holograph, after these two lines, Kerouac wrote "(end of loony Fruney Poem)." Preceding these lines by several pages in the notebook are the two stanzas that were to become the bulk of the 86th Chorus. A squiggly end mark follows the line "Peaceful and Golden" of the first stanza, indicating that he initially considered this a separate poem but later combined it with the subsequent poem that begins "A Crashing Movie." All but the first two lines are on a different notebook page.

True to his published manifesto, though, Kerouac also engaged in minor revisions of "obvious rational mistakes, such as names or *calculated* insertions in act of not writing but *inserting*" (*Portable* 485). But the nature of the revisions, particularly in *Mexico City Blues*, goes beyond these categories. This is significant because *Mexico City Blues*, unlike *Scripture of the Golden Eternity*, which he intentionally revised because it was a religious text and therefore according to his reasoning required careful editing (Charters xx), was categorized by Kerouac as jazz inspired and spontaneously generated. In the composition process, however, he indented numerous lines, cut dedications, and eliminated individuals lines and stanzas. Forty-seven of the choruses had material deleted from them as Kerouac moved from manuscript to typescript. Some of these cuts seem to have been made to avoid revealing deeply personal material. For instance, the 47th Chorus, a mediation on World War II that begins "Where is Italy?" ends in the published text with the question "What happened in Italy?" which is a variation on the introductory question. However, the poem as initially composed concludes with an answer to that query: a simple three-word line recognizing Sebastian Sampas's death in the war at Anzio. This reference to his childhood confidant may well have been too painful for Kerouac to reveal. In any case, its elimination from the typescript ironically depersonalizes the chorus by transforming the self-referent "I" into an inclusive voice of post–World War II anxiety. Revisions such as these support the project of elevating the poem from opaque, solipsistic confession to universalized, spiritual vision.

"VOICE IS ALL"

Kerouac was loathe to admit that he engaged in rewriting his texts—no doubt because the jazz improv method as he perfected it in many ways functioned effectively, and also because he may have come to believe in his own legend as iconoclastic jazz poet, especially by the later 1950s when he had become the public face of the romantic rebel Beat artist. However, the fusion of these two methods, and his treatment of them to mask the studied and literary nature of his work, enabled him to pursue a tightly focused set of objectives. As the above discussion of his Parker-like set of motifs indicates, the overarching goal was to liberate poetry as speech and song, or as James Jones wrote in his careful analysis of *Mexico City Blues*, Kerouac "wished once again to be able to sing the sign" (84). A parallel objective was to recuperate an element of the bardic nature of the poet: storyteller, musician, keeper of cultural memory, one who through sound, music, and words consolidates the communal voice of a people.

In the service of poetry as immense life force, Kerouac's writing became the instrument for the creation of a jazz orchestra, so to speak, or the universe of voices that populate our daily lives, a concept that centers *Old Angel Midnight* and the theme song for the film *Pull My Daisy*.[14] In fact, one of his most momentous epiphanic experiences, jubilantly recounted in a letter he wrote to Neal Cassady in October 1950, left Kerouac convinced that "voice is all," and he intended to "let the voices speak for themselves." He told Cassady that he wanted to write a series of books, each in a different dialect, such as bum, hip musician, cool, and American Mexican (*Letters* 1: 233). He never completed the project, but he did infuse an American choral presence into the Legend, and consequently, many of his poems as components of that Legend stand as unified, stable, and recognizable voices, ranging from the self-deprecatingly humorous to the demonic incorporating the invective and the playful, to the prayerfully elegiac, to the sermonic. These voices, especially the blues sequences, reflect Kerouac's sensitivity to the vernacular, particularly the ergot of the Beat scene, language representing the popular folk roots of the Beat ethos as swashbuckling lexical lawlessness.

These voices also convey the recognition of the poet and the poem as the mind that births the world. Like melodies, the voices that dominate the Legend's poetry are disembodied. They float inviolate, without names in many cases, unattached to signifiers of time or place and of human history and corporeality. They resonate with the mindfulness that the solitary poet is a ventriloquistic performer and the poem itself a time-space dynamic that liberates speech through variable literary form; in return, speech molds literary form. The conflagration often generates the imprint of earlier, more expansive forms, paradoxically spotlighting the soloist while muting his solitary voice among the polyphonic echoes of the texts on which he draws.

One of the most intriguing voices to solo repeatedly is probably one least associated with Kerouac or Duluoz: the demonic, heard in the "Deadbelly" poem, which is the 221st Chorus of *Mexico City Blues*. The poem purports to tell a story of the death of Leadbelly, but what dominates is the relatively uninterrupted internal rhyming of line such as "Deadbelly dont hide it— / Lead killed Leadbelly— / Deadbelly admit / Deadbelly modern cat" (223). The vowel sounds are low and long, echoing the laconic voices of the hipsters who populated the Beat scenes as well as the rough, powerful tones of Leadbelly himself. The repeated naming of Leadbelly, which in terms of root lyric forms invests both subject and object with power, becomes blurred through sound, the individual Leadbelly vanishing as the sounds in combination evoke a marginalized people, a dialogic fusion of black and Native American vernacular and white racist mockeries of that vernacular. The "ha ha ha" concluding the chorus is wickedly suggestive of *Doctor Sax,* the demonic, trickster poet triumphing over both oppressed and oppressor.

The invective voice joins the demonic in "A Curse at the Devil," a text that appears in *Scattered Poems* and features an assemblage of elements associated with magic charms. These include alliteration, word repetition, invectives, and the naming of all the terrible things that will come to pass as a result of the speaker's performance of the curse:

> Lucifer Sansfoi (the devil without faith)
>   Varlet Sansfoi
>
> Omer Perdieu
>   I.B. Perdie
>   Billy Perdy
>
> I'll unwind your
>   guts from Durham
>   to Dover
>   and bury em
>   in Clover—
>
> Your psalms I'll 'ave
>   engraved
>   in your toothbone—
>
> (48–53)

Repetition, internal and end rhyme, and nonstandard French call to mind voodoo incantation in the above lines. Simultaneously, several stanzas feature the highblown cursing of the Renaissance gentleman ("Your psalms I'll 'ave / engraved / in your toothbone—"), what Kerouac described as Shakespearian ravings "in the great world night like the wild wind through an old Cathedral" (*Blonde* 87). This voice—the mad genius infused with both God and devil—shatters time and linearity as the speaker directs its power at the hapless "you." The performative authority of "A Curse at the Devil" is augmented with rhythmic syncopation engineering frenzy or feverish movement. The effect of the rhythmic construction does not merely remind one of such movement but *creates* and *performs* it, which an oral reading of the poem surely does. Rhythm, in turn, works compatibly with the sounds to produce the demonic voice, acting as performative language to effect something: in this case, the dispelling of evil.

No set metrical pattern controls the poem, but isolated stanzas or lines in various meters exist. The third stanza contains iambics: "To Dover / and bury em / in Clover—"; the second stanza, trochees: "Omer Perdieu / I.B. Perdie / Billy Perdy." Juxtaposed with these are stanzas with no set meter. As a result, the rhythmic thread is accentual; the syllable following the word *your* in each stanza receives the stress, creating a drum-beat pushing the poem toward the final directive that defeats the devil. The rhythm of "Curse" also aptly illustrates the point discussed earlier about the accumulation of rhythm to bring the poem to its end. If one reads the lines with breath breaks indicated by the space dash, the poem is split into two parts composed of a series of phrases building upon each other and held together by the rhythm established by the stanzaic stress and breath stop. The constancy and accumulation of the rhythm sweeps each of the two sections toward conclusion. Part 1 ends with the forceful "Gibbering quiver / graveyard HOO!" Part 2, containing fewer space dashes, slows somewhat in preparation for the confident, concluding curse: "Devil, get thee / back / to russet caves."

"Curse at the Devil" also exemplifies Kerouacian rhythmic patterns that augment sound through imaginative mixing. Writing in implicit sympathy with Olson's theory of field composition, improvising by syllable and phrases rather than by metric feet, Kerouac produced relatively short poetic lines that perform as contemporary jazzlike Skeltonic verse. The rhythms often "creak" like jazz rhythms can be made to do, breaking unexpectedly, an effect Kerouac produced by emphasizing the continuous flow of the prose nature of the expository statement, "which has breaks determined . . . by syntax and sense" (Attridge 5), and then working against these rhythms with lines broken to accelerate or decelerate. Language is often in the midst of being stripped of its expository semantic-generating syntax to highlight sound and beat, while semantic content is reinserted as the poetic line moves back into expository mode.

One can appreciate this standard more fully by recognizing that the cognitive unit Kerouac used as a template for poetic expression corresponds with the intonation unit. Conjoined, this cognitive-intonation unit is what linguists call the phonological phrase (Gates, "Forging" 505). Unlike metrical verse that uses patterns of alternating weak and strong syllables, the phonological phrase is governed by points of prominence. Each phrase will have one point of prominence, determined by pitch change, duration, and loudness (Gates, "Forging" 507), which generally falls at the end of the phrase, but secondary and tertiary points may exist as well. For example, the first stanza of the 52nd Chorus of *Mexico City Blues* can be scanned as follows to illustrate the phonological phrases and their points of prominence.

```
3      2        1
I'm crazy everywhere
      3        2          1
Like the guy sailed on that ferry
     2     1
   for 3 years
3                2          1
Between Hong Kong  &   China
```

This stanza, an expository statement in line one followed with a brief commentary, is built upon lines constructed as single phonological phrases in which the normal contour of prominence dominates, the primary (1) prominence coming at the end of the line, where the speaker also pauses. Each line therefore emphasizes its semantic content rather than any musical qualities. In the second stanza, the pattern is continued with a slight variation:

```
3              2        1
The British shoulda given him
        3        2          1
    temporary residence in Hong Kong:
    3                      2
    but they didn't want any part
    1      1      2      3
    of him / first place / he didn't
    2          1
    have any money
```

What is significant in this stanza is the breaking of lines, so that some become rhythmic groups that grate against the syntactic group that moves the phonological phrase across lines. For instance, the prominence level forced onto "him" in the fourth line of the stanza forces a primary prominence on "first," creating a speechlike counterpoint suggestive of what Rosemary Gates describes in William Carlos Williams's poetry as "the movement of thought, under emotional pressure" ("Forging" 515). By modulating the poetic line in this manner, Kerouac produced a sound that remained a potent conveyor of recognizable voice types. The "creakiness" of the form is as much suited for the childlike and the elegiac as for the demonic and profane.

At times, though, Kerouac transforms pianissimo into the fortissimo of full throttle song. No Kerouac poem does this more exuberantly than "Song: Fie My Fum" and its successor poem "Pull My Daisy," collaboratively written by Kerouac, Ginsberg, and Neal Cassady. In these poems, which assert themselves as the most recognizable of Kerouac's collaborative voices, the semantic thrust of the phonological phrase is obliterated by elements of melos. Short lines and heavy stresses produce a quick, swinging rhythm. "FIE MY FUM," a shorter version of "Pull My Daisy," neatly illustrates this point:

> Pull my daisy,
> Tip my cup,
> Cut my thoughts
> For coconuts
>
> Start my arden
> Gate my shades,
> Silk my garden
> Rose my days,
>
> . . . .

Pope my parts,
Pop my pot,
Poke my pap,
Pit my plum.
(*Scattered* 2)

The poem can be read in at least two ways: the stress placed on the first and third syllable or the stress placed only on the first syllable. Either way, the poem is tightly structured. Its emphasis on short phrases; internal, slant, and end rhymes; and repetition of the imperative create a chant rhythm lifting the poem into frenzied bursts. The chant element is so strong in this poem, and even more so in subsequent versions of "Pull My Daisy," that the one break in the rhythmic pattern, the fourth line of the first stanza ("For coconuts"), is elided. "For" is read unstressed as if it were the concluding syllable of the preceding line, allowing "coconuts" to accept the stress on its first and third syllables.[15]

The presence of the disembodied voice in Kerouac's poetry underscores sound as separate from what is known as the autonomous self. This may seem an ironic undercutting of the unified, individual self that is staple of Beat ideology and Kerouac's wisdom quests, and in some respects it is. Kerouac's creation of human speech and song through poetry pushes the poet and the reader into a consciousness that attempts to escape, or at least to demystify, the illusion of selfhood, the atman. But true to his romantic proclivities, Kerouac's pathway to this awareness involved intense concentration on the personal as a vehicle to greater wisdom. Using memories, reflections, and confessions as raw ingredients, his bardic work countered the solitary, potentially solipsistic, singer, propelling him toward moments of being the other. This process led him to replace the solitary singer with a multiplicity of Beat voices fixed by the confines of linguistic play, selves that are more verbal process than the phenomenal product.[16]

"I Vow To Be Influenced By . . . Joyce"[17]

As this discussion has already demonstrated, the Duluoz Legend repeatedly conveys Kerouac's indebtedness to James Joyce's fascination with the choral, nonlinear plasticity of voice and self. The same holds true for Kerouac's poetic production, which perhaps makes the strongest case for the extent of Kerouac's Joycian inheritance, thus justifying the delay of an extended discussion of the Joyce-Kerouac connection to this point. Two long poems, in particular "Sea" and *Old Angel Midnight*, unmask Kerouac's reverence for the innovator of both high modernism and postmodernism as well as the way

Joyce's style enabled Kerouac to experiment with epistemological realities encompassed in the concept of sound.

"Sea," which appears as a coda to *Big Sur,* the 1961 fictionalized account of Kerouac's experiences in Lawrence Ferlinghetti's cabin in northern California, attempts to complete the work that Kerouac considered unfinished at Joyce's death: creating the voice of the Pacific Ocean to complement the voice of the Atlantic Ocean that Joyce had constructed created in *Ulysses* (*BS* 32). "Sea" includes direct references to Joyce, Ulysses, Penelope, and Telemachus (227), and on the basis of this evidence, we can reasonably conclude that Kerouac might have had in mind as a model the "Proteus" episode of *Ulysses,* one of the, if not the, most impressive Western representations of human thought. Through the interior monologue of Stephen Dedalus, Joyce's version of Telemachus, strolling along Sandymount Strand contemplating his self-imposed exile, his mother, and the nature of thought, Joyce fractured and forged the protean material of human perception. Stephen's mind roams freely, acknowledging what he recognizes as "the ineluctable modality" of the visible and the audible, the fluid nature of the latter swirling around him (31), including his own boots crunching shells on the seashore. With humorous lyricism, the very voice of the ocean meets the voice of *human* waters as Stephen urinates into the Atlantic. The beauty of this passage resides not only in Joyce's ability to find powerful onomatopoetic form for the voice of the Atlantic—"seesoo, hrss, rsseis, ooos"—but also in the skill with which he blends that voice with Stephen's perceptions of it. The "oo" of the water's voice echoes in the "o" of "flop, slop, slap" representing Stephen's recognition of sound and is carried into the passage's concluding phrase, the two voices mingled through the alliterative repetition of the "fl" phoneme merging "flowing, floating foampool, flower unfurling" (41). The passage captures sound perceived unavoidably as emanating from individual sources, yet to be all-encompassing.

In carrying forward the Joycian sea project, the Jack Duluoz who narrates *Big Sur* includes bits of these voices in his story, which describes the style of the sea's voice as much like the one Stephen hears: "The sea not speaking in sentences so much as short lines: 'Which one? . . . the ones ploshed?' . . . the same, ah Boom" (*BS* 32). "Sea" itself follows Joyce's lead, moving into and out of the voices of the sea and the poet, presumably Duluoz, who is both audience for the sea's performance and mouthpiece through which the sea performs. As in Joyce's "wavespeech," the two voices continue to move toward and into and then away and separate from each other. Throughout, the separation of human and oceanic voice is most often achieved by framing each in separate stanzas that talk back and forth.. For instance, the fifth stanza is the voice of the poet in Quebecois commanding the sea to speak to him: "Parle, O, parle, mer, parle, / Sea

speak to me, speak / to me, your silver you light" (221). The sea responds
in the sixth stanza:

> Rare, he rammed the gate
> Rare over by Cherson, Cherson
> We calcify fathers here below
> ————a watery cross, with weeds
> entwined ————This grins restoredly,
> low sleep————Wave————Oh, no,
> shush————Shirk————Boom plop
>   (221–22)

As short English sentences, the sea's voice in this passage is human, and as
onomatopoeia it becomes pure sound. At other points in the poem, a stanza
will combine both voices, as does the thirty-eighth stanza, which is crafted as
call and response:

> My golden empty soul'll
> Outlast yr salty sill
> ————the Windows of my jelly eye
> & fish head muck look out on thee,
> slit, with a cigar-a-mouth,
> some contempt
>   (239)

The poet challenges the sea in a duel of everlasting life, the sea answering
back cryptically that it recognizes in the poet, the "cigar-a-mouth," the con-
temptuous hubris of the human ego.

Other passages in "Sea," such as its last stanza, adopt the more subtle
blending of voices that characterizes Joyce's style in *Ulysses* working at a
highly nuanced level:

> Didja ever tell him
> About water meeting water————?
> O go back to otter————
> Term————Term————Klerm
> Kerm————Kurn————Cow————Kow————
> Cash————Cac'h————Cluck————
> Clock————Gomeat sea need
> Be deep I see you
> Enoc'h
> Soon anarf
> In Old Brittany
>   (241)

The illusion to Stephen's act of urinating in the ocean that begins the stanza
("water meeting water") reads logically as the voice of the sea (perhaps speaking

to itself as multiple forms). "O go back to otter" could be the poet overhearing and responding to the sea, which then speaks in the subsequent four lines. Interestingly, this speech includes terms that are visual signifiers understandable only to the poet himself. There is no phonetic difference between "Cow" and "Kow," both receiving the hard "c" sound; the distinction is entirely visual. Thus the two words appear to represent a fusion of the sea's voice and the poet's consciousness—in other words, the nullification of the concept of human separation from nature. The sea then resumes its solo, telling the poet, who plans to record the voice of the Atlantic ocean in Cornwall (*BS* 32), that they'll meet "soon anarf" in Brittany. The sea knows that it has no beginning and end, no east or west, no Pacific or Atlantic. It is, as it has already in Joycian voice told Duluoz, "rounden huge bedoom" (229).

Kerouac advocates a kind of nonlinearity through such voices, especially those of the sea, which can be entered at any point in its constant flux, but the poem itself is highly linear, fundamentally replicating the greater romantic lyric that emerged as a high standard for English Romantic poets, including Shelley, Coleridge, and Wordsworth, who were much read and admired by many Beat writers.[18] Within this tradition, "Sea" has a clear introduction in which the sea calls to the poet ("Cherson! / Cherson!" 219), who then situates himself physically for meditation upon or conversation with the sea ("When rocks outsea froth / I'll know Hawaii / cracked up & scramble / up my doublelegged cliff / to the silt of / a million years—," 219). The poem moves Duluoz in meditation onto another plane in which the reality of the sea's voice overwhelms the human presence. In his recognition of his own insignificance, he eventually pleads to God for help (233). But man is God, he learns, so "Save yourself, God man, / ha ha!" he hears (233). Confronted with this existential reality, Duluoz continues until he reaches a state of wisdom: it is not the sea that destroys or murders; instead the tempest that humans face resides within the human condition.[19] At that point, the poet ends his meditation, bidding the sea farewell with knowledge that he and it are one (240–41). Thus, "Sea" as a romantic lyric speaks to a Buddhist understanding of individuality as an artifice, reconfiguring this truth as a traditional narrative of human spiritual progress. Because of the dichotomy of form and subject, "Sea" stands as a paean to the interstices of Romantic and Modernist poetics in the service of Beat and Buddhist aesthetics.

Kerouac, however, eventually accepted the Joycian challenge of engaging the illusion of rhizomic voices in both form *and* content. Without doubt, *Visions of Cody* belongs in this category, but it is *Old Angel Midnight,* a collage of sixty-seven uniquely shaped poetic passages recording "the sounds of the entire world" as Duluoz heard them floating in his window (1), that most boldly builds on Joycean polyphony. The poem presents a mélange of voices from Lucien Carr, the inspiration for the poem; to the Katzenjammer Kids,

African Americans, French immigrant women, and his own Beat friends, including Ginsberg, Burroughs, and Gregory Corso. At points, sounds of an external reality, including church bells and bird song, enter the mix, but for the most part, the poem illustrates that Kerouac's "window" was his own imagination, through which language wafted endlessly.

The malleable nature of the conversational interplay in *Old Angel Midnight* clearly reflects Kerouac's reading of *Finnegans Wake*. As Campbell and Robinson have noted about the *Wake*, Joyce "had to smelt the modern dictionary back to protean plasma and re-enact the 'genesis and mutation of language' in order to deliver his message" (4). The *Wake* also reconfigures human perception of time and space. Eschewing the flat declarative sentence and the clean lines of syllogistic logic, it brilliantly counters stable character-ization and setting to thwart autonomy and linearity. On a smaller scale, Kerouac accepted the same challenge in *Old Angel Midnight,* which seeks not to represent a reality external to discourse but to create within discourse a universe in which the self as free-standing entity is exposed as illusion.[20]

Kerouac, while multilingual, did not share Joyce's mania for the collection and handling of linguistic material from dozens of languages and disciplines. He populated *Old Angel Midnight* with many languages, but he did not com-pose it as Joyce did the *Wake,* who filled dozens of notebooks with words and phrases meticulously laid on the page like mosaic tiles on grout. What Kerouac took from Joyce was a teleological objective rather than a compositional method: the disruption and rearrangement of discursively codified sound as speech into a realm where English semantics repeatedly buckles under mean-ing driven by sound and syntax alone. The results are stunningly similar. For instance, at the level of the single word, *Old Angel Midnight* contains many examples that resemble Joyce's linguistic wordplay. *Smoketacle,* for instance, is a beautiful recombinant form of *smoke* and *spectacle* —"How gruesome the smoketacle of people burning in rooms"— to create a portmanteau communi-cating the notion that burning people can be interpreted as performance (26).

It is at the sentence level, however, that the concept of the genesis and mutation of language as the process of self-creation emerges even more fully formed. The most direct expression is Duluoz's announcement in section 1 that the poem, like the *Wake,* is a creation story and that Old Angel Midnight, identified by various names throughout, including Jack, Lucien, I, Opprobrium, and Sound, analogous to Joyce's hero in the *Wake,* HCE (Humphrey Chimpden Earwicker, Here Comes Everybody, Haveth Childers Everywhere, and Haroun Childeric Eggeberth), is a masculine principle by which the world is created. "I know boy what's I talkin about," the narrator announces, "case I made the world & when I made it I no lie & had Old Angel Midnight for my name and concocted up a world so nothing you had forever thereafter make believe it's real" (1). As Sound, the creator comes home at night to "tweak his children's eyes" (2), who, the poem later implies, are birthed as language, not by Mrs. Midnight but by the Old Angel himself: "Old Angel Midnight just writes itself as it is the Hi-Is Sound" (29). Miraculously, like the acts of "Jesus in Capernaum" (29) or the dream of Leopold Bloom in the "Circe" episode of *Ulysses*, Old Angel Midnight possesses parthonogenic powers, creating his progeny, word after word spilling onto the page.

The self as textual formation is actualized in Kerouac's manipulation of the sentence. Consider this excerpt from section 36 of the poem: "eat & purr be holy kittypee pool in sand of red eyed bat bird insewecties pirking tig toont ta Ma tire free curé the school" (39). The word as signifier repeatedly travels through the syntax of the English sentence into aural signification and then back again. This dialectical movement within the sentence, the paragraph, and the composition as a whole drives the passage toward a musical rather a linguistic narrative. It is not the logic of the sentence that determines thought; instead, meaning is derived from percolating sounds, the poem implying that poets are duty bound to seek and open themselves to such sound. The sentence as melodic unit rather than semantic unit consistently, although never completely, overpowers the reader's desire for interpretive coherence. Kerouac later identified this effect as a fundamental flaw in *Old Angel Midnight*: "I began to rely too much on babble in my nervous race away from cantish clichés, chased the proton with my microscope, ended up ravingly enslaved to sounds," he determined, concluding that he "became unclear and dull . . . in [his] ultimate lit'ry experiment 'Old Angel Midnight'" (*Letters* 1: 487). Nonetheless, this semantic/aural pattern, despite Kerouac's self-doubts, laudably denudes the syntactic unit, be it linguistic or musical, as a fiction.

At this point, *Old Angel Midnight* crosses into the world of babble, a place where "the subconscious begins," as Kerouac explained in a 1967 essay on his experimental method (*Portable* 487). In this chlonthic realm, syntax breaks up, sentences stop, interpretation is abandoned, ideas are primed through unstructured sound, and the concept of individual consciousness paradoxically gestates and disintegrates. *Old Angel Midnight* declares this outright: "accorde tué, Ti Pousse, avec une belle femme folle pi vas' t' coucher—if ya don't understand s t t and tish, that langue, it's because the langue just bubbles & in the babbling void . . ." (21). The unidentified speaker, perhaps Old Angel or Jack Duluoz, tisk-tisks the ignorant Ti Pousse, Kerouac's childhood nickname that in this context suggests a mutation of self or the illusion of individuality in any form—after all, the son is but another version, or mythic Mannian succession story, of the father. The speaker's admonition implies that the child ought to know that words are unnecessary for thought and may have to be discarded if the speaker wishes to generate knowledge, that is, new life.

Sentence after sentence in the poem demonstrates this principle. The "kittypee" example above relies on "pirking tig toont ta" as the babble point, the apparently nonsensical deep breath by which the speaker gathers strength to generate new ideas. Others, such as "Dash dash dash dash mash crash wash wash mosh posh tosh tish rish rich sigh my tie thigh pie in the sky" (24), are dominated by sound piled on sound, leading to two small semantic breakthroughs: "sigh my tie" and "pie in the sky." Kerouac called this his own "awful raving madness" of language, an understandable interpretation, since *Old Angel Midnight* refuses to be anything but the naked, and therefore difficult to discern, truth of sound in relationship to thought, a poem that struck Kerouac at times as silly and slightly embarrassing yet thrilled him as "what [he] hears in heaven" (*Letters* 2: 45), futuristic "space prose" (57–69, 198), and "the flow of the mind as it moves in its space-time continuum" (487).

Kerouac's focus on voice, an eradication of conventional character and setting, in *Old Angel Midnight* announces that the universe Old Angel creates is True Nature

> . . . incomprehensibly beyond the veil of our senses & is like empty light [. . .] Why shd I fear Myself?——It's like looking at a movie high & insteada the story you see swarming electrical particles each one a bliss fwamming in the screen eternally. (13–14)

This Einsteinian portrait of reality—the Myself as waves/particles swirling through space—fashions the human self and character as linguistic matter ever slipping in and out of recognizable human form, but finding transitory stability in myth as the composite of human history and the individual psyche. *Old Angel Midnight,* just as Joyce's HCE and Anna Livia in the *Wake,* actualizes a sprawling polyglot, with Old Angel, Jack, Sound, and the I's of the text performing in their permeability that which the poem declares: "The essence of jello is the essence of arrangement. / Be nice to the monster crab, it's only another arrangement of that which you are" (18).

The notion of an external and universal essence conveyed in Kerouac's unique crab-jello metaphor addresses the idea of space that Kerouac associated with *Old Angel Midnight.* In a letter to Ginsberg in 1959, Kerouac confessed that he found "miraculous" the way in which *Old Angel Midnight* opened "a new world of connection in literature with the endless spaces of Shakti Maya Kali Illusion" (*Letters* 2: 57–69, 221). Shakti Maya, or Maya Shakti, as she is often called, names the veiling power that creates in the human ego the false belief in thingness, bringing forth the idea of the phenomenal world. Kali, or Kali Ma, is the female principle of dark nature that paradoxically eliminates the darkness of individual anger and other passions, granting wisdom and lighting the way to pure consciousness—a belief simi-lar to that espoused by gnostics and some orthodox Christians. *Old Angel Midnight,* then, extends "Shakti Maya Kali Illusion" into Western culture in its playfully persistent assault on the human voice using Kali wisdom to silence the human ego and cut through the phenomenal illusion of names and forms—the Maya Shakti.

This effort to break free from Maya's veil of the phenomenal and noumenal self is best represented in the Legend, especially the blues choruses and other poems, by a Joycian motif that I call the "partially erased name."[21] The motif takes a person's given and legal name, the most powerful cultural signifier of self, and by combining phonetic spelling and double entendre or pun, accentuates and deaccentuates the primal sign of individuality. This process challenges both the stability of the ego and the idea of language as the sacred symbol of that ego. What makes this motif most intriguing is the fact that Kerouac used his own name, *not* Duluoz, for erasure, granting himself rather than his mythic self-rep-resentation improvisational reign to transform the phonetic qualities of the French-Canadian "Jean-Louis Lebris de Kerouac" and the anglicized "Jack Kerouac" into melodies on which to riff. The improvisation establishes him as sole creator of meaning while undermining the authority of the solitary singer by destabilizing him and his literary proxies as sentient agents.

Consider, for example, the follow variations, which portend infinite semantic possibilities:

Scattered Poems—Jean-Louis Incogniteau (1);
Mexico City Blues— "Fellaheen Ack Ack" (13th Chorus),
  "Kerouaco's" (24th Chorus), "Kallaquack" (119th Chorus), "A kek
  Horrac" (137th Chorus), "Jaqui Keracky" (138th Chorus), "Ti Jean
  Picotee" (148th Chorus), and "Jean Louis Miseree" (216th-A Chorus);
"San Francisco Blues"—"Bekkek! Bekkek! / Koak! Koak! / Carra
  Quax! / Carra qualquus / Kerouacainius!" (85);
"Cerrada Medellin Blues"—"Jean Louee" (*Blues* 251);
"Berkeley Song in F Major: Farewell to My Babies"—"Jack
  Whatyrcallit" and "Jack Wittt" (*Pomes All Sizes* 86);
Old Angel Midnight—"Kee pardawac" (3), "Care—a—wack" (20),"old
  Kanuck" (23), "Kerouac—o" (30), "Crack Jabberwack . . . Onan
  Keraquack" (33), and "Quebekois Canoe (Kebokoa Kano-Kak!" (51);
"Sea"—"Wroten Kerarc'h" (223), "Karash" (231), and "Kerarc'h
  Jevac'h" (*BS* 240);
"Bus East"—"Jack Cake" (*Pomes* 2);
Some of the Dharma—"Kerouacwot" and "Kerouacvistu Aremedeia"
  (18) "Jean-Louis of Modern Prose" (98) and "John Shmerouac" (283);
Satori in Paris—"Jack Serouac" (68).

As Kerouac goofs with the hybrid nature of the sound of the name and its multilingual, material the name carries with it not only the signature of Jack Kerouac the author but also the sounds of the sea ("Karash") and rocks ("Karrak"), of *Alice in Wonderland* ("Jabberwack"), of the German ("Wroten"), Hebraic ("Kerarc'h Jevac'h"), Latin ("Kerouacainius!"), and Spanish ("Kerouac-o"). Ironically and lovingly, the name also pokes fun at the man who bears it. He is really a child ("Ti Jean Picotee"), a sad Frenchman ("Jean Louis Miseree"), a Frenchman in disguise ("Jean-Louis Incogniteau"), a masturbating duck ("Onan Keraquack"), a boat ("Quebekois Canoe"), a dessert ("Jack Cake"), a cough ("A kek Horrac"), a bird call ("Bekkek! Bekkek!), and a frog ("Koak! Koak!"), the last two being apparent intertextual allusions to the chaos of the world in the *Wake* (4) and Aristophanes' frogs that Joyce parodied.[22]

This intra- and interpoetic improvisation discloses the resonant and discordant qualities of the name, taking advantage of its plasticity as pure sound and linguistic sign. The name is always on the verge of collapsing into an amorphous swirl of ever-mutating sounds. For Kerouac—and Joyce too— whatever the human self may be exists separate from, and yet inextricably bound with, all—at the deepest level perhaps nothing more, *nor less,* than the play of names as sound and script circling on the great Spenglerian, Viconian, and Vedic wheels of time.

"THE MAGIC SOUND OF SILENCE"[23]

Coupled with his study of Buddhism, Kerouac's jazz method emphasizing song, speech, and sound eventually took him out of language and sound altogether. His reading of Buddhist scriptures heightened his belief in the illusionary quality of language, leading him to understand that sound itself is noise until one is enlightened. At that point, one recognizes all "sentient / communication" to be "emptiness and silence" (*MCB* 206). This wisdom is especially evident in "Bowery Blues," which begins with the prophecy "That the night / Will be bright / With the gold / Of old / In the inn / Within," the penultimate stanza concluding with Goethean angels addressing the singer:

"We ve been waiting for you
     Since Morning, Jack
     —Why were you so long
     Dallying in the sooty room?
     This Transcendental Brilliance
     Is the better part
     (Of Nothingness
     I sing)
(105)

Duluoz finds himself singing of nothingness, which is implied within the question "Can he or the music do that?" If so, has not the poem or song itself then ended? The illusion of song opens so wide a gap between artifice and the appearance of reality that the poem folds in upon itself and its semantic and musical roots. At this still nascent point of enlightenment, the singer/speaker accepts what he hears ("Okay"), tells the song to end ("Quit"), comments on what he has heard and done ("Mad"), and repeats the command to terminate ("Stop") (*Blues* 105). These last four lines signal the destruction of semantically based song in favor of sound, which then itself must give way to that which the angels sing—we are left with the cessation of both movement and sound: the static blankness of all. Poetry is impotent to encompass the scope of sound, which is the negation of itself.

A number of Kerouac poems make this same claim, some in more muted form than others. One of the most provocative is the 41st Chorus of *Mexico City Blues*, a four-stanza chorus published without revisions or editing in a diagrammatic structure uncharacteristic of the Legend's poetry:

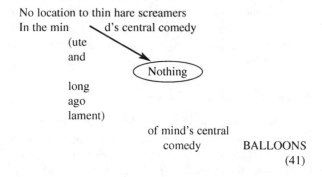

(41)

The dissection of the line "In the minute and long ago lamented's central comedy" creates a discursive and pictorial signifier of the fusion of mind ("mind's") and time ("minute"), nullifying anything perceived, even the most infinitesimal ("thin hare screamers"), between the sound of one's own thoughts (the mind) and the belief in one's special place in the universe (time). The space in "min   d's" is the visual equivalent of this sound-less emptiness, which is, as the arrow to the balloon announces, Nothing. The message is then presented linguistically in *BALLOONS,* a term and image derived from the cartoon balloon that contains a character's speech. As Jones argues, the cartoon balloon when empty, that is, recognized as Nothing, signified for Kerouac "a word hole that swallows up his intentions and dispels the illusion of permanence in meaning," leaving one to "hear only the silence of the void" (*Map* 134–35). This word hole is the equivalent of sound-as-all, what Kerouac, as in the teachings of Buddhism, named

Silence. It was a theme that he varied in *Mexico City Blues,* from the large blank space in the 11th Chorus that signified silence to the quoted aphorisms "All things are empty of self marks / If it is space / that is the perception of light" in the 234th Chorus (236). Several years later, in the essay "The Last Word," he quoted the Bodhisattva to explain the enlightened state of Silence: "All living beings who discipline themselves in listening to Silence shall hear Heaven . . . shall attain to the unattainable, shall enter the doorless, shall cross the river on the ferry and reach the other shore." The doorless world of enlightenment blots out all "pitiful shapeliness of ogroid earth," Kerouac stated, ending his essay with a Chinese proverb: "He who knows does not speak" (*Portable* 587).

What is then left when sound and voice (and presumably the ear) no longer exist? I am tempted to say the eye. But even the eye vanishes because it too is part of the Maya that taints human consciousness with illusion. Kerouac's essay "The Last Word" rings with melancholy, for while as a writer he long considered voice to be all, and speech and song anchor his poetics, his impulse to enter the great Emersonian eye drove him to create a world that remained a shape-filled wonder in which, at times, the visual took precedence over the verbal. In spite of his rational awareness of the illusion of discrete visual form, he never managed to abandon the image. Much like the poems in which he used words to inch as close as possible to music, his forays into phanopoeia sometimes moves directly from words into actual pictures—a shift that lends itself more naturally to the page than does musical composition. It was not unusual for Kerouac to illustrate his poems with delicate line drawings, such as a bulldog ("Poem Written in the Zoco Chico," *Pomes* 89), hearts ("Haiku," *Pomes* 56), smiley faces (45th Chorus, "Orlando Blues" *Blues* 242), hands (75th Chorus, *MCB*), and skulls and bones (2nd Chorus, "Orizaba Blues," *Blues* 130). He occasionally included Chinese characters as well ("Gatha," *Pomes* 51, 55). These drawings, like pictograms, are not so much representational or illustrative as they are symbolic or iconic. They sit alongside the English words reminiscent of poet William Blake's woodcut illustrations or the medieval emblem in which the verbal and pictorial work in tandem to forge a message greater than the sum of it parts. There are even lines in which the graphilect overpowers the word as bebop sound:

> Truss in dental
> Pop   Oly   Ruby
> Tobby   Tun   w d 1
>   1 x t s 8 7 r e r (
>   (*MCB* 142)

The last line of this stanza cannot be read aloud in any satisfactory way. Instead, as apparently random typing, it stands as a static image that abruptly halts the swift swing of the preceding scat. In both the holograph and the typescript of this chorus, the line was followed by an even more pronounced graphilect that looks something like this: [𝖘𝖍 𝖟𝖆𝖓𝖌𝖚𝖘]. This quasi-Arabic lettering, or pure doodle, further disrupts the stasis of the typewritten line, replacing the recognizable typewriter doodle with arbitrary script that references nothing except its own nonlinguistic presence upon the page.

Kerouac also played at times with concrete poetry. Probably the best example is what I call the bird symphony, or section 54 from *Old Angel Midnight*. Shaped like a pine tree, the section stands as a classic poetic emblem: the explicit combination of pictures and words creates a complex psychological image of the presence and significance of bird and human voices in dialogue. The structure eradicates the sense of movement in time as the voices of the birds and the poet, both speaking from a visible tree, are held in stasis within the body of the tree/word itself. The visual patterns of tree and a multitude of birds emerges as a juxtaposition of "overlapping forms" or superposition that, like pieces of a collage, creates a space in which resides the "precision of seeing" something new and the new knowledge that such sight engenders (Welsh 69). In this case, one possibility is that song resides innate in all life forms, even the trees themselves, and thus is an ancient foundational source of life and wisdom[23].

Kerouac's line drawings and concrete poems are charming, but the pairing of words and images as method never dominated his poetry. Nor did the, Apollonaire-like concrete forms hold his attention for long. He also never did much with the undecipherable doodle, although it is fair to say that his poetry with respect to this device served as a precursor to the visual emphasis of language poets such as Jackson Mac Low, Lynn Hejinian, Susan Howe, and Johanna Drucker. Instead, he remained wedded to wielding the word like paint to remold the material world. But even this focus has not salvaged his poetry from the criticism that it is weakly imaged, a flaw that Robert Hipkiss has attributed to Kerouac's method of spontaneous writing. Arguing that "poetry, depending as it does upon making every word bear a burden of meaning, is ill-suited to this technique," Hipkiss contrasts poetry with prose, the latter a form in which "an unsure statement can be built on, explained further, gone over again, until meaning breaks through. The reader of prose will wait longer for meaning in what he [or she] reads," he concludes (82). Following this logic, one can surmise that Kerouac's poetry may be more meaningful to a psychoanalyst seeking significant imagistic associations than a reader looking for aesthetic form or spiritual wisdom.

Granted, Kerouac's method of spontaneous sketching inconsistently presents the meaningful clarity and closure demanded by formalist perspectives such as Hipkiss represents. This practice, even when modified through revision and editing as his was, can discourage complete or unified thoughts.

Because of his belief in page size and associative thoughts as compositional determinants, many of his literary images can seem without destination or focus, the resulting discourse decentered and ruptured. From a formalist perspective, disruption signals a flawed text if one seeks a unified image pattern and the logical crafting of image, whether through metaphor, simile, or photorealistic description, to forge a cohesive cognitive vision or still life. Take, for example, the 146th Chorus, presented below, from *Mexico City Blues,* which portrays this reality:

> The Big Engines
> In the night—
> The Diesel on the Pass,
> The Airplane in the Pan
>   American night—
> Night—
>
> The Blazing Silence in the Night,
>   The Pan Canadian Night—
> The Eagle on the Pass,
>   The Wire on the Rail,
> the High Hot Iron
>   of my heart.
>
> The blazing chickaball
>   Whap-by
> Extry special Super
>   High Job
> Ole 169 be
>   floundering
> Down to Kill Roy

While the first two stanzas of the chorus present consistent images of powerfully swift, hot engines of both a train and a plane, the shift to the floundering 169 is unexplained and unsynchronized with the rest. Should one see irony in the juxtaposition of these images, that that which appears swift and hot is really an old engine? Or is Ole 169 being compared to the newer machines? The concluding metaphors, "blazing chickaball" and "Super High Job," allude to this possibility but reveal little about plane, train, or a plane-train combination. The poem stands as a dense series of riddles linked by sound and their physical relationship on a page.

But if one approaches the poem as a representation of the eye moving in synchronicity with the speaker's verbal thoughts—that is, the page becomes not only a stage for the performance of speech but also a canvas or screen for the projection of sight—the images convey a different significance. The ruptures replicate memory and language that defy logic to birth new or unfamiliar patterns. From this standpoint, the poem presents the speed with which both train and plane pass before the eye, as well as the speed with which the mind creates, mixes, separates, and compounds its perceptual material. Everything flies in this poem. Images and words fuse. Planes and trains are distinct yet consubstantial. Ole 169 can both blaze and flounder, and the image of train and plane against the night sky are held momentarily in the image of the "High Hot Iron" of the speaker's heart.

The hot-iron heart metaphor is a traditional poetic device, and consequently somewhat atypical for Kerouac. The visual elements in his poetry often tend toward the more playful and childlike, the unfettered imagination revealed at the level of the pun, which links the visual and the lexical. Frequently, the poems contain visual as well as oral plays on words suggesting that the punning sound generates from the visual representation of the words themselves. In "The Last Hotel," "Ghosts in my bed" becomes "the goats I bled" (*Pomes* 80), a pun that must be seen for the full effect of the trope. "Berkeley Song in F Major" contains "Eats up the fairies & *robbers* / In *Robbies* coffee saloon"; "(it all adds up to *roil* / or *royal,* one)"; and "t'all come from *ether* / And *t's'ether* / *Either* that or—What?"(*Pomes* 81, emphasis mine). These are all more visual than oral puns, the semantic shifts occurring as the visual signifier is transformed.

But there are poems that skillfully draw upon phanopoeia so that the page, as Hunt argues, becomes a space that foregrounds the eye as the primary perceptual organ muting the kind of orality featured in the above puns. To diminish the effect of musical lyrics or notes blending into each other, Kerouac would alternate longer lines with very short stacked lines, as in the 42nd Chorus of *Mexico City Blues,* below. Most of this poem engages in beboplike scatting about the breeze perceived from the speaker's position on a sailboat. But at midpoint, the poem turns to right-justified, one-word lines:

> Hear of this, fight the lawyers,
> Upset the silly laws, anger
> the
> hare
> brain
> bird
> of
> wine
> In his railroad tam o shanter

(42)

Verticality slows the rhythm, emphasizing the word as a simultaneous layering of four visual constructs: (1) physical mark; (2) linguistic code (definite articles, nouns, adjectives, prepositions); (3) signifier of images, in this case the discrete hare, brain, bird, and wine; and (4) recombinant form, the collaged visual elements. At this juncture the speaker is muted in the presence of the eye until he reasserts himself to conclude the poem with a meta-analytic expository statement: "Even on a sailboat / I end up writin bop" (42).

This line manipulation is varied slightly in the 54th Chorus, the one-word lines staggered across the page in loose imitation of images scrolling on a movie screen:

> Once I went to a movie
> At midnight, 1940, Mice
> And Men, the name of it,
> The Red Block Boxcars
> Rolling by (on the Screen)
>   Yessir
>   llfe
>   finally
>   gets
>   tired
>   of
>   living—
>   (54)

While Kerouac used line breaks to simulate moving images, the words do not create a verbal simulacrum of the visual simulacrum that Duluoz's eye perceives on the screen—that is, the boxcars in the film *Of Mice and Men* (1939). Rather, the language takes a cue from the art of film itself, flattening the object of perception into ephemeral abstractions before moving away from the visual into propositional thought as language in the concluding stanza. In effect, the scrolling words of the 54th Chorus make visible, as David Sterrit explains, "that no film has more than a part-object existence at any given moment except in the mind of the spectator who consumes each image, retains its meaning in memory and assembles those meanings into a more or less coherent whole" (*Screening* 53).

More typical of Kerouac's visual poetics are those poems in which he intentionally "sets before the mind" (*Portable* 484) an object that he sketched with words, using that verbal object as a point of meditation, a vehicle leading to fidelity of mind. This process as an analogue of painting is made explicit in the 151st and 152nd choruses of *Mexico City Blues*, which present in Matisse-like simplicity a still life of a cheap Mexican room. With careful precision, the singer fixes his eye on the physical world around him, what he calls the "simple arrangement / Of natural objects," such as a beer tray, a razorblade, a butter knife, a candle, and an aluminum cup. As the choruses move to conclusion, he envisions objects as symbolic of the ancient and ineffable, implied markers of the timeless void. In the last stanza, he awakens from his reverie to face the antithesis of the static world of art: the "real life not / still life" filled with the ugliness of cigarette butts and match tips (152).

The personal world expressed as still life emerges in self-conscious photo-realism in "A Sudden Sketch Poem," a poem that Kerouac wrote in 1956 while staying with Gary Snyder in California. The detailed description of Snyder's living quarters, with its sink, "upsidedown" teacup, frying pan, spoon, dishpan, and onions, negotiates its way into Joycian obfuscation (e.g., "squozen gumbrop") before propelling the poet to enlightenment, the illusion of thingness replaced by indivisible "magic dancing lights of gray and white" (*Pomes* 87–88). Throughout "Sudden Sketch," the speaker struggles harder than does the speaker of the Matisse choruses to assert himself as the creator of recognizable poetic visual form. A brush looks like "a red woman's hair," the faucet leaks "lovedrops," a washrag hangs like bloomers, and a hoodlatch resembles the Christian cross (87). Sometimes, though, the image eludes him, and he admits he does not "know what to say" or he stumbles into vagueness ("the sink inside or what"). However, the ego's belief that it can control the world by perceiving and naming its parts is embodied in the speaker's confident conclusion "And all for verse I wrote it" (88). In other words, *he* centers the universe.

The egocentric wisdom that the poet achieves through phanopoeic meditation in "Sudden Sketch" jars a bit when juxtaposed with the despairing naturalism of the Mexican room choruses, and neither seems consistent with Kerouac's Buddhist efforts to follow the Eightfold Path. Each, however, represents realistic stages in one's journey toward enlightenment, which the poet addresses with a more balanced spirit in "The Thrashing Doves." This poem is especially beautiful and its slightly melancholy tone appropriate for its topic: tiny caged doves in a dark Chinese market. What makes this poem powerful is its smooth transition back and forth from description of the physical objects in close proximity to the speaker, such as the hay and rice on the floor, boxes of dried fish, and opium pipes, to images conceptually linked to the fated death of the doves yet far removed in time and space—the thick Wall of China and ice in Peking. The "I" is absent from the first four stanzas, which are controlled by the perspective of a slow-motion camera that scans the immediate setting and sweeps back into history and across continents. In the fifth stanza, the more familiar declarative voice of Duluoz surfaces, and, as in the final chorus of *Mexico City Blues,* the speaker assumes the pose of guardian, seeking to warn others about death. In the penultimate stanza, this voice is replaced by a descriptive litany of the children who need his protection, the poem then concluding with the prayerful line

"For the doves" (*Pomes* 114). The three tiny words mute the egocentrism of the poet, fixing in timeless stasis the delicate image of the doves, forever beyond suffering.

As powerful as phanopoeia is in "The Thrashing Doves," it pales somewhat in comparison with the 230th Chorus of *Mexico City Blues*, in which Kerouac selected for meditation a product of his imagination. The object is "love's multitudinous boneyard / of decay" (232), a place that rivals the levels of hell in Dante's *Inferno* or Goya's painting "Satan Devouring His Son." The singer himself leaves no self-referential signature upon this poem. Voice falls away—no need for a fellow sufferer to warn those who enter to abandon hope—as each line records with photographic precision the nightmarish realities of lost love. The structure of the first twenty-five lines is ideogrammatic and incantatory, a long list of murder victims, elephant-eating vultures, seahorse glue, sliced Buddha-material, and penis apples strewn across the imaginary plain of a suffering world. The poem concludes with a dramatic shift creating a stark juxtaposition of contraries: "Like kissing my kitten in the belly / The softness of our reward" (232). The collaging of this gentle image and the horrendous inscape of mental anguish functions as does the classic haiku form or the experimental flat, plainlike surfaces of Cezanne's paintings. That is, the visual components intentionally do not report or argue a truth but rather set in motion a process whereby the perceiving individual generates the knowledge. In this respect, Kerouac was working in harmony with, whether intentionally or not, Ginsberg's theory of both haiku and Cezanne's abstract expressionism as spaces in which the perceiver of two polarized images reconciles these opposites in "a flash of recognition" (Charters, *Beat Down* 208–21). With the 230th Chorus, it is by entering the space between the grotesque boneyard and the sublime kitten kiss and discerning the truth that binds them like an electrical charge, to use Ginsberg's terminology, that a reader irrevocably destroys the dualities of good and evil, love and hate—in essence, the illusion of ego.

Kerouac's haikus, as the 230th Chorus aptly illustrates, provide dramatic evidence that he could produce the tight, crisp literary image. Many develop the complexities of intellectual and emotional form more effectively than do his longer poetic works. His interest in haiku germinated as he began to read Buddhist religious texts and Japanese poets such as Basho, Issa, and Buson. His own haikus are a variation of the Japanese. Not limiting them to seventeen syllables, he believed that a haiku should "simply say a lot in three short lines in any Western language" (*Scattered* 69). Above all, he believed "a haiku must be very simple and free of all poetic trickery and make a little picture and yet be as airy and graceful as a Vivaldi Pastorella" (*Scattered* 69). Consequently, Kerouac's haikus are much like the image poem in the tradition of Ezra Pound, capturing an intellectual and emotional complex in an instant of time, envisioning and thus knowing in a new way the beauty of indirection, as in the following:

> The summer chair
>> rocking by itself
> In the blizzard.
>>> (*Scattered* 74)

The simple image of a summer chair rocking alone in a winter blizzard is grounded in paradoxical fusion of summer within winter and the likening of the two. The image itself, capturing the movement of the seasons in time-lessness, is rooted in the riddle form. Here one discerns the metaphor with one term missing: what is like a summer chair rocking alone in a blizzard? The answer? A person caught unprepared in life, the existential isolation of a person in a crowd, the destruction of the belief in life as separate from death, a sign of one's ability to survive in a lonely, harsh environment, or possibly the belief that life is found only in death. The beauty of this haiku riddle is that it produces and sustains multiple ways of knowing through renaming specific beliefs and conditions.

Pound also identified an image poem as one in which the lyric voice tries to record the precise instant when a thing outward and objective transforms itself. The following Kerouac haiku illustrates this tenet:

> Evening coming—
>> the office girl
> Unlosing her scarf.
>>> (*Scattered* 72)

The heart of this image is the word "unloosing," the letting go, relaxing, or unbinding of something. The unloosing of the scarf holds the one moment in which the office girl abandons her nine-to-five persona and embarks on another life outside the workplace in that moment of gloaming as day turns into night. Thus the poem negotiates the complex transformation or change of masks that all humans wear everyday. In this haiku, as in the other, a riddle resides: What is like a young office girl unloosing her scarf? Again, a complex of possible answers beckons interpretation: the assembly line worker as he punches the time clock at the end of his shift, the jazz musician when he picks up his horn, the mother when she shuts the door to her sleeping child's room, the writer when he takes up his pen. Anyone, that is, who is human, being human.

The answer to Kerouac's haiku riddle epitomizes the essential function of his poetry, which I find best described by a passage from Gary Snyder's *Earth House Hold* (1957), a collection of poems, essays, and journal entries written in the early fifties contemporaneously with much of the Duluoz Legend. Speaking not of Kerouac in particular but of poetry in general, Snyder wrote that poetry is "the skilled and inspired use of the voice and language to embody rare and powerful states of mind that are in immediate origin personal to the singer, but at deep levels common to all who listen" (117). Poetry must "sing or speak from authentic experience," he continued, and those who sing or speak with such commitment live close to a world "in its nakedness, which is fundamental for all of us—birth, love, death; the sheer fact of being alive" (118). Kerouac's songs and prayers so compatibly adhere to Snyder's dictum to transform personal into communal expressions—and to read the latter in the former—that I am compelled to ask, "what better words could summarize the texts and human identities central to wisdom quests."

The essential message conveyed by Kerouac's poetry, then, is not of the eye alone but of the eye in communion with the breath and rhythm. Articulating their fundamental relationship, Snyder defined breath as "the outer world coming into one's body. With pulse—the two always harmonizing—the source of our inward sense of rhythm" (123). Through the practice of chanting, he maintained that "a new voice enters, a new voice speaks through you clearer and stronger than what you know of yourself; with a sureness and melody of its own, singing out the inner song of the self, and of the planet" (123). With Kerouac, the repetition of his own memories and fantasies as songs and prayers served him as did Snyder's chanting of "OM," "AYNG," and "AH," transforming the self known as Jack Kerouac into a shamanistic channel for dozens of other voices, even the "hummmmmhummmmm" of the earth itself that combines the bodily experience of voice, ear, and eye.

These as repeated and reconfigured through the natural human processes of memory as well as via Kerouac's unique imagination as a writer birthed the voices of Duluoz and the many, others who populate the Legend, setting in motion methods by which Kerouac effected a literary state of being that exemplifies a state of being that Snyder named the "mythological present." This world, as Snyder presented it, is a "body/mind" state suggesting "a wider-ranging imagination and a closer subjective knowledge of one's own physical properties than is usually available to men living (as they themselves describe it) impotently and inadequately in 'history'—their mind-content programmed, and their caressing of nature complicated by the extensions and abstractions which elaborate tools are" (117–18). Not so Kerouac, who be accepting the challenge of seeking sites of both physical and metaphysical ecstasy within his songs and prayers defied the limitations culturally imposed on his own body and mind, imagining God, self, and the world in ways that still baffle, exhort, thrill, and teach.

CHAPTER 7

THE FALL: *DESOLATION ANGELS*

Struggling to find definitive answers to his questions regarding ontology, spirituality, and art, Kerouac published *Big Sur* in 1961. His long-sought fame had brought him little solace, and maintaining a Buddhist posture was becoming more difficult. As *Big Sur* portrays, he retained some of the terminology of his Buddhist practices but was turning decidedly to Christianity in his orientation toward self, the world, and the transcendent. Visions of the cross that climax the narrative, leading him to declare, "I'm with you, Jesus, for always, thank you" (169), are a far cry from the bodhi tree and the individualistic wisdom of compassion taught in the Diamond and Langatavara sutras. By 1967, when he did his *Paris Review* interview, just two years before his death, he spoke as though he had collapsed into the person of Jesus all forms of religious iconography with which he had dealt. No Kerouac text directly explains this transition, but *Desolation Angels* (1956/61, 1965) a personal confession integrated with the adventure tale and travelogue, reveals some of the contours of this transition as Kerouac moved from Buddhism to a reaffirmation of Christ.

Kerouac, admitting in *Angels* that he was a Whitmanian mass of contradictions—a complex and unique character that he compared to a fevered snowflake (230)—remained steadfastly uninterested in crafting the well-wrought urn. *Angels,* an unbalanced two-part text comprising smaller units numbered consecutively, features discrete poems, songs, and other texts collaged with the main narrative that recounts Duluoz's summer of 1956 as a fire watcher in the Cascades and events of the subsequent year. The intertextual and multigenre nature of *Angels* opens it to contradictions and ambiguities, rendering it more a tracking of the *processes* of human agency than a static product *of* that agency. To this end, *Angels* relies on a number of Kerouacian prose standards, such as real events and people from Kerouac's life and adherence to a fairly discernable time line. But it swerves from these in its more transparent use of nonfiction forms, its attention to serious reflection on the spiritual significance of events and people, and its unabashed wrestling with the question of how to live a meaningful life. It is both a story told by Jack Duluoz before and after the publication of Keoruac's *On the Road* as well as a philosophical and theological meditation reminiscent of the Kerouac who much earlier wrote the *Windblown World* journals. Actualizing "what he is writing about in a shape indivisible from its content ('a poem should not mean but be')," as Seymour Krim stated in the introduction of the book (xxi), *Angels* blends life writing and fictional narrative in the service of reader edification and solace.

Standing on the periphery of mainstream culture, Duluoz outspeaks stories of his life, meaning that he apprehends or sees beyond the immediate parameters of knowledge accessible to most. The vision projected from this privileged position assumes that the world possesses meaning and order no matter how difficult living in it may appear (Landow 22). Using softly mocking or parodic self-portraits alternated with visionary statements, as well as episodic and analogic narrative structures, Duluoz criticizes the character of his readers while attempting to inspire them, relying on grotesque representations of contemporary characters, unusual definitions of seminal terminology, inductive reasoning focused on trivial objects, and an appeal to his own ethos, especially that of a flawed, guilt-ridden, confused individual (22–23, 28, 31). In recursive movement, the narrative advances chronologically, while frequently stopping time to create space in which new memories and visions surface, each one enfolding upon itself and opening out into others the master narrative of the Human Fall.

Angels unabashedly admits that it is a fall story. The trope is introduced in Book One as an exhausted Duluoz comes down the mountain from his sixty-day sojourn as a fire lookout, reminding himself that "you've had falls before and Joyce made a word two lines long to describe it—brabarackotawackomanashtopatarawackomanac!" (76). Alluding to Ray Smith's moment of enlightenment in *The Dharma Bums* when he suddenly realizes that "it's impossible to fall off mountains" (85), the statement directly references *Finnegans Wake,* Joyce's dreamlike confession of the literal (death) and symbolic (sin and guilt) fall of humankind.[1] As a twentieth-century successor of both the ancient fall story and the *Wake,* the narrative affirms both *The Dharma Bums*' Buddhist negation of the myth of human degradation and the *Wake*'s circular night dream in which humans are inevitably caught in a never-ending trap of their own (and their readers') misreadings. Incorporating a set of wisdom texts that promises no single method or doctrine of resolution and guidance, *Angels* maintains in the face of these paradoxes and refusals a heart-felt belief in the goodness of all humans, the same impulse that buoys much of the Legend. Finally, the fall is firmly established within the twentieth century's enlightenment and existential focus on the individual, doing so indirectly through the Joycian fall word to which Duluoz refers. This word is not one of the ten fall words found in the *Wake,* but the creation of a new *Joycian-like* word. Therefore Duluoz's vision of the fall, rather than a classical pastiche (or sincere imitation) of specific cultural myths, legends, and sacred stories, signifies his personal story of origin and succession. Shadows of older, universal fall stories flicker in the new fall word and, as Berdyaev maintained, can therein be discerned, but it is a distinctly Kerouacian twentieth-century story that shines forth.

Direct references to the fall in Book Two of *Angels* clarify this point. Duluoz writes that he is buoyed by the need to explain why angels "are still Falling," finding it an inappropriate topic "for an N.Y.U. Seminar" but definitely one for a writer (230). Imagining that he and his friends are falling with the Angel Lucifer into eccentric Buddhist ideals of humility (230, 261–62), he declares that before the fall he was a "Babe of Heaven" (261) torn from bliss by his fall into birth and the cruel slap that ignited his breathing (283). Asking why God would create such a miserable life for humans and wondering if it was the greed and arrogance of God's original angels that caused the fall (283), he speculates that perhaps a real devil, and not God, convinced heavenly souls to try mortality, where they were tricked into discovering themselves amid the horrors of World War II (303). Duluoz then extends the life-as-a-dirty-trick line of interpretation to imagine the possibility of a Manichaean evil Inquisitor in Space who created the human ordeal (359). Human history, he decides, is "an awful mistake" (303), a reiteration of the modernist theme of history as nightmarish, one of the more persistent and trenchant truths that the Legend argues.

As do all folk storytellers, Duluoz conveys this fall wisdom through a chorus of voices. One that sets *Angels* apart from other installments of the Legend is the voice of cultural critic. *Angels,* more so than any other, weaves explicit critique of American culture among the threads of Duluoz's adventures with friends and family. He does not pose as a Lionel Trilling, a Mark Van Doren, or a Norman Mailer, lions of intellectual hegemony during the fifties and early sixties, but this voice is prosaic and direct, although informal, as he tells the fall story. His critique of the American healthcare system, for instance, identifies the system as that "Which makes you realize the restrictions on drugs (or, *medicine*) in America comes from doctors who dont want people to heal themselves" (240), a pronouncement that does not hesitate to generalize on the basis of little empirical evidence. Without hesitation, that same secular voice critiques the then contemporary literary scene: "pretty soon [. . .] there'll be so many additional childhoods and pasts with everybody writing about them everybody'll give up reading in despair" (357)—words eerily predicting the rise of autobiography and memoir that has today trumped fiction on the American literary scene. Especially when addressing domestic and international politics, which *Angels* does repeatedly, directness is transformed into the contentious, if not paranoid, voice of the sage. "Send that message back to Mao, or Schlesinger at Harvard, or Herbert Hoover too" (340) is typical of this persona, who claims the imperative mood to punctuate what is usually an anticommunist, anti–big government, or anti-intellectual position (240).[2] In effect, Duluoz's fall story becomes that of America as damaged yet superior to all other nations.

Duluoz's narrative perspective predominantly signals comfortable familiarity evolving into intimacy with the reader, often directly addressed as "readers" or "you." *Angels* may in fact be the most complexly intimate you-I relationship in the Legend, except perhaps for *Vanity of Duluoz,* which Kerouac constructed as a direct but rather rancorous and confrontational address to his wife and his literary critics. The rhapsodic voice of the human visionary that begins by declaring Mount Hozomeen to be the Void (3) characterizes *Angels,* complementing the voice of cultural critique by providing explanations and solutions to the human dilemma of history. At an early point in the narrative, this voice is fascinatingly transformed into a literal representation of the range of human and nonhuman voices and shapes through which wisdom and visionary truths are transmitted. In this case, a meditative passage on the discriminating mind composed in standard literary English moves into apostrophic pronouncements to others ("O Ignorant brothers, O Ignorant sisters, O Ignorant me! There's nothing to write about, everything is nothing, there's everything to write about!") and then becomes a ranting stutter ("SO-SO-SO-SO-SO-SO"), immediately transformed into a line of three triangular shapes, each underscored with one of the four of the five staples of journalism ("WHO WHAT WHY WHEN"). These then become nonsense words ("ITIBITO RAT"), all of which leads to a pure doodle, without meaning and expressed as a silent scriptor on paper, the two squiggly lines signifying only their physical presence on a flat planer surface. These voices, first that of a human writer, then a sage, then a mad mouthpiece of the divine, and finally only a silent mark upon an impermanent object, ultimately return to the lyric poet who with a prophetic song calls for the world to awaken to the ancient Eastern wisdom of the "millennial rat." The call concludes with what can be read as the synesthesiac babbling sound of the color of the world: "black black black black / bling bling bling" (51–53). Although atypical of *Angels* overall, the passage encapsulates the mystic personae that Duluoz assumes and communicates consistently within the Legend.

At a more mundane level—and *Angels* is grounded in the mundane more than anywhere else—the narrative features patterns of discourse that reside but several registers below the ineffable or the mystic. At times, the narrative standpoint does not reflect an explicit and single recognizable "you" that the narrator visualizes or identifies as either himself or a silent companion. Rather, "you" is a mass of anonymous faces. A striking example of this artifice is Duluoz's description of riding cross-country, a narrative aside conveyed in a quiet sermonic voice:

> Those long droning runs across a state's afternoon with some of us sleeping [. . .] I always wake up from a nap with a sensation that *I'm* being driven to Heaven by the Heavenly Driver, no matter who he is. There's something strange about one person guiding the car while all the others dream with their lives in his steady hand, something noble, something old in mankind, some old trust in the Good Old Man. *You* come out of a drowsy dream of sheets on a roof [. . .] wondering why and looking at the driver, who is stern, who is still, who is lonesome at the controls. (259 emphasis mine)

The homiletic standard of personal experience to clarify a larger spiritual message undergirds this passage, the speaker conflating himself with an anonymous audience to convey the wisdom of trusting a fellow human being.

The confessional nature of *Angels* advances to this end, since confession depends upon the speaker's trust in the audience, and vice versa. Certainly, wisdom literature, especially that claiming to reveal human flaws, is predicated upon the audience's trust in the speaker. To establish such trust, Duluoz draws attention to his personal history, explaining that "readers who haven't read up to this point in the earlier works are not filled in on the background," so "take another look at me to get the story better," he instructs (228), including a brief autobiography, a description of his physical appearance, and discussion of his place in the Beat Generation. Presumably the assumption is that the more honest the sage is about himself and the more a reader knows about those who profess, the more likely readers will be to identify with the sage and therefore trust his or her words. Accordingly, Duluoz furnishes key historical data to identify why he writes. This is "the go-ahead confession, the discipline of making the mind the slave of the tongue with no chance to lie or re-elaborate (in keeping with the dictums of Dichtung Warheit Goethe but those of the Catholic Church my childhood)" (228–29).

In the guise of personal history, *Angels* redefines confession as a reminder of the self's profane and sacred nature. In other words, confession *links* that self with all others and conversely *removes* the self from the profane through a mediating presence purifying and thus bringing one closer to the divine. As he does throughout the Legend, Duluoz takes full advantage of this process, humbly admitting his many flaws. He is sex mad (104), has betrayed "hundreds of women" (111), has failed to help his friends understand Buddhism (151–52), is a dreamy fool who has "taken a back seat in life" (94, 168), is too shy to read in front of an audience (188), is an "idiotic sinner and stupid boaster" (243, 224), is a fearful driver (260), has become a debauched bourgeois as a result of literary fame (221), and falls far short of being a model penitent (224). These and other transgressions, specifically his mistreatment of women, generate feelings of self-loathing, which he acknowledges manifest themselves as his identification with marginalized or unpopular individuals (94, 197). The feelings are so pronounced that he imagines himself as physically ugly, the grotesque "mirror of all-the-woes-you-know" that others can see when they look into his face (125). Reflecting human crimes and indiscretions, Duluoz as a self-identified grotesque so desperately craves release from suffering that he dares to violate the implied contract between an author of fiction and the readers by openly confessing: "I know it's inexcusable to interrupt a tale with such talk—but I've got to get it off my chest or I will die—I will die hopelessly / And tho dying hopelessly is not really dying hopelessly, and it's only the golden eternity, it's not kind" (201). Unable to gamble on heaven, Duluoz implies that he also does not believe strongly enough in a nontheistic Buddhist vision of the universe to forsake the Catholic practice of confession, even if it means abandoning his persona as a published writer and the conventions of fiction demanding recognizable narrative distance between author and narrator.

This quality of confession frequently positions Duluoz as someone who depends upon prayer, which as a state of narrative isolation erases all other I-you relationships except that of the human speaker who perceives "you" as a transcendent other addressed in thanks or petition. In Catholic and other Christian orthodox as well as some Buddhist traditions, many prayers are provided for speakers, such as St. Theresa's prayer "L'amour du Prochain," which Kerouac had tacked above his bed toward the end of his life (Maher 462), and are recited in unison by large groups. Within these traditions, especially Catholicism, the penitents pray to a lesser divine being, such as the Virgin Mary or a saint, who is then supposed to intercede on behalf of the human speakers. More often, however, prayer is the spontaneous language of an individual in a heightened emotional or intellectual state, and is intended only for the divine other whom the speaker hopes will respond. For instance, Duluoz's petition "Lord be merciful, Lord be kind, whatever your name is, be kind—bless and watch" (200) creates a sense of an intimately palpable link between the human and the divine. In this sense, Duluoz effects a more gnostic or Protestant standpoint in relationship to his god, one that makes wholly unnecessary any mediating relationships between the human and the divine. This discursive space supports Duluoz's mission of conveying to his audience the authenticity of the spiritual story he presents: he is in direct contact with the divine and is thus a more reliable speaker for the transcendent; simultaneously, it confounds the atheistic Buddhist wisdom to which he still clings.

It is cinema and dream, however, that most effectively complicate the I-you relationship in support of Duluoz's persona as wisdom speaker in *Angels'* fall story. Dreams are a state in which the "I" experiences itself at its most solitary, since no one but the dreamer participates in the creation or viewing of the dreams, unless the dream is presented as the voice of a particular divinity, which is generally not the case in the Legend. While publishing many of his dreams in *Book of Dreams* (1961), Kerouac more often wove the dream concept throughout his narratives, the effect being the illustration of subjectivity and objectivity as illusions. This he coupled with the reality of viewing film and the concept of film as an intellectual device, approximating aspects of the filmmaker's and the viewer's experiences in which the "I" exists in virtual solitude, each creating the world through its own cloudy lenses while erasing the distinction between subject and object. His blending of dream and cinema results in the projection of the individual reality of living in the world of *annica*, the not-self of transiency or Impermanence.

Many of Kerouac's word paintings achieve this effect through the repetition of "I see [. . .] remember [. . .] I see," almost like a person in an altered state of consciousness who cuts through the confines of relativity to an "I" that is no more individual than a monotonous, machinelike voice (41, 57). In these cases, the filmmaker (Duluoz) imagining the scene is certainly present but also becomes one with the imagined audience (the reader) who view the film. The converse is realized in passages that eschew the hypnotic "I see" to concentrate instead on the movement of scenes *in front* of one's eyes, like a film playing in a movie theater. In these cases, the agent imagining the film gives way to the object of viewing itself, as in this excerpt from book 1:

> Ah all the rivers of America I've seen and you've seen—the flow without end, the Thomas Wolfe vision of America bleeding herself out in the night in rivers that run to the maw sea but then comes upswirls and newbirths, thunderous the mouth of the Mississippi the night we turned into it and I was sleeping on the deck cot, splash, rain, flash, lightning, smell of the delta, where Gulf of Mexico middens her stars and opes up for shrouds of water that will divide as they please in dividable unapproachable passes of mountain where lonely Americans live in little lights—[. . .] The rivers of America [. . .] all the molecules and atoms in every cell, and all the infinite universes in every thought—bubbles and balloons. (88)

In this passage, Duluoz appears to go into a reverie of sorts, evoking a rush of river water and unexplained memories of a night on board a ship. As the present recedes, the flash of disembodied memories obliterates the illusion of the viewer himself to move instead like a film montage from the scene of lonely Americans on a mountain to that of lovers throwing a rose off a bridge. The latter, a revision of the scene from *Doctor Sax* in which Ti Jean Duluoz is transformed into a spurned romantic lover, then tightens its focus on the rose, which "bleed[s] to the sea." Kerouac's hard dash abruptly cuts the scene to a panorama of "the rivers of America and all the trees on all those shores," which with microscopic precision zooms into the very cells, molecules, and atoms of this green world to illuminate the primal connectedness of all life as "bubbles and balloons." Typical of Kerouac's technique of removing himself and the reader as active agents from the text, the passage becomes the movie/dream into which self and life as transitory appearances seem to move of their own volition, separate from the viewer, yet always aware of their own nondivisibility.

David Sterrit contends that the concept of cinema/dream in *Angels* serves a polyvalent function illustrating that spiritual insights can subsume physical sight, that the biological and psychic processes of ideation have a visual analogue, and that material existence is a spectacle continually built by the impersonal totality of the universe (*Screening* 54–56). These are important insights, but Kerouac's cinema/dream constructions also reify the human constructions of time and space, parts and objects, while allowing one to see through these appearances to a greater vision of reality, specifically the Buddhist concepts of emptiness. In a sense, while Duluoz does not speak to this specifically, the manipulation of cinema/dream effects the highest form of Buddhist wisdom—the ability to recognize the world of appearances within which all must live, while simultaneously seeing, and thus living within, the life of nonattachment.

As Duluoz begins his narrative, he is embarked on a mission to spread just this kind of wisdom, trying to teach his friends the truths of the Surangama Sutra and contemplating Buddhist lectures to deliver to those in need (103). His narrative approach to recounting these efforts is the unusual literary device of *stopping and restarting* the tale—or multiple introductions, in fact three. Two appear in "Book One: Desolation Angels," and one in "Book Two: Passing Through." These beginnings are not spontaneous faltering, postmodern deception, or amateurish indecision, but folk storyteller readjustments of the narrative to fit the presumed needs of the audience, keeping them attuned to the tale, engaged in the development of characters and plot, and conscious of a lesson to be learned. In this respect, *Angels* with its multiple beginnings, reflects Duluoz's maturing sense of his role as a writer of literature intended primarily to teach rather than to entertain.

The story's first introduction features an unidentified narrator remembering his experience gazing at Mount Hozomeen in the Cascades. With geological precision, the mountain comes into focus (it is 8,000 feet of black rock), its metaphoric power and beauty ("like a tiger sometimes with stripes, sunwashed rills and shadow crags wriggling lies in the Bright Daylight") and meditative revelation exposing the illusionary nature of the life in which he participates ("just a hanging bubble in the illimitable ocean of space") (4). This section identifies the major themes of the book and allows the narrator to carry readers back in time to join him on the peak where he had encountered the "face of reality." In other words, he narrates his experience of satori or enlightenment that he shorthands as "the killing of a mouse and attempted murder of another" (4), a story that is not elaborated until the narrative has been restarted a second time. Fittingly, this early part is consistently the most Buddhist, reflecting Kerouac's immersion in Buddhism at the time he composed the early journals, which he used to write approximately the first half of the book. At that time, as the narrator (now identified as Jack Duluoz) reports, he had set out on the fire-watcher journey to learn "once and for all" the meaning of life (4). This move is analogous to that of Gautama, who searched for the bodhi tree, the perfect spot to recover his childlike experience of joyful connection with all and where he achieved enlightenment. Duluoz, however, seeks no such ordinary, childhood spot but instead the top of an 8,000-foot mountain. His move is blind, Moses-like determination to get as close to the transcendent "other" as possible or, in his own words, to "come face to face with God or Tathagata" (4). But neither God nor Buddha manifests himself, certainly not as quickly as Duluoz desires, and he remembers being left alone for months, forced to come "face to face" with only his own anguished human countenance (4).

The narrative then smoothly shifts into the present tense as Duluoz leaves behind the memories of Desolation Peak and Hozomeen, moving into a place apart where he abandons an audience of others to address himself and God. His questions and answers tumble quickly upon one another in a flood of rhapsodic anxiety and certitude:

> Does the Void take any part in life and death? does it have funerals? or birth cakes? why not I be like the Void, inexhaustibly fertile, beyond serenity, beyond even gladness [. . .] this ungraspable image in a crystal ball is not the Void, the Void is the crystal ball itself and all my woes [. . .] Hold together, Jack, pass through everything, and everything is one dream, one appearance, one flash, one sad eye [. . .] simply *be—be—*be the infinite fertilities of the one mind of infinity [. . .] This is the Great Knowing, this is the Awakening, this is Voidness—So shut up, live, travel, [. . .] And you have been forever, and will be forever. (5–6)

With the triumphant pronouncement of everlasting life, Duluoz swings back into the stance of an author speaking to his audience, describing day after day of eating, breathing, sleeping, daydreaming, and simply living life as all creatures do rather than struggling to breach the face of God, which as his Buddhist practice has taught him is a futile effort, since God does not exist.

This moment, ambiguously neither fully a Buddhist satori nor a Christian revelation, transports him into a realm where he continues meditative practice. Here, the book relies on a standard Kerouacian and wisdom technique of focusing on material details to generate greater reflections and truths. This ancient form of meditation, which in more contemporary forms is relevant to Beat writers such as Ginsberg, Diane di Prima, and Janine Pommy Vega, has its roots in the metaphysical poetry of John Donne and the romantic soliloquies of Coleridge and Wordsworth; paradoxically, it removes the individual from the material world to reveal greater insights through initial concentration on that marterial. In Duluoz's case, the focus on the minutiae of conversations he had via shortwave radio with other fire watchers, the fantasy baseball game that he and his childhood friends played, his mother's house on Long Island, the food he ate on the mountain, and his dreams all lead him to repudiate existential pessimism and fears of communist assassination plots— to instead envision America as a Western Pure Land still joyfully wild and free (19), a vast, unboundaried Buddhist void unified with compassion and laughter that he prophesies "run over the world" (20). Infusing lecture and maxims with personal experience, Duluoz lends credence to his authority as sage to define the supramundane "Power" as Buddhist rapture, ecstasy, golden eternity, dreams, and the freedom of selflessness that strips personal suffering of any meaning in the phenomenal world (28–29).

But *Angels* refuses to testify to Buddhism as a panacea to postwar pessimism and fear. Even this introduction signals Kerouac's misgivings, and while he begins one section of the introduction with the statement that noumena is "what you see with your eyes closed [. . .] and phenomena [are] what you see with your eyes open"—the former the light-within-the-dark of the undifferentiated whole immanent and beyond, the latter the lighted darkness of the illusion of the objectified—he remains unaware of what these definitions may mean in a Buddhist sense. This section includes a long list of the objects that he sees in his cabin. Product names abound (Maxwell House coffee, Chef Boyardee spaghetti, Lipton Soup) complemented by sensory adjectives to create a three-dimensional and sensual tableau realistically replicating his summer on the mountain (34–35). Cognizant that these items are nonexistent and fall short of representing anyone's or anything's life, he cannot relinquish the nagging question of why he has to endure a material existence while Hozomeen remains unburdened by such trivia and the personal memories that one attaches to them. Duluoz desperately wants a god who will give him an answer, and demands proof—the very wounds on Jesus's hands and feet, so to speak. Interestingly, this section does not end with a period. Several others end that way as well, but in this case the effect is an open-ended blankness suggesting that the answer Duluoz seeks can only be found when one's eyes are finally closed and the noumena can be seen. This emptiness hints at death of the physical body, which encompasses the atheistic belief in total obliteration and the gnostic understanding of the transcendent afterlife in which all is light, as well as the Buddhist concept of nirvana as unnamable reality beyond language.

The ambiguity of the emptiness opens the remainder of Part One of the first book to Duluoz's light-hearted memories of childhood but more predominantly to darker reflections on himself and the world. Word weariness forces him to ask what he has learned on this mountain, which he mockingly renames "Gwaddawackamblack" ("God, I'm glad I'm back," a possible mocking translation 61), and the answer is how much he hates himself (63), how his internal nothingness is worse than any illusions (63), and how powerless humans are in an amoral world (64). Now not even able to believe in the power of love to validate life, represented years earlier in his *Windblown World* journals by his sentimental thoughts about Princess Elizabeth's wedding, he terminates Part One by reverting to vestiges of Catholicism, cursing Christ in *joual: "Eh maudit Christ de batême que s'am'fend!*—How can anything ever *end?*"(65).

Roughly translated as "damned Christ who strikes down his friend,"[3] the French curse transitions him to Part Two of book 1, simultaneously returning him to the beginning of the narrative or the *second introduction,* which defines the genre of the story he is telling: "But now the story, the confession," and the point of telling it—"What I'd learned on the solitary mountain all summer, the Vision of Desolation Peak" (66). This recursive move is a genuine extension of the initial pattern of narrative discourse and a literary representation of how the practice of literary meditation and self-reflection generates knowledge. The point of return, a confluence of sorts, shelters new layers of discourse through which knowledge unfolds like a flowing stream. A narrator more conscious of his role as wisdom speaker immediately appears, and, with such agency, a narrator more conscious of readers' needs. Gone is the Jack Duluoz whose monologue about Mount Hozomeen sets him in relative isolation from his contemporaries and readers. The Duluoz who now steps forward breaks the fourth wall of dramatic illusion to instruct the audience about not only *Angels* but also the Legend: it is story and confession, fiction and nonfiction. As story, both feature plot, setting, scenes, and other conventional dramatic elements— in other words, the Aristotelian "what's happening," the development of suspense and mystery that beg to be relived and resolved. As confession, the text is personal, the eternal heart of romance reflected in historic guise. As confession and story, the narrative is connected with life itself, which, like story, is fueled by the "What Happened Next?" (238), the eternal wheel of samsara.

But it is belief in human goodness, even without knowledge of its source, that the title of the book signifies, referring to the despair of the twentieth-century spiritual seeker as well as the divine nature hidden within all. For Duluoz, this divinity is represented by angel wings that he believes all humans possess, a signature of their closeness to, yet distance from, the divine. Kerouac's frequent references to angels, not only in *Angels* per se but throughout the Legend, are most likely grounded in his Catholic upbringing, but many religions, including some forms of Buddhism, especially in the Mahayana tradition, also believe in angelic beings. The term, which became a Beat in-group trope, as Kerouac used it is a kind of logo or touchstone rather than a reference to any specific narrative or theological tradition of angels. Consequently, the term resonates across many belief systems, signifying the universal rather than any particular sect.

As a narrator with an angel nature, Duluoz then becomes someone who not only confesses but delivers an apocalypse, which is a text recording the revelations of an angel. Apocalyptic narratives can report not only eschatological events but also allegorical overviews of particular peoples, visions of the destruction of Satan, and other cosmological data (Oxford Study Bible 21). *Angels* is not a cosmological vision of the universe taking care of itself, as is *Doctor Sax,* but rather the makeup, character, comportment, and personality of the apocalyptic persona, the angelic source of the vision and the human messengers who deliver the message to others.

Throughout *Angels,* Duluoz surrounds himself with such figures, each presenting to him a different yet vital message that he decodes from their status as types. One of the most dominant is Raphael Urso, a fictionalized form of the poet Gregory Corso. Articulate, joyful, and thoughtful, Raphael is as well an iridescent tangle of contradictions: he has no qualms eating meat, although he rails against cruelty to animals (250), "somehow always yell[s]" when he talks (233), and figures himself another Shelley, although he comes from a dysfunctional, working-class Italian family. Duluoz's detailed sketch presents an impish and art-filled youthfulness that through antithesis exposes Duluoz's atrophying enthusiasms, which in turn signify the endangered condition of America's promise of youthful immigrant hope and exuberance.

This same message is transmitted in Duluoz's relationship with Old Bull Hubbard, one of the most revealing Beat portraits of William S. Burroughs as a ghostly and maimed, yet wise and tenacious, soul. Both memory and literary analogy convey Hubbard's angelic importance in *Angels*. Through his friend Irwin Garden's impressions of Hubbard as a modern-day Mycroft Holmes, the eccentric brother of the British detective Sherlock Holmes, Duluoz envisions Hubbard as a brilliant but virtually invisible spirit binding and guiding them no matter where they are (312). From memories of his own experiences with Hubbard, Duluoz constructs a strong-willed and extremely vulnerable individual: a man who kicked a heroin habit but is so desperately in love with Irwin that he literally cries on Duluoz's shoulder, confessing that he maintained his friendship with Jack only to stay closer to Irwin (313–14). Duluoz takes no offence but humorously refers to himself as "this secondbest ghost," an allusion to Shakespeare's will, in which he left his second-best bed to his wife, Anne Hathaway (314). The self-deprecating Fieldsian humor diminishes Duluoz's status as a "know-all" intellectual and artist, enhancing his self-portrait as a trustworthy everyman who recognizes how privileged he is to walk among those who suffer in knowledge of their own greatness.

However, it is the disturbingly realistic portrayal of Bill Gaines, the fictionalized version of Kerouac's friend Bill Garver, that most powerfully illustrates Duluoz's companions as apocalyptic personae. Gaines is the archetypal hipster. He has a low junky groan of "hm-m-m-m," sits hunch-backed and skinny, can spend hours reading one sentence in H. G. Wells' *Outline of History*, and is a shape-shifting confidence man. Most importantly, he articulates integral similarities between the Beat junky and the Beat artist. As he tells Duluoz, both "like to be alone and comfortable provided they have what they want—They dont go mad running around looking for things to do 'cause they got it all inside, they can sit for hours without movin. They're sensitive, so called, and dont turn away from the study of good books" (223) As this insight suggests, Gaines is Duluoz's greatest guru. Duluoz, in turn, recognizing in him vision, intellect, and tenderness, serves him as best he can, running errands for him, even humbly emptying his chamber pail. The semimonastic life that he leads with Gaines provides the serenity and focus to write. In essence, Duluoz is describing his discovery of a fellow penitent and contemplative, in whose company he forms a Buddhist-like *sangha,* or group of believers, something he lacked in his earlier pursuit of Buddhist wisdom but needs to continue his vocation as writer.[4]

The wisdom messages signified by these three characters, reflected in that of other friends including Cody Pomeroy and Simon Darlovsky (a fictionalized Peter Orlovsky), carry lessons that can certainly be transferred from Duluoz's personal life to those of readers today. We all need a group within which to share and create knowledge; we all need to recognize the wisdom of the sick and foolish; we all need to pay more than lip service to the American heritage of youthful joy. It is the responsibility of individual readers to effect such an interpretation, however, since Duluoz's stories of the lessons he learned through these characters do not explicitly present the relationships as parables of the apocalypse. Other components of *Angels* bear that responsibility, assuming the role of more overt didacticism, dramatizing inexpressible universal through personal memory and art.

One of the most stunning examples of this literary device is Duluoz's narrative of his visit to a Seattle burlesque show soon after his descent from Desolation Peak. *Angels* records that once Duluoz comes down from the Cascades, he heads into Seattle where he enters a newspaper store to look at "girlie" magazines. He also purchases the St. Louis *Sporting News* to check the baseball scores and *Time Magazine* to check the world news. From there he wanders the harbor streets, drinks wine, and eventually takes in a burlesque show, which promises more explicit sexual gratification than the girlie magazines. It is no accident that Duluoz connects erotic magazines, baseball, world events, the "seaward backalleys" of Seattle, and burlesque, since each in American culture has long been associated with male fantasies of heroism, especially those of sexual prowess, physical strength, personal pleasure, moral authority derived from pain and misunderstanding, entitlement to roam freely and widely, and an essential right to reconstruct the world. These are masculinist themes that resonate throughout the Legend. *Angels* presents these in tableau fashion, Duluoz's voyeuristic persona subsuming a racially mixed America of male and female bodies into a "tireless Joe Champion biding his time!—America is so vast," Duluoz declares, "I love it so—And its bestness melts down and does leak into honkytonk areas, or Skid Row, or Times Squarey—the faces the lights the eyes" (105). With these words, Duluoz identifies America, the horizontal expansion of the continent and the verticality of its class structure, as a metonymic bodily site within which culture and the individuals that constitute it are always under siege by practices that create values and meanings based on the subjection of the body (Butler in Leitch et al. 2491–92).

According to Duluoz, those to whom the American dream eventually trickles down are the honkytonkers, the Skid Row and Times Square "fellaheens"—those whose bodies have been discarded as useless, untrainable, or diseased. They are the unseen foundation on which the useful or socially adapted bodies exist, inextricably bound by difference. This American body appears more horizontal than vertical to Duluoz. In other words, it is a vast plain upon which identities of self, especially gender oriented, move with a plasticity that counters the mundane representation of the desired self as fixed by historical boundaries. It is the burlesque that showcases this more nuanced vision of the American body. Kerouac devotes three short chapters (nos. 66–68) to this mainstay of Victorian through Beat American culture, creating what might be one of the few extant texts written from the perspective of a typical viewer of 1950s burlesque.

Burlesque has long functioned as an at least minimally tolerated underground in which men and women challenge hegemonic social codes. Specifically, the burlesque encodes in the female body sex in its most blatant form, appropriating the female body for both titillation and cultural critique

(Latham 11). The male comedian, a staple of burlesque, functions somewhat similarly. His frequent depiction as childlike, lazy, selfish, and lascivious reifies images of lost, discarded, or disabled manhood while providing a site from which mainstream prescriptions for masculinity, such as the man in the grey flannel suit, are parodied. These parodies often rely on old minstrel routines that employ the "black-faced" comedian against which to set or debunk exterior social codes.

Interestingly, Duluoz introduces the burlesque as both an "oldtime" form of entertainment and a "delicate art." By the mid-fifties, Americans had long since rejected burlesque as a delicate art, although Kerouac correctly assessed its historical significance as a legitimate art form. Burlesque emerged on the American scene in the 1860s, when P. T. Barnum brought Lydia Thompson's British group to New York to stage *Ixion*, a mythological spoof that became a tremendous hit. This form of burlesque developed in early British Victorianism in response to repressive middle-class prudery and served a similar purpose in the United States. Many of the early burlesques spoofed highbrow entertainment, such as Shakespearean drama or classical Greco-Roman texts, through feminine wit and female costuming that pushed the boundaries of decency. Women, for instance, often wore pants on stage. Middleclass and wealthy men and women were frequent patrons of these shows, but by the 1880s, burlesque in the United States was becoming the disheveled cousin of vaudeville, which was itself by that time the raunchy training ground for actors wanting to break into the entertainment business. Burlesque in those days began to feature more familiar working-class scenes, such as courtrooms, barrooms, and street corners (Kenrick 6). It also spoofed middle-class social conventions, particularly using blunt comedy to mock middle-class language, and focused more on sexual titillation, by the twenties embracing striptease and cooch dancing (a sexually provocative form of belly dancing). Working-class men were also the primary audience.

By the twenties, burlesque had also been damaged by the advent of the follies, Florenz Ziegfeld's tour de force that established the stunningly slim, beautiful, and talented female body as a code for the ideal feminine. By pioneering what some historians have called the mechanized chorus line—twenty perfect legs, arms, and buttocks moving as one—the follies effectively erased the focus on the individual woman as speaker and on the plumpness of female burlesque performers. The twenties also gave rise to some of the most potent efforts to wipe out burlesque. Various feminist and religious groups found burlesque unwholesome and unchristian. Their efforts were unintentionally aided by the advent of film and television, which soon replaced vaudeville, and by a male sexually oriented erotic and pornographic magazine culture spearheaded by Hugh Hefner's *Playboy* magazine, which first appeared in 1953. Those who opposed burlesque certainly did not succeed in wiping out sexually explicit entertainment, but at midcentury burlesque had been reduced to seamy soft-pornographic female routines accompanied by a few pathetic attempts at corny male comedy.

When film replaced burlesque as a popular entertainment, it did so ironically in part by absorbing standards of the live burlesque act into celluloid image. Vestiges of burlesque were embedded in the earliest of American films, establishing an accessible venue from which male and female bodies were subjected to "useful," that is commercial, purposes. The one image that appears repeatedly in the Legend and is especially relevant to this discussion is the film persona of W. C. Fields, the Fields/Dean/Cody/Duluoz configuration discussed in earlier in this book directing one to the emerging importance of fictional Hollywood signifiers of American masculinity—formulaic phantasms based on the burlesque body transformed from a living stage performance into a flash of photons on a blank screen: images of images that move one closer to the realization that no ontological status exists for the gendered self outside these stylized performances.

Angels's description of the Seattle burlesque includes both the Fieldsian male comedienne and the female stripper. It is the latter that opens the show. Duluoz notes that the first dancer is not "dirty" enough for the audience, explaining that her job is simply to introduce the comedy act, which consists of a character named Abe feigning grotesque faces and smacking his lips at the girls. His straight man, Slim, is described as erotically good-looking. This prefatory trio, a white female that hints of sex but withholds it and a white, two-man comedy act that exaggerates heterosexual desire as primitive while hinting at homosexuality, wastes no time blurring the distinction between the exterior culture's rules for the useful body and the interior being's desires and parodic responses (Butler in Leitch et al. 2495). Abe and Slim are then joined by a female comedian, a Spanish dancer named Lolita, and the three tell feeble sexual jokes. One places Abe on trial for being found in a graveyard. When the judge, played by Slim, asks, "What you been doin out in the graveyard?" Abe replies, "Burying a stiff." The judge states that such behavior is prohibited by law, but Abe retorts "Not in Seattle" and points at Lolita, who coyly remarks, "He was the stiff and I was the under-taker" (106). Duluoz admits that the audience gets involved in the comic troubles that Abe and Slim face, especially the way Lolita's punch line mocks Abe, demonstrating female sexual power over him while sustaining her role as sexual object. Abe and Slim's routines are followed by an African American male tap dancer who is so old that he can barely finish his routine. In sympathy, Duluoz remembers that he "pray[ed] for him to make good," imagining the dancer to be something like himself: "He is just in from Frisco with a new job and he's gotta make good somehow" (107), Duluoz presumes and applauds enthusiastically.

But the strippers are the main attraction. The first, Miss O'Grady, triggers Duluoz's memory of the Fields' movie *Never Give a Sucker an Even Break* (1941), in which Fields mocks a middle-aged, overweight, and assertive waitress by asking her, "Ain't you an old Follies girl?" The sarcastic line sustains the slim ideal of woman by castigating the more normal aging process of the female body. It also effectively silences her discourse. Simultaneously, though, the humor jabs at the larger cultural belief in youth and beauty as the norm for femininity and at the American dream of financial success: The waitress gets stuck with more than her fair share of wooden nickels as tips. For Duluoz, the allusion primarily signifies Miss O'Grady's sharp-tongued and nonerotic persona. Miss O'Grady, whose proper stage name parodies chaste unmarried womanhood, still manages to excite the audience by showing her breasts, but she fails to be risqué enough for the male crowd. It is "Sarina the Naughty Girl" who gets the house rocking by slinking and bumping her way on stage where she mimes the act of intercourse on her back. Sarina's lascivious come-on—a performance of femininity that far exceeds mere middle-class female "naughtiness" at the time—such as cutting one's hair, wearing short skirts, staying out past curfew, or kissing boys—becomes the desired extreme of the female body encoded as the sex act itself.

Interestingly, Sarina's generic performance of female transgression becomes an act that allows Duluoz to reconceptualize both male and female roles. As he watches Sarina's bumps and grinds, he imagines her in a magic castle constructed of cement and beer bottles by a mad Spanish king. In this realm of exotic fantasy, the transgressive world that had opened itself to an image of the female as solely a sexualized object obliterates that very subjection of the body. This is effected as Duluoz envisions the king and Sarina each lying dead in their juiceless graves. The sexual impulse has ended.

In that vessel, a fusion of mortality and ever-lasting life where individual human identities disintegrate into a universal atomic structure, Duluoz collapses human history, specifically the practices of religious and cultural mythologizing by which gendered identities are embodied in iconic figure. "The whole world," he remembers, naming Jesus, Buddha, Mohammed, the Devil's serpent, and Hellenic queens, roars in the theater. A vision of Blakean apocalypse and wisdom punctuated by the crash of "broken glass" transforms this protean swirl into a "white snowy light permeating everywhere" (109–10). Out of this Buddhist no-thing-ness, Duluoz next regenerates himself in direct physical contact with the resurrected Sarina, imaginatively performing the fulfillment of his masculinist desires for the carnal world by having sex with her, yet also denying that definition of masculinity by imagining that he has become her chase romantic protector, shielding her now-vulnerable and precious body with his kisses and his heart, symbols of male bodily care of the subordinate female. In this complex scenario, the parodic performance of coitus by a female engenders parodic creation and performance of multiple modes of masculinity and femininity within heterosexual discourse—as well as a culturally acceptable explanation of why this flux of gendered identities exists: the illusionary nature of ego-based distinctions.

It is the material, rather than the ethereal, vision that ultimately dominates Duluoz's burlesque experience, first through Sarina concluding her stage performance by showing the crowd her "naughty teats" (110). Here, of course, the nipples are not innately naughty, but Duluoz interprets them as such within the burlesque context, a reminder of how her act has transgressed the exterior code of the useful female body and how much audience gratification rests on that transgression. Secondly, as Duluoz exits the theater after the show he encounters cast members heading home or to bars, including the African American dancer who now appears not only old but also sickly. The inevitable degradation of the human body is revealed as a facet of a gendered and racialized world.

The conclusion of his burlesque experience also foregrounds Duluoz's empathy with individuals whose occupations are vilified by the larger culture. Through his gaze, the performers are seen as sad and simple and yet as the fabric of fantasy and dreams, the essence of a human's performative ability to re-create itself apart from what others demand of it. White women can use their bodies to dominate and be dominated in this world, an old African American dancer can wield his aging feet to draw loud applause, and a decrepit comedy team can taunt repressive laws and beliefs regarding expression of human sexuality. In Duluoz's memory, burlesque is not a disgusting underworld of sexual depravity but a necessary space in which male and female fantasies can be verbalized and acted out, and visions of alternative personal and social desires can be recontextualized, at least for a few hours.

The burlesque is also the world itself stripped of the illusions of respectability, where the social strata are exposed in all their material ugliness. Dancers and comediennes are ordinary men and women making a living under difficult, impoverished circumstances, particularly the females, almost entirely at the mercy of a male-dominated burlesque industry in its last days, and the male patrons attend primarily for the nudity and sexual arousal and release, Duluoz included (he remembers seeing condoms in the alley outside the theater). As a man with money in his pocket and a mother at home to feed and house him, Duluoz depicts himself as somewhat indifferent to the lived hardships of these people, while at the same time his confessions and fantasies indirectly acknowledge those hardships. In effect, he portrays the burlesque as an inclusive snapshot of an America where race, sex, and class are ugly yet provocative reminders of the malleability of the human condition.

The Seattle burlesque is an example of parody that produces laughter and a sense of sadness, both responses to the realization that the original or stable "other" that is gender, and I can add race here as well, is only a copy of an ideal that cannot possibly be embodied. Its ontological cause cannot be said to reside solely in Duluoz's self, since he is not the sole actor, although the narrative to some extent situates him as the existential source of these slippages. It is through the lens of the burlesque as cultural artifact that the unstable "political and discursive origins of gender" materialize (Butler in Leitch et al. 2497) as systems that rely on control of the physical body to maintain agency. In this respect, *Angels* demonstrates that the gendered body is always, as Butler argues, a body in drag or a state of imitating or performing something other, whether it be the norm of the useful body or the acts of the transgressive body. Duluoz's burlesque, both his memories of what he witnessed on stage and the fantasies that he substituted for what transpired on that stage, illustrates "useful" and "non-useful" gendered behaviors that in combination denaturalize gender. Certainly as apocalyptic messengers they "trouble" the distinctions between what is normal and what is not, what is reality and what is not.

Whether in the cosmic company of angelic actors such as Sarina, Abe, Slim, and the elderly tap dancer or in that of close angelic friends such as Cody, Irwin, Hubbard, and Gaines, Duluoz consistently uses his narrative to position himself as an apocalyptic messenger, a characterization that instills in him a conflicted sense of self. Caught between perceiving himself as not only human teacher but also divine seer of the fall mythology, he realizes that he is unworthy compared with the angels with whom he associates. In keeping with this tripartite consciousness, he represents a human being who out of extraordinary ordinariness sees more lucidly than others. Consequently, the set of terms that *Angels* implicitly and explicitly develops is that of a story/life from which humans inexplicably "fall" into life, and in this life, which he repeatedly likens to dreamlike environment, one's hopes, fears, and the confessions inevitably and repeatedly appear and ascend, descend and disappear.

Duluoz identifies this living world of angels as, first, the "Inferno," an obvious allusion to Dante's levels of hell and, second, an illusion in which he sits "upside down on the surface of the planet earth, held by gravity, scribbling a story." Confessing that there's no need to write a story of any kind (life itself does that, so one need not worry about being a writer) and that it is not enough to contritely confess one's sins ("my sorriness wont help you, or me" [67]), what remains is "an aching mystery." This, then, is Duluoz's answer to the purpose of human life: Humans have no reason to exist but to discuss this mystery, the "horror and the terror of all life" and the "vicious" cycle of Buddhist impermanence (67), in affirming a human terror that in Christian confessing wears angelic wings. In the end, all the sage can do is speak or write the story. The audience must, in Buddhist and gnostic-Christian fashion, come to their own understandings of the universe. What remains central, the core values that Duluoz wants his readers to recognize and thus to return to, is the need to express one's fear of that impermanence, to see one's own and others' angel wings, and to use language to connect with others by telling stories of the mystery.

At this point, *Angels* returns to the earlier story of the satori that Duluoz has experienced on Hozemeen: the "face of reality" telescoped as "the killing of a mouse and attempted murder of another" (4). This recursive realignment is a time-tested oral technique of not only folktales but also more formal discourse such as political speeches, sermons, and formal academic writing: the initial announcement of what the speaker intends to say provides just enough direction to convince the audience that the rest of the read is worthwhile. Elaboration is then offered at various points within the body of the text. Duluoz, however, does not elaborate on everything from the initial description of this satori but focuses on the most critical part, the murders of the mice. In this extended version, he relies on grotesque characterization to provide the details of how he killed a little mouse that was hiding among packages of Lipton's Green Pea Soup, hitting it with a stick, watching it eyes pop out, and trying to disassociate himself from the act. He then kills a second one by drowning it in a pan of water. Guilt overwhelms him in both cases, leading him to decide to let a third mouse live. These events are recounted in a complex construction of past- and present-tense moments moving so frantically that Duluoz seems to believe that he is once again in that moment. The past, that awful mistake called history, is very much alive in the present. Arguably, though, it is the mystical experience of reliving the past that enables Duluoz to expel that past. Forced to question his previous feelings of spiritual superiority, he pessimistically concludes that the idea of a personal god blessing the good is silliness. The world is malevolent emptiness in which a mouse is just like a human who feels fear, and all beings are murderers (the mouse he let live was eventually killed by a rat) who must "stop murdering," or they will be forced to return to suffering in another life.

With Book Two, the narrative presents its *third introduction,* restarting once again to expand on Duluoz's desire to find the peace that he had experienced on the mountain, "a kind of cloistral fervor in the midst of mad ranting action-seekers of this or any other 'modern' way" (219). This peace, he insists, he will develop for the sake of his art, an implicit teaching to others, *and* for the sake of simply meditating (220). As with previous introductions, this one recognizes that the narrator intentionally restarts as a device to pull the narrative forward. Acknowledging what he assumes as readers' knowledge of the story up to that point, he telegraphs a reference to the week of revelry that immediately followed his fire-watching experience, expanding the explanation of the story's purpose by stating that he was determined "to prove" he could lead the Tao life in the "world of society," not just alone on a mountain top (219).

This final restart clarifies the fallen life manifested as the ideation of appearance, reality, and layers of textuality. Two metaphors in particular, photography and masks, most clearly make this case. The former is best exemplified by Duluoz's reflections on a photograph of himself with Irwin, brothers Simon and Lazarus Darlovsky, and Raphael Urso taken in Mexico. Likening the image of his Beat gang to Thomas Brady's photographs of Civil War soldiers, "proud captured Confederates glaring at the Yankees but so sweet there's hardly any anger there, just the old Whitman sweetness that made Whitman cry and be a nurse" (241), he reconstructs the image of Confederate soldiers imaginatively fused with Whitman as a nurse, the composite laid atop the actual photograph. The results transform the young men into mythic martyrs embodying resilient yet outdated national pride, staunch fraternal fidelity, and Christian humility. The certainty of a sturdy reality undergirding the simulacra vanishes, leaving only the ephemeral layers of texts, whether internal or external images, to be read, reread, and thus rewritten eternally, or as long as an image lasts.

Angels also contends that in such a world individuals are condemned to go through life making, carrying, and wearing their own faces—false representations that, like a flesh movie as Duluoz describes it, deceive the wearer and the spectator, a static "you-face" mask that one creates to be read by all who encounter it (298). Although Duluoz does not elaborate philosophically on the mask metaphor, it seems to function much like an existential self that individuals assume in order to conform to an objectified reality, thus falling into the Sartrian trip of "bad faith," or unwitting belief in a subjectivity that does not exist. In this state, humans can appear as blind and egoistical, as do the American counsel representatives whom Duluoz encounters in Tangiers, refusing to dirty their hands to learn how fellahin people truly live (320). They can appear trapped in meaningless jobs out of love and duty toward others, as does Duluoz himself who knows that he has to support his mother (354–55). They can manifest as disappointments to others: Simon disappoints when he selfishly urinates on the street in front of strangers (204), and Duluoz disappoints himself when he leaves his mentor, the Bill Gaines, to suffer and die alone in Mexico. Even those with the capacity to care for others exhibit passivity and escapism that perpetuate suffering and death, exemplified by Raphael's and Duluoz's vocal consternation over seeing caged doves waiting in Chinatown. Each merely, as Raphael states, "don't wanta dream about wilted pigs and dead chickens in a barrel" and go home to sleep (170–71). One can argue that Kerouac countered this passivity by choosing to assume the mask of writer, using the experience as a catalyst for one of his most powerful poems, "The Thrashing Doves," which as I discussed in the previous chapter, resurrects the flesh-and-blood birds as eternal birds-of-words. But *Angels* insists that art does nothing to stop the cycle of samsara in Duluoz's world, and it does nothing to quell his feelings of guilt or his need to recover from his fall.

At the same time, Duluoz repeatedly insists upon seeing within this flawed human shell bits of everyone's angel wings. Many stories in *Angels* reveal processes by which humans exact this discovery, or at least try to. One is by reading the manifest world, even the commonest of experiences, as transcendental script. This central belief of romanticism privileges the poet as an individual with the ability to decode the universe for others. The writer as sage works with trivial facts and events, endowing them with value and deciphering layers and layers of meaning from them (Landow 31). *Angels* is a treasure trove of such thinking. For instance, while on his second visit to Mexico with Irwin, Simon, and Lazarus, Duluoz observes a number of ant villages, anthropomorphizes the insects, and expresses distress when Lazarus tromps carelessly through their lives. In this scene, Duluoz reads a much greater story of humankind and its god: "So, as Lazarus walks thru villages, so God walks thru our lives, and like the workers and the warriors we worry like worrywarts to straighten up the damage as fast as we can" (244). The reportage of an event that to most people would have been a *non*event Duluoz transforms into a parable teaching that the human compulsion to worry is unnecessary: God will walk through the world whether one wants him to or not.

A variant of the practice of exegetically reading a cosmos presumed to have a supernatural order is Duluoz's habit of reading himself into the lives and stories of past heroic figures, be they from popular culture or classical mythology. From grand narrative and iconic forms, he extracts smaller truths about himself or others. In the figure of baseball legend Ty Cobb, he deduces that he, like Cobb, has tremendous talent but is not a likable person: "I'm no Babe Ruth Beloved," he admits (197). In another instance, a pantheon of classical Greek gods and heroes becomes the material of a narrative knitting himself into the fabric of his Beat gang, while distinguishing each from the other. Raphael he calls Socrates; Irwin, Zeus; their cabdriver, the Athenian statesman and general Alcibiades (ca. 450–404 BC), with a history of shifting allegiances; and himself, both Priam, the ill-fated king of Troy during the Trojan War, and Croesus, the ill-fated king of Lydia whose hubris led to his defeat by the Persians around 574 BCE (202). However, interpreting his friend Cody Pomeroy through the narratives of Duluoz's own family and the film narratives of W. C. Fields is perhaps the boldest example of Kerouacian correspondence. A flawed angel who feels little for those weaker than he, Cody gambles compulsively, cheats on his wife, and physically abuses his daughter (363–64), but through the veils of Duluozian cinematic and immigrant history is championed as a bemused and beleaguered American dreamer, the literary twin of Fields.

This exegetical practice can legitimately be regarded as a manifestation of Duluoz's egotism, especially when he repeatedly refers to himself as Shakespeare, Balzac, and Buddha. However, stories such as those of flawed or suffering humans, including Ty Cobb, Priam, Croesus, and Fields reiterate the dangers of believing in self-sufficiency or grandeur—as Fields said, life is "fraught with imminent peril." At another level, Duluoz acknowledges a known narrative, refers to it, and, by inserting himself into it, reads the present metaphorically. In other words, the conceptual links appear to accentuate his ego and the subject-object dichotomy, but in reality the difference between subject and object is elided as the story, whether elucidated in detail or evoked by the power of the single name of its protagonist, is recontextualized to emphasize the fallibility and tragedy of human power. This comparative process often functions in *Angels* to strip away the facade of time that frames the human belief in the individual self, and thus works to negate that very concept.

Angels treats history in just this way: persistently grounding truth in as individual's history as rendered through memory, yet distrusting history as human artifice and simultaneously working imaginatively to obliterate it. *Angels* questions the extent to which the story of fallen humans can be explicated through communal history or personal memory. Ironically, the latter, Kerouac's primary material for literary construction, Duluoz negates as important, a point that he makes in the context of his contemplation of one of the most important persons in his life, his father: "I say 'Poor Pa' really feeling him and remembering him right there, as tho he could appear, to influence—Tho the influence one way or the other makes no difference, it's only history" (172). History, as Duluoz suggests, is impotent to change people's lives.

Duluoz also understands history as a fundamentally sinister artifice that humans manufacture (305). The nature of this artificial world is mediated through his quoting of Irwin's comment that "the universe is on fire and a big swindler like Melville's confidence man is writing the history of it on inflammable gauze or something but in *self eradicating ink* on top of all that, a big hype fooling everybody, like magicians making worlds and letting them disappear by themselves" (239). It is this Spenglerian trickery that Duluoz seeks to avoid, perhaps most often in the essential Beat trope: the act of hitching rides in a car. In keeping with the eternal quality of the Shrouded Traveler as Kerouac developed him, the "good old" men who ferry Duluoz across continents reflect the kernel of goodness and nobility that he nostalgically associates with humans as a timeless (that is, outside history) species (259). A considerable part of Duluoz's life is spent trying to replicate this timeless quality. He does not seek death, a simplistic interpretation

of Kerouac, but rather seeks through material practices release from the anxiety and alienation produced by his recognition of time and space as origin-
less simulacra.

Of course, one cannot ride forever in a car driven by the Shrouded
Traveler, and the second book of *Angels* argues that part of Duluoz's unrest
stems from his blindness to the possibility that the world can lead him
astray (220). It is only later, as he describes his ocean voyage to Tangiers,
that Duluoz interprets his condition as an opium-induced "turningabout"
that reconceptualizes the physical and metaphysical worlds and his place in
space and time. Reading himself into the greater context of the archetypal
American experience of perpetually seeking a new frontier, he exposes the
invisible converse of that dream: there really is nowhere else to go. The literal and metaphoric road has so reached its end in his own mind (300) that
he speculates that even the Sacristy, the Catholic term for a room in which
sacred artifacts are kept, affords no hope for the lost: all faith in the rock
of St. Peter to protect fragile human life vanishes (315–16, 339). Duluoz's
Catholic-Buddhist experiences as well as interpretations of his life and the
world have foreshadowed this bleakness, since both traditions have failed
to provide the assurance, peace, and authentic artistic and spiritual life that
he desires.

While he does not blame either Catholicism or Buddhism per se, what
resonate throughout *Angels* are noneradicable beliefs in a personal god and
the authenticity of the individual. The personal god, reified in the figure of
Christ on the cross in *Big Sur*, is foreshadowed in *Angels* as Duluoz's unstable concept of the void, or sunyata. This is not the clearest sign of the dwin-
dling power of Buddhism in his life, but it is a motif that floats along the
narrative of *Angels* as a morphological indicator of the imaginative process
by which one seeks definitive knowledge in an epistemological flux. For
example, on one hand, Duluoz genuinely desires to accept the Buddhist
teaching of sunyata. Several of his descriptions of the void as indivisible,
fire, and pure energy come close to the Buddhist understanding (155, 201).
Additionally, his definition of infinitude as "empty space and matter both,
it doesnt limit itself to either one" (70) echoes the Heart Sutra, which
explains that sunyata is not vacuity but rather everything and that it exists
everywhere. However, Duluoz more often uses the concept to reify his own
existential crisis, an act that often grossly misrepresents sunyata. Sometimes
"void" simply refers to empty space or the blankness that he feels in his own
life. Used this way, "void" connotes desire to obliterate the concept of form
or "thingness" altogether, an erroneous interpretation of sunyata but a
telling expression of Duluoz's attitude toward the physical world. Even more
often, "void" is personified with attributes of indifference, maliciousness,
viciousness, understanding, and greed (69, 70, 72, 115). It smiles, amuses

itself (70), and warns that all will die in horror (359). In this state, "void" appears as a malignant object, something like *Doctor Sax's* Great Snake, divorced from the material world. Such personification serves as a tool to explain difficult ontological concepts. In Duluoz's case, the personified void more closely resembles the wrathful Hebrew god Jehovah than anything like the paradoxical universality of sunyata. Consequently, it functions as a shadowy representation of his own Judeo-Christian heritage and as a linguistic extension of his fears of and desires for a transcendental other. In these shapes, the deconstructive motility of the term "void," each definition residing upon the present absence of the others, mirrors Duluoz and Kerouac's personal intellectual and emotional conundrum.

This personified void, however, emerges as the most distinct footprint of the concept of a personal god that Duluoz critiques in *Angels* while incessantly flirting with, and eventually claiming, it as more satisfying than the flickering images that compose his void. At the most superficial level, language such as "Lord," "He," and "God," establishes immediate connections to a personal god, and Duluoz occasionally attributes worldly events to this source, as he does to describe the tumultuous sea storm that he survived on the trip to Tangiers: "God chose to let us live" (302), he explains. Christ is also cited in *Angels*, now replacing Buddha as Duluoz's "first" hero, solidifying the direction to which his spiritual journey is taking him (362). At a deeper level signifying the marriage of spirituality and art, God is revealed as the Christian god through reference to Paul of Tarsus, whose letter to the Corinthians Duluoz quotes regarding the divine power of writing "which the Lord hath given me to edification" (286). This declaration is predicted early in Book One via the Christian cross that Raphael gives Duluoz to wear. The object hangs round his neck through drunken orgies and while sleeping alone under the stars, a tangible and sacred symbol of Christ's mission to bridge the corrupt and the celestial (150–52, 192). The cross also operates as an even more potent signifier of the power of human connection in the immediate present, Duluoz remembering that as he, Raphael, and Irwin readied themselves for the famous *Mademoiselle* photograph in which Kerouac was wearing the cross, he "realize[s] the greatness of Raphael—the greatness of his purity, and the purity of his regard for me—and letting me wear the Cross" (196). With Kerouac one is never sure how to interpret the initial uppercase, but in this passage, the capitalization of "cross" likely indicates the special power of that object at a personal level.

The deepest level of signification of Duluoz's preoccupation with the concept of a personal god is the explicit discussion of that very topic. Several of his memories of Cody serve this function. Decidedly not Buddhist, Cody takes a gnostic and theosophist approach to the metaphysical, enthusiastically sustaining a belief in the dualism of material reality and the soul. He expounds on the theosophical distinction between the physical body and the astral ghost, which at death must travel through levels of the known planetary universe until reaching final salvation. God clearly exists for him on a personal level, although, as he tells Duluoz, "that sonumbitch trail to heaven is a *long* trail!" (153–56). Other friends, such as David D'Angeli (based on Philip Lamantia), a Catholic himself, lecture Duluoz on his misdirected Buddhism, which D'Angeli perceives as "nothing but the vestiges of Manichaeism" (186).[5] While D'Angeli's argument that Buddha could not bring enlightenment because he was not outside the natural order strikes a cord with Duluoz (187–88), Duluoz resists public declaration of Christian faith, particularly in later discussions with Cody and Raphael in which Raphael pokes holes in Cody and his wife's middle-class Christian biases. By not supporting Cody, Duluoz tacitly aligns himself with Raphael's more rational than faith-based position (211–12), but he later abandons it, confiding privately to Cody that "Christ *will* come again" (213). Although he finds it difficult to discern the logic of an innocent, newborn baby being condemned for "personal reasons" in a world of suffering (283), he is compelled to declare that "God must be a personal God because I've known a lot of things that werent in texts" (285). This mystically based avowal severs his earnest ties to the empirical individual-focused teachings of Buddhism and solidly aligns him once again with mystical Catholic faith in the dualistic separation of corrupt humanity and pure divine. By taking such a stance, Duluoz again affirms the romantic primacy of the truths of physical and mental experience rather than the neoclassical tendency to privilege generalization and doctrine.

Inherent in this stance is a foundational distrust of doctrinal language. Now, as Landow argues, as a culture "falls" from God and nature, its language degenerates and this corruption becomes a predominant theme, especially in twentieth-century wisdom literature (128). The speaker of wisdom, whether prophet or sage, will concentrate upon definitions of terminology, striving to rejuvenate language appropriate for the needs and reality of the contemporary audience and to call them back to the presumably purer language of the past that embodies moral values from which they have strayed. In this regard, ironically, Kerouac is the one writer of the Beat generation who has been most vigorously accused of representing the fall of culture because of his corruption of the English language. Contrary to Landow's findings, however, Kerouac inverts the paradigm, seeing not degeneration in language but a false refinement that prohibits honest expression and therefore the discovery of truth: "The requirements for prose & verse are the same," he wrote, "i.e. *blow*—what a man most wishes to hide, revise, and unsay, is precisely what Literature is waiting and bleeding for" (*Letters* 1: 516). His point is that culture itself has already fallen in part because it strayed too far from its natural voice, language, and expressive mediums. To counter the fall of American culture, he calls for a more natural poetic voice and method of writing. As I discussed in the last chapter, he associated these with musical forms and the ancient bardic tradition; in *Angels* he reiterates this call while revealing more about its imaginative and spiritual nature as reflected in spontaneous prose.

This method as already noted, he likens to oral storytelling in which author and audience share an intimate exchange of knowledge that eschews craft (of a particular kind) and allows for the occasional production of what Duluoz calls "gibberish" in the service of expression of the soul (280). This definition centers artistic production in the hustle and bustle of a world teeming with life, and it is this connection between language and the world that Duluoz emphasizes. It is poetry that rescues him at critical moments. Life, in essence, *is* poetry for those willing to see that, *Angels* contends. For instance, he gleefully pulls himself back into life when he realizes that he is "making poems out of nothing at all, like always, so that I were a Burroughs Adding Machine Computer I'd still make numbers dance to me" (299). These pronouncements embody the classic bohemian and Beat understanding of the dialectical nature of art and life. Like the Buddhist concept of sunyata, which does not distinguish between form and void, art and life are indivisible.

In fiction, Kerouac took this a step farther, presenting the human soul as emerging most authentically with all of its wrinkles and angel wings in those moments of the spontaneous production of living art/artful life. It is this purest expression of the soul that Duluoz connects to Paul of Tarsus, who in a letter to his followers in Corinthia stated that corresponding to them from afar allowed him to use his writing talents for their benefit rather than their destruction (286). In this context, Duluoz's language and writing take on a prophetic quality that he alludes to as he tells the convoluted story of his final spiritual "turningabout" and the storm at sea "I feel I didnt explain that right," he rethinks after presenting the experience of the storm, "but it's too late, the *moving finger* crossed the storm and that's the storm" (302, emphasis mine). The "moving finger" fits elegantly within the framework of his identity as spiritual quester, writer, and sage. The phrase most directly evokes the four-line poem that is part of Omar Khayyam's *Rubaiyat:* "The Moving Finger writes, and, having writ, / Moves on: nor all thy Piety nor Wit / Shall lure it back to cancel half a Line, / Nor all thy Tears wash out a Word of it." Nothing, in other words, can change either the storm itself or the reality of Duluoz's attempt to describe the experience; a greater power has created them both. Less directly, the "moving finger" is intertextually linked to the Old Testament story "The Handwriting on the Wall," in which Daniel, a wise man and visionary, accurately interprets for the Babylonian King

Belshazzar a prophecy of doom written on the king's wall by "the fingers of a human hand" (Daniel 5:5, Oxford Study Bible, 920). In combination, the wisdom of the *Rubaiyat* and the story of Daniel's prophecy name the divine source of the natural world, the retribution that one must expect for sinning against God, the importance of the human visionary who delivers these truths, and the poet as that emissary from afar.

By linking his horrific experience at sea, his storytelling method, and the "moving finger," Duluoz implies that divine vision resides within himself as well as in the methods of recreating and conveying the specifics of his life experiences, emotions, and thoughts. He recreates and defends the pursuit of art as well as spiritual truth, that is, his own life's work, by writing about the source, function, and power of language itself. By implication, his self-characterization as a somewhat average, flawed being suggests that all forms of language exist to guide one to salvation. Significantly, this literary representation of the wisdom persona does not negates faith in either a transcendent personal god who gifts the world with salvation or the individual's power to fashion his or her own salvation. Duality and nonduality reveal and obscure each other.

The "moving finger" passage embodies the romantic roots of contemporary wisdom literature that emphasizes an epistemological position highlighting personal experience, the storyteller as word painter, and expression of the experience complemented by emotional effects within a predominantly perceptual frame (Landow 133). The method, approximating the immediacy of visual and cognitive expression, is deceptively indirect, and Kerouac's attention to the wisdom of authentic language also makes this point, particularly in Duluoz's relationship with Raphael. Presented as a Socratic foil, Raphael at one point in their travels righteously ridicules Duluoz's theory of absolute spontaneity and cites Shelley as an example of a revered poet who "didn't care about theories about how he was to write 'The Skylark'" (280). His last shot is to call Duluoz "an old college professor" (280), implicitly invoking the cliché "those who can do, and those who can't teach." Duluoz's response is to deride university life, an indirect defense of his poetic talents, but he leaves uncritiqued the reference to Shelley. Unspoken is the fact that Shelley thought a great deal about composition methods and the function of the poet; his *Defense of Poetry,* for example has long been a canonical mainstay of literary theory and criticism. Raphael's misstatement is left uncorrected, subtly undermining Raphael's credibility as a literary historian and affirming Duluoz's theorizing while disassociating him from the then conventional academic practices, such as the New Criticism. The episode deftly sends the message that poetry and theory can be authentic forms of language and that traditional forms of learning from one's wise elders, whether in a library or by talking with established writers (Raphael ironically ends the argument by leaving with Irwin to visit the

writer Carl Sandburg), can genuinely promote acquisition of valuable knowledge leading toward truth.

In no more personal, dramatic, and no doubt unexpected form does Duluoz
convey this message throughout *Angels* than the "Trope of the Wise Old
Woman." This figure appears as early as Kerouac's *Windblown World* journals
in an undated entry probably referring to domestic scenes from his childhood
in Lowell: "I believe the old crones around that sewing table, I believe they are
as old and wise as nature" (137). His "old crone" is a recombinant construction of four ancient stereotypes: the woman of wisdom, such as Sophia and
Athena; the pure source of life, such as the Virgin Mary and Gaia; the beautiful yet dumb or treacherous female, such as Delilah and Pandora; and the evil
hag, such as Lilith and Eve. In popular culture, the Wise Old Woman is manifest as angelic mothers and nurses, Hollywood movie stars, old maids, frigid
high school teachers, Halloween witches, and many others. Frustrating many
Kerouac readers, all four frequently appear. The hag, especially, often emerges
in the Legend in one of three forms: a creature unable to overcome her biological urge to procreate and thus unwittingly sustaining death; a dumb object
of male sexual gratification; or a desexualized nag unable to comprehend the
male artist's need for adventure and solitude. In this guise—variants of
Kerouac's infamous line "pretty girls make graves"—his female characters are
misogynistically constructed. One must bear in mind, however, that Kerouac's
agenda was never to present a utopian vision of gender equality. Through
Duluoz, the depictions of women operate to illuminate his narrator's efforts to
achieve wisdom about the self and human nature.

This literary and epistemological move is achieved not by focusing on a
girlfriend or wife, neither of which centered Kerouac's life, but rather on his
mother—Gabrielle Levesque Kerouac, *Ma*, as Kerouac called her, or *Memere*,
which means "grandmother" in Quebecois and is the name by which readers
best know her. No single volume of the Duluoz Legend provides a lifelike,
biographical portrait of Memere, and readers should not expect to find the
"real" Memere in *Angels*, the one reported to have been anti-Semitic and to
have despised Ginsberg, Burroughs, and Cassady as well as any woman
Kerouac brought home. As Memere is developed, her character becomes
more complex as Kerouac's writing becomes more autobiographical and self-
reflective. From the first sketchy image of her as the wise and nurturing aunt
in *On the Road* to whose cloister Sal Paradise repeatedly returns for peaceful
solitude, Memere is transformed into the nurturing, mystical, ribald, hopeful, and suffering homemaker, wife, and mother of *Doctor Sax* and the
embodiment of the "intrinsic Buddha" in *Some of the Dharma* (190). In these
and other texts such as *Angels,* she remains an uneducated but wise, demanding first-generation American[6] with great faith in Catholicism, her only sur-
viving son "Ti Jean," the American dream of prosperity and moral goodness,

and her own wisdom gained over years of hard work, both at home and in the factories of Lowell. Fearlessly yet humbly weaving the story of his relationship with Memere through the narrative, Duluoz narrates his private experiences with his maternal sage that communicate for the edification of himself and for readers' generalizations regarding the values to which America and Western culture must return. In this respect, Memere stands as an abbreviated representation of reality and as a literary device to explore Duluoz and the greater world.

Duluoz calls Memere "the most important person in this whole story and the best" (334). Unlike any other person in the world, she is a gleeful soul who lovingly provides companionship and solitude for him. In his mind, everybody loves her (283–84). Yet the short biographical material that he integrates in the narrative illustrates that she is no doubt, like thousands of working-class immigrant women, seeking a better life for her family in an early twentieth-century America that provided few if any social safety nets. She is the one person whom Duluoz truly seems to both respect and fear (286), but he admits that she can be a "suspicious paranoid" about his friends, and he often ignores her admonishments to abandon them (283–84). Despite his love for her, he is bothered by the fact that he remains so close to her: "Even Genet the divine knower of Flowers said a man who loves his mother is the worst scoundrel of them all [. . .] and all the time I'm sitting there enjoying and *in*-joying the sweet silly peace of my mother" (337). The reference to Genet, a writer for whom Kerouac had great respect, is a telling indication of the depth of Duluoz's concern, recognizing in others' reactions the taboo of his relationship with Memere.

But his defense of her as the mother of the sixth patriarch in the tradition of Chinese Zen Hui Neng (638–713) and as the embodiment of "the actual true 'Zen'" wisdom (334) transforms her into the exotic other. Captured in this gaze, she is no longer a working-class mother, but a soul of ancient and wise origin. She also strikes him as "a Head Nun in a remote Andalusian or even Grecian nunnery," a mystical but existential exotic who, when she says her rosary beads at night, thinks, "Who cares about Eternity! we want the Here and Now! [. . .] Eternity? Here and Now? Wat they talkin about?" (360). The combination of Christian and Buddhist wisdom, Memere is the person to whom he turns for answers regarding the horror and unhappiness of life. Her response is commonsense folk wisdom: people have to "do right" and return home to the families, or "make yourself a *haven* in this world and Heaven comes after," she counsels (360). But the counsel of the wise old woman is generally denigrated by American patriarchy in which youth, beauty, and material success reign, and there is little in the Legend or Kerouac biographies to suggest that others saw Memere as a Sophia figure. Consequently, she is a highly problematic figure in his life. Representing the attainable/unattainable center of his world, she is one who knows him best, the one he most trusts, yet the one whom society tells him he must abandon if he is to achieve American masculine adulthood.

Much of Memere's story appears toward the conclusion of *Angels*. Therefore, even though Duluoz mentions Memere throughout, her story reads as a major digression, almost as if Duluoz has been holding back revelation until the impulse to confess his love for her can wait no longer. In so doing, he uses her as a vehicle to criticize "most of [his] fellow writers" who hate their mothers but use those "big Freudian or sociological philosophies" as material for the writerly fantasies (334). In contrast, he signals the way he himself manipulates his mother as a character. First, as he reveals indirectly at the conclusion, he is defending her: "I always wanted to write a book to defend someone because it's hard to defend myself" (364). Thus she becomes a surrogate for himself, much like Duluoz is a surrogate for Kerouac. Secondly, she is a site of fantasy, like the mothers that other writers hate; but as a site of love and wisdom she must be read differently from those, the implication being that Memere reveals critical elements of human nature. He recounts, for instance, that during his second trip to Mexico he thwarted a group of thieves from stealing his jacket by announcing that if he lost it his mother would be extremely upset (286). The episode conveys the reality of Mexico as dangerous—not entirely the liminal world of bliss presented in *On the Road*. But it also exposes Mexicans, often maligned as ignorant peasants, as sensitive and insightful: even the thieves of the world have mothers they love and respect. Memere, then, is not nearly so much Duluoz's flesh and blood but the signification of personal connection linking human beings across cultures.

Memere also must be seen as a mirror of Duluoz. Through her he reconstructs himself so that the trope of the Wise Old Woman teaches him that he must strive to be a better person. The wisdom of staying at home that Memere teaches leads him to realize that he needs to be more like her— "patient, believing, careful, bleak, self-protective, glad for little favors, suspicious of great favors, [. . .] make it your own way, hurt no one, mind your own business, and make your compact with God" (340). In one respect, his relationship with her allows him to understand more lucidly his extreme mistreatment of other women, convincing him to confess that he has betrayed two wives and "hundreds of lover-girls" (111). Part of his effort to remain celibate, a dominant theme in *Some of the Dharma* and *The Dharma Bums*, comes from his guilt and genuine desire to reform—knowledge reified in both the physical body of Memere and his metaphoric vision of her.

But the trope of the Wise Old Woman is more than a female Sophia, Virgin Mary, Athena, or St. Theresa de Lisieux whom Duluoz must strive to be *like*. She is also that which Duluoz himself must *become*. *Angel*'s early chapters reveal that Duluoz has at least internalized the possibility of that cognitive transformation. Remembering that while still on the mountain he would wake in the morning to see his mop, he writes that the implement is "still drying on the rock, like a woman's head of hair, like Hecuba forlorn" (16). A metonym of the Buddhist belief in carrying on the menial chores of one's life as right living, the mop, reconfigured as the ancient Greek heroine Hecuba who refused to commit suicide even though her family and country had been destroyed, symbolizes female perseverance in the face of great suffering. The mop as an extension of Duluoz thus connects Hecuba's courage to Duluoz. Daringly, he later transforms himself into that Wise Old Woman, like Hecuba forlorn claiming life to the end. In a striking self-portrait, he imagines himself in a fellahin world without America or any other nation state, hiding in a cave as "the last old woman on the earth gnawing on the last bone in the final cave and I cackle my last prayer on the last night before I dont wake up no more—Then it'll be bartering with the angels in heaven but with that special astral speed and ecstasy so maybe we wont mind at all then, seems" (99–100). With nothing left but himself, self-transformed into the body of the grotesque old woman, he lastly imagines the future as the space in which the writer as prayerful penitent—the descendent of Shakespeare, Joyce, Melville, and himself-as-woman—will inevitably triumph: "Gad," he declares, "the greatest writer who ever lived will have to be a woman" (271). This tropic pattern synthesizes Kerouac's fascination with escape from civilization and its history and his belief in a transcendent afterlife, coupled with skepticism about the metaphysical realm as any better than suffering on earth. Duluoz's imaginative gender play elides the separation between epic history and the present and future, mythologizing himself through others as aerial sublimes who expose the generative radical of America as an ancient, wise, and eternal.

With such knowledge, Duluoz the grotesque Wise Old Woman writer "lost in the unutterable mental glooms of the 20th Century Scrivener of Soul Stories" (364) can do nothing greater or less than confess and teach through a flawed life and soul. Other angels have delivered their apocalypses to him: Irwin's is to use art for public good; Cody's is to keep living but remember that bad deeds will haunt one; Gaines's is that death triumphs in the end; Memere's is that home and family ensure reward in heaven. Duluoz's message is that the imaginative act of literary self-transformation enables one to pursue knowledge and life. For Duluoz, that life concludes as a "peaceful sorrow at home" (366), a belief in a transcendental afterlife, a commitment to life in the present, the realization that the typical American will always have wanderlust but will have nowhere to go (300), and that self, security, and creativity lie within the home, the ancient and elemental foundation of culture. Here, as the angel of desolation, Duluoz hunkers down, writing on to warn others and teaching others about the ineffable: Why do we exist, why do we suffer, and why does God, if there is a god, not care? The answer to these questions Kerouac had already penned some ten years earlier to both himself and America in *Some of the Dharma*: "This writing will not rot like a body because it will always partake of the vision of the unborn—" (279), an affirmation of self, culture, and the very redemption of fallen human nature itself in the language of the contemporary prophet and sage—Jack Duluoz, Aremideia the Paraclete.

NOTES

INTRODUCTION

1. "Aremideia" may be a Kerouacian version of "Ariya Metteya (Pali) / Maitreya (Sanskrit)" associated with Burmese and Sri Lankan buddhisms. "Ariya" (or "Arya") is a common Sanskrit phrase that means "noble" and can be applied to anything worthy of praise. Kerouac, then, seems to be calling himself the next noble Buddha.
2. See Lardas for a cogent discussion of the New Vision.
3. In Atop an Underwood, Paul Marion notes that Kerouac referred to Lin Yutang (1895–1976) in an October 1942 notebook that identified authors with a special sensitivity to the "individual sensation of Life" (82). Kerouac may have read Lin's *The Importance of Living* (1937), *My Country and My People* (1935), *The Wisdom of Confucius* (1938), or other works of his—the record is not clear at this point.
4. See, for example, Theado, who maintains that "as recognition for Kerouac's artistic achievement increases, the Duluoz Legend outgrows the genre of autobiography and becomes an intimate chronicle of a writer's stylistic maturation" (5).
5. See Rubin.
6. Some psychologists claim that all human knowledge is grounded in stories constructed on past experiences; new experiences are interpreted through the old stories. See Schank and Abelson.
7. For lucid discussions of theoretical stances on this topic, see Hinchman and Hinchman.
8. Swartz's rhetorical analysis of *On the Road* represents this trend in communication studies. His use of fantasy theme criticism to examine "the implications of Kerouac's role in influencing American society" (4) highlights the conventional Beat themes of social deviance, sexuality, and fraternal relationships.
9. In a general sense, my reading of the Legend parallels that of Brendon Nicholls, who calls it a mythology of self rather than autobiography.
10. This synopsis of the primary narrative of American culture comes from Hoffman's *Form and Fable* and other sources including Manning Marable's work in African American history and cultural studies, including a lecture that he gave at The College of Wooster in September 2006.
11. See http://en.wikipedia.org/wiki/Jim_Bridger and http://en.wikipedia.org/wiki/Johnny_Appleseed, as well as "Johnny Appleseed: A Pioneer Hero" *Harper's Magazine*, November 1871.

12. Richardson makes a convincing argument regarding Sal and Americanness in the context of writers such as Richard Wright, James Baldwin, and Jean Toomer.

13. Daniel Hoffman's work on folk traditions in American literature helped me see Kerouac in this light.

14. Marco Abel presents a fascinating reading of *On the Road* from the perspectives of Deleuze and Guattari, acknowledging folk and language issues somewhat connected to my reading of Kerouac's search for truth that results in multiple and contradictory meanings. However, Abel's dehistoricized insistence that "Kerouac's entire oeuvre" or his "poetic project was to invent—not represent—a new, missing people" (246) is a gross misreading of Kerouac's letters, journals, and *Legend*.

15. Gallup poll questions have changed dramatically over the years; the phrasing of the questions is unstable, some are eliminated, and some new added.

16. See http://poll.gallup.com (Oct. 24–26, 2005).

17. See *The Social Contract, Discourse on the Origin of Inequality,* and *The New Heloise,* as well as Lloyd's insightful discussion of reason as a gendered concept.

CHAPTER 1

1. Ann Charters argues that Kerouac's new style was also influenced by Burroughs' autobiographical writing and by John Clellon Holmes' first novel that drew liberally upon real events in his life (*On the Road,* xviii–xix).

2. See James T. Jones's *Map of Mexico City Blues* for a discussion of the significance of the "oo" sound.

3. See, for example, Arnheim, Russell, Kosslyn, Shepard and Cooper, and Block.

4. See George Dardess's insightful essay on Kerouac's sketching process.

5. Andrew Welsh's *Roots of Lyric* contains a thorough discussion of the lyric elements.

6. See Hunt's "Kerouac's Dialogue" and "Voicing the Page."

7. The film to which Kerouac alludes could be the William S. Hart directed *The Square Deal Man* (1917), in which Hart played Jack o' Diamonds, a gambler who puts his trust in love and wins (http://www.imdb.com/title/tt0008623/). In British and American folk tradition, Jack o' diamonds also refers to whiskey.

8. Additional differences between the notebook and published versions demonstrate that even at the sentence level, Kerouac manipulated his use of English and French (much of the notebook is composed in French), punctuation, and description to craft Duluoz and Maggie as distinctly fictionalized figures.

9. John Shapcott elucidates this feature of Kerouac's method by explicating Duluoz's use of diegtic sound (i.e., heard and recorded on the tape by Duluoz and Cody) and discussion of music they had listened to in the past to refresh Cody's memories. Also see Weinreich for an insightful discussion of the tape and memory (82–83).

10. Tytell also notes the similarity between the "Circe" episode and *Visions of Cody,* although he does not discuss them at any length.

11. In a 1961 letter to John Montgomery, Kerouac attributed this explanation to Leon Trotsky commenting on Celine's writing (*Letters* 2: 287).

12. Duluoz's draft autobiography is located in LM 1, one of the uncataloged Kerouac notebooks in the NYPL Berg Collection. Kerouac noted at the head of the text that it was written in Mill Valley, California, April 6, 1956.

13. Maggie Cassidy Notebook 3, NYPU.

14. See, for example, 7, 25, 265, and 396 in *Cody*.

CHAPTER 2

1. See *A Farewell to Arms*, in which Hemingway wrote, "The world breaks everyone and afterward many are strong at the broken places."

2. When dealing with letters such as these as literary texts and as primary sources to elucidate the composition and interpretation of other texts, one must be cognizant of the letter as a public document. No matter how closely connected the writer and addressee may be, the letter, even when the author has no intention of ever sending it, is a document intended for consumption by another, a construction of a self that the writer wishes to present to another. A power dynamic is always present as a writer seeks to establish, modify, sustain, or end a relationship.

3. Brinkley erroneously states in *Windblown World* that Stephen Dedalus directs his statement to the boys in the class he is teaching. In actuality, Dedalus makes the comments to Mr. Deasy, his supervisor, who has engaged him in intellectual sparing (Joyce, *Ulysses* 28).

4. It is not clear which Carlyle text Kerouac was reading at this time, but it may have been *Sartor Resartus,* Carlyle's spiritual, fictive autobiography.

5. See Donald Stockton's lucid overview of Spengler as well as John Lardas's *Bop Apocalypse* for a discussion of how Kerouac, Ginsberg, and Burroughs used Spengler. See also Robert Holton's essay on *On the Road,* which draws intelligently on Spengler.

6. Joe Mitchell, a writer for the New Yorker, chronicled Joe Gould's life in "Professor Sea Gull" (*New Yorker,* Dec. 12, 1942). At the time, people believed that Gould's "Oral History" was a real Proustian endeavor, but after Gould's death, it was found that a publishable magnum opus did not exist. His diary of approximately 1,100 pages, however, is now housed in the Fales Collection at New York University (http://www.villagevoice.com/news/0014,miller,13818,1.html).

7. Gould was committed to Pilgrim State Hospital in 1952. His death and funeral were reported in the *Village Voice* on August 28, 1957.

8. Gerald Nicosia discusses the balloon image, and Jones in *Map* draws upon Nicosia's interpretation. See *Memory Babe* 483.

CHAPTER 3

1. See http://www.autry.com/html/home.php and http://www.cow-boy.com/musaut.htm#ed for filmographies and discographies. Autry also owned the Los Angeles Angels (later called the California Angels, then the Anaheim Angels, and now the Los Angeles Angels of Anaheim) baseball team from 1960 to his death in 1998.

2. Newly restored versions of Autry films are now readily available through his estate.
3. "Proverbs from Hell," in *Marriage of Heaven and Hell.*
4. See my discussion of Kerouac's narrators as feminized males in *The Feminized Male Character.*
5. Rob Holton, in *On the Road: Kerouac's Ragged American Journey,* states that "the image of the pearl is an ancient one, a symbol without precise reference but implying wisdom, purity, and beauty" (31).
6. Kerouac did not regularly attend church, but see his letter to Neal Cassady dated January 1, 1951, which indicates that he spent time in St. Patrick's Cathedral in New York City listening to novenas and meditating.
7. Eddie Dean Glosup (1907–99) was one of Hollywood's "Singing Cowboys." Dean, who was called "the golden-throated cowboy," appeared in westerns and may be best known for his recording of "One Has My Name (The Other has My Heart)."
8. For instance, see Lardas, Holton, Theado, and Grace (2000).
9. See *Some of the Dharma.*

CHAPTER 4

1. Tytell briefly connects *Sax* and the Snake with gnostic ophitic groups.
2. Theosophical beliefs include mystical knowledge of God combined with karma, reincarnation, the evolution of the spirit, and the ultimate perfection of all life.
3. See the Theosophical Society Web site for a thorough overview of these beliefs; http://www.theosophical.org/theosophy/faqs/index.html#Q5.
4. The term "gay" is most likely a reference not to homosexuality but to flamboyance and happiness; the derogatory terms used in Kerouac's day for homosexuals were "queer" and "fag."
5. The caduceus in classical mythology is a winged staff with two serpents entwined on it, which symbolized Hermes and Mercury, both messengers of Zeus, and so it is an image with masculine and feminine connotations.
6. In my preparation of this chapter, I found very helpful two articles by Fiona Patton (see bibliography). Her objectives in both differ from mine, but her insightful Bakhtinian analysis of Kerouac's language advanced my own thinking about *Doctor Sax* and the rest of the Duluoz Legend.

CHAPTER 5

1. Jeanne Malmgren, "On the Road to Enlightenment," *St. Petersburg Times;* Lee Ann Sandweiss, "Inside the Mind of Beat Generation's Jack Kerouac," *St. Louis Post-Dispatch (Missouri),* October 29, 1997; Tom Clark, "Kerouac's Inner Journey to Find Light and Meaning." *Washington Times,* September 7, 1997, Part B, p. B8.

2. See Gargan and Hoffert's short review, which states that "those who persevere
will be rewarded with interesting insights into Kerouac's struggle with alco-
holism, his occasional thoughts on suicide, and his disturbing tendency
toward misogyny."

3. See Falk.

4. The typescript is housed in the Berg Collection.

5. *The Encyclopedia of Ephemera* discusses the advent of scrap manufacturing and
scrapbooking; the latter has become a major middle-class hobby in early
twenty-first-century America.

6. *Beat Culture and the New America 1950–1965* provides an excellent introduction to Beat-associated visual arts.

7. See Albright.

8. 2004 World Almanac, Martain Bauman in *The Dharma Has Come West: A
Survey of Recent Studies and Surveys* at http://www.urbandharma.org/udharma
/survey.html, U.S. Census Reports.

9. Kerouac's published statements regarding Zen are contradictory, so one can
understand why a discussion such as Sterritt's would imply that Kerouac was
a follower of Zen Buddhism (*Screening the Beats* 50–56). Kerouac's wide-rang-
ing Buddhist readings informed him about Zen, and texts such as his October
1960 column written for *Escapade* magazine present Zen favorably (*Blonde*
166–68). However, *Some of the Dharma* attributes to Zen Buddhism "sinister
disciplinary undertones" (114) and in *Desolation Angels* Zen is called "nothing
but the Devil's Personal war against the essential teaching of Buddha" (267).

10. The Hinayana and Mahayana traditions support monastic as well as more
community-oriented spheres, so there is no clear distinction between the two
based on the election of a life of solitude.

11. Cassady discusses this in her memoir *Off the Road*. Nicosia also notes that
Kerouac expressed some skepticism about, if not distaste for, Cayce's mysticism (457–59).

CHAPTER 6

1. "The Beginning of Bop" in *Blonde*, 117.

2. See Joachim E. Berendt's *Jazz Book* for an insightful discussion of the early history of European musical improvisation (152–53).

3. *Vanity of Duluoz* also includes the musical directive "Allegro, the composer
should write here" (192).

4. Mexico City Blues Holograph Notebooks—Box 18b, New York Public
Library Berg Collection.

5. In the published section 4, the phrase "& Burroughs and Ginsberg were
asleep" originally read "& Burroughs was asleep with Ginsberg." This and the
first fifty sections of the prose poem were composed in five small breast-pocket
notebooks, now housed in the Berg collection at the New York Public Library.

6. These techniques are from Hartman's discussion of Konitz's technique in *Jazz
Text;* my discussion of jazz is deeply indebted to his original work.

7. Weinreich makes this argument regarding Kerouac's biography, not the literary motifs that I have discussed.

8. "The Quoter and His Culture" by Krin Gabbard (92–111) in *Jazz in Mind: Essays on the History and Meanings of Jazz*, Reginald T Bruckner and Steven Weiland (eds); Detroit: Wayne State University Press, 1991; also *Bebop: the Music and the Players*, Thomas Owens, New York: Oxford University Press, 1995.

9. "Essentials" in *Portable*, 485.

10. Mexico City Blues Holograph Notebooks—Box 18b, New York Public Library Berg Collection.

11. This reading draws on Homi K. Bhabha's discussion of stereotype in *The Location of Culture*, 80–81.

12. My argument counters that of James Jones, who claims that by following the notebook page Kerouac "gives in to the power of circumstance, to the determination of whim . . . [opening the] poem to the qualities of randomness, coincidence, and inevitability that are commonly attributed to experience in life" (*Map* 141). The form is more constraining than Jones acknowledges, evidenced by the uniformity of the holograph and published poems. Seventy percent of the choruses contain twenty-one to twenty-five lines, a standard for the blues poem identified by Kerouac in *Some of the Dharma* ("A Blues is a complete poem . . . usually in 15-to-25 lines," 342). Stacked blocks with relatively short lines and an average of three to four short stanzas also contribute to uniformity.

13. These are choruses 70, 76, 83, 86, 129, 132, 133, 143, 146, 192.

14. The film (1959) was directed by Robert Frank and Alfred Leslie and written and narrated by Kerouac. It features Ginsberg, Corso, Larry Rivers (as Milo), Orlovsky, David Amram, Richard Bellamy, Alice Neal, Sally Gross, Pablo Brank, Delphine Seyrig. The theme song "The Crazy Daisy" was written by Ginsberg and Kerouac and performed by Anita Ellis.

15. A very different effect, haunting and dramatic, was created when this poem was set to music as the opening song for the film *Pull My Daisy* sung by Anita Ellis.

16. James Jones makes a similar observation regarding *Mexico City Blues,* arguing that the poem creates "a self that dissolves" (128) and that "the self that exists in the poem proves that the self writing the poem is not a fixed entity but a flow and flux that exists only by inference from its creations" (*Map* 128–29).

17. *Atop an Underwood.*

18. See "Structure and Style" by M. H. Abrams.

19. See Jones's discussion of "Sea" in *Kerouac's Family* for insight into Kerouac's allusion to Shakespeare's *Tempest.*

20. *Old Angel Midnight* was originally titled "Lucien Midnight" after Lucien Carr. For publication, Kerouac changed the name, finding inspiration watching Charles Van Doren on television talking about an "old angel" in heaven (*Letters* 1: 173).

21. James Jones calls these "Kerouactonyms," writing about them in broad strokes, identifying only a few, arguing that Kerouac used them "to transcend words by means of words" (*Nine* 75).

22. In the *Wake*, Joyce includes " Brekkek kekkek Kekkek Kekkek! Koax Koax Koax!" to signify the chaos of the fall and the underworld (Campbell 32; Joyce 23).

23. Michael Hrebniak insightfully writes that this poem is "Patterned upon isolated snap-units and dense word conjunction" (142).

CHAPTER 7

1. See Campbell and Robinson's still highly insightful reading of *Finnegans Wake* as dream and myth.

2. I suspect that Kerouac was referring not to Herbert Hoover (1874–1964), who was president from 1929 to 1933, but to J. Edgar Hoover (1895–72), the then director of the FBI.

3. My thanks to my colleagues Carolyn Durham and Sharon Shelly for providing this translation.

4. A *sangha* is any community of four or more fully ordained monks. In general, ordained or laypeople who take Bodhisattva vows or tantric vows can also be said to be a sangha.

5. The gnostic reference, unexplained by Duluoz, may refer to the Eastern elements of Mani's gnosticism that presented Jesus as the light of wisdom who revealed knowledge to awaken and free people, in defiant rejection of baptism as the method of salvation (Barnstone and Meyer 507).

6. Maher's biography includes a chronology of Kerouac's ancestors.

BIBLIOGRAPHY

Abel, Marco. "Speeding Across the Rhizome: Deleuze Meets Kerouac *On the Road*." *Modern Fiction Studies* 48.2 (2002): 227–56.

Abrahams, Roger. "Folklore and Literature as Performance." *Journal of the Folklore Institute* 9 (1972): 75–94.

Abrams, M. H. "Shelley and Romantic Platonism." *The Mirror and the Lamp: Romantic Theory and the Critical Tradition.* New York: W.W. Norton, 1958. 126–31.

———. "Structure and Style in the Greater Romantic Lyric." *From Sensibility to Romanticism: Essays Presented to Frederick A. Pottle.* Ed. Frederick W. Hilles and Harold Bloom. New York and London: Oxford University Press, 1965.

Adler. Ed. *Departed Angels: Jack Kerouac.* New York: Thunder's Mouth Press, 2005.

Albright, Daniel. *Lyricality in English Literature.* Lincoln: University of Nebraska Press, 1985.

Allen, Robert C. *Horrible Prettiness: Burlesque and American Culture.* Chapel Hill, NC: University of North Carolina Press, 1991.

Amram, David. *Offbeat: Collaborating with Kerouac.* New York: Thunder's Mouth Press, 2002.

Armstrong, Karen. *Buddha.* New York: Penguin Books, 2001.

Arnheim, Rudolf. *Visual Thinking.* Berkeley University of California Press, 1969.

Attridge, Derek. *Poetic Rhythm: An Introduction.* Cambridge and New York: Cambridge University Press, 1995.

———. "Rhythm in English Poetry." *New Literary History.* 21.4 (1990): 1015–37.

Bakhtin, M. M. *The Dialogic Imagination.* Ed. Michael Holquist. Austin: University of Texas Press, 1981.

———. *Rabelais and His World.* First Midland book ed. Bloomington: Indiana University Press, 1984.

Ball, Gordon. Ed. *Allen Verbatim: Lectures on Poetry, Politics, Consciousness by Allen Ginsberg.* New York: McGraw-Hill, 1974.

Barnstone, Willis, and Marvin Meyer. *The Gnostic Bible.* Boston: Shambhala, 2003.

Begnal, Michael H. "'I Dig Joyce': Jack Kerouac and *Finnegans Wake*." *Philological Quarterly* 77.2 (1998): 209–19.

Berdyaev, Nicolas. *The Meaning of History.* Trans. George Reavey. New York: Charles Scribner's Sons, 1936.

Berendt, Joachim E. *The Jazz Book: From Ragtime to Fusion and Beyond.* Trans. H. and B. Bredigkeit, Dan Morgenstern, and Tim Nevill. New York: Lawrence Hill Books, 1992.

Bhabha, Homi K. *The Location of Culture.* London and New York: Routledge, 1994.

Blake, William. *The Marriage of Heaven and Hell.* London and New York: Oxford University Press, 1975.

Block, Ned. Ed. *Imagery.* Cambridge, MA; MIT Press, 1982.

Bloom, Harold. *The American Religion: the Emergence of the Post-Christian Nation.* New York: Simon and Schuster, 1992.

Boatright, Mody Coggin. *Folk Laughter on the American Frontier.* New York: Collier, 1961.

Bruckner, Reginald T., and Steven Weiland. Eds. *Jazz in Mind: Essays on the History and Meanings of Jazz.* Detroit: Wayne State University Press, 1991.

Buckler, William E. Ed. *Prose of the Victorian Period.* Boston: Houghton Mifflin Co., 1958.

Butler, Judith. *Gender Trouble: Feminism and the Subversion of Identity.* New York: Routledge, 1990.

Campbell, James. "Kerouac's Blues." *Antioch Review* 57.3 (1999): 363–70.

Campbell, Joseph, and Henry Morton Robinson. *A Skeleton Key to Finnegans Wake.* New York: Viking Press, 1972.

Carus, Paul. *The Gospel of Buddha.* Peru, IL: Open Court Publishing Co., 1997.

Cassady, Carolyn. *Off the Road: My Years with Cassady, Kerouac, and Ginsberg.* New York: Penguin Books, 1990.

Charters, Ann. Ed. *Beat Down to Your Soul.* New York: Viking, 2001.

———. "Introduction." *On the Road.* New York: Penguin, 1991.

———. *Jack Kerouac Selected Letters 1940–1956.* New York: Viking, 1995.

———. Ed. *Jack Kerouac Selected Letters 1957–1969.* New York: Viking, 1999.

———. Ed. *The Portable Beat Reader.* New York: Viking, 1992.

———. Ed. *The Portable Jack Kerouac.* New York: Viking, 1995.

Clark, Tom. "Kerouac's Inner Journey to Find Light and Meaning." *Washington Times.* 7 Sept. 1997, part B: B8.

Conze, Edward. *Buddhism: Its Essence and Development.* New York: Harper and Row, 1975.

Coolidge, Clark. "Kerouac." *American Poetry Review* Jan.–Feb. 1995.

Coomaraswamy, Ananda. *Buddha and the Gospel of Buddhism.* Bombay, India: Asia Publishing House, 1956.

Dardess, George. "The Delicate Dynamics of Friendship: A Reconsideration of Kerouac's *On The Road.*" *American Literature* 46.2 (1974): 200–06.

———. "The Logic of Spontaneity: A Reconsideration of Kerouac's 'Spontaneous Prose Method.'" *Boundary* 2.3 (1975): 729–46.

Deleuze, Gilles, and Felix Guattari. *A Thousand Plateaus: Capitalism and Schizophrenia.* Trans. Brian Massumi. Minneapolis: University of Minnesota Press, 1994.

Deschner, Donald. *The Films of W. C. Fields.* New York: Citadel Press, 1966.

Deveaux, Scott. *The Birth of Bebop: A Social and Musical History.* Berkeley: University of California Press, 1997.

Dopkins, Stephen. "The Role of Imagery in the Mental Representation of Negative Sentences." *American Journal of Psychology* 109.4 (1996): 551–65.

Eburne, Jonathan Paul. "Trafficking in the Void: Burroughs, Kerouac, and the Consumption of Otherness." *Modern Fiction Studies* 43.1 (1997): 53–92.

Ellman, Richard, and Charles Feidelson, Jr. *The Modern Tradition: Backgrounds of Modern Literature*. New York: Oxford University Press, 1965.

Emerson, Ralph Waldo. "The Over-Soul." *The Selected Writings of Ralph Waldo Emerson*. Ed. William H. Gilman. New York and Scarborough, Ontario: New American Library, 1965, 280–95.

Epstein, Ron. "Clearing Up Some Misconceptions about Buddhism." *Vajra Bodhi Sea: A Monthly Journal of Orthodox Buddhism*, Feb. 1999: 41–43.

Falk, Jane E., "Journal as Genre and Published Text: Beat Avant-Garde Writing Practices," *University of Toronto Quarterly* 73.4 (2004): 242–47.

Feurerbach, Ludwig. *The Essence of Christianity.* Ed. E. Graham Waring and F. W. Strothmann. New York: F. Ungar Pub. Co., 1957.

Fisher, Philip. "American Literary and Cultural Studies since the Civil War." *Redrawing the Boundaries of English and American Literature*. Ed. Stephen Greenblatt and Giles Gunn. New York: Modern Language Association, 1992, 232–50.

Frank, Robert, and Henry Sayre. Eds. *The Line in Postmodern Poetry.* Urbana: University of Illinois Press, 1988.

Fraser, Kathleen. "Line. On the Line. Lining Up. Lined with. Between the Lines. Bottom Line." *The Line in Postmodern Poetry.* Ed. Robert Frank and Henry Sayre. Urbana: University of Illinois Press, 1988.

Frye, Northrup. *Anatomy of Criticism: Four Essays*. Princeton: Princeton University Press, 1957.

———. *The Critical Path*. Bloomington, Indiana: Indiana University Press, 1971.

Gargan, William, and Barbara Hoffert. "Jack Kerouac. Some of the Dharma." *Library Journal* 122.13 (1997): 87.

Gates, Henry Louis, Jr. *The Signifying Monkey: A Theory of African-American Literary Criticism.* New York and Oxford: Oxford University Press, 1988.

Gates, Rosemary. "Forging an American Poetry From Speech Rhythms." *Poetics Today* 8.3–4 (1987): 503–27.

———. "T. S. Eliot's Prosody and the Free Verse Tradition: Restricting Whitman's 'Free Growth of Metrical Laws'." *Poetics Today* 11.3 (1990): 547–78.

Giamo, Ben. *Kerouac, The Word and the Way: Prose Artist as Spiritual Quester.* Carbondale and Edwardsville: Southern Illinois University Press, 2000.

Glasscock, Jessica. *Striptease: From Gaslight to Spotlight.* http://www.clotheslinejournal.com/burlesque.thml (accessed Sept. 22, 2005).

Goddard, Dwight. *A Buddhist Bible*. Foreword by Robert Aitken. Boston: Beacon Press, 1994.

Goethe, Johann Wolfgang von. *Faust: A Tragedy.* Trans. Walter Arndt. Ed. Cyrus Hamlin. New York: W.W. Norton, 1976.

Grace, Nancy M. *The Feminized Male Character in Twentieth-Century Literature.* New York: Edwin Mellen Press, 1995.

———. "A White Man in Love: A Study of Race, Gender, Class, and Ethnicity in Jack Kerouac's *Maggie Cassidy, The Subterraneans,* and *Tristessa.*" *College Literature* 27.1 (2000): 39–62.

Grace, Nancy M., and Ronna C. Johnson. *Breaking the Rule of Cool: Reading and Interviewing Women Beat Writers.* Jackson, MS: University Press of Mississippi, 2004.

Griffin, Paul J. *On Being Buddha*. Albany: State University of New York Press, 1994.

Harris, Oliver. *William Burroughs and the Secret of Fascination*. Carbondale: Southern Illinois University Press, 2003.

Hartman, Charles O. *Jazz Text*. Princeton: Princeton University Press, 1991.

Hassan, Ihab H. "The Character of Post-War Fiction in America." *Recent American Fiction: Some Critical Views*. Ed. Joseph J. Waldmeir Boston: Houghton Mifflin Co., 1963.

Hawthorne, Nathaniel. *House of the Seven Gables*. Bantam Classics Edition. New York: Bantam/Random House, 1981.

Hemingway, Ernest. *A Farewell to Arms*. New York: Charles Scribner's Sons, 1969.

Higgins, Brian, and Hershel Parker. *Critical Essays on Herman Melville's "Pierre; or, The Ambiguities."* Boston: G. K. Hall & Co., 1983.

Hinchman, Lewis P., and Sandra K. Hinchman. Eds. *Memory, Identity, Community: The Idea of Narrative in the Human Sciences*. Albany: State University of New York Press, 1997.

Hipkiss, Robert A. *Jack Kerouac, Prophet of the New Romanticism*. Lawrence: Regents Press of Kansas, 1976.

Hippolytus. *The Refutation of All Heresies*. http://www.earlychristianwritings.com /text/hippolytus5.html (accessed Feb. 9, 2006).

Hoffman, Daniel. *Form and Fable in American Fiction*. New York: Oxford University Press, 1961.

Hoffman, Katherine. Ed. *Collage: Critical Views*. Ann Arbor, MI: UMI Research Press, 1989.

Holmes, John Clellon. "The Philosophy of the Beat Generation." *Beat Down to Your Soul*. Ed Ann Charters. New York: Viking Penguin, 2001, 228–38.

Holton, Robert. "Kerouac among the Fellahin: On the Road to the Postmodern." *Modern Fiction Studies* 41.2 (1995): 265–83.

———. *On the Road: Kerouac's Ragged American Journey*. Boston: Twayne Publishers, 1999.

Hoover, Paul. Ed. *Postmodern American Poetry: A Norton Anthology*. New York: W. W. Norton, 1994.

Hosek, Chaviva and Patricia Parker. Eds. *Lyric Poetry: Beyond New Criticism*. Ithaca and London: Cornell University Press, 1985.

Hrebeniak, Michael. *Action Writing: Jack Kerouac's Wild Form*. Carbondale: Southern Illinois University Press, 2006.

Hunt, Tim. "Jack Kerouac. Some of the Dharma." *Review of Contemporary Fiction* 18.2 (1998): 233.

———. *Kerouac's Crooked Road: The Development of a Fiction*. Berkeley: University of California Press, 1996.

———. "Kerouac's Dialogue of the Aural and the Visual." American Literature Association Annual Conference. Boston, MA, 2005.

———. "Voicing the Page: Inflection in Jeffers' Poetics." American Literature Association Annual Conference. Boston, MA, 2003.

James, William. *The Varieties of Religious Experience*. New York: Longmans, Green & Co., 1923.

Johnson, Ronna. "*Doctor Sax:* The Origins of Visions in the Duluoz Legend." *Review of Contemporary Fiction* 3.2 (1983): 19–25.

Jonas, Hans. *The Gnostic Religion*. 2nd ed. Boston: Beacon Press. 1963.

Jones, Jim. *Jack Kerouac's Nine Lives*. Boulder, CO: Elbow/Cityful Press, 2001.

———. *A Map of Mexico City Blues: Jack Kerouac as Poet*. Carbondale: Southern Illinois University Press, 1992.

Joyce, James. *Finnegans Wake*. New York: Penguin Books, 1999.

———. *Ulysses*. Ed. Hans Walter Gabler. New York: Random House, 1986.

Kaufman, Geir, and Tore Helstrup. "Mental Images: Fixed or Multiple Meanings." In Roskos-Ewoldsen et al., 123–50.

Kaufman, Walter. *Existentialism from Dostoyevsky to Sartre*. New York: Meridian Books, 1956.

———. *From Shakespeare to Existentialism*. Garden City, New York: Anchor Books, 1960.

Kayser, Wolfgant Johannes. *The Grotesque in Art and Literature*. Trans. Ulrich Weisstein. New York: Columbia University Press, 1981.

Kenrick, John. *A History of the Musical: Burlesque*. http://www.musicalsl01.com/burlesque.htm

Kerouac. Prod./Dir. Antonelli, John. Videocassette. New York: Mystic Fire Video, 1995.

Kerouac, Jack. *Atop an Underwood: Early Stories and Other Writings*. Ed. Paul Marion. New York: Viking/Penguin, 1999.

———. *Big Sur*. New York: McGraw-Hill, 1981.

———. *Book of Blues*. New York: Viking/Penguin, 1995.

———. *Book of Dreams*. San Francisco: City Lights Books, 2001.

———. *Book of Haikus*. Ed. Regina Weinreich. New York: Penguin Books, 2003.

———. *Desolation Angels*. London: Andre Deutsch Limited, 1966.

———. *The Dharma Bums*. New York: Penguin Books, 1984.

———. *Doctor Sax*. New York: Grove Press, 1959.

———. *Good Blonde and Others*. San Francisco: City Lights Books, 1994.

———. *Heaven and Other Poems*. San Francisco: Grey Fox Press, 1977.

———. *Lonesome Traveler*. New York: Grove Press, 1988.

———. *Maggie Cassidy*. New York: Penguin Books, 1993.

———. *Mexico City Blues*. New York: Grove Press, 1990.

———. *Old Angel Midnight*. Ed. Donald Allen. San Francisco: Grey Fox Press, 1995.

———. *On the Road*. New York: Viking, 1957, 1991.

———. *On the Road; Text and Criticism*. Ed. Scott Donaldson. New York: Penguin, 1979.

———. *Poems All Sizes*. San Francisco: City Lights Books, 1992.

———. *Pull My Daisy*. New York: Grove Press, 1961.

———. *Satori in Paris; and, Pic: Two Novels*. New York: Grove Press, 1988.

———. *Scattered Poems*. San Francisco: City Lights Books, 1973.

———. *Scripture of the Golden Eternity*. San Francisco: City Lights Books, 1994.

———. *Some of the Dharma*. New York: Viking Penguin, 1997.

———. *The Subterraneans*. New York: Grove Weidenfeld, 1981.

———. *Vanity of Duluoz*. New York: Penguin Books, 1994.

————. *Visions of Cody.* New York: Penguin Books, 1993.

————. *Visions of Gerard.* New York: Penguin Books, 1991.

————. *Windblown World.* Ed. Douglas Brinkley. New York: Viking, 2004.

Khayyam, Omar. *The Rubaiyat.* http://classics.mit.edu/Khayyam/rubaiyat.html (accessed Jan. 15, 2006).

Knight, K., Remy Lafort, and John M. Farley. *The Catholic Encyclopedia.* Vol. 5. New York: Robert Appleton Co., 1909. Online edition, 2003. http://www.newadvent.org/cathen/05013a.htm (accessed Feb. 9, 2006).

Kosslyn, Stephen Michael. *Ghosts in the Mind's Machine: Creating and Using Images in the Brain.* Cambridge, MA: W. W. Norton, 1983.

Landow, George P. *Elegant Jeremiahs: The Sage from Carlyle to Mailer.* Ithaca and London: Cornell University Press, 1986.

Lardas, John. *The Bop Apocalypse.* Urbana and Chicago: University of Illinois Press, 2001.

Latham, Angela J. *Posing a Threat: Flappers, Chorus Girls, and Other Brazen Performers of the American 1920s.* Middletown, CT: Wesleyan University Press, 2000.

Layton, Bentley. *The Gnostic Scriptures: A New Translation with Annotations and Introductions.* Garden City, NY: Doubleday, 1987.

Leitch, Vincent B., William E. Cain, Laurie A. Finke, Barbara E. Johnson, John McGown, and Jeffrey J. Williams. *The Norton Anthology of Theory and Criticism.* New York and London: W. W. Norton, 2001.

Levering, Miriam. "Jack Kerouac in Berkeley: Reading *The Dharma Bums* as the Work of a Buddhist Writer." *Pacific World. Journal of the Institute of Buddhist Studies* 3.6 (2004): 7–26.

Lin, Yutang. Ed. *The Wisdom of India and China.* New York: Random House, 1942.

Lloyd, Genevieve. *The Man of Reason: "Male" & "Female" in Western Philosophy.* 2nd ed. Minneapolis: University of Minnesota Press, 1993.

Mackey, Nathaniel. "Sound and Sentiment, Sound and Symbol." *Callaloo* 10.30 (1987): 29–54.

Maher, Paul Jr. *Kerouac: The Definitive Biography.* Lanham, Maryland: Taylor Trade Publishing, 2004.

Malcolm, Douglas. "'Jazz America': Jazz and African American Culture in Jack Kerouac's *On the Road.*" *Contemporary Literature* 40.1 (1999): 85–110.

Manning Marable. Ed. *Dispatches from the Ebony Tower: Intellectuals Confront the African American Experience.* New York: Columbia University Press, 1983.

Marsalis, Wynton. "What is Jazz? An Interview with Wynton Marsalis." *American Heritage* Oct. 1995. http://www.american heritage.com (accessed July 6, 2005).

Mast, Gerald, and Marshall Cohen. *Film Theory and Criticism: Introductory Readings.* New York and London: Oxford University Press, 1974.

McGrath, Alister E. Ed. *The Christian Theology Reader.* 2nd ed. Oxford, England: Blackwell Publishing, 2001.

Melville, Herman. *Pierre; or, The Ambiguities.* New York: Harper and Brothers, 1930.

————. *Pierre; or, The Ambiguities.* Ed. Henry A. Murray. New York: Hendricks House, 1949.

Merton, Thomas. *Mystics and Zen Masters.* New York: Noonday Press, 1967.

Miller, Henry. *Crazy Cock*. Forward by Erica Jong. New York: Grove Press, 1991.

Mitchell, Joseph. "Professor Sea Gull." *The Greenwich Village Reader*. Ed. June Skinner Sawyer. New York: Cooper Square Press, 2001.

Montgomery, John. Ed. *Kerouac at the Wild Boar*. San Anselmo, CA: Fels and Firn Press, 1986.

Mortenson, Eric R. "Beat Time: Configurations of Temporality in Jack Kerouac's *On the Road*." *The Beat Generation: Critical Essays*. Ed. Kostas Myrsiades. New York: Peter Lang, 2002, 57–76.

Munitz, Milton K. *Cosmic Understanding: Philosophy and Science of the Universe*. Princeton: Princeton University Press, 1986.

Murray, Joseph M. *Working the Spirit: Ceremonies of the African Diaspora*. Boston: Beacon Press, 1994.

Nicholls, Brendon. "The Melting Pot That Boiled Over: Racial Fetishism and the Lingua Franca of Jack Kerouac's Fiction." *Modern Fiction Studies* 49.3 (2003): 524–49.

Nicosia, Gerald. *Memory Babe: A Critical Biography of Jack Kerouac*. Berkeley: University of California Press, 1983.

———. Untitled interview with Allen Ginsberg. University of Massachusetts Center for Lowell History—Oral History Program. Lowell, MA. Undated transcript.

Owens, Thomas. *Bebop: The Music and its Players*. New York: Oxford University Press, 1995.

Pagels, Elain Hiesey. "Augustine on Nature and Human Nature." *St. Augustine the Bishop: A Book of Essays*. Ed. Fannie LeMoine and Christopher Kleinhenz. New York and London: Garland Publishing, 1994. 77–108.

———. *The Gnostic Gospels*. New York: Random House, 1979.

Panish, Jon. *The Color of Jazz: Race and Power in Postwar American Culture*. Jackson, MS: University Press of Mississippi, 1997.

"Paraclete." http://www.newadvent.org/cathen/11469a.htm (accessed March 2004).

Paraskevopoulos, John. "Conceptions of the Absolute in Mahayana Buddhism and Shinran." *Journal of Shin Buddhism*. http://www.nembutsu. info/absolute2.htm (accessed June 9, 2005).

Paton, Fiona. "Reconceiving Kerouac: Why We Should Teach *Doctor Sax*." *The Beat Generation: Critical Essays*. Ed. Kostas Myrsiades. New York: Peter Lang, 2002. 121–54.

Phillips, Lisa. Ed. *Beat Culture and the New America 1950–1965*. New York: Whitney Museum of American Art, 1995.

Phillips, Rod. *"Forest Beatniks" and "Urban Thoreaus": Gary Snyder, Jack Kerouac, Lew Welch, and Michael McClure*. New York: Peter Lang, 2000.

Plimpton, George. Ed. "Jack Kerouac." *Beat Writers at Work: The Paris Review*. New York: Modern Library, 1999, 97–133.

Pound, Ezra. *ABC of Reading*. New Haven: Yale University Press, 1934.

Powell, Michael. "The Locomotive Poetic of Jack Kerouac's *Mexico City Blues*." *Notes on Modern American Literature* 9 (1985): 8–12.

Rexroth, Kenneth. "Discordant and Cool." *New York Times Book Review* Nov. 29, 1959.

Richardson, Mark. "Peasant Dreams: Reading *On the Road*." *Texas Studies in Literature and Language* 42.2 (2001): 218–42.

Rickards, Maurice. *The Encyclopedia of Ephemera.* New York: Routledge, 2000.

Rosenblatt, Louise. *The Reader the Text the Poem: The Transactional Theory of the Literary Work.* Carbondale: ILL: Southern Illinois, Press, 1996.

Roshi, Sojun. Untitled lecture. http://www.berkeleyzencenter.org/Lectures/january 2003.shtml (accessed Jan. 2006).

Roskos-Ewoldsen, Beverly, Margaret Jean Intons-Peterson, and Rita E. Anderson. Eds. *Imagery, Creativity and Discovery: A Cognitive Perspective.* Amsterdam: Elsevier Science, 1993.

Ross, Nancy Wilson. *Buddhism: A Way of Life and Thought.* New York: Alfred A. Knopf, 1980.

Rousseau, Jean Jacque. *Discourse on the Origin of Inequality.* Ed. Roger D. Masters and Christopher Kelly. Hanover, NH: University Press of New England, 1992.

———. *Julie, or the New Heloise: Letters of Two Lovers Who Live in a Small Town at the Foot of the Alps.* Hanover, NH: University Press of New England, 1997.

———. *The Social Contract.* Trans. Richard W. Crosby. Brunswick, OH: King's Court Communications, 1978.

Rubin, David C. "Beginnings of a Theory of Autobiographical Remembering." *Autobiographical Memory: Theoretical and Applied Perspectives.* Ed. Charles P. Thompson et al. Mahway, NJ: Lawrence Erlbaum, 1998, 47–67.

Russell, Peter. *The Brain Book.* New York: Penguin Books, 1979.

Russo, Mary. *The Female Grotesque: Risks, Excess and Modernity.* New York: Routledge, 1994.

Sartre, Jean-Paul. "Why Write." *The Norton Anthology of Theory and Criticism.* Ed. Vincent B. Leitch. New York: W. W. Norton, 2001, 1336–49.

Schank, Roger C., and Robert P. Abelson. "Knowledge and Memory: The Real Story." *Knowledge and Memory: The Real Story. Advances in Social Cognition.* Vol. 8. Ed. Robert S. Wyer, Jr. Hillsdale, New Jersey: Lawrence Erlbaum Associates. 1995, 1–86.

Shapcott, John. "'I Didn't Punctuate It': Locating the Tape and Text of Jack Kerouac's *Visions of Cody* and *Doctor Sax* in a Culture of Spontaneous Improvisation." *Journal of American Studies* 36 (2002): 2, 231–48.

Shepard, Roger N., and Lynn A. Cooper. *Mental Images and Their Transformations.* Cambridge, MA: MIT Press, 1986.

Smith, Huston. "The Reach and the Grasp: Transcendence Today." *Transcendence.* Ed. Herbert W. Richardson and Donald R. Cutler. Boston: Beacon Press, 1969.

———. *Beyond the Postmodern Mind.* New York: Crossroad, 1982.

Snyder, Gary. *Earth House Hold: Technical Notes and Queries to Fellow Dharma Revolutionaries.* New York: New Directions Books, 1957.

Spengler, Oswald. *The Decline of the West.* Vols. 1–2. New York: Alfred A. Knopf, 1939.

Stein, Gertrude. *Tender Buttons: Objects, Food, Rooms.* New York: Claire Maire, 1914.

Sterritt, David. *Mad to be Saved: The Beats, the Fifties, and Film.* Carbondale and Edwardsville: Southern Illinois University Press, 1998.

———. *Screening the Beats: Media Culture and the Beat Sensibility.* Carbondale: Southern Illinois University Press, 2004.

Stockton, Donald. L. "Oswald Spengler's Uneven Legacy." http://www.bayarea.net/
~kins/AboutMe/Spengler/SpenglerDoc.html (accessed March 15, 2004)

Stumpf, Samuel Enoch. *Socrates to Sartre*. New York: McGraw-Hill, 1966.

Suggs, M. Jack, Katharine Doob Sakenfeld, and James R. Mueller. Ed. *The Oxford
Study Bible: Revised English Bible with the Apocrypha*. New York: Oxford
University Press, 1992.

Swartz, Omar. *The View from "On the Road": The Rhetorical Vision of Jack Kerouac*.
Carbondale: Southern Illinois University Press, 1999.

St. Teresa de Avila. *The Life of St. Teresa de Avila by Herself*. Rpt. ed. New York:
Penguin Classics, 1988.

Taylor, Bayard. Trans. *Faust; A Tragedy*. Johann Wolfgang von Goethe. Boston: James
R. Osgood and Company, 1873.

Theado, Matt. *Understanding Kerouac*. Columbia: University of South Carolina
Press, 2001.

Thompson, Charles, et al. Eds. *Autobiographical Memory: Theoretical and Applied
Perspectives*. Mahway, NJ: Lawrence Erlbaum, 1998.

Tillich, Paul. *The New Being*. New York: Charles Scribner's Sons, 1955.

Toulmin, Stephen. *The Return to Cosmology: Postmodern Science and the Theology of
Nature*. Berkeley: University of California Press, 1982.

Tyler May, Elaine. *Homeward Bound: American Families in the Cold War Era*. New
York: Basic Books, 1988.

Tytell, John. *Naked Angels: The Lives and Literature of the Beat Generation*. New York:
Grove Press, 1986.

Van Den Heuvel, Cor. *The Haiku Anthology*. New York: W. W. Norton, 1999.

Wallenstein, Barry. "Poetry and Jazz." *Black American Literature Forum*, 25.3 (1991):
595–620.

Warshow, Robert. "Movie Chronicle: The Westerner." *Film Theory and Criticism*. Ed.
Gerald Mast and Marshall Cohen. New York: Oxford University Press, 1974.

Weinreich, Regina. *The Spontaneous Poetics of Jack Kerouac: A Study of the Fiction*.
New York: Marlowe & Co. 1995.

Welsh, Andrew. *Roots of Lyric: Primitive Poetry and Modern Poetics*. Princeton:
Princeton University Press, 1978.

Wheeler, Leigh Ann. *Against Obscenity*. Baltimore, MD: Johns Hopkins University
Press, 2004.

Wolfram, Eddie. *History of Collage: An Anthology of Collage, Assemblage, and Event
Structures*. New York: Macmillan, 1975.

Yanni, Nicholas. *W. C. Fields*. New York: Pyramid Publications, 1974.

INDEX

NANCY M. GRACE is professor of English at The College of Wooster in Wooster, Ohio. She is the co-author of *Breaking the Rule of Cool: Interviewing and Reading Beat Women Writers*, the co-editor of *Girls Who Wore Black: Women Writing the Beat Generation*, and author of *The Feminized Male Character in Twentieth-Century Fiction*. She has published articles and given papers on Jack Kerouac, James Joyce, interdisciplinary studies, gender studies, and rhetoric and composition. She is also one of the founding members of the Beat Studies Association.

Printed in the United States
105437LV00004B/5/A

9 781403 968500